No Better Day

Timothy J. Elliott

iUniverse, Inc.
Bloomington

No Better Day

This is a work of fiction. All of the characters, names, incidents, organizations, and dialogue in this novel are either the products of the author's imagination or are used fictitiously.

iUniverse books may be ordered through booksellers or by contacting:

iUniverse
1663 Liberty Drive
Bloomington, IN 47403
www.iuniverse.com
1-800-Authors (1-800-288-4677)

Because of the dynamic nature of the Internet, any web addresses or links contained in this book may have changed since publication and may no longer be valid. The views expressed in this work are solely those of the author and do not necessarily reflect the views of the publisher, and the publisher hereby disclaims any responsibility for them.

Any people depicted in stock imagery provided by Thinkstock are models, and such images are being used for illustrative purposes only.

Certain stock imagery © Thinkstock.

ISBN: 978-1-4697-6391-0 (sc)
ISBN: 978-1-4697-6393-4 (hc)
ISBN: 978-1-4697-6392-7 (e)

Library of Congress Control Number: 2012904485

Printed in the United States of America

iUniverse rev. date: 6/1/2012

DEDICATION

To you, Mom, with love. My memories of you will live forever.

PROLOGUE

The splashdown occurred around sunset. The brilliance refracted in the beads arcing from the impact, then settled to a calm in the ocean. Various times of the day had been tested. The procedures were new. This time proved best—when wavelength and photochemical properties transitioned daylight to twilight. There were many unfolding mysteries in the universe, revealing how things really worked. Light was a marvelous tool when used adroitly.

The one about to become female considered a lot all at once: the number of souls scattered across the lands here, personalities she'd be meeting, their various moods and unique behaviors. Best of all was the tantalizing concept of how many memories she'd be collecting. That's what really got her excited about the mission. There were going to be so many.

As the last freckle formed on her skin, she saw the evening's first star—in the eastern sky, away from the sunset.

Gorgeous, she thought. *Fitting.*

There was beauty here. Also darkness. The sight may have been her personal welcoming gift.

She couldn't dawdle. She'd received the first instructions already. She was to make her way to the designated location for the "chance" encounter. That would take a while.

Five small children happened to be playing together on the beach when this all transpired. They were unaware anything peculiar was taking place at first, attention fixed instead on constructing sand castles along the lapping shore. That changed. The quintet felt a psychic tickling of sorts, as if feather dusters were reaching into the deepness of their minds and brushing around, searching for what couldn't possibly be mined yet.

The children stopped, setting aside their plastic trowels and buckets, and came together, standing shoulder to shoulder to stare out at the sea, facing the sunset. That was the direction they were drawn to, the western light.

Up on the dune, their parents also paused. Paused because they were watching their children, who were inextricably staring out to the ocean's horizon, as if in a trance. This caused the adults some degree of concern. They had no idea what their little dears were doing. This ended their discussion of the latest bad news from around the globe, ended comparisons of personal hardships they'd been enduring recently. They thought: What was holding their kids' attention? Nothing was out there.

Except an exquisite sunset. A sunset like no one had ever seen.

Then, something even stranger occurred. At once, their children lifted their arms to the glorious panorama, as if trying to touch its beauty. After another minute, the children all began turning their hands at the wrists, in circles—around and around and around.

Human pinwheels… honoring the splendor.

Back in the tots' souls, their spirits were soaring, happier than they had ever been. Happier than learning they were coming to the beach in the first place. The children laughed with joy at the sunset, sated by a super-love flowing into and out of them, celebrating as if there was going to be no tomorrow.

They weren't far off the truth.

Their first abilities to store lasting memories bloomed into existence. Something of great significance had arrived. And it was past due.

CHAPTER 1

Trevin Lambrose went slack-jawed before the Internet, scrolling through the terrible headlines, recoiling as each horror hit his senses like a hammer. He'd wandered off the Photoshop assignment, wanting to see what was going on in the real world, once again drawn into the dread of what was happening out there. The story chronicling the 45 shootings and 9 murders in the city over the weekend almost gave him a stomach ache.

With the exception of the constant drama in a deteriorating society, life in here—in the office—had become a drag. He craved more from his vocation, from his own life. Plain and simple, he needed a change, and he wanted to take those he cared most about with him. Maybe his new "girlfriend" (*Could he call her that yet? Was it too premature?*), would help calm his growing unease. She'd been his shining light since they'd met at the book store a couple of months ago, the one thing keeping him on track. When he got depressed, like now, he thought of her smile, her unbelievable smile, her truly, uniquely captivating smile. Truly, there was something almost magical about it, the way it entranced him. He couldn't wait to behold it again, churning up those alluring freckles, so countless on her face, so incredibly enticing.

"Look!" an intern called excitedly, snapping his reverie. "The colors are even weirder today."

Trevin knew what was in the sky, everyone did. The weather had become very unusual lately, light, color and diffusion so strange it took one's breath away, especially toward the end of the day. The intern was expressing how bizarre things had become—again. No meteorologist had yet sufficiently explained the phenomenon.

His mind still foggy, Trevin reflected on the particularly spiritually uplifting sunset the evening before. The effect on him had made it tough to come into work this morning, the anticlimax of a new, boring day positively hum-drum. The effect had triggered so many wonderful memories from his youth that he'd become completely lost in them, almost spilling his drink off the balcony.

Sweet memories from his youth …

The riotous interns were once more gathered at the agency's largest window overlooking the city of Chicago, gawking at the vivid display like children. Trevin became too distracted to work any longer. He put his computer to sleep and disappeared into the men's room for a reality check. There, in the mirror, he saw in his angular face a betrayal of unexpected wear and tear for a man of only 36.

To himself, he flatly said, "Three years. Three years I've been here already. An eternity. But… I should be grateful to have a job. This recession's a freakin' killer."

There was a newspaper on the counter, the front page reading: "How Long Will It Last?"—a blatant reference to the eroding state of the economy. With the ongoing wars, violence and despair spreading around the globe, Trevin couldn't answer that question to save his life.

Never quit a job without one lined up, he heard in his mind, a mantra recited to him from various colleagues throughout his adult life over and over. Maybe joining the interns at the window would have done him good. Man, he was in a foul mood today …

Somebody tried the door and gave up. Good thing he'd locked it. After splashing cold water on his face, Trevin rightly returned to his boring cubicle, slipping on the iPod and immersing himself in Beethoven and work. Art had to get done. Commerce had to be made.

A few minutes later, when he was almost in an Alpha state, someone approached from behind and rudely plucked the earpiece from his head, causing him to first flinch, then whirl in his swivel chair angrily. The fantastic art he was generating for a logo design dropped from thought.

"Glen!" Trevin barked. "Didn't I tell you never to do that again? What the—?"

A cloying smirk greeted him. "Take it easy, Tarzan," Glen said, motioning with his hands for Trevin to relax. "I'm just messing with ya …"

"Exactly!" said Trevin.

Ignoring the jab, Glen asked, "Got here early again today, huh? Trying to suck up to Solorio? Someone said you got here by seven."

Trevin considered the imposition of the remarks. He was always a nice guy. Firstly. "Glen," he said smoothly. "I don't suck up to Solorio."

"Why not?" said Glen. "He's the boss."

Trevin braced himself, staring at his peer's fleshy fat face. "Glen, if anyone's sucking up to the boss… Not that I care, but we've all noticed you spending a lot of time in his office recently."

"Just keeping in the loop," Glen said, then sideswiped an argument by changing the subject. "He decided on no layoffs, for now at least. Hopefully that luck keeps up."

Trevin changed the subject also, keeping his voice low. "Interns didn't finish anything. Again."

Glen looked at the gaggle at the window, drawing a guess. "They're mesmerized. Do you blame them? The skies are eerie, man."

"How's the copy coming along, Glen? Solorio needs this mock-up ASAP. We need more accounts, money's drying up."

The pudgy 35-year old took a step back, assessing his colleague. "I'm on top of it," he answered. "Saw you surfing the net, looking at the shitty headlines again. You gotta take your mind off that crap, guy, you'll drive yourself crazy."

"And you're watching what I'm doing on my computer. Thank you, Glen; I'll consider your advice."

"Someone woke up cranky. If you were a woman, I'd say it's that time of the month."

"Glen …"

"It's humor, Trev, humor. Laugh a little. Try some, you've lost it."

"I… better get back to work." Trevin half turned back to his screen.

The copy editor backed off, disengaging. Suddenly, he raised his voice at the interns and starting clapping his hands together. "Okay, everyone, you don't get paid to gawk at the clouds! This isn't a nursery school!"

They scattered. One of the brash youngsters muttered, "Interns don't get paid at all …"

Before vanishing into his own office, located at the corner, Glen added one more irritating remark to the muscular artist: "Have fun at the old folks' home tonight, better you than me."

Trevin smoldered like a sunburn, waiting for everyone to leave the main office area. He finally got up to take a peek at the splendor taking place over the city. It was positively otherworldly up there. He'd never seen anything like it.

Compassion, he thought to himself. *There needs to be compassion.*

Glen was an all right guy. Trevin recalled the troubles the nattering butterball was currently having at home with his wife. Glen had told Trevin of the woes often enough.

Yeah… maybe Trevin's recent "female acquaintance," Constance, could teach him how to be a little more compassionate …

* * *

By five o'clock, Trevin rushed the door like a cheetah, politely waving goodnight to the temporary receptionist behind the front desk. He hadn't bothered checking on the interns—as was his assigned duty—monitoring them, making sure they'd been pulling their weight, helping to create samples in order to drum up the much-needed new business. And Trevin didn't care. Not tonight anyway. His heart and mind just wasn't here, in the ordinary. He had his precious seniors to connect with.

Glen shot out of his office, catching him at the last second. "Trev! Seen the boss?"

"Nope," Trevin answered quickly, gripping the door handle. "Not once all day. Hasn't that been Richard's way as of late? Gotta run."

Glen went to say something, but Trevin was gone. Befuddled, Glen went back to his own work, but when it came his time to leave, he made sure to leave a Post-It note in the big man's office, letting him know exactly what time their star graphics guy had left the building. It was a tattle-tale message scribbled under the company logo—Lightning Strikes Advertising.

* * *

Like a pro, Trevin negotiated the Kennedy Expressway in his 1997 Chevy Blazer, through the horrendous rush hour traffic, working his way northwest as fast as possible. Around him, he saw—in quick glances—the general anger and irritation painted on drivers' faces. Heads shook, horns honked and rude gestures flew. In his estimation, the sights were part and parcel to his personal theory: People were hurting to the breaking point, emotions ramping up.

When a dense layer of low clouds broke, the powerful sun suddenly blasted through, glaring off his windshield, and Trevin was temporarily blinded. He had to lock up the brakes when traffic ahead suddenly halted. By the time he got going again, his nerves were shot, and he finally passed the clogging construction with frayed nerves and sweat trickling down his neck. The back of his buttoned shirt, and his collar, were now soaked.

After pulling into the massive Lakebreeze Healthcare Campus parking lot, he motored all the way to the back, where he shut off the engine and decompressed, pulling his thoughts together. His heart was still hammering from the near accident. He parked where he always did—just before the forest preserve, where no one was around him. Soon, he knew, the swarms of visitors would be arriving, filling the lot. Currently, there were only a dozen vehicles here, and they were way up, by the front entrance.

As he labored to slow his breath, peeling his back from the upholstery, he gave it his mental all, working the psychological tension out, visually drinking from the serene scene before him. Since it was late spring, almost summer, there was still plenty of light left before nightfall. The funny clouds had mostly left, but more were brewing in the horizon, in the west, where the hint of yet another dazzling sunset struck and soothed his troubled soul. At least he was here—one of the few places he found solace anymore. He got out, listening to the vivacious birds in the trees behind him. He always parked facing west now. It had become his weird little idiosyncrasy, always desiring to be pointing in that glorious direction. To the sunset. To infinity.

This was still the city, and the developers had done a great job melding the facility's form with function. Despite the massive recession (more of a depression, Trevin believed), this was one of the more decently funded institutions around. A lot of private dollars saw their way in here.

But these residents deserve a place like this, he reminded himself. *They're better than us, the younger generation. Look what we've done to the world. We're no stewards.*

He grabbed his black tote bag full of art supplies and began the long mosey into the building. A particular scent caught his attention straight away, jogging his memory. Someone had recently mowed grass—the lush acreage where he sometimes saw a resident or two wheeling about. The aroma struck a chord, instantly catapulting him back to the days of Little League baseball, where his father and mother would drop him off at the edge of the freshly mowed playing field, and he'd run free as the wind to join his pals. In his mind, he could still hear his parents shouting after him, telling him they'd catch up after parking.

Like the current weird weather conditions, this phenomenon—this transportation and complete immersion back into his wonderful memories—had been occurring all the time now. It seemed to be occurring especially after staring off into the western light, into desire, after wishing he could go back to the those better days… forgetting all about his present problems.

God, he wished he could go back.

Chicago definitely could use some rain. The days had become so hot and dry. The long-range forecast hadn't much of it in sight, unfortunately. It had become this way since the formations had started billowing in. Another unsolved mystery. By the time he passed through the automated double doors and into the blessedly comfortable lobby, the euphoric running through the baseball park, cicadas buzzing, friends cheering him on, had been eradicated. Industrial strength carpet sanitizer replaced the grass scent, and Trevin had to shake off the cerebral cobwebs with considerable effort. He now stood in locked formation at the sign-in desk.

"Mr. Lambrose, hello," chirped a young aide manning the station. "Welcome back, the residents are ready for their art lessons." Then the female employee darted a look past him into the lot and formed a wry smirk. "Parked as far away again as possible, I see. Trying to set a record?"

"I just like the walk. Tough day," Trevin replied, sighing. He liked this woman. He liked all the employees here. He wished he could be one of them. Setting the tote bag down, he signed in, letting her reach across the desk and slap the adhesive name-tag on his chest, giving it a tap for good measure.

"Sky still goofy out there?" she asked innocently.

"It's diminished somewhat," he answered. "But it looks like it might be another good sunset. You should get some of the residents outside. Is Allison on tonight?"

"Yes, she's around. Want me to page her?"

"No, I'll run into her, thanks. Can I go in?"

"You sure can. Have a great one, Mr. Lambrose, have fun with your pupils."

"You can call me Trevin, you know." And then he was going to say more, but he realized in his daydream up to the door, he had forgotten her name. She had a smile button over her name-tag. Embarrassed, he thanked her again as she went back to the phones, and he walked past the desk, around and into the front atrium, where he momentarily didn't know which wing to navigate.

Another friendly male staffer, a maintenance man, startled him, making Trevin's decision for him, pointing. "Yo, Picasso! You're down there tonight. You went the other way last week."

As Trevin thanked him and cracked a joke, he made his course correction.

"Creating more masterpieces tonight?" the man asked after him, seemingly genuinely interested.

"Something like that," Trevin answered, still foggy with kernels of happiness from his memory.

It didn't take long to get blindsided by another. Immediately in front of him, a very old resident was being gently pushed in her wheelchair by a loving set of adults. Trevin stepped to the side to let them pass and froze, disproportionately moved by the sight. He recalled his own beloved grandmother; a person whom he was very close to but was now gone. Trevin said hello to the three strangers as they continued onward, secretly watching as their forms—framed by the entrance—turned to silhouettes against the wavering heat lines in the parking lot, creating quite a picture. So much tenderness there. The feeble woman pointed out her favorite fish in the lobby's aquarium.

Trevin found himself whispering his grandmother's name: "Nan... I miss you ..."

Never could he walk into a nursing home and at some point not compare the facility to the one his grandmother lived in briefly back home in Rochester before her death. Before he had a chance to fly in from Chicago and see her before she passed away in the hospital. He'd never found peace in that heartbreak.

Consequently then, Trevin's stroll through the hallowed complex became more or less a continuation of the dreamy amble in this evening, taking an even keener note mentally recording everything he saw and felt, trying to absorb the love that surrounded him. Even the tropical plants, spread out evenly throughout the hallway, and the nice art he wished he'd been commissioned to paint, appeared brighter and more supporting this evening. Some sights he'd grown accustomed to: Families talking low in private quarters, caregivers assisting the frailest, nurses checking blood pressure. His heart reached out to all the residents, hoping their days were filled with happiness and fulfillment.

Unlike what he was experiencing these days ...

Trevin rounded the bend and saw his first destination of the visit: a private room all the way down on the end. The door was open and a sliver of light from the outside was shedding illumination onto the carpeting, as if calling him. Across from that was the bay window to the courtyard, facing west. *Facing west, of course.* The sun was just starting to set out there. The hallway was beginning to glow.

Gladys Embery—the super-sweetheart—was in there. A peach in her upper eighties, and as far as anyone knew, had no family to look after her. She was all alone. That's what Trevin had been told anyway. That had always killed him, and he didn't want to take another step before preparing. He loved seeing her, and he had to demolish the miserable daily news from his head and instead concentrate on just benefiting from her wonderful presence. This was invigorating, she was invigorating. From the day they'd met, there was something about Gladys that was utterly engaging. Kind of like his Constance.

Maybe someday the two would meet.

He got to her door and poked his head in. This was how he always first saw her. Her back was turned, her marshmallow white hair pulled into a bun, doting tenderly on potted plants on immaculate sills, watering soil and separating leaves with thin, pale fingers. Gladys was dressed in her typical (and somewhat funny) pink robe and fluffy slippers. It was not hard to imagine the other end of her life as a pony-tailed teenager, almost 70 years ago, maintaining a neat room for her parents' inspection.

Trevin hoped to be as resilient when reaching her age. *If* he reached her age.

As Gladys turned, she lit up like a chandelier, delighted to see Trevin standing there. She set the spray bottle on the bureau by her bed and scurried to the door to cup her tutor's face. "Trevin, oh Trevin. It's our lesson for the month—you didn't forget. I sure didn't."

Trevin was already laughing as they hugged each other. "Gladys, how are you, my dear?"

He used as much warmth as possible, seeing how the now-setting sun behind them was reflecting in her signature bifocals. Despite its brilliance, the light was still unable to hide her worldly, crystal blue eyes.

"I wouldn't forget you," he said. "How could I?"

She ushered him in with wild waving. Trevin set his heavy bag on the standard-issued sofa. There was one of them in each single room. "Oh, I love this time," Gladys crooned. "I wish we could do this art therapy of yours for hours. Let me put everything away."

Trevin stopped her. "No, your room is spotless. Let it be, Gladys, let it be. We're always running out of time."

He then set up his supplies as she fetched a hardbound sketchbook from a top drawer. He promised to himself that he would always, always protect her—whatever that meant—while she prattled about the drawings she'd done in his absence. The apartment's square footage was adequate for the activity they were about to engage in—about the size of a single hospital room. The bed was the mightiest obstruction to deal with.

"Thank you again for buying all of us these beautiful sketchbooks," Gladys said, getting comfortable. "I happen to know everybody loves them."

"For my favorite pupils," he said, "anything goes."

Within minutes, they were doing art together, two peas in a pod, Gladys sketching in her book while Trevin gave her pointers, occasionally going to his work. They had a great time, reacquainting, catching up, talking about the great things Lakebreeze had done for the residents lately. And Gladys was never short of compliments.

"Everyone loves you here, Trevin," she said. "It takes a creative mind to think of a volunteer program like this. I'm glad you came to us."

"I don't think everyone's a fan, Gladys. Mr. Joseph doesn't love me. All that man does in our lessons is give me a hard time. I'm seeing him next."

"Eugene's a curmudgeon. Don't take anything he says or does personally."

"Not everyone's as easy going as you are, dear. You make this an absolute pleasure."

"That's because I'm just an old bitty waiting to die."

"Gladys!" Trevin scolded. "Don't say that! That's morbid."

"I don't see it as morbid, Trevin. Someday an angel's going to come for me. I'm just looking to move on to a better place."

Trevin almost said "'You too, huh?'" but instead opted to just stare at Gladys, thinking about her words, taking in the fantastic person she was. He'd heard her speak of the afterlife before, and her belief in a great paradise beyond this plane, but he had to push it all out of his head. He just couldn't handle the heavy stuff from anyone other than himself tonight. Gladys stopped drawing to stare out the window, at the lawn and forest on her side of the building.

"Get your inspiration from out there?" he asked.

"I don't have much time left, Trevin," she answered, ignoring the question. "I can feel it. But it's okay, there's people waiting for me. I miss my mother and father so much." Then, changing tone, "Looks heavenly out there, doesn't it? The light. It's communicating to us."

"What's it saying?" Trevin asked tenderly.

"It's signaling a change."

"A good change?"

"I think so."

Trevin's heart raced to her. But to stay focused, he commented on her lovely plants.

"I take care of them the best I can," she responded with pride. "They're living, too."

Trevin's hand went to the rubber tree plant by him, and he paused at a single leaf. "May I?"

"Sure," Gladys said. "That's my rubber tree plant. They like a human touch."

The texture was soft and slippery. "It's so smooth," he said.

Gladys went back to her sketching. "My mother taught me to polish the leaves of a rubber tree with mayonnaise."

"Mayonnaise?"

"Nutrients. Old farm trick."

Trevin raised his eyebrows, amused. "Stealing jars from the kitchen, Ms. Embery?"

Gladys laughed again, the sound disarming. She said, "The chefs give them to me, silly. I ask for them."

Trevin chortled, shook his head. "I know, dear." Then he asked for indulgence. He was in the mood to see what she'd been doing on her own. One sketch in particular had him extremely impressed: the bird feeder hanging from the tree just 15 feet from her window. In the drawing, a cardinal was perched on the feeder, pecking at seeds. The execution was more meticulous and intentional than her previous work.

"Wow." He compared what she'd done to real life. "This fellow with the feathers. That's this view out there."

She nodded. "You get an A-plus. That cardinal posed for me. It was around when I woke up. I did that this morning."

"Great composition. Good weight given to the bird's shadow."

"I wanted to capture its spirit before it flew away. Like you've been teaching us: Concentrate on subjects that make us happy. I used to draw things like this when I was a little girl."

As they went on with their session and conversation, and Trevin slipped deeper and deeper into apparent rumination, Gladys noticed, reaching out to pat his hand. "I think tonight is about teacher. I think tonight is about you, Trevin. You obviously have so much on your mind. Is work not going well?"

Trevin became embarrassed, and balked with a shrug and a mumble. Knowing he was uncomfortable, Gladys gave him a break, asking how he came to enjoy working with "old fuddy-duddies" in the first place.

And so he obliged, regaling the story of an intern at Lightning Strikes who'd mentioned visiting his grandfather at one such retirement home. The residents there apparently liked hearing about the world of advertising, and the proverbial light bulb went off over Trevin's head. And it didn't hurt that his beloved grandmother, Nan, had been treated well in the short time she was in one. "And so one thing led to the next," Trevin summarized, "and now here I am. Good thing Allison was open to my suggestion."

"Well, Allison's the program director here," followed Gladys. "She's supposed to take in good ideas."

"True enough," said Trevin.

"Speaking of your grandmother," Gladys continued, "what do you remember most about her?"

"Her tireless love for her family. And sharing tea with her whenever I came home from college. We had some good talks."

"She's in your memories, but does she come to you in dreams, Trevin?"

"Interesting question. Not yet. Why?"

"Well, she will," Gladys said. "Like my theory on the weather out there—dreams also communicate."

Trevin laughed, shook his head. "You're a clever whip, Gladys. That's why I love coming here and working with you. You've turned the deal on me—this was supposed to be about you tonight. I live in my head too much, that's my problem."

"The only problem we have is running out of time, my dear," said Gladys. "Let's get some work done."

And the two worked on in silence.

* * *

Twenty minutes later, Gladys and Trevin's rapt attention to their craft had consumed them. They were both still drawing in their sketchbooks, talking about nothing in particular, happy just to be with each other. Trevin was feeling much better than he had all day. When he paused to see what she was doing, he was surprised to see she'd just been executing circle after circle on the blank page, grinding graphite to paper like a machine.

"Gladys, I thought you were adding something to the cardinal sketch. What are you doing?

Why are you drawing all those circles?"

It took her a moment to come around. This was the first Trevin noticed her perception seemed to have drifted. He became a little worried.

"Oh …" she answered slowly. "It gets my good memories percolating. I do this sometimes. I'm not sure how I picked it up. It's dumb, I know."

He carefully took her book. Flipping back further, he came across dozens of pages just like it, some circles bold, some very light. Some had wings and halos around them.

"You didn't show me these, Gladys," he said. "It's fascinating. You know, this might also sound weird, but I've been seeing circles a lot lately myself. I mean, not to stimulate memories, but I've been noticing them, too—in nature, out in the world as I walk around. Speaking of dreams and communication, you're onto something here. There's something about that shape—that motion—that's important." He handed the book back and chuckled at himself. "We're a pair, aren't we?"

But she didn't answer the question, and instead took to doodling more circles, letting her mind wander, a far-off expression coming to her face. "I let them take me back to better times," she said. "The future loves the past, Trevin. Take me away, take me away …"

He was going to interrogate his protégé further, but a sharply dressed female holding a clipboard had appeared at the door with her eyebrows raised, a look of relief on her face.

"Allison!" Gladys said happily, setting her work aside.

At this, Trevin stood up at attention, feeling a little guilty. After all three exchanged greetings, the attractive young woman with the cropped blonde hair pretended to be upset at her instructor.

"Trevin, you've been here with Ms. Embery all this time?"

"We were just wrapping up," he said. "I'm going to see Mr. Joseph next."

"It was my fault, dear," Gladys interjected. "I kept him longer than I should have."

"It's okay, Ms. Embery," said Allison, "I was just joking." Then she checked her watch. "But he does have others to get to tonight. Time can get away from all of us. I just want to make sure Trevin sees who's expecting him—they've been asking about him."

Trevin gathered his supplies. "Gotta go, Gladys, sorry. Great talk tonight."

Gladys groaned to her feet, Trevin assisting her. Allison leaned into the doorway, bringing the clipboard to her chest. "Honestly, I'm not cracking down on you guys. We're having fun here, everything's okay. Ms. Embery, we have a movie in the recreation room in a half hour."

"I won't be doing that tonight, Allison," said Gladys. "But thank you for telling me. I'm going to bed early."

As Trevin hoisted the tote bag over his shoulder, he noticed Allison's official business. "What's that?"

"I just need your John Hancock on more of these forms," said Allison. "We forgot them when you started. Legalese, sorry. Want to step out with me?"

"Sure."

Trevin and Gladys said their bittersweet goodbyes, hugging again, and just like that, the sweet-natured senior simply detached, grabbing her TV remote and turning the set on to a game show, the volume instantly drowning out any further dialogue in the room. Allison waited for Trevin in the hallway, saying goodnight to Gladys, and hooked his arm as a friend would when they were out of sight, leading him away. The last thing Trevin saw was Gladys transitioning back to isolated reality. His heart broke at once.

When the two reached the end of the hallway, where the foot traffic was busier with added visitors, Allison acknowledged his obvious ruefulness. "Gladys is fine, Trevin, I've come to know that look from you. We take very good care of her here."

He stopped her. "I know you do, I didn't mean to suggest otherwise. But she *has* been happy? She *has* been all right?"

"Yes, of course. Something to be concerned about?" Allison queried.

"No. She just seemed a little… preoccupied tonight."

"Can you elaborate?"

Trevin thought about it, but drew the conclusion it wasn't his place to psychoanalyze. "I'm sorry, Allison, I just grow attached to some of them. I read into things."

Allison laughed knowingly, maneuvering around a large potted fern plant. She had to move a branch out of her face. "Trust me," she said. "That's something you have to get used to. We all love Gladys, who couldn't? But she's safe and warm and lacks for nothing. We're her family."

Trevin thought about the comment. He wouldn't exactly say she lacked for nothing. Some of the mystifying and poignant things she was talking about …

"So," he said, changing the subject, "let me do what I need to do."

Allison handed him the clipboard with a pen, tapping the spots he had to address. "Sign there and there. This is a waiver stating you won't sue us if a meteor lands on your head while you're here on the grounds."

As he took the forms and did as requested, "Maybe getting hit by a meteor would do me good."

But Allison was smug this evening, and she began eyeing him capriciously. He noticed, and stopped with the pen. "What?" he asked.

The smirk grew large on her face. "A little birdie told me you're dating someone. Who's the lucky girl?"

Handing back the clipboard, he feigned annoyance. "Who said that?"

"Word gets around." He was furrowing his brow, not budging. "Oh, come on, Trevin—we're friends—you can tell me. You've quite the rapport with the female residents here; you must've said something to one of them during your lessons."

"I say a lot of things," he replied.

"So who is she?" Allison pushed. "Maybe you two can double date with Robert and me sometime."

"Allison, we're not ready to join you and your husband Technically, I *am* seeing someone, but I don't know where I stand with her yet. She's a mysterious woman."

"Ooh, that's intriguing …"

"Ha ha. She's brand new to town and we haven't had that much face-time together."

Allison smirked. "Where'd you meet her?"

"In a bookstore."

"What's her name?"

"Constance Summerlin."

"Constance? That's a pretty name," Allison said. "Well, good luck with that! Truth be told, it's a relief to hear, I was desperately trying to think of who I could set you up with. You've taken the pressure off."

"Glad to have been of assistance," he countered. "But I'll put the pressure back on by asking if you could get me in here full time. I really love working with this population group, and as you know, I've run out of steam in the advertising world. I think I'd be an asset to Lakebreeze."

"You would be," Allison responded quickly, "but we're broke. The state owes us a ton in operation costs, and private donations are drying up. Times are tough, bucko, sorry. We'd love to have you as staff."

Trevin couldn't hide his disappointment. "Getting out of Lightning Strikes is all-encompassing. I'm just dead there, Allison. I can't get excited over anything about that place anymore."

"Be careful what you wish for," she warned. "You don't want to be out on the street with nothing lined up."

He went to say something more, but suddenly, the end of a walker—rubber caps and all—came poking slowly out from behind the massive fern, previously hidden from view. It was trying to tap him in the balls. Trevin jumped back. Allison jumped, too, also alarmed.

The crazy old coot behind the stunt made his grand entrance.

"Mr. Joseph!" Trevin exclaimed loudly. "*What the hell?*"

Maniacal laughter filled the hallway. The short man sporting a scruffy white beard and moustache slowly emerged fully from his covert hiding place, pushing the walker with effort. Through the wheezing, he said, "Been listening and waiting for the moment, sucker. Thought you were gonna be yakking with Ms. Allison here all night. Good evening, beautiful!"

Trevin said, "You son of a ..."

Mr. Joseph got up in his face, staring him down. With a grin, he formed a fist and held it under Trevin's chin. "What're going to do, boy, put up a fight?"

Trevin laughed it off, backed up a step. Allison played into the joke.

"You snot-nosed schlub," Mr. Joseph continued at Trevin. "What were you going to do, blow right on out of here without giving me my lesson? You missed me last time, chowderhead, you're not getting away easy tonight."

"Go at my balls again, pal," warned Trevin, "and you'll never get another one."

The cantankerous man, his atrophied body half stooped, flexed a bicep for display. "I'm scared. You'll get these: the guns."

Finally, a laugh was shared by everyone. Allison got between them. "Get going, you two. Trevin, I'll see you on the way out. Mr. Joseph, behave. We don't want to have to spike your Metamucil with a cow tranquilizer."

Mr. Joseph cackled uproariously, drawing attention from the lobby. "That couldn't stop me from asking you on a date, darling. How about it? You're tired of your husband anyway."

"Next time, Romeo," Allison said, wagging a finger at him and walking away. Mr. Joseph stared after her, lasering in on her buttocks. Allison called back to Trevin.

"Bring your lady next time, Mr. Lambrose."

When she was far enough away, Mr. Joseph said to Trevin. "Love to watch 'em walk away." Then he tried poking Trevin. "Mrs. Pertina has quite the bod, doesn't she? Too bad she's married." And finally he threw a fake punch. "Ready, chump? I got something for you to do. I don't want to stand out here all night."

Trevin swept with his hand, rolling his eyes. "By all means, sir, lead the way. I can't wait for our time together."

* * *

Trevin admired the Playboy pin-up that Mr. Joseph had taped to the inside of his closet. He'd seen it as the old man opened the door to fetch his sketchbook, proudly gesturing at it.

"Nice addition, Mr. Joseph," Trevin stated. "Your family seen it yet?"

"Wouldn't care if they did."

Mr. Joseph was on an uncharacteristic mission. He quickly set up his kitchen table for the two of them to work. The layout of his apartment was exactly as Gladys Embery's—a single occupancy. Again, Trevin reflected on its simple yet functional design, configured with no severe angles; lots of neutral colors with a large living room window to allow light in. And speaking of light, there was hardly any left. Twilight had set.

When everything was ready to go, and Trevin's belongings and supplies were where they should be, and the obnoxious walker was out of harm's way, they got down to business. Mr. Joseph frantically dug through his sketchbook to find a page, Trevin patiently waiting to see what the big reveal would be. Normally, there'd be a card trick or a dirty joke first, but tonight, Eugene had something going. Trevin saw the multitudes of sketches—mostly boats and planes, pretty competently rendered, too.

"You've been going at it, like Gladys," said Trevin, trying to start a chat.

"This is about me now, boy. Focus! Focus!"

"Last time you mentioned your family coming for a visit, Eugene. What of it? They going to be here?"

"What are you, the Spanish Inquisition? I *need* you to draw something for me. Please."

Trevin folded his arms. "At least you said 'please'."

"I'm serious, wiseguy."

"So, what's the 911? What do you want me to do?"

The book was shoved at Trevin and Mr. Joseph started explaining. "I had a weird dream the other night. It told me I'm going to live to be 115."

"Oh?"

Trevin spread the pages with his thumbs for better viewing, and then was surprised and impressed at seeing a full-body self portrait. Mr. Joseph had drawn himself in a very intrepid way: depicting himself standing atop a cragged mountaintop, donned as a frontiersman, Daniel Boone-style. Most striking was the absence of the walker.

"You did this?" Trevin asked.

"No, Tootie Fruit and Jack the Bear did. Of course I did it, clown. I want your version next to mine."

"Why?"

"Is there never an end to your questioning? Maybe you, Trevin, being a *real* artist, could make it come true if you did your version next to mine. There's magic in the air these days and I want to be there for my grandchildren."

Trevin was looking at him oddly.

"When you're as old as me," Mr. Joseph defended, "you're willing to try anything. Some cultures believe depictions have supernatural influence. And don't laugh at me, Trevin, this is my only time I'm going to be nice to you. I'm a broken pile of bones."

Trevin was still marveling. He didn't know where to start. "Where'd you get this idea?"

Mr. Joseph huffed. "Just start drawing, Trevin. I'll tell as you go. We're both on the clock."

So Trevin went at it—with his set of pencils—replicating what he saw, adding his own style and flair. Mr. Joseph watched with wide-eyed attention, leaning close. Trevin explained the approach. "I'm lowering the horizon line from what you did to make you even more dominant in the frame. See? You're bigger and better than ever, Mr. Joseph."

"I'll use that line on Allison some day."

"You promised to talk about your inspiration," Trevin responded flatly.

The old goat got serious. "When I dreamt of me that way, I felt the most incredible love I've ever felt. Came straight from God, I think. He was trying to tell me something, maybe. Those mountains are the Adirondack Mountains in New York State. We went there with the grandkids when they were small."

"New York State?" said Trevin, taken aback. "I'm from Rochester!"

"You going to interrupt?"

"Sorry."

"I played marbles there with my granddaughter, Becca. On a mountain just like that. One of the happiest moments in my life. We had a picnic blanket. She brought her marbles from home—a bag of brilliant blue ones. I can still see them shining in the light. We told the rest of the family we were having lunch, just the two of us. Becca always was an independent person with a strong will, still is. We're still close, even though she lives far away. Wish I could live in that memory forever."

"Where is she now, Eugene?"

"All grown up, living in Atlanta, Georgia. I really miss her. As a matter of fact, her parents are picking her up at the airport tonight."

"Oh, really?"

"Maybe, they'll stop by. Becca lost her job recently and she's on edge, poor girl. She's coming home for a much-needed break."

"Sorry to hear that." Trevin had never seen the salty dog so wistful. It actually made him feel better about Eugene. Between Gladys and the coot, Trevin had experienced a lot of unexpected tenderness tonight. And that was about the best thing he could have hoped for.

Mr. Joseph continued. "She not happy down there anyway. She's talked with me about moving back, but she doesn't want me mentioning anything to her folks. She thinks they'll think her indecisive. They told her that before, when she was a little girl. That always made her mad. She'd been dating a jerk down there, too, but she ended it. If I met him I'd crack him in the snout."

Trevin finished, handing over the version. The likeness was much more truthful and rich. Mr. Joseph was more than delighted. He was blown away. "It's perfect," he exclaimed.

"You see? This'll make it happen; this'll make me like the guy in my dream. You have the touch, Trevin, this is exactly what I was looking for."

"Glad you like it," Trevin said, hanging his arms behind his head. "I'll keep my fingers crossed."

Fifteen more minutes into their lesson, the jarring intercom announced that visiting hours were over. Guests were asked to make their way to the lobby. Mr. Joseph was still riding from the thrill of Trevin's drawing, and said goodbye with a macho pose of both biceps. Then he pretended to punch Trevin in the gut. "115, Lambrose, I'm going to 115."

"You do that, Mr. Universe. Hope Becca and the tribe show up."

* * *

By the time Trevin had returned to the Lakebreeze parking lot, a crowd had gathered, and they stopped him cold by their unnatural, preoccupied body language. They were staring and pointing up into the night sky. A highly unusual occurrence was up there. Allison came out and stood beside him, before he even thought of walking to his car.

"Wow ..." she said, awed, touching his arm. "It's at night now, too."

Trevin had never seen anything like it.

The best way he could imagine describing it—in case he ever had to for reference—was like an Aurora Borealis on steroids. Northern lights gone haywire. Sheets of green and yellowish light were rippling from horizon to horizon, like a giant shower curtain being pulled back and forth across the heavens, shimmering and eerie, partially obscuring the cresting half moon, due east. The effect was undeniably breathtaking, mesmerized the eyes against the otherwise black, starlit backdrop.

Trevin looked around. Residents were being led out. Friends and families were temporarily halted from going home. It seemed the younger folks were the ones who seemed daunted. The elderly... were calm.

"What is that?" asked Allison. There was worry in her voice.

Trevin answered. "I don't know. If it's an Aurora Borealis, it's colliding charged particles high up in the atmosphere, coming in from the Northern Hemisphere. Or it could be something utterly alien, and we're all going to be sucked up into it."

The semi-joke fell flat to Allison's sensibilities. She was too freaked out, and she reached over and grabbed his forearm. "It's not natural. I'm not sure if I like it."

"I don't think it's anything to be worried about." But Trevin wasn't sure.

The air was still hot, very rare for this early in the season. The rippling seemed to be trying to converge into a pattern, Trevin was sure of it. Slowly, the arcing tightened near the moon, and a leisurely rotating circle became visible, turning fairly opaque, blocking out most of the stars there. It drew audible gasps from the crowd.

"I'm going to go call Robert," Allison said, and went inside.

As Trevin started to walk to his car—still parked alone by the edge of the forest preserve—his ground-based attention was caught by an elderly person who had apparently passed out. There was commotion, and he rushed over to see if he could help. Apparently, the senile woman had become so excited at the lights in the sky that she had reached up to them with her hands, and when she tried to stand from her wheelchair, the blood left her head. After a bit of an alert, Trevin and the others were told she was fine. There was no need to call an ambulance. The episode had given everyone a good shock—one too many for the night—and it was time to disperse and go back to where everyone was coming from or going to.

By the time Trevin climbed into his Blazer and threw the tote bag in the back seat, the phenomenon in the sky was almost over. He leaned forward to the dashboard and was staring at it dissipating up there, disappearing into nothingness.

At once, a burst of happy memories shot through his mind, taking his breath away, filling his head with incidents he hadn't thought of in years. Childhood parties, good friends who had come and gone from his life, his parents' warm laughter, his grandmother's loving attention. And so he sat there in his car, wallowing in his own personal slice of paradise until the enchantment subsided, the shimmering anomaly above having faded completely. It was only then that he was able to drive home.

CHAPTER 2

Solorio was absent again. No boss. And the interns were dawdling. Again. They were slouching off—boats without rudders—waiting to be told what to do. Trevin was sick of their behavior. They had grown to become a liability. They should be taking their assignments more seriously, taking more initiative, but they weren't. Trevin didn't know what their problem was, but he did know they were adding to his workload. That comprehension, combined with the great letdown he was experiencing from not having last night's high anymore from staring into the Aurora Weirdo-alis, made him not even want to lift a finger.

Having arrived early again to the Lightning Strikes office, Trevin was already tired, and he shifted the rest of his attention to his rarely-seen Constance Summerlin. For some reason, he really needed to see her. Whatever happened the night before had served to awaken the urgency to address some serious stuff in his life.

The pretty temp receptionist (who the also-absentee Glen had been giving so much attention to lately), was at least performing her duties. Trevin had seen her calling FedEx to pick up the spec work that he'd done to send out to prospective clients, and she'd already organized the scheduler for the week. And that had been hard. There were lots of holes—precious little business. One intern was complaining that he couldn't hook up his Wii Station to the conference room monitors. He wanted to do some virtual bowling. That's when Trevin got up.

"Might not want to get into that just now," he cautioned the youngster upon approach. "When Mr. Solorio gets here, we're having a meeting.

Remember, you guys are supposed to be trying to rustle up ideas, too. It's a team effort around here."

Wii Boy put his toys into a drawer. "Sorry, man," he mumbled.

Trevin started to walk away, knowing he'd better start worrying about his own future here. *Why had Richard hired so many interns?* he thought. Certainly, this was not a wise strategy for a struggling agency.

"You know what? Why wait?" corrected Trevin, then addressed the lackadaisical group. "Everyone in the conference room. Let's go."

He stood at the door as each funneled past, pads of paper and pens in hand. Someone asked where the copy editor was. Trevin said he had no idea and not to worry about it. The kids all took their places at the round table and Trevin entered the room, lowering the track lighting before joining them in his usual seat, putting his hands on the table to set the tone.

"Okay," he started, making eye contact with each. "We *are* trying to generate business for Lightning Strikes. This is what we do. Things have been bad, we all know it, we don't have to act like it. We've had some new leads in the past months, but so far, they haven't worked out. We're holding on with the accounts we still have, but we have to do better. The economy is terrible, but we have to work through that. Mr. Solorio needs everyone working as hard as possible, creating samples, brainstorming, coming up with new marketing ideas that will help all of us—*all of us*—to get back on track. Richard may have promised some juicy work, but sometimes that work comes from us and our efforts. He's trying. I know you guys are doing this for school credit, but you have to try more, too. Let's try to conduct ourselves a little bit more professionally, okay?"

Goth Girl, a Bohemian punker with a sylphlike face and a medley of ringlets in each eyebrow, held her hand up.

"Yes?" said Trevin.

"Do you believe what you're saying?" she asked. "I mean, we've all noticed you looking real bummed out all the time."

Trevin felt like he'd been pushed to the floor. He stifled a look of embarrassment, and withheld growing angry. He didn't know her name, but Goth Girl had been gracious before in the past, so he tried to answer her straight. "Yes, I do. I'm sorry if I've come off distant lately. Stress takes its toll. I remember this firm in easier times."

There was a lull, and Goth Girl again raised her hand. "Want me to make some coffee?"

Trevin coughed. "That would be nice, thank you."

She set off.

The large oak cabinets in the room, looming large against three of the four walls, appeared threatening to him all of a sudden, as if closing him in. Trevin really didn't want to be here. Goth Girl had struck a nerve too close for comfort, and he flashed on the resumes he'd already sent to other companies. He simply had to take steps to control his destiny before someone did it for him. Hopefully, big changes were going to come his way soon.

"That's probably why Mr. Solorio isn't here at present," Trevin added, not sure where to take the meeting. "Glen told me yesterday he had a good lead. A very good lead. He's probably with them now, working for you, working for me. He usually pulls off exactly what he says he will."

Wii Boy dared Trevin. "What is it?"

"Something you should all be familiar with if you've been in Chicago a while," Trevin answered. "He should be in soon."

"Call his cell phone," challenged another intern.

"I don't think I'll do that," said Trevin.

They all sat and stared at one another. Trevin heard the coffee pot brewing. He had to look persuasive. He knew, just as Glen did, that Lightning Strikes had been out of most paying work for some time now. Wii Boy slapped the table.

"So, Trevin, you've been here for three years. We've never seen your portfolio." There was a haughty arpeggio in his voice. "What do you say you show us while we wait? We heard it's rocking."

This tweaked the flock. They became agitated, like mice sniffing at a sack of grain. Trevin remembered the spare book he'd buried under the DVD player, locked up and stored away. When the pressure became too much, he got up, took it out, dropped it soundly on the hard table in front of the people, and let them swarm around the black case like sharks, ripping the zipper open.

"Easy, easy," he cautioned, watching them study the first page of samples.

Goth Girl vacated the java machine to join in.

"It's 'Andrea,' right?" Trevin asked, suddenly recalling her name.

"Yeah," she said, and dove in.

Necks craned and eyes widened. The interns went from sheet to sheet, sometimes someone holding off turning the page. Within minutes, they were blown away. Trevin was an amazingly gifted graphic designer. There, before him, Trevin saw his glory days and perhaps his happy times here never to return. He became melancholy, and longed for some of those sweet memories formed not long ago. There they went: his award-winning ads, brochures and annual reports, sliding by his eyes like dusty beckonings from his past.

Shit, he had to get himself happier!

"Awesome, dude," someone said.

"Thank you."

Thinking of Gladys and Mr. Joseph, Trevin's thoughts went nomadic again. They landed in the proverbial muddy waters he believed he was falling into. They'd led happy lives. They'd made great memories. Certainly, he had so much more life in front of himself, hadn't he?

Just then the door flew open, the knob crashing into the faux finished wall behind it, plaster chips splintering to the carpet. Everyone jumped, including Trevin. The portfolio slid across the table. Richard Solorio had entered the scene.

"Morning all," Solorio barked in a harried state, voice tightened from the scalding latte he'd been slurping, still tightly gripped in one hand. Immediately, Trevin switched places with him, and the pear-shaped owner could barely squeeze into the same chair. The latte splashed as it was set down. Thank goodness it didn't cover Trevin's portfolio.

Trevin put it away as his superior acknowledged him. "Morning, Trevin."

"Morning, Richard."

In his other hand Solorio held a dozen folders. He started almost throwing them at each intern, covering the round table. Trevin was the last to get his. To the interns: "You guys learning from the best? Good." A compliment, *to Trevin.* That was rare these days. "Well, pay attention, no more play time. We got stakes on the table. I have something here."

The door wasn't shut so Solorio kicked it closed, creating another loud boom—not a pleasant introduction. Trevin noted the impact scuff on the wood his shoe print left.

Richard was gliding into his mid-forties, sporting salt-and-pepper flecks in his wind-mussed hair. He was the type of business person who always did his best to dress in sharp suits, no matter what was happening, and this occasion was no exception. Richard moved his tie out of the way as he launched into content-discussion, throwing around the company name "Handy Beaver" with pride and dignity. "As you *don't* know," he bleated to everyone. "I've been wooing these guys for some time now. I think I got them. That's what these folders are about."

There was name recognition. One of the interns said, "Handy Beaver? Isn't that the home-and-garden chain?"

"Why yes it is," said Solorio, barely looking at the kid. "The very same."

The intern laughed and kicked back in his chair. "Man, I love those commercials! That psychotic rat they have for a mascot is the bomb. I see it all over town."

"It's a beaver," corrected Solorio, "not a rat. And it's ironic you bring that up. That's the first thing we're working on—re-doing that mascot. It's old and it's outdated and it scares children. If we do this first assignment right, we could get the whole advertising campaign they're launching. Their business is hurting, but they're willing to shell out big bucks to get it going again. They hate competing with the big stores. They're looking for a major overhaul of their brand image, and I've told them we're just the ones to do it. That's who I was meeting with this morning."

Trevin looked at the interns, throwing a *See? I told you so* expression their way.

"It'll be spec work at first," said Solorio, flipping through his own notes, "but this could be big. Learn everything about Handy Beaver in those folders. I've bragged about you guys, so don't let me down. They'll be here in three hours."

"What?" the interns shouted in unison.

"Handy Beaver will be here in three hours?" Goth Girl asked, making sure.

"That's what I said," said Solorio. "Trevin, get these people to clean out their ears." To the group: "I got 'em, you keep 'em."

Everyone sprang into jotting notes as Solorio discharged vital information. He informed all of a jingle Glen had written for a radio spot. "They loved it; I read it to them, played some music so they got the idea of how it would sound. Handy Beaver's still run by the grandson and his wife, and they like old-fashioned things, old-fashioned values. That's who'll be here in a short while."

Wii Boy was staring at the old mascot atop a letterhead. "Yeah, this critter always gave me nightmares, holding a saw in one hand, a hammer in the other. Looks like he wants to kill me. And that maniacal grin looks murderous."

"Then come up with something better," said Solorio, then to Trevin, "You're team captain. Get everyone going, delegate responsibility. We need this one."

"Okay, Richard," Trevin said calmly.

Solorio saw the old mascot. He pointed to it. "That nose needs to go. It looks sexual, like a po-po." This drew a round of laughs. Then Solorio said, "So don't stand around all day staring at the weird clouds we've been having—work your own magic. That's what I pay you to do."

"You don't pay us," said Wii Boy.

"Shut-up," Solorio yapped. "They're looking at a couple other agencies, everyone, we have to seal this fucking deal. Oh, and one more thing. You're all employees today. We have to look like we're fully staffed—everyone's on the payroll—we have work coming out our asses."

"Why's that, sir?" someone asked.

"Image, man, image. Perception is strength. Now everyone out, I have calls to make!"

Solorio stood, accidentally hitting the table with his fat stomach, sending his latte spilling onto the floor. "Clean that up!" he ordered an intern, then stopped Trevin as the graphic designer was the first to try to leave. "Trev, try not to leave early today. It sets a bad example."

Trevin was thrown, and blinked. "What?"

"I have ears and eyes in these walls. Someone told me you left early yesterday, and you're my shining star."

Trevin knew who it was—Glen. The hypocritical prig! "I'm getting to work, Richard," he said, and excused himself.

"And stay off the Internet during hours, please," Solorio called after him. "Unless it's work-related."

As Trevin left the conference room and headed toward his cubicle in the middle of the main floor, Glen was just coming in, bouncing a foot-long submarine sandwich wrapped in a bag off his trousers. Trevin shot him a foul look. The snitch shook it off and started flirting with the receptionist.

* * *

By the time Handy Beaver arrived, they were upset. Husband and wife, plus an account executive with an attitude the size of Iowa, were ready to rip the group to shreds. They were furious because someone from Lightning Strikes had taken the initiative—later found out to be Wii Boy—to "screw with the beaver's nose so much it looked like a phallus!" as the missus put it. They'd received it as an attachment from an anonymous e-mail just prior to leaving.

"A what?" asked an intern not knowing the word, posing as an assistant manager.

"A penis," Trevin said to her in private, seething under his breath.

Lightning Strikes was on the verge of almost losing the account already. The husband was at the door, still gripping his belt and laying into Mr. Solorio. "I'm telling you, Richard, we won't have a dick for a nose." A few interns giggled in the background, listening in. "That beaver was drawn by my grandfather, right when he came back from the war! If you guys want to make a joke of this whole thing—we'll find someone else!"

Trevin, from the cubicle, actually felt sorry for his boss. He was watching the puffy man perspiring, assuaging the trio hell bent on chastisement. And the interns were an embarrassment, overdoing their role-playing. They were scurrying about, pantomiming feats of office fervor, and one was actually standing on the sill, cleaning the window panes with a Shammy. Trevin had to tell him to get down and get serious.

"It was a mistake," Solorio assured. "The sample didn't mean to go out to you, we're fixing it." Then he spotted Trevin's face over the partition. "Trev, did you get to come up with anything?"

"I did," Trevin answered, coming forth. "I have it on the computer right now."

"Let's take a look." Solorio ushered the three to his star's cubicle.

When the four had a chance to look at Trevin's few mock-ups, they calmed down. Trevin had done a better job than the overzealous and misguided intern, but no one was sure if the fires had been put out. "We'll get back to you," muttered the wife, asking that they leave. "We won't have our beaver besmirched."

The interns in the background giggled again, running into the conference room to prevent being seen.

* * *

It was eight in the evening, and the interns had long bailed, leaving Trevin with the remainder of the "Hail Mary revisions," and Solorio's stern comments still ringing in his head. Trevin had created the best he could, but also wanted to punch Glen in the head for snitching on him. Fortunately, Handy Beaver had agreed to give Lightning Strikes a second chance. The penis-nose was gone but the hammer and saw still remained, and that had pulled the plug on Trevin's reserve for the night. He figured there shouldn't be a maniacal logo going out into an increasingly maniacal world. But who was he to care?

Alone—or so he thought—he took a break and went to the window, hoping to see something spectacular in the sky out there. Sunset would be arriving soon, and perhaps with it, a new batch of tingly sensations. But nothing was coming, and the cityscape didn't look any more unearthly than it usually did. The colors were so plain he could forget about them …

… and think about Constance.

When would be the next time he'd see the amazing woman he'd been fortunate enough to go out on a couple of dates with? Not soon enough, he knew, thinking of her smile—her amazing, amazing smile. It dazzled any room it appeared in, and instantly had him hooked. She did say she wanted to go out again, when she was less busy. She was stoic at first, but her defenses came down with time. One thing was clear: she loved hearing about his past but preferred not dwelling on hers.

A finger reached out and tapped Trevin on the shoulder, almost making him hit the ceiling. As before, he whirled, and again saw his annoying co-worker standing there, sporting an insufferable grin. Trevin was livid.

"Glen, how many more times do I have to tell you to stop doing that? What are you doing?"

"Didn't like that look you gave me earlier. Didn't know what it was, but figured I'd wait till you cooled down to ask you. I knew it wasn't good. Been locked in my office, just came out now, saw you standing here."

"You seem to come and go at will, Glen. But you made sure I'd be here, didn't you?"

"What do you mean?" Glen subconsciously backed up.

"You know what I'm talking about," said Trevin, controlling his temper. "You told Solorio I left early yesterday."

Glen shrugged his shoulders, diverted his eyes. "Don't know what you're talking about, buddy. We're not prisoners, you know."

"Whatever, Glen, I don't want to argue with you."

"There's nothing to argue about. But if that's what you were upset about …We're all right now, though, right?"

"Yeah, sure, Glen. Just let my business be my business."

"I… I …"

"Save it, Glen, I'm burned out. I'm out of here for a workout, while I still have energy." Trevin walked from the window, fetching his gym bag from under his desk. Glen followed after him, hovering, obviously with something else on his mind. Glen was a great hoverer. When Trevin couldn't take it anymore, he faced the man.

"What is it?"

Glen shuffled his shoes and lightly kicked the partition. "Buddy, could we talk?"

Uh oh. Trevin didn't like this. He'd been here before with the copy editor. "What about, Glen?"

"Look, I know I've been talking with you about my personal problems lately, but this is about Janelle."

"You're wife?" said Trevin. "I told you, I'm not a marriage counselor."

"We're having problems, man. I don't want to go home to see her right now. You're set—you don't have a family, you don't have anybody to go home to."

"And I'm supposed to feel good about that?"

"Well, you got that new broad you said you're seeing. Don't marry her, marriage sucks."

Trevin bit his tongue, tapping into all the restraint he'd been raised to value. His parents' teachings had served him well. "Let's keep this brief," Trevin said, and set his bag back down.

Glen lit up with glee, happy to have someone to confide in. In the next 10 minutes, Trevin played therapist, Glen bemoaning everything, from his life to his wife. Trevin stuck up for the woman he'd only met a few times, for Janelle, professing she wasn't a nag at all—as Glen put it—but a lovely person, worthy of Glen's attention and love. She didn't deserve to be talked about in such a fashion. Glen argued that Trevin had only seen Janelle's nice side, at parties, and everyone put on a front when they had to. "I think she's going to leave me," he finally said. "She's said things."

This switched the tone. For all Trevin's opposition, his empathy reached to the poor guy. He softened, and apologized. "I pray that doesn't happen, Glen."

"I wander my neighborhood," Glen said. "I don't know what to do." The glow from the ordinary sunset filled the sad sack's face like a golden washcloth, accentuating the wetness forming around the eyes.

"Glen, go home. Go for one of those walks and take Janelle with you. Talk it out. Life's too short. Look at the shit in the world. We have a lot of work to do here in the office, and we need you in your A-game."

"I needed a friend."

"I'm being one, Glen. You're going to have to trust me." Trevin was already forgiving the bastard.

Glen looked mournfully into the cityscape, out the window. "Maybe I should just jump," he said, shocking Trevin.

"Glen, listen to me. Don't ever say that. I'm sure actual counseling from a real counselor is covered by our insurance—what's left of it. Ask Richard, he'll help. These talks have been getting worse. Trust me, I'm sympathetic, I know what nerves are, like how I'm stressing out over this job search."

Glen snapped to this. "What? You're looking for a new job?"

Oh, shit. A shiver ran Trevin's spine. What did he just do? How could he have been so careless? He didn't want that information getting out, especially to Glen. The blabbermouth was the last person Trevin wanted in on his affairs.

"So that's what you've been up to," Glen said, drying up. A knowing grin once more burst forth on his face. "I knew it. Don't let Solorio find out."

"Glen, please, it was an analogy, I didn't mean—"

"—No, you're serious. Tell me about it, Trevy. You're leaving Lightning Strikes?"

"I didn't say that …"

Glen pointed a finger. "Didn't deny it, either. Trevin Lambrose is moving on. How're you doing it? Can I have your cubicle?"

The good will once more eroded away. Duped again, Trevin told himself he wasn't going to discuss this. He warned Glen to keep his mouth shut, to not spread rumors, and bolted toward the door, dragging his gym bag with him. The automated door chime peeled loudly throughout the space as he busted out of the office. Glen called after him—"Your secret's safe with me!"

CHAPTER 3

⟨——⟩

When he hit the downtown streets, Trevin had to shake off the bitterness he was starting to feel about Glen. His co-worker's recent obnoxious behavior was getting on his nerves, and the last thing Trevin needed was more mental garbage clogging his brainwave activity. He switched the gym bag to the opposite shoulder, pointed himself in the right direction, and did what any sane working stiff would do after putting in a grueling 13-hour work day: He hit the club for a grueling two-hour workout. He hadn't driven to work today—he'd taken the el train—and he was glad about it. The mixture of cement under his shoes and smell of the city at night helped move him away from his funk.

In the gym, he exhausted himself to ruins. Pedaling fiercely on the ellipticals, he'd nearly gotten himself hypnotized by staring at the other cardio machines' circling rotational movements.

Yep… there was something to that circling motion. Virtually every muscle in his body was pumped by the time he left.

As he walked to the train station to head home, he noticed that the light pollution ruined any chance of him viewing something interesting against the stars tonight. Searching for some kind of high, a golden idea hit, and he grabbed his cell phone and left a long, rambling message on Constance's voice mail, asking her to call back and let him know how she was doing. It had been a week and a half since they'd last corresponded. One of the things bothering him in this early stage of trying to date her was what seemed to be a reticence on her part to take the initiative and call him. It was always the other way around. But… voice mail was enough… the sound of her husky voice warmed his spirit. He knew she wasn't going to pick up. She mostly went missing during the work week. What was she doing?

He was just about to enter the terminal when his attention was caught by a dreadful sight at the corner.

With caution, he approached.

The crime scene was nameless and faceless. There was a strong police presence with squad cars and strobing lights keeping a gathering crowd back. Officers were combing the scene; two smashed cars with blown-out windows had rammed the side of a building. An ambulance was blocking most of the ugliness. Already, the *Do Not Cross* tape had delineated barrier, mapping the worst of it. Trevin saw a detective examining bullet casings on the asphalt.

A sense of horror entered Trevin's body. A stranger's voice shattered his silent prayers.

"What's this—another shooting?"

Trevin turned. He hadn't noticed the priest—in full garb—striding up alongside him. The 60ish man, as slender as a votive candle, carried a rosary in one hand, a gym bag in the other.

"I don't know what this is," Trevin answered bleakly.

The priest stared at the trouble, shaking his head. "This is beginning to be a common sight. All over."

Trevin thought he'd seen the priest at the club over time. But that didn't matter. This wasn't the time or place to get into a breezy conversation.

"Heard someone say road rage," the priest continued, rubbing the rosary in his fingers. "I wanted to help, maybe administer Last Rites, but I was asked to step back. What's becoming of this world?"

Trevin grew disturbed. "There has been too much of this. I can't make sense of any of it."

"We need help …" the priest said. "From above."

Trevin had the most unique angle on the palatial terra cotta renovation the two found themselves standing under; a direct contrast to the repulsion not far away. The building was beautiful. "I think of that constantly," he said up to its magnificence. Then, feeling more charitable, he turned and extended his hand. "Trevin Lambrose. I think I've seen you once or twice in the gym."

"John Garren." They shook hands.

"*Father* John Garren," Trevin joked.

"Yes, I'm a member," said the priest. "I'm finding I must keep my body, mind and spirit as healthy as I can these days. We all should. Something big's coming."

That was an ominous comment. Trevin went to ask about it when church bells cut into the city din, tolling loudly two blocks down. The sound put an ironic twist to the melancholy. Both of them, in unison, looked around and located its source: a historic Lake View Catholic church, towering high above the storefronts it sat behind. There was a disarmingly charming clock face set into its steeple, lit up like the full moon.

"I love that sound," said Trevin. "Always did."

"Me too," said the priest. "Reminds me of peace."

"Exactly," agreed Trevin. Then, paradoxically, one of his happy memories from childhood hit, providing inspiration. "In fact," he added, "it reminds me of the sound the church bells that I grew up by made at night. Talk about peace. The church is still there, sits on a hill. You can see it from my parents' backyard." Trevin could hear and see it clearly in his mind, staggering in how real it was. "What a feeling that conveys in the dark …"

Then, as if letting go of a Vatican secret, the priest asked, "Mr. Lambrose, do you believe in End Times?"

Trevin didn't know how to answer. "Do you?"

"Yes," the man of the cloth answered, somewhat validating Trevin's own suspicions. "And it's ramping up. Humankind cannot carry on like this. Just look at what we see across the street. The skies are showing us."

The new chill leaking into Trevin's body was not coming from one of his fond memories, but from his morbid curiosity. "The skies are showing us?"

"The Lord is saying enough is enough. He's trying to show us His beauty to make us correct course." When he looked at Trevin, and saw his expression, he smiled. "Nice to meet you. Sorry."

Trevin didn't laugh. Or budge. "It's okay."

"I get carried away."

"Father," Trevin dared. "Have you been thinking a lot lately about your memories from the past? Any happy memories you may have had from childhood? If you *did* have happy memories? Or not even childhood—from any happy moment you remember fondly?"

"Not any more than usual."

"I've been distracted like crazy with them. Things have been making me wish I could return to the best times of my life, literally. I just want to get away from this time. I've always been nostalgic, but this is different, this is off the charts. I wonder if something's affecting my brain."

Father Garren scratched his chin, nodding. "There does seem to be a need for escape. Try not thinking of your past too much. You can't live in it."

"Not yet anyway," Trevin shot back, drawing a stare from his newfound ally.

"I don't know, son," said the priest. "Right now, I'm caring more about those souls across the street."

Trevin felt guilty being so self-indulgent. He looked away and blew out a breath, processing. "Now I'm sorry," he said with a smirk.

The priest concluded by shaking Trevin's hand. "I'll be off." He stated how nice it was to meet his fellow gym-goer and get a name. "See you at the club, Mr. Lambrose, if we make it to then." Father Garren made the sign of the cross at the depressing scene anyway, and they parted ways.

Trevin watched him disappear in the direction of the church, its tower still pealing hauntingly. The clock face's Gothic-plated steel hands moved too slowly for perception, but he could plainly see the time was way late. He performed the sign of the cross himself, and went into the terminal. Time to sleep.

CHAPTER 4

Trevin wanted to do something good. Something real good. Whatever that meant. Even he wasn't sure. It was an impulsion that had been creeping up in him for some time, the inner drive to strive for something higher. Father Garren's ominous words from a few days ago had remained lodged in his head, tapping away at his psyche. End Times… Prophecy… "something big's coming …" It didn't make him want to kick back and take it easy.

He had gone into Lakebreeze this evening with that very intention. He had driven to Lightning Strikes that morning so he could sail (or crawl) up to it straight after work. But all his expectations of immersing himself in meaning were derailed when he heard the news: Eugene Joseph had died. The cantankerous scrapper never made it to his 115 years of age. Trevin's portrait hadn't worked.

Allison was on her third cigarette by the time Trevin found her to console her. She had taken the news hard, and was crying outside the facility by the many pine trees there, perfectly placed for hiding. She was still wiping the tears when he put his arm around her and said how sorry he was. For 20 minutes, they said nothing. He had a clean linen in his tote bag for wiping charcoal, and he gave it to her so she could blow her nose. As much as the crab had given all of the staff grief over the years, they still loved him and would miss him.

"He just went down for a nap after lunch and never woke up," she said after Trevin asked what happened. "This is the part of the job that I hate. It happens sometimes."

Trevin thought about Mr. Joseph. Thought about the happy talks they had together after he got him to finally simmer down, and thought of the cryptic way Eugene had been musing in their last few visits. Some mysteries would never be solved, Trevin knew. He also acknowledged the fact that their feelings were subjective. Some fellow residents would mourn Mr. Joseph's passing, some wouldn't think anything of it, and some still wouldn't even know the man's name if asked—or know their own. Last week, the liver-spotted jokester was so alive, so full of piss and vinegar, swapping memories of the Adirondacks and Becca. But tonight… he was gone.

"You're on top of the mountain now, my man," Trevin said, looking up into the evening sky.

"What?" Allison looked at Trevin strangely.

"Nothing."

Allison went on to inform Trevin that Mr. Joseph's family was here, *now*, at Lakebreeze. They'd received the news hours ago and rushed immediately to the healthcare campus to collect his belongings. Trevin wondered if Becca had shown.

Allison ground out her last cigarette and hesitated, almost going for another one, but she had to get inside, get on with work and life. "I have to get back," she said. "I don't know why I do this to myself."

"Because you're a kind and caring person," Trevin assured. "You're good for these people."

She made a funny grumbling sound, sniffling. "Whatever. I hated his womanizing, the prick."

"Come on," said Trevin, guiding her forward. "I better go inside, too. Do you think I can have a look at his room, one more time?"

"Sure, if you don't interfere with his family."

"Just to say goodbye in my own way. One artist to another."

* * *

As usual, the Lakebreeze staff efficiently conducted their duties. Guests and visitors roamed about in typical fashion, meeting with loved ones to brighten their lives. By the time Trevin reached Mr. Joseph's deserted room, a deep sense of sadness had come over him, his heart breaking, and he almost started crying. He took one step inside, observing the drawn curtains pulled tight to keep the night out. The room was mostly empty. Boxed crates were stacked against one wall; crisp new linens had replaced what was there on the already flawlessly made bed, ready for the next customer. The space felt unbearably clinical, the pillows removed.

Just out of curiosity, Trevin stepped inside further and checked the inside closet door. The girlie-poster had been taken down. Remains of the adhesive tape were still there, however.

Trevin wondered if the coot's sketchbook was still around somewhere. He hated snooping, and felt icky being this far into the room, but he wanted to see if he could find it. He didn't want that prize to go to waste. He could give it to Allison to give to Becca. It would be a grand keepsake. Maybe it was still in the top drawer of the dresser.

Trevin dared going into it, but there was nothing. All the drawers had been emptied. He lingered at the piece of furniture, gliding his hands over the bare and dusted surface, remembering his friend. He wondered if, perhaps, Eugene's aura was still hanging around, staring at some cute female staff member, making salacious comments from another dimension. Suddenly, there was a scuffle of shoes behind him in the hallway. Trevin turned, and went red with embarrassment at the sight of who must've been Mr. Joseph's family.

Shit …

"What are you doing?" said the patriarch, the others behind him.

Trevin didn't recognize any of them. How could he?

"Nothing," he quickly answered, stepping away from the dresser, moving to the center of the room. "I'm Trevin Lambrose. I'm the volunteer artist who gives the art lessons to some of the residents here. I was a friend of Mr. Joseph."

The lot filled the doorframe, squeezing in to stare at Trevin. Trevin felt as though he was technically being blocked: five against one. They all had tears in their eyes, faces awash with grief. The youngest ones in the back had more orange moving crates to bring into the room, carrying them in their hands. "Are you his family?" Trevin asked, voice cracking.

"We *are*," replied the matriarch, a woman of about 60. Mascara had smeared down her cheeks. "Were you just in that drawer?"

Trevin felt awful. "No—I mean, yes!" he responded sharply. "It's not what you think. I am so sorry for your loss. Allison Pertina told me what happened when I came in tonight."

"We know Allison," the matriarch followed. "Did she tell you to come in here?"

"No, I was looking for his sketchbook on my own. I mean—I was going to give it to her."

"It's right here," the husband said, pointing to it under his arm. The man looked eerily like a younger version of Mr. Joseph, which made things weirder. He opened it to the versions of the frontiersmen—one Eugene's, the other Trevin's—and asked, "Is this what you did with him?"

"Yes, it is," answered Trevin. "We did that a week ago."

There was an awkward pause. Trevin didn't know what to say. The family just glared at him. The man held the book to himself, comparing the two versions, then said into it, "Thank you for working with him." Looking up, "He was my father, he enjoyed your visits."

Even though Trevin was a little relieved to hear the compliment, he still felt like a sitting duck. The group stood there, as if in a trance. Trevin was mortified, just wanting to leave. The three young adults behind the parents—two females and one male—looked the worst, their eyes especially puffy and bloodshot. The youngest girl, who must have been Becca, looked like she'd been crying for a month.

"I'm so sorry," he repeated to her specifically.

No registration.

Dad and mom stepped in at that point and had the others follow, setting the crates down. Now Trevin was really penned in. The father extended his hand. "Ben Joseph."

"Nice to meet you, sir," Trevin said, shaking his hand reluctantly. Becca was boring holes through him with her glower.

Trevin switched places with them, moving around so he was in the doorway. The family filled the room and started shuffling the boxed crates, seeing what was left to be collected. Trevin got the distinct notion they were subconsciously shielding their grandfather's property from the stranger. Becca was a pretty girl, as Eugene had described her: college age, black hair, blue eyes, tattoos that were questionable, visible on her arms.

No use maintaining eye contact, this wasn't a stare down. Trevin went to exit. "I'll get out of your way."

But Ben Joseph spoke up, and caused Trevin to pause. "Thank you for everything," he said with genuine gratitude. "Art was important to my dad."

Trevin was going to say "You're welcome", but instead met Becca's fierce stare again, thinking of her grandfather's love for her. *Maybe he should say something?* Trevin supposed. *Leave her with an anecdote that would make her smile.* "Becca, right?" he said.

She straightened defensively, mouth like an upside down crescent roll. "How'd you know my name?"

"Uh… your grandfather told me. He bragged about you. You're the granddaughter from Georgia. He was happy you were moving back to Chicago."

The family froze, all eyes going to Becca. Becca turned aghast. Then Trevin remembered how he wasn't supposed to mention anything about the move to anyone.

Double shit …

Becca's face slowly contorted into fury. She shot one fast look her parents' way, then rocketed back to Trevin.

"Becca?" her father said, surprised. "You're moving back?"

Aiming wrath at Trevin, Becca hissed, "Granddad said that to *you?*"

Trevin felt like a total idiot. He became defensive. "We shared things, I—"

"Becca?" Mom chimed in. "You're giving up already?"

Becca had become livid. Without answering her parents, she demanded of Trevin that he tell her exactly what her grandfather said.

How could he have been so stupid? For whatever reason, the two had wanted this kept a secret, and he'd blown it for them. Trevin stammered. "I-I shouldn't have mentioned anything, I'm sor—"

"It was none of your business!" Becca barked.

Dad stepped in. "Becca, that's enough. Stop."

But she didn't stop. The combination of grief, embarrassment and personal reasons reached a head. Becca went off like a nuclear bomb, creating a scene, blaming Trevin for butting in where his nose didn't belong. The argument was only fueled by her brother, who bemoaned to the other siblings how Becca was "quitting again." Becca kicked crates, erupted with new tears.

"I'm not quitting anything, damn it!" she yelled. "Granddad and I were just talking! I'm not giving up! Dad—stop looking at me that way!"

Then everyone began shouting over one another, blaming this one and that one for not communicating before. Obviously, this was a long-standing issue, running deep within the nuclear family. It was when Becca called Trevin an asshole and ordered no one to listen to him that Trevin cautiously backed out and made his getaway down the corridor—the lout on the loose.

So much for doing good.

* * *

Trevin was hiding in a quiet reflection room at a remote point of Lakebreeze when he heard the commotion. It was Becca. She had tracked him down and was looking to lay into him some more. And she did. Loudly and wildly. For whatever reason, he had become the subject of her wrath—or her grief—or both. Death did that to people. If it wasn't for Becca's family running her down and dragging her away, Trevin didn't know how far into hysterics she would have taken things. Too many prying eyes and horrified looks from guests and residents convinced Trevin that it would be best to end his evening early and go home.

There'd be no Gladys tonight.

Trevin found Allison—who heard what happened, factually and literally—and told her he needed a break. He wasn't sure if he'd be in for a while. She let him go with much understanding and personal embarrassment, and apologized for an unprecedented episode. Nothing could have been more "unprecedented" than Trevin's current state of mind.

He dodged out of the building, loping to his Blazer all the way in the back of the lot, all the way to the edge of the forest preserve—where no one else had parked—and looked to the western heavens for solace. Was any up there? A weird formation or hazy-floaty thing that would help trigger escapism through reminiscing? He wanted to go back to his roots, to his happy days of yore, and hit the reset button.

It was a romantic notion, of course, but he took it to heart. He really needed a break. He took off in his vehicle like a bat out of hell, flying over the speed bumps in the entrance road, the stars above twinkling down at him.

CHAPTER 5

—⟨ ⟩—

Trevin turned his Blazer off the main boulevards onto Salmon Street, a quiet little side lane that ran alongside the Metra community train tracks. Immediately on the next corner, half a block up, was Munnison—his street. There he took a right and immediately started looking for street parking. His nerves were rattled, and he just wanted to put his head on the pillow. Munnison was nestled in the comfortable, residential neighborhood of Jefferson Park, on the northwest side of Chicago. This family neighborhood had always been a treasure, upholding lots of historic homes and traditions for generations. Trevin had done himself well. He'd found a great apartment atop a two-story renovation at the corner. Well, it was almost three-stories: there was also a full basement with garden level windows!

The first thing he noticed was that the streetlight on his corner, directly across from the house he rented, was out again, just like it had been for a while now. Just when the bulb had been replaced by the city—*pop!*—it went out again, seemingly at the slightest weather provocation. What this did was isolate his corner of the street with an ominous darkness at night, particularly given the fact there was also an industrial-looking cement factory right there on Salmon, at the curving away point of the Metra. In other words: His was the one dark hole on the block.

"Son of a bitch," he said aloud. "Is that thing timed to blow out?"

The comment was of no use. No one was around to hear it. And there was no parking at his corner tonight. That was typical also. The increasing hassle of trying to find street parking late at night in a residential neighborhood had grown to be a tremendous pain in the posterior over the two years he'd been here. He continued driving slowly eastbound, doing a U-turn under a train trestle—*the Chicago Transit Authority's* tracks—and grabbed a lucky spot when another car pulled out. Small miracles did happen.

The city had clamped down on commuters who didn't live in the neighborhood and were parking on Munnison and Salmon, and then walking to the trains, but there were still vehicular headaches. There were a lot of cars with permits belonging to the families on the block, still taking up most of the spots on both sides of the street most of the time, and on occasions idiot drivers who didn't belong there looked to cut through to avoid the main roads.

Such was life …

Trevin climbed out of his Blazer and faced a stroll back to the opposite corner.

There were many old and stately trees lining this provincial layout. The homes themselves were mostly brick bungalows and foursquares. From what he'd picked up over time, no neighbor was particularly fond of his rental: a twin-level clapboard, partially renovated, with an enormous zigzagging staircase going up the front of the house instead of the back. And he was the only tenant. The first floor was long under construction. The owner—Trevin's landlord—had mostly given up for now on fixing it up because of the terrible economy and the bursting of the real estate bubble.

That didn't exactly make his house very popular on the street. He could see it from here, in the dark: a big, hulking behemoth cloaked in shadows by the trees and faulty streetlight.

As he approached with his tote bag bouncing off his weary shoulders, he looked around, wondering who most of the people in these houses were. He still hadn't reached out in a friendly or neighborly way. Nor had they to him. Trevin kept to himself, doing his business, desperately trying to carve out a better future. When he reached his corner, the dominating balcony stretched full length overhead, casting even darkness below. Yes, it was easy to understand how his landlord's house could be construed as a colossal eyesore.

And speaking of his landlord, apparently the guy didn't have a good reputation on the block. Trevin had heard of arguments between the man and a few locals, grievances over loud construction and bad attitudes. That's who Trevin had to write his check to every month.

Trevin got his mail from the first-floor landing and made his way up the staircase, one clunking stomp after another, pausing midway up to peer into the first-floor windows. There were yet to be curtains or blinds hung to impede his view or any stranger's. That definitely wasn't good. But it was quiet here, and that's what Trevin valued immensely. He could see the same grimy toolbox shoved in a corner, gathering dust atop an unfinished hardwood floor.

When he'd reached the balcony, Trevin propped open the outside screen door with his foot and looked for the proper key, looking over his shoulder to take in his dramatic view. Over the concrete factory he could see the commuter Metra tracks, and beyond that, the Kennedy Expressway. The cars flew there, creating an omnipresent sound like ocean waves. This was absolutely a pivot-point to the city and suburbs.

From the direction of where his Blazer was parked, a hot rod had suddenly turned onto Munnison and was blasting its way up toward his corner, shattering the stillness of the night. Surely it was one of the idiots Trevin had considered. The car shot by, barely slowing as it took a violent right on Salmon. "Slow down, jackass!" Trevin shouted after it, adrenaline raking his bones.

"Nice pipes," said a male voice, coming from the darkness.

Trevin looked around. It came from his right, maybe next door. Trevin crouched, feeling suddenly embarrassed, peering through the banisters of his balcony to the house next to him. There was an overhang. Under it, he could partially see the front porch of the next house. That's where the voice had come from. There was a man sitting there, on a swing with a woman. One small candle illuminated a card table set in front of them.

Shit. Trevin hadn't seen them. "Sorry," he called out.

"Don't be," the male answered, lifting a wine glass in his direction to salute. Obviously, the couple could see him and had been quietly watching. "Good to know people on the block care. We'd like to see the street permanently cut off. We hate those morons racing through."

Trevin felt relieved at the humor. Still crouching, trying to see the forms, he said, "Yeah. I'm afraid something's going to happen one day. Something bad."

"Don't say that. We've had a couple of near-misses."

Trevin had been here two years and he didn't know who his next-door neighbors were. Or the neighbors after that—the ones he was addressing. They seemed nice, they looked normal. Trevin figured they were middle-aged, the man heavy, the wife skinny. Perhaps a friendly comment was in order. "I didn't mean to disturb your peace," he said with a mellow tone.

"You didn't," the female chimed in, also saluting him with a wine glass.

Trevin straightened, turning around to go in. He heard the man's voice start up again. "Hey, when's your landlord finally going to finish that first floor of his? It's been, what, two years? Jiminy Cricket."

Trevin winced. He called back. "Mr. Fovos? Who knows? He says soon."

"Yeah, he says that a lot. He's said it to all of us."

Trevin dared looking again. The man set his drink on the table, got up, and walked over so he was standing right below the balcony. He could barely be seen in the low light, but a distant streetlight on Salmon reflected off his eyeglasses. Trevin watched him give the staircase deliberation. "Man oh man. This is the ugliest thing I've ever seen on the front of a house."

Trevin had no comment.

Then the man struck up a cigarette and Trevin could see him better. The man lifted his chin and blew the smoke into the air, exposing a fat belly beneath an untucked Hawaiian shirt. Trevin could also see big feet in big sandals. "Your landlord's not the friendliest guy," the figure spoke. "How does it feel to be the lone occupant in his big house?"

"I like it," Trevin answered boldly, slightly put off by the imposition. "Have a good night." But Trevin was stopped again. "Peter Bebziak," the man said, then gestured to his lady. "My wife, Ruth. We live here, that's our house."

Ruth waved, said hello. Trevin said hello back. He could discern that she didn't come close to matching her husband's girth. Or his brusqueness.

Figuring it a good time to prove he wasn't completely antisocial, Trevin set his bag down and met the man on the sidewalk, shaking hands and introducing himself. Trevin was astounded by the man's height. The chap must've been six foot four or five, thick beard and moustache giving him a moose-like appearance. Ruth may have had red hair. And that was pulled into a ponytail.

"Sorry," Trevin said. "I don't see my landlord much. He doesn't come around much."

"No, he doesn't."

Trevin was prepared to dismiss the man quickly. He had way too much on his mind, particularly the disaster he'd just experienced at Lakebreeze. He was still swirling from Becca's shouting but the conversation started to flow, Peter taking the initiative. And soon enough, Trevin was convinced the burly man wasn't someone to avoid. Peter turned out to be affable enough, but didn't know much about personal space. Trevin had to back up twice to acquire it. Peter told him he was a computer programmer who'd been reduced to contract work because of cut-backs. Ruth worked in a florist shop, but currently wondered if she should quit after a robber broke in after-hours and trashed the joint. Mayhem and malaise were everywhere. When they found out Trevin was an artist, they couldn't avoid the usual insulting comments about becoming famous only after death.

When Trevin politely excused himself, Peter brought up the subject of the extremely hot weather perhaps bringing more cretins racing through the neighborhood. "Heat does crazy things to people," he said, puffing on his second cigarette. "I talked to the alderman. He's done shit. Typical politician."

"Stay off of politics, honey," his Ruth coached.

Trevin started up the staircase, apologizing for not introducing himself earlier.

"Well, if you want," said Peter after him, "we're starting up a neighborhood watch program. You can meet a lot of us neighbors."

"A neighborhood watch program?"

"Didn't you hear what happened down the street?"

Trevin stopped, balancing against the railing. He hadn't heard anything. But whatever this was, he knew it wasn't going to be good. "No, what?"

The big man pointed to the end of the street. "Down where you parked? That green house with the pine trees on the side of it? It was hit by a prowler a month ago. Never caught the asshole."

Trevin was disturbed. He looked to the better lit end. "Was anyone home?"

"Hell yeah, someone was home," Peter answered, agitated. "Mrs. Dombrowski. She's only about a hundred years old! Lived there her whole life, poor lady. She's still by herself, has been for years."

Already, Trevin dreaded the story. To hear of an elderly person getting attacked …

Peter continued. "Hubby's been gone a long time. We try to look out for her on the street. There's only so much we can do. The prick broke in in the middle of the night, she wakes up, encounters him in the hallway; she nearly dies from a heart attack as he runs out, stealing crap. Silverware and a stupid radio. We're lucky to still have her."

Despite his horror, Trevin couldn't help but note the egotism in Peter's voice, as if he was glad to have been the one to break the story to the neighbor. "That's… terrible," Trevin said, feeling his blood pressure shoot up. "Never caught him, huh?"

"If we had we would've strung 'im up."

"How is she now? Mrs. …"

"Dombrowski. She's okay but she never comes out anymore. Who can blame her? She has no children. That's why we like to know who's who on the block. We're vigilant; we don't want any more crap."

"No, of course not." Trevin had grown unexpectedly furious. "God, I'm sorry to hear that. But I gotta go; it's been a long day. I'll keep the neighborhood thing in mind."

Ruth Bebziak stood up, saying good night. And then she collected the wine and the glasses and headed inside, urging her husband to join her. After she was gone, the bear-man once again got too close, lowering his baritone voice. "Maybe you can tell your landlord the next time you see him that we're all on this block together. He should fix this place up. Between that damn streetlight and this being the darkest corner, we don't want the house attracting anymore fucks. We're glad you're here, but we just want things safe. I don't mean to be forward."

"I work late hours," Trevin defended. "I'll keep an eye out. Goodnight, Peter."

"If you need us, you know where to find us."

Right, thought Trevin, cynically.

The final thing Peter wanted to impart on his new friend was an invitation to the upcoming Fourth of July block party. Peter encouraged Trevin to come, bringing anybody else he wanted to. The annual bash was in a little over a month, and a good time was promised. A flyer in the mail was assured. Trevin remembered the ruckus from previous years. He escaped it all by going to the movies. Trevin went into his apartment and shut and locked the door, feeling again like a heel for not playing a little better with his fellow citizens.

* * *

Trevin was dead asleep when his cell rang, blasting him awake with its set spectacle of flashing lights and clanging tones. He smacked his head on the vaulted ceiling inside his studio. He'd never made it to his bedroom. After

Peter Bebziak, he'd dropped the tote bag, plopped on the sofa in the front room and passed out, leaving the world to its wicked devices.

It was Constance! The time on the DVD player read 3:30 a.m.!

"Constance?" he practically yelled, jamming the TALK button and slapping the piece of cell phone plastic to his ear. "Is it you? Is everything all right?"

Her sweet, sweet voice hung back, at first chuckling with humor. "Uh… yeah… it's me. I'm all right. How are you, Trevin?"

Trevin sat up on the sofa, trying to get his bearings. He was ecstatic his mystery woman had called, screw the time. And he was talking to her in his favorite room—the studio—with the vaulted ceilings and skylight and TV and all his art supplies surrounding him like a womb. This space was why he'd jumped at the place when he saw it. "I'm, I'm fine," he said, rubbing his eyes. "What's going on?"

"It's about time I called you back, sorry for the delay. You probably thought I'd ditched town already."

Trevin had grown to love her voice, and it sounded particularly magical tonight. He laughed, reveling in her words. "I know that's not you."

"Did I wake you?"

"Yes, as a matter of fact, you did," he answered. "But I don't mind."

"Do you not want to talk?"

"No, no—yes I want to talk, I've been worried about you."

"Worried?" she exclaimed. "Why?"

The skylight above the drafting table enabled the city's night glow to filter in, bathing the apartment in burnt orange. It made him feel relaxed. "Never mind," he said.

"I can take care of myself."

"I'm sure you can. But I've left several calls—including that latest stupid one."

"I thought it was cute," she giggled. "I want to thank you for the longest message I've ever heard."

"You're welcome," said Trevin in retort.

He had the air conditioner blasting already. The place was cold. The floorboards under him awakened his bare feet. This wasn't a dream. He checked the shawl to his right; hung over the strange octagonal window there to make sure no one could see in. A view straight into his studio was accessible from outside on the balcony. This was the one feature of his apartment Trevin had become unsettled by. He couldn't relax thinking people could see in.

"What are you doing so late?" he asked.

"Receiving."

"Receiving? What are you talking about?"

"Oh, nothing. Just receiving ideas for what I'm to do with you."

"What? What does *that* mean?" What a strange comment. Trevin got up and made his way to the swivel chair at the drafting table, sitting on it to sharpen his senses. Piles of his own sketchpads filled the tabletop.

But Constance ignored the question. "Trevin. We definitely have to get together soon. It's been too long since our last date."

He laughed in disbelief. "Anytime. When do you want to?"

"You have to work tomorrow?" she asked.

"Of course, don't you?"

"Yes, but the agency's sending me elsewhere. I'll be downtown."

"That's good."

"Not too far from my perfect apartment I found," she said. "South Loop, great view. Got a great deal with all the distressed real estate. It's up high where I do my best work."

"I don't know what you mean by that, either," Trevin said. She sucked in a deep breath and let it out, sighing. The sound was almost musical. Trevin fell in love with it.

"The city's so beautiful at night," she said. "I can see some stars right now."

"Anything unusual up there?"

"Nothing out of the ordinary," Constance answered. "But I did see something the other night. Shimmering colors and light, right over the moon. It was incredible."

"I saw the same thing," he said, almost mentioning Lakebreeze, but he didn't want to ruin the moment with a bad flash. "What do you think it was?"

She didn't answer this, either, just laughed some more. All of this intrigued Trevin. He had to be careful: He didn't want to be smitten so early in a possible relationship.

"I've been thinking of you," he chanced.

She cooed. "Tell me about it."

"You've made quite the impact in just the short time we've known each other. That smile of yours. It's… killer."

"That's sweet. I'm glad you like it."

"So where are we going to meet tomorrow?" he pushed.

"How's about Buckingham Fountain in Grant Park? Even a tourist like me knows where that is."

"You'll get to know the city," said Trevin, heartily agreeing to the meeting point. It was an excellent choice. Tomorrow evening, after work, by the lakefront.

"Where the water meets the sky," Constance said.

"Where the water meets the sky," Trevin repeated. "I love that. Are you a poet?"

"No," she answered, "I'm the new girl on the block."

CHAPTER 6

———◄ ►———

Trevin looked like a bleary-eyed puff fish the following morning at Lightning Strikes. The late-night chat with Constance had cut tremendously into his beauty sleep. He'd been up for the next hour after getting off the phone with her, thinking of their meeting tonight, and the tragedy at Lakebreeze. What a contrast. When he'd see her, things would improve, he knew. Daydreaming about her, he stared into his hot java, steam overheating his face, preparing for whatever bullshit was going to come his way today.

Of course, it was no big surprise that none of the interns were in yet. They'd probably been out partying hard the night before, disregarding their responsibilities. Did no one want a brighter future anymore? Trevin had to tell himself not to be so judgmental, it wasn't virtuous. And Glen wasn't in either. In the distant corners of his mind, Trevin wondered if he'd gone on that walk with his wife, Janelle—kissing and making up. But why should he care?

Because he was a caring kind of guy.

When the door burst open and the chimes pealed, the stampede entered. So now the youngsters were here, ruining his ponderings. Like sharks to chud, they went straight at the conference room, attacking the pot of coffee he'd made. The clinking of mugs was like a tribal symphony. *What a minute,* he realized. *Where was Wii Boy?*

He followed into the room and asked.

After a "'good morning,'" Goth Girl told him that Mr. Solorio had told the colleague not to come in anymore.

"Why?"

"Because of the Handy Beaver thing," she replied, playing with her lip ring. "Guess Mrs. Handy couldn't get over that dick-thing. She called Mr. Solorio personally to complain more."

"So he's gone?" asked Trevin.

"He's gone."

Suddenly Trevin felt responsible. "But I fixed the logo. They saw it, we sent it over. I thought everything was fine."

Goth Girl said, "Guess she needed someone's head to fly or she wouldn't continue considering giving us the business."

"How do you know all this?"

"Text," she answered. "Got it from Max this morning." (Wii Boy) "Wanna read it? It's full of expletives."

"No, thanks," said Trevin, looking at the floor in confusion. "I believe you." He left, going back to his cubicle.

Just then Glen came strolling in with the pretty receptionist, chatting away idly. Glen called to him when seeing him, "Trev, did you hear Richard let go one of the interns?"

"I did, Glen." Trevin sat down, going about his work, confused. When Glen walked over, he leaned on the partition.

"Richard called me late last night and told me. Shame. I liked the guy's Playstation."

Without looking, Trevin said, "I guess you're his go-to guy now." There was no way he was going to get into a discussion with the sneak; Trevin was still mad at him for the remarks about his job hunting. Glen punched him lightly on the shoulder, trying to get him to loosen up.

"Thanks for our talk, buddy, Janelle and I made nice with each other— at least for one more night."

"That's nice, Glen. Did Richard tell you what we're supposed to do now with Handy Beaver? What's the news on it?"

Glen leaned in, whispering. "Hey… what do you think of our receptionist? I'm thinking of asking her to lunch."

Trevin stopped what he was working on and slowly turned. "For real, Glen? Really? Are you serious? After what we talked about? After what you came to me about?"

Glen backed off, drumming the top of the partition with his fingers. "I didn't say I was going to do it, I'm just thinking about it. Lighten up."

Trevin was going to let him have it, verbally. He couldn't handle it anymore. He was so tired of the pettiness and the hypocrisy he'd been experiencing from people lately that he was just going to give the sycophant a piece of his mind. He was about to open his mouth when the cell phone in his pocket started going off. Both could hear it buzzing loudly from Trevin's hip.

Glen grinned snidely. "Better answer it; it's either your new job or your mystery woman calling to say how much she misses you."

Trevin stood, purposefully nudging past Glen, getting out of his way before something bad happened. As Trevin excavated the phone from his slacks, he somewhat recognized the number. It seemed to him to be familiar, and it was a downtown locale. Maybe it *was* an agency calling. The call went into voice mail, and as Trevin stood by the door, it buzzed again, signaling a message had been left. He had to answer it. He had to get out of here and find some privacy.

"I'll be right back," he told the receptionist, who was setting up for the day behind the front desk.

Glen said loudly after Trevin as he left the premises, drawing attention from the receptionist, who giggled without knowing what she was laughing at. "Let me know how it goes!"

* * *

The call was from Malligan and Totnes, a competing advertising agency Trevin had sent a cover letter and resume to a few months back. He'd nearly forgotten about it—as he had most of the firms he'd sent information to—inquiring into whether or not there might be a position available.

After listening to the start of the voice mail, competing against the loud noises from the city street under construction at the base of his building, Trevin looked for a quiet hiding place. The dissonance was assaulting. He had to relisten to the message with no obstruction, and react to it, but this spot was impossible. He'd only heard the intro from Thomas Archer, the creative director, inviting him to come in and meet, before he was off to the races, sprinting across traffic, almost getting hit. Trevin headed toward an isolated alley between two skyscrapers.

His blood pressure was spiking, his adrenaline surging. Trevin couldn't believe how something as simple as a phone call from a possible lead could cause him to get this agitated. It wasn't healthy, but he was this desperate. His mind was racing a thousand miles per hour.

It was hot here in the middle of Chicago's Loop, with the sun already beating down onto man-made canyons and pedestrians below. When Trevin entered the alley, not exactly clean and fresh, he had to angle toward one side but not get his clothes dirty, keeping in shadow, the rays pounding where it could, as if trying to reach him. Trevin ran further in than expected, all the way to a back pocket, where dumpsters, fire escapes and the stench of urine surrounded him.

Displeased, he looked around and then up, seeing the clear blue sky through the four skyscrapers towering above him. There were only a few puffy clouds drifting by. Thank goodness the din dropped off here.

Flapping his cotton knit shirt back and forth to relieve the perspiration, he played the message over, one finger plugged in his free ear. Thomas Archer was stating how they were just now getting around to calling people back. "We reviewed your site," the professional voice said, "and we're interested in talking to you. You may have caught us at the perfect time. Some good fortune came our way in these rough times and we're thinking of expanding a little bit. We're in need of a few hungry wolves. I'm going into a meeting now, but will be available at the end of the day, say, four o'clock. Why don't you call then or try tomorrow if that works better. Thanks." End of call.

No one said "goodbye" anymore.

After saving the message, Trevin filled with enthusiasm, wondering if this could be a break. First Constance, now this—Malligan and Totnes. He almost dropped into a stupor.

He wanted to share the good news, even though it was way premature. His first impulse was to call Constance. Or his parents. He hadn't spoken to them in a while. There'd been no good news; he'd felt bad. Mom and dad were always worried about him—God bless them—and they knew how unhappy he'd become in recent times. Pressure, pressure, pressure. Probably more self-imposed; they hadn't put any on him. He'd always wanted to please. To make right. To be the savior.

He'd have to call Mr. Archer back at four o'clock; he didn't want to wait. He had to find a way to get out of the office to make the call. This was going to be tricky. Trevin wanted his boss to get the Handy Beaver account, but he also wanted to get the hell out of Lightning Strikes. He had to grab his future when he could.

And that being the case… Trevin started fantasizing about a better job and better days. Happier moments and future memories, where he'd again be laughing and joking, satisfied in life and work… Constance Summerlin by his side.

Then something extraordinary happened. As he was letting his imagination go wild, drawing upon make-believe happiness, a particularly low and bulbous cumulonimbus cloud appeared overhead, cloaking everything in an even darker shadow, filling the space between the four buildings. Trevin froze, snapping out of his reverie. It was as if a giant dirigible had come out of nowhere, settling over the spot he was at, shattering the ordinariness of the blue sky. He wasn't sure if it was real, but thin wisps broke off its belly, and started a very strange downturn creeping along the sides of the skyscrapers toward him. Trevin looked around to see if anyone was witnessing this. He was alone. The threads grew and turned in space (circling?), until it became like a funnel, blotting everything else out, subtle and odd colors inside, twinkling somewhat.

Troubles melted from Trevin's mind. He suddenly felt so relaxed that his heavy spirit lifted. Before it enveloped him, his beloved grandmother flashed into his mind. And she was waving and smiling at him from the terrible wheelchair she'd been stricken in for the last years of her life. He wanted to talk to her, ask her how she was doing, hug her. Raw sentimentality took over with the strength of a hurricane, and Trevin began to cry.

* * *

The next thing Trevin was fully cognizant of was splashing his face with faucet water, back in the Lightning Strikes men's restroom. He was aware something strange had transpired outside—and quite well remembered the phone message from Thomas Archer—but passed the woozy obfuscation off to stress and running around in the heat. Whatever had transpired… he was emotionally drained. He only hoped it wasn't obvious on his face as he went back to work in his cubicle.

By this time everyone was well underway with the day, and Mr. Solorio was in his office, diligently placing phone calls. Trevin could see him through the window there, even though his blinds were half drawn.

Trevin's phone rang at his desk. It was Glen, calling from the corner office. Trevin picked it up and the voice immediately asked, "How'd it go?"

This guy doesn't let up, Trevin said to himself. "Glen, you better have called for something else."

"Chill, bro, everyone knows you want out of here."

"Goodbye, Glen." Trevin went to hang up, but Glen stopped him. Trevin said, "What do you want?"

"The interns think you hate them."

"What?!"

"They said something after you walked out."

"What did they say?" Trevin kept his voice low, looking around the office at them. He was growing outraged.

"Nothing specific. It's your body language, the way you talk to them."

"Glen, why the hell are you even entertaining this? I don't hate the interns. Don't go spreading petty and erroneous gossip; I don't want any of this getting back to Richard."

"Just thought I'd give you a heads-up."

"Glen, I'm asking you for the last time—as a friend—and we've been through a lot together—please keep your mouth shut."

"I am being a friend, this is what friends do—warn."

Trevin swallowed, composing his words carefully. "You know, I liked you better the old way, Glen. You've changed. You can be a real asshole when you want to."

"*I've* changed?" said Glen, suddenly indignant. "Look at you! You walk around here, miserable, not caring about Lightning Strikes anymore. You take off to make a phone call and don't come back for two hours—"

Trevin checked the time. Glen was right! He had been gone for two hours! *What the hell?*

"—And you've grown hyper-sensitive about everything. I'm only trying to help you, too."

Trevin couldn't believe it. *Two hours?* What'd happened to him? He grew instantly weary of the argument, and begged to get off the phone. "Look, we'll talk again, Glen, sorry if I've snapped at you, or anybody. I didn't mean it. Bye."

As Trevin put the phone back in its carriage, he bent over, rubbing his face, straining to understand what had become of the time. A little wobbly, he became dizzier still when Solorio's door opened and the boss of the agency called him in.

* * *

Solorio closed the door behind Trevin as Trevin took one of the two guest chairs that faced the huge cedar desk. As Trevin settled into it, he felt ill at ease. Solorio made his way around to his high-backed chair, where he also took a seat and immediately folded his hands, looking tense himself. The ridiculous bust of Julius Caesar also glowered on the shelf past Solorio's shoulder from Trevin's perspective. Trevin had always hated that effigy. Such affectation. He waited for his boss to speak first.

"Trevin." That was Richard's form of greeting when there was something serious to talk about.

Trevin followed it with, "Richard."

Anxiety filled the air. Trevin had been here in this office hundreds of times—brainstorming, making presentations, talking projects—but this was different. Something was wrong. He didn't like it one bit. There was an aura that signaled danger. Normally, light rock would be playing from Solorio's satellite radio receiver. Today… nothing. Paranoia swept Trevin's psyche, and he began to wonder if anything bad had been discussed between Solorio and Glen. He didn't trust the dynamics of the firm anymore. And Richard was having a hard time making eye contact.

Trevin folded his hands as well and crossed one leg over the other knee. "Is everything all right?"

Solorio sighed. "We didn't get Handy Beaver."

"What?" Trevin felt a blow to his stomach. He was devastated. His heart immediately sank. Getting that account was crucial. "What happened?"

"We didn't get it," Solorio repeated. "I just found out an hour ago."

"I… thought we corrected course."

"I thought so, too," said Solorio. "But apparently, it didn't work. They decided to move on to another agency."

This was bad. Real bad. "I'm… I'm sorry," said Trevin, downplaying his shock.

Solorio's face contorted into a series of odd shapes, obviously thinking about something difficult to discuss. Leaning forward on the desk, he said, "Trevin how long have we known each other?"

There was way too much subtext in that question. "A long time, Richard. Three years."

Richard grabbed a pencil and started tapping it into his free palm. "You're my go-to guy, you've done great work. I'd like to know what you've done to my interns."

"Excuse me? I'm not following you." Now dread was positively forming inside Trevin's body.

"You didn't have anything to do with that attachment that punk sent over?"

"You mean Max? The mascot-thing?" The insinuation was offensive. Trevin clenched his hands. "If you're asking if I was somehow responsible for him sending that over, the answer is 'no.' You know that, I wouldn't do that. I hope you're not serious—"

"We all know you haven't been happy around here lately. I see you moping, looking like you've lost your best friend. You're on the Internet constantly—"

"That's not true—"

"You spend way too much time stewing over headlines and news rather than being that guy I used to know …"

Trevin wanted to apologize but what was there to apologize about? This was an exaggeration on Solorio's part, a stretch. Something really awful was going down here and he'd better brace.

"Trevin, we needed that account. It would've saved us, at least for a while."

"Excuse me, sir, but what does this have to do with the interns and me?"

"They look up to you; you're supposed to be leading by example."

Trevin actually shook his head. "I don't understand—"

"You're looking for another job, I know," Solorio interrupted, raising his tone. Trevin sank psychologically. "It's no secret; I know what happens around here in my firm."

It wouldn't have taken a scholar to figure out that Trevin's associate had ratted him out. His worst fears had been realized, his instincts correct, and he wanted to scream. "Richard," he said calmly, "instead of accusations that only cloud our problems, shouldn't we be forgetting about Handy Beaver and thinking of other ways we can bring money into Lightning Strikes?"

Solorio's perfectly trimmed eyebrows pulled together in a pinch. "Trevin, come on, we're grown men. You can be honest with me. What job are you going for?"

No longer able to withstand the strain, Trevin point-blank asked, "What the hell has Glen been feeding you?"

Solorio put the pencil down and leaned back again, smirking wisely. To him, it was as if he'd cracked a secret code. "So, are you taking it? I know you've been in communication with someone."

Trevin's insides were a mess. It felt like someone had reached into his intestines and wrenched them around. But being the no-nonsense, tough individual he was—some would say "lone wolf"—he decided he owed it to himself to be honest. He'd never been a coward. "Someone's called me,

Richard, that part's true. But that doesn't mean anything. Don't listen to Glen, he hasn't been himself lately."

"Neither have you," said Solorio curtly. "Will you be leaving us?"

Richard was out for blood. That was quite apparent to Trevin. People were changing, he thought, the world was getting meaner. "Richard, please don't jump to conclusions."

"Who is it? You can tell me."

"Uh… I'm not comfortable with that."

Solorio steepled his fingers. "I'm disappointed you didn't tell me first."

My sweet God, Trevin thought, sweat pooling at the small of his back. "What was there to tell?"

"I think using my time to search for other jobs is a bit dishonest, Trevin. What, is the weird weather clogging your judgment? Fucking with your head? You're a talented guy, but you've been on complete disconnect mode. I gotta be honest, there's plenty of fresh fish who'd work for less."

Trevin was astonished. This was what they called "being railroaded." "Sir… let's both calm down. We all need money in this economy, I'm grateful for this job—"

"You have a funny way of showing it."

Trevin was ready to lose it. He stood, unsure of what he himself was going to do. Solorio followed him with his eyes.

"I have to anticipate, Mr. Lambrose," Solorio said with an icy touch.

Mr. Lambrose? Trevin thought of only a single strategy: Make that call at four to Thomas Archer at Malligan and Totnes. If only that interview was already set up. Mr. Archer had said they were hiring, right? There was nowhere to go for Trevin, not yet anyway. "Richard," he said, staying collected. "I have to ask: What kind of arrangement's been made between you and Glen?"

"What are you talking about?"

"Something's going on, I know it. This… interrogation is wrong. You're not like this, we've known each other, we're friends. You guys have talked something out, he's covering his ass."

Now it was Solorio's time to stand. Even though Trevin was lean and muscular, and Solorio was fat and soft, Richard seemed like a giant to his younger employee. He lowered his voice. "Get back to work—now."

Trevin lingered, not knowing what to do. He wondered how everything in his life seemed to be imploding as it was—people, stress, frightening talks with priests, the world. He wanted to turn over Solorio's desk, and watch the man get buried under the weight of it, but naturally, he walked out instead. The awful affair ended.

* * *

Trevin found Benedict Arnold in his corner office and wanted to beat the shit out of him. Of course, the copy writer was feigning innocence, working with his back turned at his desk, the overhead lights off, only the desk lamp creating a necessary pool of light in an otherwise cave of a setting. Mellow New Age music was playing from his iPod port. Trevin pushed the door open further, looming in the doorway. This was *not* how he stood at Gladys Embery's entryway.

When Glen did turn, he acted surprise. "Oh, Trevin, how goes it? What's up?"

Trevin answered with a growl in his voice. "I felt sorry for you, Glen. I did. I genuinely cared about your well-being. Thanks a lot."

"What's the matter with you?"

Trevin's blood pressure shot through the roof. He looked around, made sure no one was watching and stepped in, shutting the door behind him, throwing a shadow over his colleague. "Stop playing dumb, Glen. Don't act more stupid than you have been."

"That was rude."

"Keep faking it. Shows how much you valued our friendship."

Outside the door, the receptionist knew something was up. She motioned to Goth Girl and a few of the interns, who also knew something was awry. They collected nearby for the show.

The two co-workers stared at each other. "Trevin," said Glen, not getting up. "Whatever your problem is—take it elsewhere. That infamous temper of yours will ruin you someday."

"I'm not going to do anything, Glen; I'm just telling you how disappointed I've become with you. It's a bad enough world out there, man, you've made it worse."

Glen turned his back on him, going back to work. "Drop the shit, Trev; I don't know what your problem is."

"You told Richard about my phone call from the agency. You've been aligning yourself with him for a while now. I don't know if it's to protect your job or make yourself look better, but you're putting me at risk, you're throwing me under the bus. Something bad's going down with the lack of business and you're hatching a scheme. You know we didn't get Handy

Beaver. When trust breaks down, it's everyone for themselves. You didn't have to go that route, we could've worked together. You've contributed nothing good to this, Glen."

Glen slapped off the music, this time acting mad. "It slipped, for fuck's sake, I'm sorry. It was nothing intentional, we were just talking. Richard asks me things, no harm was intended."

"Where do you have these chats, Glen, at his favorite bar a few blocks over?"

"We go there at times, yeah. Christ!"

"I won't be your sacrificial lamb, mister, and I won't be a party to you cheating on your wife, either. Don't come to me with your problems with Janelle. Stay away from the receptionist."

Glen turned to face him. "Don't get pious with me. Who do you think you are?"

Trevin couldn't help it; he banged the door with a fist, making everyone in the office jump. Solorio opened his door. When he asked what was going on, they pointed to Glen's door. Richard stormed in, immediately seeing the proverbial powder keg about to go off.

"Trevin, that's enough!" he yelled. "Get out of here." Trevin faced his opposition.

Richard must have seen the fire, as he flipped the tie over his shoulder and wildly pointed to the front door. "For the day," he ordered. "Glen, get back to work."

In Trevin's mind, things began to blur. Everything became surreal and dreamlike. This was not happening—*had* not happened. Trevin wrestled control back, understanding that he'd crossed a line. He gingerly walked out, put his computer to sleep, gathered his gym bag, and left, walking past the gauntlet of stunned expressions. Solorio remained fixed on the spot, shaking like a leaf. When he saw everyone standing around, he barked at them, scattering them back to duty.

* * *

But Trevin never went home. He'd raced back to the alley where he'd listened to the message from Malligan and Totnes, where he'd been swallowed up by whatever the heck had descended down from the sky, making him calm, making him think, making him relive magical moments from yesteryear. He'd been out here all afternoon until four o'clock—which was now—

searching against hope for the same phantasmagorical relief, praying it would just suck him up and take all his worries away.

His grandmother did not come back to him this time. The skies were clear. Trevin called Malligan and Totnes after performing relaxation exercises, desperate to set up that interview. He didn't know what Solorio was capable of now. He didn't know if his position was safe. A perky receptionist answered. All he discerned was the slurred pronunciation of the firm with one long, unintelligible greeting. He had to plug his ear against the noise.

"Trevin Lambrose for Thomas Archer. He called earlier, I'm returning his call."

Immediately, he was put on hold, forced to listen to jejune, programmed music. After a minute, the crap cut out and the same professional voice as before came on. "Thomas Archer."

"Mr. Archer! Trevin Lambrose calling you back."

"Trevin, yes, you got my message."

"I did, sir, thank you for calling. Hope I'm not catching you at a bad time."

"No, this is fine. Did you think about what I had to say?"

Trevin answered with a crack in his voice. "I did, and I'd love to meet with you."

"What's your schedule look like?"

"Uh, let's see …" He pretended to check. *I have to land this gig!* "It's fairly open."

"Good, let's set something up," said the voice. "By the way, Lightning Strikes is a fine outfit. Why do you want to move away from it?"

"Uh, I'm looking for a new challenge, Mr. Archer."

"Call me 'Thomas,' Trevin."

"Okay, Thomas. You said you're expanding, right? That's what you said."

"We are, surprisingly in this recession. When would you like to meet?"

Trevin was sweating worse than before. They set up an appointment for the following morning. Trevin had a lot of personal days. He could get away with it. An approaching garbage truck blew its horn and almost disarmed the attention.

"What was that?"

"Nothing," Trevin answered. "I'm by a window."

Trevin was given Malligan and Totnes' address, and was asked to bring his portfolio. "Tomorrow morning then," Trevin finished with. "Nine a.m. sharp. Thank you, Tho—"

He was hung up on, again. Trevin lifted his shirt to wipe his face. As he did, a disgusting piece of trash flew in and stuck to his bare stomach, startling the bejeezus out of him.

At least he had that interview!

* * *

And the day got worse from there. Trevin had to call Constance (and leave a message, naturally), asking if they could meet the following evening. He used the excuse that he wasn't feeling well, which wasn't horribly a lie, but he simply couldn't face someone he wanted so badly to start a relationship with being this rattled and dismayed. And by the time he arrived home (he'd driven again, performing reckless maneuvers on the expressway); Solorio had left an awful voice mail. He'd decided to suspend Trevin's full-time status following the outburst. Trevin wasn't to come in again at all until further informed. The message ended telling Trevin to expect his "stuff" sent to him via FedEx. Trevin had never heard or felt the cell ringing in the Blazer—it had been on the seat next to him, music blasting.

The full gravity of the situation caught up to Trevin as he was ascending the staircase at home and accidentally dropped the cell from his hand, lugging the gym bag up. He watched it slip through the slats of the balcony, and continue the same way all the way down to the soft dirt under the first-floor landing. Infuriated, he slogged back to retrieve it, crawling on hands and knees in the dank nether region, where he smelled old fertilizer and saw the creepy, cobwebbed basement window staring back at him like the Cyclops from Greek mythology.

It was official. He'd been thrown to the wolves.

As he stood up, brushing himself and the phone off, the thought of his dear parents once again sprang to mind. His recent foul moods had been a deterrent to call them and keep them up to date. What was he going to say to them now? They were going through their own issues: the economy in Rochester, the troubles at dad's plant, mom's work hours at the library being slashed …

I've worried them so much, he thought, cursing the day he was born. Trevin knew they had so much love in their hearts for their only child.

That broke *his* heart, failing like this. He remembered them opining for years that they wanted him to have more than they were afforded. That was going to be a reality. Not presently, that was.

He'd wait until he landed that job at Malligan and Totnes… and then call them!

He trudged back upstairs, went inside, and slammed the door.

* * *

But his parents called him anyway. That evening. Trevin had been on the balcony in a rickety lawn chair, observing bizarre "sun dogs"—or mock suns—sparking up in the hazy, swirling clouds flanking the actual sun. Four flaring points of prismatic glory were at their peak, creating an illusion of a giant Christian cross in the sky. Trevin remembered reading how old sea-faring civilizations used to witness this very phenomenon in awe, believing God was signaling to them.

Carl Lambrose's 67-year old voice sounded as rich as ever, soothing Trevin's soul. "How're you doing, son?" he asked. "It's been a while since we talked. What—two, three weeks?"

"A little too long, dad, sorry," Trevin replied.

"Is this a bad time to call?"

"It's never a bad time to hear from you, dad. What's up?"

"Your mother and I were watching the news. It was so terrible we had to turn it off. We wanted to talk to you, we were thinking of you. So here we are. How are you?"

"I'm doing okay, dad. Where's mom?"

"She's loading the dishwasher; she'll be on in a minute."

That had been a long-standing tradition in Trevin/mom-dad phone calls. First one got on, then the other grabbed the other line.

"So how are you, dad, everything all right?"

"Sure," answered his father. "How are you?"

Trevin noticed two of the wooden balustrades on his balcony railing looked loose. He put his hand on them and shook. Yes, they weren't attached as solidly as they should be. That wasn't good. He figured he'd better have his landlord Louie Fovos check that out ASAP. "Uh… fine," Trevin finally answered.

Dad said, "I don't like the 'uh.'"

Trevin smiled. "I'm not stammering."

"How's everything at Lightning Strikes?"

"Um, fine. Summer's coming. How's the garden coming along?"

"I'm just planting now, I was out before dinner. Should be a good one if we ever get rain. The almanac's calling for an unusually hot summer."

"Been a hot spring already," said Trevin, going back to the sun dogs, which triggered an inadvertent recollection of himself as a young boy, play-wrestling dad in the house, mom shouting at them to stop. Trevin laughed to himself, asking his father about it.

"Wrestling?" queried dad. "Whatever made you think of that?"

"I'm just growing nostalgic in my old age."

"Your mother hated when we did that. I got in a few good licks."

"You were lucky," said Trevin, sending the two men chuckling together.

"Wait—" said dad, "Your mother got on. April! Your son's bringing up times we used to wrestle in the house."

"And it's a good thing you two outgrew that," said his mother, voice cheery and upbeat. "Hello, Trevin." Trevin smiled again and greeted her back. It was so good to hear her. April Lambrose was a year younger than his father. "We were getting worried," she said. "You haven't called."

Trevin apologized a second time. He knew he'd have to explain how busy he'd been, hiding the real facts.

"No gym tonight?"

"Not tonight, mom. I need a break."

"How's that new lady you're seeing—Constance?"

"Funny you should ask, mom. We're getting together tomorrow night, as a matter of fact. After work." He winced as he said "work."

"Well, good luck with that," she said. "You've told us of her. She sounds like a nice person."

Not wanting to feel any worse about Constance, Trevin turned the tables, asking about them. With heavy voices, they filled him in on their trials and tribulations. They were saying rosaries every night, going to Mass constantly—the usual. They agreed to stop interrogating each other when they realized they were sounding grim. Enough was enough. Happier days would present themselves. They told Trevin of their power walk excursions.

"Your father has us out a lot," mom said, switching gears.

Trevin was delighted to hear it. "That's good, you guys, keep healthy."

In fact, dad thought it a good idea to go on one now. They had an unbelievable sunset going—being on Eastern Time, an hour later—and he didn't want to waste it. Dad had been finding the sunsets inspirational lately, something Trevin found highly intriguing. And understandable.

Mom said, "I know you must be enjoying the strangeness in the skies, Trevin. Have you painted anything about it yet?"

"No, not yet, mom."

"They're like glimpses of heaven."

Trevin paused. "That's beautiful, mom—wow—I'll remember that."

"That's who you get your imagination from, son," said dad. "April always was in touch with poetry."

"Carl, no I'm not."

"On that note, son, we'll let you go."

"Okay, dad. I have to eat some dinner anyway."

His mother pounced. "It's seven-thirty and you haven't had dinner yet? Trevin, what's wrong with you?"

"Mom, I've been busy."

"What an oaf," dad joked, bringing an even brighter smile to Trevin's face.

"Want a shot in the jaw, dad?"

"You could try it if you were here," dad countered. "But you'd lose, sadly."

Mom stopped them. "That's it, we're ending this. We love you, Trevin. Let us know if you're thinking of coming home soon. We'd love to see you. We'd pay for the ticket."

"Oh, no you wouldn't," said Trevin, immediately. "I've been thinking about coming home, waiting for the right time. It'll be soon, I promise. Love you guys, too."

After they hung up, Trevin still felt the battery acid-like taste in his throat, probably bile from all the covering up. The firmament was showing its first hints of nightfall. The sun dogs had gone away, replaced by a mammoth halo forming tighter around the sun as it was absorbed by the horizon. He decided to try to take its beauty and vision into the land of sleep with him tonight. His sanity depended on it.

CHAPTER 7

The train blasted past, nearly sweeping Trevin off the platform. A watchful commuter reached out and held him back, warning him to be careful. The el eventually ground to a halt some distance ahead, leaving Trevin and the other commuters at the back of the herd. The screeching made his jaw clench—an ugly, grating reverberation shattering his last nerve. With one hand, he blocked the brilliant early morning sunshine. With the other, he gripped his alternate portfolio as tightly as he could. Already he was perspiring. He hated wearing this stuffy button shirt, tie and slacks, but he had to make the best impression possible with Malligan and Totnes. He was lucky he got any sleep at all.

When the doors opened, the rush of humanity piled off and on. At that very moment, Trevin felt the cell phone buzzing in his pants pocket. As much as he hated the fear of being late, he stepped back from the crowd, checking to see who was calling.

It was Malligan and Totnes. He didn't like the pit in his gut.

Letting the current train go, Trevin answered, plugging his free ear. Announcements were making it difficult to hear. "Trevin Lambrose."

"Mr. Lambrose?" It was a different, perkier representative than the day before. "My name is Brenda from Malligan and Totnes. I'm calling on behalf of Thomas Archer. Yesterday, you'd set up an appointment with him." She was saccharin, well-rehearsed.

Trevin grew suspicious. "Yes?"

"How are you this morning?"

He didn't want to be rude, but it felt like his knees were buckling. Nervously, he chose the response, "I'm fine, Brenda. I'm stepping on the el to come down now."

"That's what we're calling about. Mr. Archer wanted me to reach you before you did. He's sorry if we're inconveniencing you, but there's no need to come in this morning."

Trevin choked, coughed. "What …?"

"Sorry for calling at the last minute."

"Brenda. What happened? Is this a cancellation?"

"Yes. Mr. Archer wasn't happy about it, trust me."

Trevin's tongue went dry. "What's going on?"

Brenda sighed, but remained intact. "Something's happened to the designer position we were interested in you for."

"*Were* interested? As in past tense?" This was his worst fear manifesting.

"Mr. Lambrose, we had an unexpected snag pop up last evening. It caused us to have a meeting well into the night about it. We thought we had certain accounts, but a key player backed out at the last minute. We're looking into legal matters now. It was too late to call you last night."

Trevin felt massive sinking in his stomach, his extremities going numb. "Uh… does this mean things have… changed?"

"Things have changed, yes. We're sorry if you took time off work. Thomas didn't see this coming, none of us did."

Another train was roaring in, adding to the stress. Trevin strained against it. "When will Thomas—Mr. Archer— be ready, Brenda?"

"We have no way of knowing at this point. Just sit tight at your current job and we'll be in touch."

The words echoed painfully in his head: *Just sit tight at your current job.* Didn't everyone know he didn't have one anymore? Trevin knew he was in a dire predicament. "Brenda—this is important for me to know—*do* you think he'll be in touch?"

"Mr. Lambrose, I can't answer that with certainty. We're putting out fires, lawyers are involved."

"So you're saying I shouldn't come in?"

"I'm saying you shouldn't come in, yes."

In a last-ditch effort, he appealed on a personal level. "Brenda, do you have influence there? Do you think you can make sure he does call when he can?"

"Mr. Lambrose, I have to go, thank you for your interest in Malligan and Totnes. Have a nice day."

"But I—"

She hung up, leaving Trevin fearing facing joblessness and holding what he thought of as a cursed piece of plastic to his head. As the grind of the mincing metal once more assaulted his ears, he started to hyperventilate. It became impossible to breathe. He had to think quickly about what he was going to do. This was a vital decision.

* * *

Trevin went to the interview anyway. He'd taken the next el downtown, and was now bursting through the double glass doors at the advertising competitor, Malligan and Totnes. Immediately, he was struck with its much-glitzier interior than his traitorous Lightning Strikes—the waiting area alone was glamorous as hell. The receptionist desk was momentarily unmanned. There was a monolithic half-wall behind it with frosted glass partitions to the sides hiding the bulk of the agency from view. He looked above the half-wall, wiping the sweat from his forehead, noting the exposed duct and pipe work and track lighting—a renovated factory loft. Very chic. Would he love to work here!

Only a few paces to the front desk …

He shot forward, leaning on the counter and looking around, trying to catch someone's attention. Pop rock played from a tiny radio beneath him, pens scattered atop a day planner. Legally speaking, he was trespassing, he knew. But someone was close, he could hear them, and this was way too damn important to back away from. The smell of brewed coffee reminded him of Goth Girl, and her readiness with a pot at his former place of employment.

The rat bastards …

A young woman appeared from behind the frosted glass wall to the right. She said hello with a surprised look, saying she didn't know someone had walked in. Trevin tried to compose himself. She was flawlessly dressed, just the right amount of makeup. She could be Brenda, he wondered, the one who'd ruined his last hope. Maybe it was his glare that had her averting eye contact. She took a seat behind the computer and asked how she could help.

"Trevin Lambrose," he replied, lifting his portfolio as proof. "I'm here for Thomas Archer. Are you Brenda?"

"I'm not," she answered. "Brenda's busy."

This might've been a lie. In his current state of mind, Trevin thought of many conspiratorial things. He strained not to come off as a psycho. "He's expecting me."

She said, "I don't believe he's seeing anyone this morning."

"I'll wait," he said, adding a "'please,'" and then smiled at her.

Perhaps reading bad intentions, the pixie-woman quickly eyeballed around, as if looking for an escape route. Blobs of shadowy figures were coming and going behind the frosted glass like an exotic Kabuki theater show. Trevin wondered who was who. She checked the planner. Trevin sighed uneasily. Obviously not seeing the guest name, she picked up the phone, telling Trevin to hold a moment. She pressed an extension. Trevin heard a male voice come on within seconds. She turned in her chair and whispered. Trevin heard his name said twice. There was obvious confusion. She was given instructions and she hung up, standing. With remarkably polished fingernails, she pointed at the chairs behind him. "Can you wait there?"

"Of course." Trevin turned around and parked himself in the nearest one, portfolio resting on his lap. She then disappeared into the depths of the organization.

Trevin waited, unable to convince himself that what he was doing was not only possible professional suicide but a sure sign he was cracking. He hadn't planned anything here beyond demanding—well, asking—to see the big shot who'd raised his spirits yesterday, and have that interview, and prove to him he'd be insane not to hire Trevin.

The 50ish cool cat himself eventually appeared, trying to hide his noticeable suspicion, followed closely by the receptionist, who was now mousy, trailing like a frightened lamb. Trevin thought they were eyeing him like the Frankenstein monster. Like his neighbor Peter Bebziak, this man was also a giant, perhaps six-foot-five, but as skinny as a rake. Extending his hand, they met in the middle of the reception floor as Trevin stood, each introducing themselves.

"Didn't... Brenda say for you to not come in today?" asked Mr. Archer.

So it is Brenda, thought Trevin. *The sneak.* "She did," he answered.

Mr. Archer still seemed bewildered, looking Trevin over. "So... forgive me for sounding blunt, but why are you here then?"

"I was in the neighborhood," Trevin lied.

"You just happened to have your portfolio?"

Trevin shrugged. He was unable not to notice the creative director's wacky tie. It was at eye level, with stars and planets all over it, very goofy and very cosmic. Perhaps the gent had a sense of humor. That might be good. Mr. Archer held back a twinkle of irritation.

"It was important to meet," Trevin said. "I know things are crazy here—they're crazy for me, too— but I wanted to meet in person, at least show you what I could offer."

Brenda leaned in, asking, "Want me to call someone?"

Mr. Archer told her to get back to work. A few other "creatives" were about now, meandering in and out to see what was going on. They must've been tipped off. Trevin believed himself to now be entertainment for the troops. *How many are interns?* he considered.

"Mr. Lambrose," Mr. Archer reiterated coolly, "let me be clear. We've explained our situation. This has been a personally embarrassing one for me, but things have changed since we spoke yesterday. I appreciate your determination, but you know the facts now."

"I understand," Trevin said, dread flooding in. "But with all respect, sir, determination is something you can't read on a CV. Just allow me to give you a preview of what I can—will—be able to do for you. Please."

The human skyscraper pursed his lips, mulled a few things over, and checked his watch. Then, perhaps to mollify the amped-up stranger at the door, returned a pleasant front. "Come with me."

* * *

Trevin gave it his best shot in the (vastly more impressive conference room than Lightning Strikes, of course), fighting hard to keep sweat from appearing and dripping on his pages. He turned them for Mr. Archer. Trevin gave a great pitch, explaining style, strategy and result.

But it wasn't enough to shake the reality of the situation …

He wasn't getting the job.

During the futile exercise, he had the distinct feeling the tall man was also keeping one watchful eye on him, determining whether or not he was a malfunctioning idiot.

"I'm screwed," Trevin muttered to himself as he left Malligan and Totnes and waited for the elevator. Through the double glass doors inside the office, Brenda's eyes could still be seen over the reception desk, staring at him, judging him.

Trevin did what any lad would do in a fractured state, facing a jobless future with no prospect in sight during the worst recession in eighty years, worried about an increasingly deteriorating world: He threw up in the lift on the way down.

CHAPTER 8

Trevin shrunk into a downtown alley—hoping, praying, wishing—to return to better days. Return to times when life was breezy and rich and happy. He had a terrific childhood, with great parents and a kind grandmother. And many great friends, a couple of loving girlfriends, and wonderful times he couldn't possibly all remember. *What were memories for anyway?* he asked the sky. *To torture people later in years? To remind them of how things used to be, as opposed to how they are now?* He didn't want to wallow in self pity—that was immature—but he felt like crap. He yearned to have joy in his heart again. Oh, to live in that euphoric state of his happiest memories forever.

Memories, sweet memories. At least he had them. He imagined poor souls who were brain dead, or who had Alzheimer's. Where did their memories go? Did they have them? Surely, the universe wasn't *that* cruel…

He ended up staying downtown, baking in the heat, walking around in a daze. A bright spot flared into his consciousness—Constance! He was going to see her tonight! Thank God he hadn't forgotten! There was no way he was going to let anything get in the way of seeing her. She was inspiration… solace… light.

But he'd have to tell her she was dating a bum. A jerk with no job.

He was not going to meet her in his current mental condition—full of rage and despair, crying out to the heavens that seemed to be saying something back.

He wasn't that far from Lightning Strikes. Solorio's bar was somewhere nearby. The one where Glen had conspired with Richard.

Trevin checked the time on his cell. It was approaching late afternoon. The rummy may be on a bar stool by now, sucking down his beer and a basket of wings, devising a scheme to screw his next victim. After another turn, Trevin found it.

Over its entrance, the cheap awning flapped like a film prop from a bad *noir* potboiler. Trevin approached it, grabbing the rusted, sun-baked handle on the warped wooden door, deciding whether or not to go in. Adrenaline was raging, making him fantasize of all kinds of vengeful acts. He had to get that out of his mind. Maybe Trevin could turn this nightmare around, appeal to Solorio's better half, get his position back. It was worth a shot.

Trevin yanked the metal lever and walked in.

It was mighty dark in here. The place stunk like a cave of rancid cigarettes with mopped liquor stains on the floor. As the door shut behind him, Trevin teetered, waiting for his irises to adjust to the lack of light. There were handfuls of scrubs in the joint, some playing pool in a back room. Sure enough, he spotted his ex-boss, alone and lost in the television mounted high behind the bar: a home stand with the Cubs.

Trevin proceeded forward, the clacking of billiard balls brittle and taut. He regretted not being able to ditch the portfolio: a sure sign he'd been out peddling. Normally, he would've enjoyed absorbing an environment like this for morbid reference, but today, things were far from normal.

Solorio didn't see him at first. Trevin saddled up alongside and waited. Finally, his presence interrupted a sip.

"Well, look who it is," said Solorio with surprise. "What're you doing here?"

Making sure he hadn't carried filth and muck from the street onto himself, Trevin remained as calm and as diplomatic as possible. "I was around. I remembered you came here. Just walked in. I was wondering if there's any way we could talk. Cooler heads prevail, you know."

Solorio stared. He set his half-empty bottle of beer on the bar and leaned away, broadcasting coldness. "I don't think talking through things is possible, Trevin."

Given the precarious nature of his mood, Trevin deemed it best not to be combative. The bartender addressed him, and Trevin asked for ice water, downing the glass like he'd been in the desert for a week. Solorio filled with disquiet. He caught the portfolio by Trevin's leg.

"Where were you?" Richard asked.

But Trevin didn't want to discuss that. He tried again. "Richard, we need to talk. Please."

"Don't do this, Trevin."

"We can be gentlemen."

Solorio crumpled a napkin and wiped his lips, trying to ignore the bother. "I made up my mind, Trevin." Then he turned his back to check out the billiards game.

Trevin didn't like the puffy man turning his back on him. Trevin didn't like anyone turning their back on him—figuratively or literally. "Things were heated, Richard—abnormal given the time we've known each other."

Solorio glared at him. Really glared. "Trevin, I have enough stress in my life. I've hired someone else. There, I said it. The deal's done."

Trevin almost gave an audible gasp. "What?"

"One of the interns. Not the Handy Beaver idiot—don't worry there."

Trevin almost couldn't speak. He felt the blood drain from his head. "You let me go and then you hired an intern? *Already?*"

"He's not making what you did."

"That's not the issue."

"Just deal with it, Trevin. Now that you've tracked me down, I'm telling you like it is."

"I'm not tracking you down, Richard, I'm trying to make amends, start anew. You were very happy with me for a long time. I've made some mistakes that I'm sorry for …"

"Save it," Solorio scoffed, acquiescing to a bag of pretzels. "Things change."

"So it's a done deal?" asked Trevin. "You could've asked me to take a pay cut."

"We've parted ways, Trevin," Solorio said, fixating now on the Cubs game. Trevin stood his ground, he couldn't leave. Without looking at him, Richard asked, "What happened to the gig? You can't be here 'cause it's going great."

Red was all Trevin saw. How could he have let this manipulator have so much power over his livelihood? Unwisely, he hissed, "Worry less about me and focus instead on the suck-ups who are ruining your agency."

"That …" Solorio said with deliberation, smacking the bottle on the bar, "… was rude."

The bartender warned the two men to calm down.

Trevin was shaking, not knowing what to next expect from himself. He was aware he was losing control, and he hated it. He couldn't believe the irreversible damage he was inflicting to his reputation. Richard knew a lot of people. Trevin could kiss away any good reference.

"Oh, that was rude, Richard? Really? Don't think I don't know what rude is. Don't think I don't know you're getting all that free labor from the interns, and billing the clients for their services. They should be paid for that, at least once in a while. You're turning ruthless, Richard. Glen's kissing your ass to save his neck. You two conspired to get rid of me, looking for ways to save money. Is that what I became to you—a financial burden? What happened to loyalty? I have to live, too."

The images from the television flickered off of Solorio's eyeballs, giving him a diabolical appearance. He said, "Do you have any idea how much worse you're making things, Trevin?"

"You've got to contribute positively, Richard, things are out of balance."

Solorio snidely laughed. "How about this? All this time, I never knew I had a soothsayer in my midst. I'm not blind, Trevin, you've had nothing but disdain for me, my company and others for a while now. You're a wreck and you bring it in every day."

"That's an exaggeration."

"Is it?" Solorio finished his beer and prepared to head out, throwing a few bills on the bar. When he stood, he met Trevin's frown and dropped the magic question. "You didn't get the job, did you?"

Trevin remained still. That said it all.

"Oh fuck—that's it, isn't it?" Solorio shook his head. "Rule Number One. Never quit a job unless you have another one lined up, definitely. School of hard knocks, one-oh-one."

Trevin's hand reflexively lashed out, latching onto the smart mouth's wrist. The bartender warned again, saying he'd call the police. Solorio advised, "Let… go."

Trevin eased his grip. Solorio shook his wrist free, headed out the door.

Trevin remained fixed, shaking uncontrollably. Unable to restrain emotions, he went after his ex-boss, catching up to him on the bustling sidewalk.

"Don't even think about it, Trevin," Richard cautioned. "Don't get crazy."

Both were shielding their faces from the blasting sunshine, squinting their eyes. Trevin was screaming to himself in his head: *What are you doing? Stop. Stop!*

Solorio tried getting away, opening the distance without jogging, weaving in and out of pedestrians, bumping into a few.

"This is how you repay me?" Trevin chided out loud. "After all the hard work I did for Lightning Strikes? We won awards! Prospered! Hell, I went to your house for Thanksgiving the first year. Art is my life, Richard, you know that!"

"This is how you're repaying *me,* Trevin—look at you! You're going to physically assault me? Is that why you didn't get the job—you turned into a madman for them, too? Word travels fast, fella. The world sucks, Mr. Lambrose, accept it."

"Let's be reasonable."

"You first! Go to your old people and bitch at them! They don't have anything better to do."

They stopped at an intersection. Pedestrians gathered. Trevin imagined cold cocking the wuss as they waited to cross. The angry ruby traffic light fueled Trevin's fury. Solorio couldn't wait. He stepped off the curb and ran across the street, a box truck blasting its horn, missing him by inches. Bystanders shook their heads, someone calling him a stupid ass.

Trevin would never see the spineless worm again. It was just as well. He had become a wild-eyed maniac, pleading for mercy. Another abyss he'd fallen into. He headed off in the opposite direction, against the grain of the still-balanced.

CHAPTER 9

—◄ ►—

Trevin was unable to comprehend what he'd nearly driven himself to do. He did not need to lose his humanity, although it felt humanity was losing him. Up until yesterday, Solorio had been the man who'd put food on his table for the past three years. With the Chicago skyline at his back, he stared out to a calm and glittering Lake Michigan just before sunset, feeling horrible about himself, sensing the ebbing light behind him gearing up for another dazzling display. The lake itself reflected a time of day—a precise and fleeting singularity—where the water was actually lighter in tone than the sky. At the horizon due east, twilight had already crept in.

In other words, the mood was sacred.

Mostly, he had the place to himself on this favorite Grant Park bench. Only a few bicyclists zipped by on the path designed for them, disrupting the panorama. A jogger and a dog walker also moved past. The gulls cawed as the waves lapped the shoreline. A thin breeze snapped up, mercifully cooling his skin. He could hear the rush hour traffic on Lake Shore Drive. He should have felt peace. Instead, he felt dread and guilt. Constance would be coming soon, and she wouldn't know she'd be entering the presence of an almost-maniac/ loser. Glen had been right—he did have to get a check on his own temper.

Closing his eyes, Trevin meditated, pretending an invisible barrier of protection was surrounding him, stopping the really bad stuff from ruining the moment.

Someone was watching him. He sensed it. It was the most extraordinary supernatural sensation. He climbed off the bench and turned around, hit by the spectacle. The sunset's rays were blasting upward behind the skyscrapers like giant, straight fingers, reaching to the wild clouds forming overhead. It was a pageantry of visual splendor. His eyes drank it like nectar, his breath stolen. But he still knew that someone was studying him from afar.

He discovered adults presiding over laughing children way down in the park to his right. The little ones were running around like happy little hornets, tagging each other with elfin hands, blissfully unaware of the world around them. Maybe the sky was protecting them. When he looked back, there was someone there, at Lake Shore Drive's edge: a contour female form in a flowing spring dress.

Constance.

She hadn't been there before, had she? Regardless, Trevin recognized her shape immediately—her perfect shape and whipping, mid-shoulder length hair, blowing distinctly against the speeding vehicles behind her. It actually made him smile for the first time in forever.

He held up a hand and waved. *Remember this picture*, he ordered himself. *Remember it for the future.* Constance waved back and began the long trek toward him, traversing the lush expanse of public lawn. When she halted in an engaging pose feet away, hands on hips, head tilted, she also smiled. And as he remembered, it was its own force of nature. The sunset only enhanced her natural beauty. He wished to express all he felt—awe, dawning love, relief—but that would have been inappropriate. Not this early. Her husky voice took the initiative, and she opened with a joke.

"What's a looker like you doing alone in a park like this?"

The day's revulsion shattered. "You're… beautiful," he said, slack-jawed.

She laughed. For a moment, it sounded literally like musical tones to Trevin's ears. He shook the crazy notion off and composed himself.

She came close. "Wow. Now that's an opening line." As he beheld her magnificently freckled face, her expression changed, but she read him on a deeper level. "What's wrong?" she asked sympathetically.

This stunned Trevin. He stuttered. He wanted to tell her about all the bad he had done, had been done to him. "Nothing, nothing. Sorry about last night."

"Don't worry about it. We're together now."

He fell into her and hugged her suddenly, kissing her on the cheek, touching the side of her head with his cupped hand. She was surprised, but hugged back, smiling again like no one's business. The scent of her hair was heavenly, her bare shoulders and back like a treasure from God. When he released her, he said, "Hope that wasn't too forward."

She considered him with her limpid brown eyes. "No, it was sweet. Sorry I was late. I had to finish up at the office."

"You're not late."

"But something's wrong."

He was so distracted, unable to get off the unique planes of her face. She wasn't much shorter than him, only an inch or so, but her aura approached giantess status. "Put it this way," he said, "you're the best thing I've seen all day."

She arched her eyebrows. "Wow again."

"Tell me, Constance, do you have to work on that smile or does it come naturally? It could move mountains."

"I'm just glad to be here, Trevin. Stop with the compliments."

"I have to tell you something. Sit down, please."

He led her back to the bench, where they both sat facing the ever-deepening colors of Lake Michigan, looking more magical by the minute. Trevin figured he'd better get all the mucky stuff out of the way now. If he was going to lose her so early on for being an idiot, why not get it over and done with? "I'm going to come straight out and tell you something… it's difficult for me to say …"

"Spit it out, Trevin, now you're worrying me."

He took a deep breath, blew it out and blurted, "I lost my job today. Well, yesterday, actually. It's a crazy story and I don't understand how it all happened, but everything was fine when you and I talked on the phone the other night—well, not so fine. Anyway, I thought I had a new one lined up, but as it turned out… I didn't. And I can't get my old one back—although I tried with nearly disastrous results. I'm upset, frightened, depressed, and I don't blame you if you get up and leave now. I threw up in an elevator."

Her eyes blinked a dozen times. "You lost your job because you threw up in an elevator?"

He almost laughed, almost able to find the humor in her joke. He shook his head no. "No, I lost my job because things got real messed up. Save me."

Her expression changed several times, trying to figure him out. A corner lifted on her great lips. "Save you? From what?"

"I don't know why I said that."

"Trevin, look, you lost your job. So what? It's not the end of the world." Funny she should say that. It was beginning to feel that way to Trevin. "And you think I'm going to walk away because of it?"

"I don't know. Some would. This is incredibly humiliating."

She took his hand. "Trevin, we might not know each other very well yet, or know what this is—you and me—but I can tell you I know a winner when I see one. I am so sorry I've not been around or returned many calls. That's what happens when you're the new kid on the block—you get sidetracked. You're the first person I've wanted to know here in Chicago. We met for a reason. I'm sorry you lost your job, but there's no judgment here, not from me. That's happening to a lot of people right now. We can move on from this."

Millions of pounds lifted from his shoulders. This woman also had the knack to always say the right thing. What a gift. He laughed instead, the sharp result of a catharsis. She spotted his portfolio.

"Is that your artwork? Can I see?"

"With what light's left, we can try."

Handing it over, he unzipped the case for her, opening to the first page, where she was immediately blown away by the advertising sample. Page after page, she studied his craft, listening to what he explained about each one. She didn't understand the lingo, but did understand real talent when she saw it. She said as much.

"You've really been handed a gift," she said afterward, snuggling up close to him.

He was on cloud nine, and vowed he wasn't giving up until he landed that next gig.

"Good," she said. "Don't. A good struggle is a divine struggle. Maybe that's why I was allocated to you."

The term stopped him cold. "Allocated?" Her gaze bore into him.

"You're on a path, Trevin. Everything—and I mean everything—happens for a reason. Good and bad."

"So… you're a fatalist," he said.

"Sort of. Like the day we met at the bookstore: I saw good things for us."

To keep his heart from leaping out of his chest, he diverted back to the eastern horizon, where a slow-moving boat was way out, going on a straight line. A single onboard light winked off and on, creating a visually serene and most artistic distraction. "What little I know of you, Constance, I can tell you this: There's tremendous light inside you."

"That is so nice," she replied. "Aren't you a peach? Thank you. What do you say we go for a walk along the lake? Let's not waste this magical lighting."

"Let's go," said Trevin.

* * *

They learned more of each other—walking arm in arm—talking backgrounds and interests, the trek taking them along the beautiful scenery of the shoreline path, heading north toward DuSable Harbor. Trevin hadn't felt so satisfied in months. He asked her how she liked temping. She said it was fine, while she figured out a few things. He told her how he'd marveled at her incredible optimism, and how it had inspired him when they were together. And tonight, she explained how she'd moved to the Windy City to explore other parts of the country. Life in small-town California wasn't all it was cracked up to be. Chicago had a rawness she'd heard of—a realness—and she wished to experience it. Here was a reputation for its natives to be the "salt-of-the-Earth types."

"Some of them," Trevin corrected.

He had a thousand questions, but his head had moved into a thankful state, and an interrogation would've been inappropriate. He did ask if she was thinking of sticking around Chicago.

"For the time being," she answered.

"Been married? Kids? Leave someone in California?"

She hadn't, and even chuckled at the question. "I'm a late-bloomer, I guess, I'm just starting to open up. I've always been shy. Why— got something in mind?"

Trevin laughed back, blushing. "I'm sorry, I don't mean to pry. I'll shut my mouth now. Best not to be a guileless goat."

"By all means," she said flirtatiously, squeezing his arm, "bleat away."

* * *

They'd been together for an hour and had covered a lot of ground, conversation-wise and around the Grant Park area. Their journey had also taken them into the night, where the lights of the city sparkled like diamonds. And Michigan Avenue—the Magnificent Mile—seemed to be even more alive with its zipping cabs and dazzling window displays.

She hadn't driven, she didn't own a car, and in front of the Art Institute, where they decided it best to call it a night, Constance was prepared to hail one of the taxis. Trevin wasn't going to have her pay. "I insist," he said. "I asked you here."

"But you didn't twist my arm, Trevin," she said. "I wanted to be here. Don't be ridiculous."

By the time they flagged one down, the open spots in the sky had filled in with strange, thickly-shaped clouds, like it was threatening to rain. But it hadn't done so in so long that he wasn't worried about it, and mentioned so. She had no reason to wish she had an umbrella.

"It would be nice," he said, "but it's done this for months now, then it clears up. I'm not worried about getting wet on my way home. You shouldn't either."

This had been great for both of them, a definite departure from their usual hectic schedules. Trevin had even forgotten about his awful predicament for the time being, and even felt a little bit confident he could land on his feet quickly with Constance around. He couldn't believe how extreme he'd seen himself get, and he wanted to work on that. *Everything will work out,* he told himself. *Right?* At least she made him feel that way.

Her eyes glittered as she looked around at the sights of the city, the cabbie impatiently waiting to get going. She asked if he thought he'd ever get his work in the Art Institute.

"Maybe after I'm gone," he answered kiddingly. "Like the tired old joke."

She looked at him curiously, cocking her head. "I've never heard that joke."

"Never mind," he said, and gestured at the driver to be cool when he huffed and puffed and told her to get in. "Before you go, Constance, just tell me something. Tell me *one* thing that you love in life. I want to take that home with me."

"Memories," she answered, hand on the open door. "I love memories more than anything else. *Your* memories. I want to hear about them. We'll have time… I want you to tell me about them, no holding back. We can do something with them."

He looked at her, awestruck. "We can do something with them?"

He thought of her answer, not knowing what to say. It was one of the most unique replies he'd ever heard.

As if reading his thoughts, she added, "I know you've been sentimental—nostalgic—lately. Reminded of better days. It's written in your eyes. Your distress today is already a memory. A bad one, but it's a memory. Let it dissipate. The future loves the past." She shrugged her adorable shoulders. "Guess I picked the right person to be with."

Her gaze tunneled into his very soul. Then suddenly, an enormous whitish flash split the clouds, lighting the entire sky up, scaring him. He actually ducked and swore, then apologized when he saw she was hardly fazed. The cabbie was even looking up through his windshield, trying to figure out just what exactly that was.

"What was that, lightning?" he said, shocked, not expecting an answer.

Her face was serene. "I don't know."

Trevin felt stupid.

She got in and powered her window down, telling him she hoped to see him again soon. He handed the driver some money as she explained to the cabbie where she needed to go. Trevin leaned into her window and gave her another kiss on the cheek.

"You're also very cryptic," he said, then smirked.

"You won't be left in the dark for long," she said, then winked at him. "Stay strong."

He stepped back from the curb. As the taxi pulled away, making an illegal U-turn heading south on Michigan Avenue, she called back, "Don't keep me waiting—let me know what your schedule's like."

And she was gone. No chance to decode the conundrum. His attention shifted to the sky.

CHAPTER 10

Some small fireworks were already wowing the crowd at twilight. Roman candles, flying spinners and fire fountains shot off from the opposite end of the street, where Trevin's thoughts went to poor Mrs. Dombrowski, the old woman who'd been attacked some time ago. He'd received the invitation Ruth and Peter Bebziak had promised, even as attempts at getting together and just being generally neighborly with them hadn't been made.

What kept Trevin from fully letting himself go here at the Munnison Street Fourth of July block party was the fact that he hadn't yet landed a job. And he'd tried. National unemployment levels were at record highs. It was almost two months after the night at Grant Park, where he'd told Constance about Lightning Strikes. But true to her word, she was still with him, and still hadn't acted the least bit concerned about any of his hardships. In fact, she'd constantly reminded him to stay positive and alert, collect his unemployment benefits with dignity, do bang-up jobs with the few freelance gigs he'd landed, and never, ever give up.

To her puzzlement, she'd asked why Trevin had kept matters from his folks. She'd learned how close he was to them and how she thought it best for him to be truthful. He'd told her they'd been through enough—he was waiting for the moment to spring the news.

What was most splendid at the moment was the fact that Constance Summerlin was on his arm. He still felt like he was on top of the world when she was with him.

As they shuffled further into the thickening crowd, he asked her if she was okay. A few drunks and rowdies were already stumbling about. Most were behaved.

"Of course," Constance answered, wide-eyed and giddy. "I'm having a great time. I love this!"

The noise and over-stimulation were factors. To Trevin, at least. On both ends of Munnison, wooden sawhorses set the boundaries, a few city police cars parked there to boot. In order to make room, all the neighbors had their vehicles berthed the next block over.

Trevin and Constance agreed they'd never witnessed so many families gathered in one stretch—grills and barbecues lighting up individual lawns, the smell of delicious meats permeating the air. Cotton candy, corn on the cob and many other assorted summer treats enticed and teased. Lawn chairs were everywhere, reminding Trevin of some modern art installation. He told Constance that maybe he should've brought his camera, and she laughed and beamed, soaking in the surroundings like a vacuum cleaner.

Men gawked at her. Who could blame them? She was a sight. Trevin had to stifle the ugly barbs of paranoia and insecurity that kept creeping up inside him as they made their way through the gauntlet. He hated himself for feeling jealous, and tried not to let it show. He didn't need to make himself more insecure.

Tiki Torches and string lights blazed from sidewalk and stoop. Hammocks swung between trees, and older citizens lolled about on porch swings, sipping lemonade and watching the scenes. Seeing diehard baseball flags and banners flying proudly from eaves, Trevin opened up the next round of get-to-know-me's. "By the way," he asked Constance, speaking loudly, "are you a Cubs fan or a White Sox fan?"

"Who are they?"

"You're kidding."

"Or *what* are they?" she added.

Charmed, he tried to explain Chicago baseball dynamics, which confused and baffled her. Her freckles crinkled. She battled to understand. A band of overweight schlubs fumbled by, knocking into them, holding each other up while belting out "God Bless America." Trevin ultimately gave up, noting that it was unimportant and inconsequential.

Midway into the block was a large wooden platform—a built stage for a night concert. Already homegrown roadies—mostly middle-aged men—were running cables and taping them down, testing microphones, tightening snares and setting electric guitar stands. Constance was overjoyed to see this.

"We're dancing when that thing gets hopping!" she squealed. "You do dance, right?"

"Uh …"

She tugged his arm, demonstrating her amazing physical strength. "You better be ready!"

Farther down on the other side of the platform, there were small rides and games for tots. Some were already on them, screaming with delight, surrounded by doting parents.

Trevin said, "I haven't seen anything like this since I was a kid in my old neighborhood."

As Constance strode up to the miniature carousel, orbiting a candy cane hub, she stopped, suddenly becoming very taken by its circular motion, eyes locking on the demonstration. Trevin watched her. After a minute, she began mimicking its rotation very subtly with her hands—as if subconsciously—turning her wrists, lifting her arms somewhat. This was all very curious.

"What're you doing?" he asked.

"Nothing," she answered, and continued.

The more Trevin stared at her hands, moving around in pace with the carousel's rotation, the sharper a very special flashback to the good old patriotic days of his youth came to mind. He remembered a particular childhood Fourth of July, where nearly every tree trunk on his street was wrapped with red, white and blue streamers. American flags were everywhere. Hula Hoops were tossed into the air, one getting stuck high on a branch in front of his parents' house. A sponge football spiraled over the swarms—male friends chasing after it, girls in packs watching them go. Trevin was back there, in greater detail than he could have recalled intentionally, reliving the joy and ease and freedom and wonder.

Constance stopped, turning to him, and smiled. She was a little embarrassed. "Sorry."

Trevin came out of his flashback, and remembered the circles Gladys Embery had been doing in her sketchbook, and her analysis of the shape—or motion—meaning something.

Constance said, "Just caught up in all this fun."

"I see," said Trevin. "You getting hungry? I could eat. Food tastes better outdoors."

"Lead me where your nose goes."

Trevin spotted Peter Bebziak at the arresting aroma of rib's point of origin. The fat man was slumped in a lawn chair with a half circle of neighbors surrounding him—a pack bridging two houses. There was a grill there next to everyone with smoke rising. All were engaged in beer drinking. Peter's wandering eyes happened to find Trevin's at that moment, and he stood so fast he knocked over his chair. Peter starting waving as Trevin grew uncomfortable knowing he hadn't reached out.

"Hey you!" Peter called out, slopping the beer on the person next to him. "Trevin! Get over here!" He waved like a mad bear, an explosion of guffaws exploding from the group.

"Who's that?" Constance asked.

"The neighbor who invited us. We should go over. Be warned—he's kind of loud."

The couple broke past a new blockade of people sitting on the curb while Peter was already making room, ordering the other neighbors to move, dragging new chairs into the cluster. Peter was obnoxiously dressed, wearing an Elvis Presley blue and gold mambo shirt, and was even more animated now that he was inebriated. Trevin didn't know the others they approached.

The clique sucked in the newcomers, the men gawking at Constance like they'd never seen such a woman before. Peter sprung at them, clapping Trevin on the shoulder so hard that he nearly knocked him over. Then Peter put Trevin in a headlock, knocking his skull like a woodpecker. Trevin almost gagged at the smell of his armpits. Ruth, a couple of chairs over, ordered her husband to calm down, immediately apologizing to Constance, who stayed back. When the shenanigans ended, Peter loudly introduced them to everybody.

"This is Trevin, the International Neighbor of Mystery I was telling you rummies about at the meeting. Trevin's the artist who lives in our corner house up there, landlorded by the dickweed."

This started a row. A volley of complaints shot up about the house like more of the fireworks going off. "That's one hideous staircase!" slurred one drunk, followed by diatribes against "the jag-off owner who never acknowledges us." Trevin wished he never pulled Constance into the trap.

Peter had the two sit next to him. Constance sat demurely with hands folded, eager to accept everybody and everything. They gravitated to her and she smiled—at everyone—telling them how nice it was to meet. The ebullience stopped the group cold. For a moment... they had sobered up.

Trevin took note. *Like a defense missile,* he thought.

Then, multiple questions fired at Constance all at once, everyone wanting to be in her attention. Already, Trevin was old news. The neighbors wanted to know where Constance was from, where she lived, what she did and where she did it at. One lady leaned forward, studying her, asking if she'd had her teeth whitened.

"No, I just brush them," Constance answered, looking at Trevin for approval.

Eventually, Peter threw up his arms and slapped his male buddies in a Three Stooges shtick. "All right, assholes, lay off her already! She wants to enjoy the party!"

The street band addressed the crowd via a hand microphone and this broke the group's rapt fascination. Everyone settled in, getting comfortable as the local musicians began their first set, rocking out to Frankie Valli and the Four Seasons. The sound boomed, dynamic and delightful. The alliance once more operated freely. But now it was difficult to hear, and drunken Peter nudged Trevin, shouting over the performance. "Where've you been, dude?"

"Around," Trevin shouted back, noticing Constance adjusting to the raw energy of the music, wondering if he'd done the right thing dragging her into this.

As it was, she seemed enthralled, studying not only the band but the middle-aged folks of the block who gathered at the stage and danced freely. With attention split, Constance fielded even more questions—also shouted at her—people wanting to know if she'd ever been to a Chicago block party. She did her best, answering over the volume. She had them in the palm of her hand. All of them. It was as if the band wasn't there. The men boasted to her of their exercise routines (what little they did), their cars, and some even got into memories. Great ones.

She really did have some kind of gift, Trevin recognized, captivating without effort, as with that day with him in the bookstore. He remembered what she said to him about loving memories. In fact, their conversations always got around to memories—his!

This is getting odd, he thought, equating her to the sun, holding people in a geosynchronous orbit by her gravity. Ruth touched him on his forearm. "Don't let go of her, Trevin, she's a keeper."

"I know, Ruth, thank you," he said.

Over plates of scrumptious ribs, bratwursts, corn on the cob and coleslaw, someone brought up the neighborhood watch program, which the neighbors had still been working on getting implemented. Trevin was informed of all the meetings he'd missed, the police blotters describing the crime in the area—robberies, theft, drug arrests—and how the average citizen was becoming more leery of going out at night. It was disturbing news to be sure, diametrically opposed to what was around them tonight. Trevin asked Constance if it was too much to hear. She assured him it wasn't.

When Peter announced that it was Trevin who yelled months back at the careening car—something that almost everyone heard in their homes—he became an instant celebrity. They loved it, and he got attention he did not want.

Constance had never been informed of this tidbit.

Peter explained. Constance listened. Trevin removed himself for more food, unwilling to re-experience the embarrassing chapter. When he returned, Constance was smirking at him. "You did that?" she quipped. "How valiant."

"Moving on …" Trevin said.

But a man named Fred shook Trevin's hand anyway, to honor the act. Fred could hardly see straight and fell off his chair, dropping all his food on the grass. A cunning dachshund shot in from beneath a shrub, snapping up what it could—especially the bratwurst—and ran off like a bullet, creating hysterics. A lady ran after the pet, swearing like a sailor, thus saving Trevin from further discomfiture. But this only lasted so long because Constance and Trevin, as a couple, became the next topic of investigation.

Constance let Trevin field the subject, sitting back to watch how it would be defined, keeping a wicked laugh from erupting at his unease. In the middle of his thesis, the bottom dropped out of his cheap chair, sending him halfway to the lawn, legs splayed like a circus clown.

After another round of hysterics, a number of neighbors rushed in to help. This time Constance couldn't hold back and exploded into laughter, drawing angry looks from Trevin, who said he'd get even with her later. When things got back to order, "Drunk Bob," as Trevin later referred to him, grabbed his eighth beer and seized the opportunity to chat Constance up.

"There's plenty of drama on the street, not all tragic," he slurred, and began pointing. "That house there? That's the Kowalski's. They're not here tonight 'cause he's at the casino, gambling every last red cent. He just lost his job. She works. They'd have lost the house if he hadn't won big recently—thinks it's a legitimate way to earn cash. Don't get near him, he'll steal you blind." The woman next to him, probably his wife, didn't like the gossiping.

"Bob, that's enough."

He dismissed her. "Over there is the Morgans. He sleeps in the basement, his wife upstairs. She kicked him out of the bedroom two years ago, been that way ever since. They won't get a divorce."

"Bob, shut up."

"Hon, everyone knows about it, you shut up. Clark Morgan thinks it's funny; he's the one who told me. You should see the bunions on his feet." Making a cork-sized hole using forefinger and thumb, "Huge, like this. They belong in the Guinness Book of Records—looks like red olives on a pink salad."

"That's it!"

Bob's woman got up and smacked him good, ordering him home. The hysterical laughter of the group became louder than the music. Bob cackled like a hyena himself, blowing everyone a kiss as he staggered off like a hobo, giving his beer to a teenager.

This was not how Trevin saw things unfolding with Constance this evening. She squeezed his hand, giving a reassuring wink—an indication she was fine.

* * *

Trevin couldn't remember the last time he sat on a street curb, watching Independence Day fireworks. Constance was cuddled next to him, more than happy to hear his stories of block parties like these in days gone by in Rochester. The memories were warm and tender, speaking of them as they were. He bent the tips of his gym shoes on the asphalt, rocking them back and forth—the happy person he once was. She had her arms folded about her knees, seeming very much enchanted by each morsel and anecdote, experiencing his emotions as if they were her own. Occasionally, she would look to the stars, as if the recollections were inspiring her to think of something cosmic.

There weren't as many party-goers on this end of Munnison—his end. The band that had been playing most of the night announced they were taking a break while the finale boomed. As things were readied, the aging rockers left the stage, and opportunity presented itself.

Two male adolescents, both wearing Goth tee shirts, jumped onto it and commandeered the music system with a mammoth boom box, blasting techno-rave. This created quite the combination—shuddering firework explosions in the sky above the party, mixed with ultra-loud, spellbinding Electronica. Coming out of their hiding spots, mobs of youngsters spilled into the street, replacing all who'd gone absent, and transformed Munnison into a mosh pit of razor sharp chords and psychotropic frenzy.

This sudden shift thrilled Constance. She literally jumped up and began bouncing around, yanking on Trevin's arm to get him to join in. That was the end of Trevin's reminiscing. "Come on!" she squawked. "I said you'd be dancing! This music's awesome!"

Before he could argue, she pulled him a quarter of the length down the street, back to center, where they joined the throngs of twisting, shaking young folk, already entranced by the overpowering chords. What was fair was fair, Trevin rationalized—he'd have to give in to her. Titillated like he had never seen her, it was her turn to lose her mind. Constance went crazy, dancing wholly uninhibited, their clothes literally rippling from both the bass and the fireworks overhead. She looked from sky to Earth more dominantly now, grooving and moving, seductively wrapping arms around Trevin, pulling him in.

He watched her lock in on a young man and woman, both around 18, cloaked in shadow under a large oak, kissing passionately, their fingers raking each other's hair and neck, no prudish parent to break them up. Constance stared like she'd never witnessed that before.

Eventually, the rocker front man—now sporting a huge Uncle Sam hat—regained control of the music, turning the boom box down to a sane level, asking the block if they were having a good time. The masses went nuts. Cheering, screaming, pumping fists. Fun was being had by all.

A new Electronica jam was even faster and even more extraterrestrial-sounding. The kids inadvertently encased Trevin and Constance in a sort of sensory cocoon, pumping them up further. Constance planted Trevin's hands on her hips, fixing them there. Trevin felt his sweat slap off her. He was within inches of her lips, mentally melting watching her move. Each quavering and undulating arpeggio cleansed and purified, granting her more permission to let go.

He wanted to hold her forever …

When the last firework lit up the night, her eyes snapped alert as if bursting with purpose, and she bolted from the scene, breaking through the crowd and running away up Munnison in the direction of Salmon. It took a moment for Trevin to register what was going on. He yelled after her, then gave chase. She took a right on Salmon and kept going, heading to nowhere. She was fast, but Trevin was faster. His head was filled with confusion and distress.

He eventually caught her a block down, grabbing her by the arm and pulling her to a halt. Together, they were huffing like two runaway trains, Trevin sweating like a mad bull. "W-what a-are you doing?!" he panted. "W-what the hell's wrong?"

"N-nothing …" she reported. "Nothing. I-I'm all right… I'm all right…" He highly doubted it. She seemed consumed by guilt of some sort, and started raving, "C-can't be doing that… I'm getting too worked up… not supposed t-to…"

"You're not supposed to what, Constance? What aren't you supposed to do?"

"I'm sorry. Please forgive me… p-please forgive me…"

"Forgive you for what? Who are you apologizing to?"

She never answered. Trevin had no idea what was going on. After several more minutes of getting nowhere, he gave up, letting her be. She embraced him, shutting her eyes, the sweat from each other's bodies soaking into one another. The party faded away, logic entangled by a single circumstance. No dialogue, no morass, only delirious mystery. She said in his ear, "There hasn't been a minute gone by that I haven't thought of you."

Further out, other neighborhoods were sending up their finales, horizons lighting up with burst of color and delayed sonic booms. Constance had taken Trevin to some wild places of the mind. He had ascended to the stars, too.

CHAPTER 11

Trevin took Constance up his staircase after the block party had ended. It was probably around midnight, he didn't know. Nor did he care. He was nervous to show her his apartment. "You'll be the first guest I've had," he said, checking the black holes of the first-floor windows.

"Well, it's about time," she responded. "We're always meeting on neutral ground. But I'm flattered."

When they got to his balcony, she stopped to look around, impressed. "You can see everything from up here. I like it up high."

He was fumbling with his keys. He could barely work his fingers.

"What's that?" she asked, pointing to the cement factory, looking ominous as usual.

"That's fully operational during the day," he explained, telling her what it was as well as describing the unique layout of the neighborhood—a definite advantage for a commuter—and checking the streetlight on his corner at the same time. It had behaved all evening, even during the fireworks thundering.

She got closer to the edge, leaning over to get a better view of the stragglers still on Munnison. Only diehard laggards were roaming about, chattering and still drinking. A few were already picking up the street. He propped the screen door with his usual lead foot.

When he looked, she was leaning too far over, and he saw the loose balcony balustrade strain against the weight. He rushed to her and pulled her back. "Watch that! It's loose. I still have to call my landlord to get that fixed."

Just before going in, he asked if she was all right. He was still concerned about her running away episode.

"I'm fine," she said. "Embarrassed, but fine. I don't know what came over me."

Not wanting to press the issue, Trevin inserted the key into the lock, but paused. "Well… shall I show you my etchings?" It was a tease. A jape. She totally didn't understand it.

"Is that a line?" she asked.

"Never mind," he said, deflating. Then he paused again. "Ready?"

She understood that he was stalling, though. "Trevin, open the door."

They entered, revealing the shadowy depths inside. Trevin gamboled his hand around to the dimmer switch in his studio and turned the track lighting to low, creating a mellow glow. She immediately cooed.

"Ooh, I love it, it's so nice in here. What a great place!"

He tossed the keys onto his drafting table, letting her look around. "I love the sanctity here," he said. "The peace. It's great for my art, what little I do of it now."

He shut the door, plunging them into silence except for the air conditioning unit chugging away, smelling the intoxicating fusion of what was left of her perfume.

"Feels great in here," she mentioned, studying his workspace and drafting table.

"That thing's been running a lot already this year," Trevin said, referring to the air.

"This is—without a doubt—an artist's lair," Constance continued. "I love the vaulted ceiling and skylight."

He was proud.

She saw the shawl pinned over the octagonal window. "Interesting."

"I don't like people being able to see in. That shawl was my grandmother's."

"Even more interesting," she said. She saw his sketchpad, sitting lonely atop the drafting table, and asked if she could look at it. "I can't get enough of your work."

But she didn't have to flatter him. He'd let her do anything she wanted. He even snapped on the overhead lamp light for her and moved aside the rolling taboret containing his paint tubes and brushes. Before flipping the first page open, she looked at him, giving him one of her stunner smiles, ripping his heartstrings apart. Then she began her journey into his sketches.

She gasped at their beauty. The images—some in color—were mostly surreal landscapes. "Straight from my head," he explained. "My dreams, actually."

One after the other, she moved through the creations of her man, drinking in their integrity and imagination. They really were fantastic. She stopped at the one that struck her the most: an Eden-like paradise painted in pastels, depicting incredible depth of field. There were hills and valleys, giving way to massive mountains, rolling back to infinity. Flourishing rivers and streams cut from the foreground all the way backward, lush trees of magnificent scope gracing the land. The colors were those of one of his favorite sunsets.

"Tell me about this one, please," she swooned. "Tell me now."

Reluctantly, he went into detail, moving up alongside her. It was somewhere he imagined his grandmother was now—without her wheelchair. "It's a place I'd rather be, to escape into... forever. It's a place where all my happiness could be. I'd walk with Nan there."

She closed her eyes and felt his words, holding the sketchpad dear.

"I guess it would be my idea of Heaven," he concluded.

When she reopened her eyes and looked at them, he wanted to kiss her. Like a nuclear reactor, he was on fire. But he held back... he didn't want to be too forward. He'd been raised a gentleman.

"Oh my..." she said.

He asked, "Want to see the rest of the place?"

* * *

After the remainder of the apartment tour, Trevin and Constance returned to the art studio and sat on his sofa there, not knowing if they should touch each other or not. There was plenty of raw, sexual tension passing between them. It was obvious to both parties. To divert, Constance described how she loved his spacious kitchen with the bedroom directly off it. "It's really a great layout," she said. "You have the whole top floor to yourself. I like these half walls here dividing the studio from the rest of the apartment."

"Yeah, but I can't see into the kitchen from here unless I lean forward."

"I think it makes the room cozier," she said. She also commented on the back porch—right off the kitchen—and how hot it was when Trevin opened the door to show her.

"It's enclosed with no vents," he said. "I only go back there to store stuff and when I go down into the basement to do laundry."

"It's dark," Constance included.

That somewhat confounded Trevin. He wasn't upset with her, just at the amount of comments like it he'd heard since opening up to the neighbors. "Don't you start," he pleaded, explaining everyone's alleged fascination with the house he lived in, and how foreboding some thought it appeared. "Everyone talks about how gothic it looks. I love it."

Drumming her knees with her hands nervously, Constance scanned the art studio again, landing upon a small book shelf to her left that appeared to contain a set of large photo albums. "Are those …?"

He read her mind as she stared at them like sizzling steaks. "Photo albums? Yes."

She wanted to see them, desperately. Trevin was tired of talking about himself, and demanded to know more of her. She didn't want to go that route. She said once again how boring she was, her background.

"That's your response all the time," Trevin said, not holding back his frustration. "One of these days, I'm going to find out."

"Trevin, show me the photo albums."

"It's late," he countered.

"No, it's not. You want to go to sleep?"

He did not want to go to sleep. So he grabbed a couple of bottled waters from the refrigerator in the kitchen and yanked out all the albums from their shelves in the studio, cursing himself for bringing them to Chicago in the first place. They combed through each one, Constance forcing Trevin to explain nearly every snapshot, looking like she was eating up the memories for dinner. She couldn't get enough. She was ravenous to hear about them, even asking Trevin to explain the emotions he felt at the time. It was actually bizarre. It was like a fetish.

"This is what made you who you are," she said. "The memories sculpted you."

Trevin was tiring of the exercise, but couldn't resist her. Her magnetism was enough to unhinge all the screws in every appliance in the apartment.

They went through friends he grew up with. She asked if it was tough leaving them.

"They knew I wouldn't stick around," he answered. "They told me I had a wandering soul. I suppose they were right. They were like brothers."

Old girlfriends and prom pictures came next—portraits of beguiling teenage innocence. This piqued Constance's interest, fascinated by the dated hairstyles and clothes from the time. There was no cattiness in Constance's summary, only respect. She asked, "Are you sorry you're not still with them?"

"Life moves on," Trevin answered. "They were important to my life then."

"What's happened to them?"

"They're both married with kids, living somewhere in western New York." This spurred specific tenderness and soft moments. "They were great. I wish them the best."

Next—the sports pictures. Football, wresting, baseball. Constance stared at the scenes, wanting to hear about the best touchdown and the quickest double-play to win the game. Brain surgeons studied MRIs this way. The cellophane sheets holding the pictures in place had yellowed, the dry plastic brittle at the edges.

"You were quite the athlete," she said as he moved from that section.

"'Were' being the operative word."

They even went through his high school art awards and exhibitions, which earned him a scholarship to art college, bringing him to Chicago. Grade school instructors had early on discovered his talents, encouraging his parents to enroll him in special art classes. He'd ultimately followed that path to pursue his dreams. A corner had been turned within the nuclear family. The nest had been abandoned. What an unprotected thing it was, opening his past to a new personality—a lifetime interpreted in minutes.

And finally… his hometown street and the house he grew up in—the one his parents still resided at: a split-level nestled beneath verdant shade trees—mostly oaks—common witch hazel and red chokeberry shrubs lining an attractive front porch. "We got rid of some of those trees," he reported. "A weeping willow in the backyard crept into the septic tanks. That had to go."

She loved the name of his street: "Sweet Briar Road."

Trevin smiled. "Quaint-sounding, isn't it? It was a great place to grow up. Great neighbors."

"When's the last time you were home?" she asked.

"Not for a while," he answered. "Mom and dad want me to visit. I think they think something's up. I owe them a visit."

"What are you waiting for?"

"The right time."

She was staring at him, wild-eyed and serious. "They miss you," she stressed. "They love you. You *have* to do it."

"Soon, Constance, soon."

Constance saw photographs of Trevin's Nan, and saw how close grandson and grandmother were. She was a small, frail lady with solid white hair and a kind face, apparent even behind the wire-rimmed spectacles. There were several of the two sitting together at a card table, laughing and joking, holding mugs of tea up for the picture taker. Nan was often seen in her wheelchair, body slumping. "The poor woman suffered so with arthritis and many other things," Trevin said painfully. "God bless her."

Constance became transformed by the images, asking the most private questions about his emotional connection to these happy times. She seemed to get so worked up by the discussion that when Trevin asked if she was going to flee again, and if he'd have to chase her down in street all over, she suddenly leaned in and kissed him. Hard. Trevin experienced his own fireworks. His fingers made their way through her silky mane, and she felt his strong back. It was more than he could have imagined. Then, she suddenly pulled away, leaving him in the lurch, and went back to the albums, asking more questions. Trevin was dazed… discombobulated… disarmed. Their first kiss.

"Tell me more of Sweet Briar Road," she said.

Trevin almost couldn't. It took a few moments to collect himself, then his fingers began tracing more photographs of his beloved neighborhood. "That picture there reminds me of the no-fear I had walking home from school when I was a kid, or anywhere close by. I'd round Sweet Briar's bend and see that angle. Sweet Briar's a circle—well, an oval, really."

Almost a circle, Trevin thought… curiously.

"Keep going," she insisted.

"That one was from the end of my high school career, when it was all over. It was when we walked out of our high school for the last time. Look at that red tone on our faces and everything. Must've been near sunset. You can also tell by the shadows. I don't know who took the picture."

She pointed at another. "What about this one?"

"Back to Sweet Briar. There used to be a meadow where the dead end street going away from our driveway stopped. We referred to it as "the fields." As kids, we'd play there for hours. It's not there now—it's a new housing tract."

Constance said, "Sometimes memories are triggered by certain sounds, certain scents."

She was right. He grinned, recalling some. "We'd hear crickets night and day coming from the fields. I loved that sound. Always associate it with that freedom. I'd leave the window open at night and be lulled to sleep by them."

"There are also memories in looking in different directions. Like how you love the west."

His mind traveled farther into the beyond. "Yeah, there's something consecrated about that."

"North, south, east and west," she said, her voice soothing. "There are distinct moods to each. Sometimes I line myself up to their harmony. It's spiritual."

"Yes it is, Constance," Trevin agreed. "Order and purpose."

"Which we seek."

He chuckled, working his way back to reality. When he looked at her, she said, "I get sentimental. Your descriptions are beautiful."

"*You're* beautiful," he emphasized.

"Your memories are going to do you a world of good," she said. "Trust me."

Ignoring the crypticism, which he'd been growing used to being around her, he spouted, "You're the most amazing woman I've ever met."

"Who's this devilish-looking young man?"

Constance had once more ripped Trevin out of the moment, focusing instead on a new album, and a new set of childhood pictures.

"That's Tommy Porch," he answered. The photograph had both the new guy and Trevin in the same frame, both wearing baseball uniforms and donning caps. Tommy was marginally taller than Trevin. "One of my best friends," Trevin continued. "Still is. We were both 17 there, right before a game. Your assessment is right—he is one crazy dude. Proud recipient of the 'class clown' title in high school."

"Class clown?"

"Tommy will forever be a teenager. I can't believe he's married with kids now. Sometimes I feel sorry for his wife. He's a handful."

Wanting to get through the album, Trevin reached over her and flipped to the next page, curious himself as to what was there. He stopped on a dime at what he saw next. "Well I'll be …" he said aloud to himself. "Nutty George …"

"Who?"

"Nutty George. I mean, Mr. Tavalier. Like 'Cavalier.' Tava-*leer*. Geez, haven't thought of or seen that guy in eons."

"Who is he?" Constance asked, leaning close to study the picture Trevin was gawking at.

The snapshot had been taken from Trevin's parents' front lawn on a bright summer day, with Tommy and Trevin throwing a baseball around by the street. Trevin explained his father was the camera operator. In the background, in front of a high wall of shrubbery, partially obscuring the house across Sweet Briar, was a funny-looking man looking over at the boys in a scowl, mowing his lawn. Young Tommy and Trevin were unaware the man was glaring.

Trevin became saddened by his own stupidity. "That man back there was a neighbor, that's his yard. Lived across from my parents forever, still does. We made up that stupid nick name for him—'Nutty George.' I don't even know how we came up with it. We were jerks. His name isn't even George."

"What is it?"

"I think it's 'Cecil,' if memory serves me correctly."

The man was probably in his early forties at the time. Due to him being small within the frame, it was impossible to discern precise features, except for the balding head and beach ball belly bulging out from under a yellow Polo shirt.

"He's throwing daggers at us with his eyes," Trevin muttered. "He hated us. And who could blame him?"

"What happened?"

Trevin explained how they harassed him—how all the kids in the neighborhood harassed him—and how sorry he was for all of it and how he wished he could make amends. "Nobody really knew them. Not even the adults made much effort to socialize with them after they blew off the block parties, speaking of block parties. They had no kids—Cecil and his wife. I definitely don't know her name. And they probably hated us for it. This isn't a happy memory."

"Not all of them are," Constance pointed out.

"But they were neighbors, still are. I'm always going off about the state of today's world. That's how it started—right there in the past—when chances were squandered. The Tavaliers turned into recluses. She ventured out rarely. Can't remember ever seeing her more than a handful of times. They just wanted to be left in peace and we treated them like nutballs. Everyone figured he planted those hedges to make a point. See how it looks like a fortress? Tommy and I pulled a few pranks on them."

"What did you do?"

"Rang their doorbell and ran, made crank calls, sent pizzas to their house. With all the bad in the world, we made it worse. One of the most obnoxious things Tommy and I did was throw cookies at their house. So disrespectful."

"You threw cookies at their house?"

"That's probably why he's looking at us—he knew it was us. Haven't thought of that in years. God, I wish I could take that back."

"You can," Constance said. "You *can* make amends. When you go home. While you're there, apologize to Cecil and his wife."

One o'clock had hit. Trevin took the book from her and put the whole pile aside. "I can't do this anymore," he declared, and stood up, rubbing his head.

Constance conceded, and stood up with him. Putting her arms around him, she said, "Thank you for the amazing stories. There's one more thing I need tonight …"

Trevin squinted his eyes, not knowing what to anticipate.

"I need one of your photos for myself. To have at home. Let's go make a copy."

"Now?"

"Now," she said. "I'm teaching you that memories can be virtuous, among other things. Help me make my first official evening at my honey's house complete. Let's go."

Honey? The word melted Trevin's heart. He suddenly found the wakefulness to do as she requested. "Pick one out," he said.

* * *

At the 24-hour service bureau, Trevin and Constance had to wait for the only employee's availability to fix the color copier machine so Constance could get what she came for. She'd chosen a photograph of Trevin in his final year of high school, shaking hands with a corporate sponsor, where he won a major prize at a regional art contest—the wall behind them showcasing his award-winning work. It was the moment he'd learned of his scholarship. "Your whole future came to you at that moment," she'd explained on the drive over. "That's why I wanted it."

They were sitting away from everyone in the curiously busy store, people-watching, not believing how many there were here this late on a holiday. But… that was okay, they were actually having fun. Despite the hard, sterile plastic seats by the front entrance being uncomfortable, the couple studied the strangers in secret, trying to guess who they were and why they came in. What truly mattered was that they were together, touching up against one another. Trevin made her laugh, commenting on how crazy the stark overhead fluorescent lights made him feel, reminding him of Lightning Strikes—something he was still working hard on to forget. He didn't bother adding that the machines reminded him of just how many times he'd been without her, hard-copying one resume after another, sending them out in hopes of landing a job.

Things got interesting when a minivan, driven by a woman transporting a cargo full of Little League boys, pulled up in front, idling by the door. There was a scramble of motion inside, the kids still in their uniforms. Trevin figured it must've been a tournament running excessively late. There were six boys, all eager to get out.

The boys were having the times of their lives, and as the doors slid open, they piled out like giddy rats leaving a sinking ship, rushing into the store already, one having a slower time climbing out on the opposite side from where Trevin and Constance could see. The window's concrete ledge blocked their view of the group from their waists down.

"What's this?" asked Constance. "The last one's taking a while."

"I don't know," said Trevin, growing interested.

The boys in the store had a digital camera, and were hounding the same employee Trevin and Constance needed fixing the color copier. Obviously, the children did just come from a game, and were eager to have their photographic representation of it printed out. Outside, the woman—definitely the last boy's mother—was gathering her belongings behind the wheel, saying something to the loner-boy through the window, who by now had made his way to the front door, waiting. His gait had a waddle. He wasn't wearing a uniform, just regular summer clothes, and he behaved magnificently—much more subdued than his colleagues.

Constance sat up, keying off her sympathetic nature. "Something's up."

At the same moment, also in the parking lot, an elderly man had just come from his car, shuffling to the entrance with a cane, badly bent from years living with a degenerative disorder. Carrying a folder in his other hand, he came up from behind the loner-boy and tried reaching over his head to open the door. The loner-boy saw him, and at first stepped away, giving the elderly man a once-over, empathetically studying his condition. Pleasant words were exchanged, and the boy moved in, making the effort to hold door for his aged counterpart—displaying wisdom far beyond his years—allowing the man to shuffle on in. Mom got out, checking her purse, not seeing any of it.

Now mom held the door for her boy. He wobbled in, clearing the ledge blockade, granting Trevin and Constance full view. The child was also disabled—severely so—metal braces clamped to both malformed legs from the knees down. Together, mother and son joined the rest of the boys.

Trevin was amazed. What an unforgettable moment. He leaned in, about to whisper into Constance's ear. He saw that she was quietly starting to cry, so moved by the event.

"Babe, what's wrong? Are you okay?"

Constance went into her purse, yanking tissues out. Embarrassed, she wiped her eyes and blew her nose. "I'm fine, I'm fine," she said. "I'm sorry... that was just so... beautiful. The understanding in that boy's eyes, the understanding between both of them. The love in their hearts ..."

He put his arm around her, looking to see if anyone was staring. They weren't. "Is that what you took from that?"

"Yes, I did. I *felt* it."

He stared at her. "Wow."

As they basked in the warmth of the shared tenderness, and became fueled by their own toward each other, they eventually had their machine fixed, and they received the color copy they'd driven here to get. Trevin paid, but Constance saw something on her own that she purchased—for Trevin, as a "memento of the monumental evening."

"That's not necessary," Trevin said.

"I want to," she insisted, pulling the trinket out of the bag and giggling at it. Her eyes and face were still slightly flushed from becoming over-emotional. "The end of a perfect night. Plus, it fits."

It was a goofy toy figurine: a palm-sized gnome with two opposing faces. Both sides had the creature in a shirt and tie, but the dispositions were polar opposites. With placards hanging from each neck, one read: HOW I FEEL AT WORK—the character miserable and dejected. Turning it around: HOW I FEEL AFTER WORK—the face now bursting with glee, eyes bugging out of its head.

Trevin loved it, thanking her profusely. "May I get to know either again …"

"When you're dreaming up your next great vision," she said. "And always have the happy side facing you."

On the way out, Constance saw the loner-boy with the leg braces. He was by himself, turning a card stand, looking at the eye-catching designs. The mother and the others were huddled at a digital printing kiosk, talking with the employee. Constance caught his eye. The boy melted in her presence, stopping and waiting for anything she had to say. Trevin stood back, again observing.

"You're a good boy," she said to him discreetly. "You are so very special and so very loved."

She raised one hand, just a tad, and used it to trace a circle twice in the air, then unleashed a stellar smile. It was subtle. It was private. But the boy lit up like the sun and smiled back until his face looked like it would crack.

CHAPTER 12

A few days later Trevin walked back into the Lakebreeze Healthcare Campus for the first time since the Becca Joseph incident. With Constance. It was an edgy move. He still hadn't fully recovered from the whole thing. In fact, he was looking over his shoulder every step of the way, half expecting the furious and grieving granddaughter to fly at him from around any given corner. He'd told Constance the story on the way over. She thought it tragic. But he had obligations to uphold, and he needed to keep any artistic effort moving forward.

Of course, Constance was dressed to the nines, razzle-dazzling everyone who saw her, especially the old male coots who were always seated in the lobby—who up until now had been snapping newspapers in disgust at the day's news. What accented Constance's beige blouse the most was the lavender quartz crystal necklace she had around her neck. Trevin stared at it again as she signed in, the same way he'd stared at it helping her into the Blazer. They'd brought in with them the pungent, gritty air from yet another muggy day. Summer had arrived full force. The heat on them quickly dissipated in the near-freezing temperature inside.

Everyone was delighted to see Trevin. They missed him so. He had more friends than he thought—staff and residents alike. Most had heard of the ugly incident that had cast him out for a while and apologized on the Joseph family's behalf. He assured them none was necessary. Some asked why he'd taken so long to return. He lied, claiming business reasons were at fault.

Little do they know, he thought dismally.

Introducing Constance—as he knew would happen—they swarmed around her like she was a Rodeo Drive celebrity. She charmed them instantly. Here it went again, just like the block party. She chatted them up with spunky rapport, connecting with them, making them laugh, telling them how much she'd heard of this fantastic place!

Allison Pertina bounced in by happenstance, hearing the commotion. Falling upon her favorite volunteer with a bright hug, she thanked Trevin for coming back at all. The Joseph episode "just didn't happen here, not in our home." He didn't bring up losing his job in the interim—that just wasn't right. Maybe he'd look into opportunities here later.

Within minutes, Allison and Constance were best friends, absorbed in girl-talk and happy exchanges. Allison threw an adamant "thumbs-up" to Trevin—a total approval of Constance—when Constance turned at the tug of an elderly woman, wanting to know her name. Allison broke up the gang, redirecting everyone back to their posts, and gladly escorted the pair to where Trevin should start the night, giving him carte blanche to go wherever he needed. Many had asked about him. Trevin asked right away about Gladys.

"She was devastated," Allison reported. "She definitely could stand to see the sight of you. She was afraid she'd never see you again."

Trevin's heart went out to the frail lady. "She's mainly why I brought Constance," he said. "For some reason, I think the two will hit it off."

Allison caught Constance's necklace. "Ooh, pretty. Matches your personality, girl. You're a nuclear reactor!" Then, punching Trevin on the shoulder. "You *did* bring her! Constance, we love this guy, we don't want to lose him again. Make sure he doesn't get lost."

"He won't," retorted Constance. "I'm his compass."

"Oh, really?" joked Trevin.

After an introduction with more seniors who'd been flocking around, delighted to see such nice-looking young people, Allison left to her business—and left Constance and Trevin to deal with the residents launching into memory after memory of all the magical and wonderful times they had when they were that young. Trevin was overwhelmed. Constance was intoxicated.

Trevin had to excuse himself. He had to get at things. He asked Constance if she was all right. She was, and said she'd catch up with him in no time.

With some concern, he left.

No Better Day

Constance found Gladys Embery while exploring on her own. She'd been on her way to finding her man, but in so doing, she'd collected other sights and sounds, cataloging experiences. Not all of them were happy. Some were heart-wrenching. Constance saw residents bedridden and sick, some talking to themselves. Her heart soared to them. She embraced the moments without interfering. After all, that was the reality of life.

It may have been by happenstance, but Constance knew at once where she was and who she was in the presence of: the noted and dignified woman Trevin loved so much, reminding him of his Nan. There was no one in the long corridor as the visitor stumbled across the room. Constance halted, peeked into the apartment, grew fascinated. The elderly woman was alone, tending to odds and ends, humming under her breath, a game show murmuring away on her television screen. Spying would have been too strong a word—this was admiration. At once Constance filled with a love and understanding for the gentle spirit she'd recognized from Trevin's descriptions.

Gladys had no idea anyone was there. At first.

The sunset's light from the adjacent courtyard was charged with nectarine and peach-colored radiance, striking the entire hallway like a guiding flare. Constance remembered Trevin invoking this very scenario. Indeed, it was to be savored… deemed therapeutic …

Gladys sensed someone there. Setting the mister down on the small kitchen table, she took a look at the door, took a sip of water from a glass, and turned to stare out her window to admire the unique view of a tree there with an empty bird feeder. Crickets could be heard from the outside world: another of Trevin's great memory catalysts. Gladys remained contemplative as the sunlight cleared the top of the building and bathed the lawn with the most fantastic glow. A prismatic spectrum spread across the crazy clouds out there in the distance.

There was a commercial break on TV, and Gladys reached for the remote, shutting off the set. Silence grabbed hold of the milieu, other guests and visitors far away. Gladys turned again to the door. "I know you're out there—" she said with a kind and almost playful voice. "—Whoever you are. You can reveal yourself. Don't worry—I won't bite."

In the hallway with her back to the wall, Constance flushed. She'd been had. Figuring she'd better make herself known, she took a deep breath and launched herself forward, stepping into the limelight, offering

Gladys an immediate, Grand Canyon-sized smile. Again, Constance was over-emotional—a most curious detection—finding herself fighting back tears of joy.

Gladys' eyes went wide as she froze, recognizing that something great had just entered her world. "Hello," she said quietly.

"Hello," Constance greeted back. Her voice was also soft.

"Who are you?"

"My name is Constance Summerlin. You must be Gladys Embery."

"I am."

"May I come in?" Constance asked.

Gladys responded, "By all means …" Then, "You've arrived."

* * *

By the time Trevin found the two, Constance and Gladys were sitting mostly in the dark—the only light coming from the hallway overheads. Night had fallen, and it was not a stretch to say he was surprised to see them this way. They were laughing and joking like the best of friends, sharing the kitchen table, both enjoying a glass of ice water. Walking in, Trevin turned on a floor lamp. "There you are, Constance," he said. "Well, hello Gladys."

They barely stopped their conversation as they said hello back, squinting as their eyes adjusted to the increased light. Gladys needed her hug right away. Setting his bag down, Trevin obliged, asking Constance, "How'd you find her, babe?"

"Exploring," Constance answered, sitting back, watching the two so happy to be reunited.

Trevin knew Constance was self-reliant, but the initiative the girl took. The next words out of his mouth were, "What was I interrupting?"

"Nothing," answered Gladys, telling him to pull up a chair. "Your lady is quite remarkable. It's like we've known each other our whole lives."

"That's what it looks like," he said, settling in. Gladys offered him some water, but he turned down the offer. Constance was the vision of calm, giving her man an assuring wink.

Trevin said, "Well, I hope the two of you have been having fun. I don't need to give everyone's back-story—you already caught up. I had to see some people first, Gladys. I wasn't going to miss seeing you tonight."

"Oh I know, Trevin, I know."

Constance interjected, leaning forward to take Gladys' hand in hers. "I've learned so much of this sweetheart, Trevin. She's just like you said: very strong and very independent. I've learned that she never married, never had children, and is quite fine with all of it. She's helped so many others that they were her family and she enjoyed her career as a florist, running a business with a friend's daughter."

Gladys nodded, grinning. "That's me."

"We've talked about many things since we've known each other, haven't we Gladys?" Trevin added to the point. Then he said in all seriousness. "And I want to personally apologize to you for not being around. You know what happened to me the last time I was here."

"I do, Trevin" Gladys said, brushing it off. "What a terrible mistake that young girl made. But she was in such grieving. Her grandfather meant so much to her. Poor Mr. Joseph. I feel bad for the whole family. I said my prayers."

"God rest his soul," Trevin said. "I hope he didn't see his Becca yelling like that."

Gladys reached for Constance's necklace—the amethyst—and played with it in her fingers, holding the facets to the lamp, watching the reflective surfaces shimmering and gleaming. Her pale, liver-spotted hands steadied as Trevin had never seen. "I think Mr. Joseph is part of the light now," she said.

Constance and Trevin shared another clandestine glance.

"There are so many great things in the light," Gladys continued, staring into the necklace, speaking lucidly. She seemed to be addressing them both… and no one. "There are people that are filled with light even before they go. It's most rare. It's the memories that have made them that way. Great memories. I've shared a lot here with Constance tonight, already. She just brings them out. I told her about my childhood home, my parents."

"Want to share it with me, Gladys?" Trevin asked. "I'd like to hear it, too."

"It's all a circle," Gladys said. "Everything's… interconnecting."

Gladys asked Constance to grab the sketchbook behind her on the bureau. Constance did so, and as the old woman thumbed through the pages, looking for the sketch she wanted to show Trevin, Constance caught glimpses of her creations, fascinated. Gladys turned the sketchbook around to present to him—like pupil to a favorite teacher. "Here's my latest. I just drew it yesterday morning. This was the living room in my parent's house. It was the happiest house I ever knew."

It was far more complex than any he'd seen her do. And it was loaded with crisp detail.

"Mother put these plants around," Gladys said, pointing to some of them. "This is how I first became interested in botany. That's why I tend to them. Our neighbor had flower gardens. I'd water them. A good neighbor can be the best thing. Oh, I loved our house. Mother wanted the living room painted blue, but I preferred green. I've always loved the color green—olive green probably being the least fun."

As she spoke, both Constance and Trevin could see the lady's mind trailing away. A million miles away and decades in the past. It was amazing how reminiscing did that, Trevin thought. For the first time, he wondered if that's why Constance had him doing it all the time. It was transcendental. Constance's thesis of memories being a form of a time machine could be accurate.

Constance smiled, caught in the moment. "We'd quibble, we were broken records. But she loved me. I'd get my way in the end. We ended up with pine green, not too emerald. I told her our neighborhood was like that, just look around. There were many trees. You see, father and I went to the store and bought the paint. We walked, held hands the whole way. He had such strong hands, I felt so safe when I was with him. There were big drop clothes all over the place—we had to wear our tatter clothes."

Gladys had become totally relaxed. She finished her story, shaking away the mental cobwebs, and brought herself back to the present. "I can still smell our house with the paint and plants. It wasn't bad. There are splatters on father's face."

Are? Trevin thought. Maybe she was actually there still, Trevin wondered—even though she was here with them in the room. When Gladys looked up at the two, Trevin said, "You left us."

This made Gladys laugh, and she apologized to Constance for touching her amethyst necklace.

"It's perfectly all right," said Constance. "I'm glad you like it."

Gladys put her hand under her chin, and sighed. "I could live in those memories forever. I hope Eugene's in his, existing in his happiest memories. Wouldn't that be something? Wouldn't that be Heaven? We'd make up our own paradise—all personally constructed from our best times. God and all His Creation would certainly be busy with all that."

Gladys gave the sketchbook back to Constance to put on the bureau.

Trevin said, "That would be something, Gladys."

Constance just looked at the two of them, intensely.

The three chatted for another fifteen or twenty minutes. Time passed all too fast. Gladys saw that she had devoured their allotment of time talking, and apologized, worried that Trevin had wanted to get in some art lessons.

"I think this was a good way to begin again," said Trevin. "Next time, my dear."

Trevin confirmed that they did have to move on, and he and Constance stood, gathering their belongings, preparing to exit.

"Come back and see me again, won't you, Constance? I did enjoy our time together."

"I will, Gladys," Constance said.

"Maybe we have known each other forever."

"Maybe."

"And my dear Trevin," Gladys said. "You, too. We just sat back and enjoyed our time together. I just wanted you to be here. It means so much to me when you're here."

"Thank you, Gladys," Trevin said. "I love you, too."

* * *

The exodus of visitors moved out like shuffling cattle under the moon's light, drawn to the pasture of SUVs and minivans. Trevin had slipped into an extremely contemplative mood now, and he keyed in on the loose kernels of blacktop occasionally kicking up as the rougher shoes of the masses scuffed the cooling pavement.

Before Trevin got Constance into his Blazer (in the rear of the lot, of course), he stopped to listen to the trilling crickets. "There it is, my beautiful crickets. So enchanting. Gladys really moved me tonight."

"Me, too," said Constance. "I'm so glad I finally got to meet her. Thank you for taking me."

"You're welcome. I hope she's going to be okay."

"She is," said Constance.

"How do you know?"

"Because I believe people like her will be."

Trevin continued to listen to the sounds of the night, watching the cars pull out. He truly was in a miasma. He guided Constance into the passenger seat, and before he closed the door, she said, "I want to buy you another gift."

"No, Constance, that's not necessary."

"Come on. You're not ready to go in yet, I can tell. I know just the place."

Before he had a chance to protest, she kissed him. When the magnificent moment ended, she pulled from him, tilting her head to the moonlight. "You can't refuse now."

It took an effort to catch his breath.

"But we'll have to hurry," she said. "It closes soon."

The evening had elevated him to a better place. Before he drove away, he checked the sky for any sign of a swirling aurora borealis. There was nothing up there tonight.

CHAPTER 13

"A New Age bookstore? You kidding me?"

Constance bought Trevin a huge chunk of quartz crystal. A heavy one. Lavender in color. That's what she had decided upon. That's what she had planned all along, since Gladys had been fascinated by her necklace all evening. Like Trevin, Constance had been inspired, and she knew just the late-night bookstore that carried them. They drove all the way to the trendy Lincoln Park neighborhood, getting there just before closing time.

The first thing Trevin had commented on before going in was how the neighborhood shops had barely managed to survive, given the recession. The second thing was how dark and abandoned the street seemed. Maybe it was only a matter of time. Maybe everything was going to collapse, as it appeared it was. This chic little neighborhood just hadn't caught it yet. But it would.

Constance told him to stop being such a sourpuss and a downer—especially after such a great night at the Lakebreeze Healthcare Campus—and "go with the flow," letting Constance be his guide. With her chocolate-colored eyes and face full of the most enticing freckles he'd ever seen, Trevin gave in to his lady, despite being overwhelmed in the store by the incense, aromatherapy concoctions, aura cleanser spray, occult board games, metaphysical books and posters of dolphins sailing over the planets in the solar system.

The place was a cliché.

"What am I supposed to do with this?" Trevin asked, holding the football-sized slab in his hands. He'd taken it out of the bag just after she'd purchased it and had it stuffed into the plastic bag by the sole goateed employee who hurried them out afterward and closed and locked the doors. When the lights went out, they found themselves once again alone on the street.

"What I really wanted was a pan flute," Trevin joked.

"Oh, hush!" Constance said.

He saw the smile, but she was dead serious. She wanted to prove how in-the-spirit she was of her mystical connection with dear, old Gladys. That was worth a gift right there, by her calculations. She took the chunk from him and held it up to the streetlight. "Did you see how Gladys was holding my necklace to the light? She had a point. I want you to keep this somewhere where it can inspire you, make you think of this night, help you to move yourself into a better future. They have trapped energy locked inside them—from the time the Earth was forged."

"You're a geologist—that's your background. That's why you haven't told me."

"Trevin, stop." The crystal *was* dazzling. Inside, there was a universe of bottle throat sparkles and transcendental fractures. "Do you like it?"

"It's beautiful," he said, also looking at her dreamily in the night.

"Interstices so minute," she said, "you'd need a microscope to see some of them. Quartz is the most abundant mineral in the continental crust. Billions of years of heat and pressure. It'll help ground you."

"I need grounding?"

"Trevin… I need you to accept a quest."

"A quest?"

She gave the chunk back to him, and put her hands on his shoulders— "aligning" him—repositioning him a few steps this way and that. When she was satisfied she had him where she wanted, she said, "Perfect. Now picture me as your west—your favorite direction."

"That's cool. I like that idea."

She stepped back, careful to make sure she wasn't falling off the curb. Clearing her throat, she said, "Trevin Lambrose, you've received this gift as a future memory. I want you to remember me getting it for you—in this shop, at this hour. I want you to commit it to your being… its qualities appreciated… because of how I appreciate you."

"Okay, I—"

"Shh."

Trevin became eerily aware of an extraordinary union taking place between them. An abstract notion, sure, but it made sense to him in an oblique way. With her standing there the way she was, saying what she was, every building and every object in sight was where it should be. Perfect order.

"Will do …" he said, whispering.

"And… commit *me* to memory," she said, tilting her head. "Forever."

Trevin's heart soared. "Forever."

Having finished her inauguration, she said "Amen," and then she laughed. "We're a weird couple, aren't we?"

"But at least we're a couple," he said, deeply gratified.

As they drove off, Trevin had one, even more overriding notion pressing on his mind: *Don't screw this up.*

* * *

The parking situation here was even worse than in his neighborhood. He was hoping to be invited up, but Trevin somehow knew that wasn't going to happen. Not tonight anyway. He had only been in the South Loop a few times since its gentrification before the big crash, but it still held up as being mighty beautiful—and mighty congested. Even if he had been fortunate enough to be asked, there was nowhere to drop the Blazer. Permit-zone posts were everywhere, and the last thing he'd need is a hefty fine given his current financial position. He was already tapping into his savings.

"Now I know why you don't have a car," he said, shaking his head.

She laughed at his remark as he double-parked in front of her fancy entrance, in the rococo round-about, staring at the inviting chandelier inside her lobby. This was one of many high-rise conversions. A uniformed man at the sign-in desk was checking a ledger, bathed in the corona of light. "I'm impressed," Trevin said. "My first time here."

"It's not as expensive as you might think," Constance responded. "There were lots of great deals given how many foreclosures there are in the area. People just want to rent their places to get any source of money coming in."

"Which floor is yours?" he asked, doing his up-through-the-windshield thing into the towering structure.

She pointed to the top floor. "All the way up there, at the top."

The night had turned very hot and muggy, and he opened the sun roof so they could see it without straining. At this late an hour, things were quiet. "I love the sound of the outlying traffic on Lake Shore Drive," he said, trying to distract himself from thinking improper thoughts about her. He couldn't help it. "Sounds like the ocean."

"It does, now that you mention it," she said, herself stalling.

The architecture was marvelous around here, his eyes gliding over the lavish 1920s façade. "Must be a great view up there."

"It is," she answered. "I had to get a place up high. I do my best thinking up there. There's no one else on my floor."

"You're kidding."

"Nope. It's nice. Well… you know."

Now there were strange-forming clouds in the sky. Some were coming down low, almost surrounding the building she lived in. Trevin thought of Father Garren's words, and the mysterious incident that happened to him in the Chicago alley while making the call to Malligan and Totnes. "Constance, have you ever heard the term 'End Times'?"

She took on the most bewildered look. "I think so. What made you think of that?"

"I had a priest a while back say some pretty wild things to me. I wonder if it's coming true. I don't want it to all end—now that I've met you."

Constance wasn't sure where to start. "I can see what your friends growing up meant—you're a pretty intense guy, honey. But I love that about you. I'm not sure what to add, except I will say this …" She pointed straight overhead, through the sun roof. "Beyond those clouds… past the stars… that's where we're all heading, I believe."

"You believe that?"

"I do."

There was no denying he was frustrated, in more ways than one. And he thumped the steering wheel involuntarily to work if off. "How about fate? Or God? Do you believe in God?"

She leaned in, touching his bottom lip. "I most definitely do. To both questions. You're a gift from God."

Now it was his turn to laugh. "I'd say that's a stretch." Then, suddenly remembering something, he dug into his pocket, lifting his hips up from the seat, and presented her with a shiny new key.

"What's this?" she asked.

"To my apartment. It's a key to it, speaking of gifts. I forgot to give it to you earlier—you beguile me so much. I want you to have it." As she took it, "Take *that* as a sign."

"I… I don't know what to say."

"To make you feel safe, if you ever need it …"

Constance grew delighted. She looked like a child being given her first birthday present. "Thank you," she said, folding her fingers around it, holding it to her heart. She took in a mouthful of air, blew it out. "We have to look out for each other."

"We do," he said.

After kissing him passionately, she thanked him for a great evening and got out, walking—no, skipping—to the front entrance. Trevin waited for her to get inside, seeing that she had some good will words for the illuminated doorman as she punched the button of her elevator, waiting to go up.

* * *

Trevin set the bag with the quartz crystal rock in it on the balcony by the front door as he heard his cell phone ringing inside, lighting up the studio inside the window like a UFO on steroids. In the quest to run out and grab Constance's photo, he'd forgotten his cell, and figuring it was now his sweetheart calling to thank him one more time for the best evening she'd ever had (ha ha), he threw everything down to untangle the web of his own keys and get inside, to answer the damn thing.

He dropped them. They fell all the way through the slats to the bottom landing, then slipped through those, and landed in the black hole under the staircase—the creepy patch of dirt that had never been planted with grass seed.

Running all the way down, he begrudgingly got on his hands and knees, crawling under the first-floor landing. Once more, the black eyes of the basement window stared at him, almost threateningly. He didn't like it down here very much with the lack of light. Suddenly, a cat shot out from the corner and scampered off, scaring the hell out of him. He almost jerked up and cracked his head on the underside of the landing, which wouldn't have been good—there were exposed nails up there.

He heard the cell phone ringing again, and raced to the top once he found his keys. Now crazier thoughts were in his head. Maybe it was his parents calling for an emergency reason. He'd suddenly remembered the horrible call he'd received years ago at this time when his grandmother had been rushed into emergency surgery from the retirement home. She never came out. In all the scenarios now flashing through his head, Trevin finally made it inside, absent-mindedly leaving the bag where it was and snapped up the cell, just in time to catch it before it again went into voice mail.

"Where were you?" It was Constance. She'd sort of become worried.

"I dropped my keys. I left my cell here. What's going on? Is everything okay?"

"Yes, everything's fine. I just wanted to tell you how touched I was by you giving me a key to your apartment. That's a really huge step. I just hope you didn't regret it."

She *was* calling to say something extra-special. "Constance, I don't regret it. You mean everything to me, more than I can put into words. I don't want to scare you off."

"You're not going to scare me off. Really—I'm here for you."

Her sweet voice was the best thing he could have asked for. It would be the last thing he'd think of before drifting off to sleep. He had to shake off the reminder of never having made it back to Rochester in time before his grandmother passed away. That was one memory he'd always wanted to forget.

They talked for a few more minutes. It seemed things were inching his way, the universe finally stopping laughing at him. Recognizing the shabbiness of the shawl on the octagonal window, he pulled it down when he got off the phone, putting it back in the closet, folded. Nan was not going to be relegated to a makeshift curtain. He went to bed, thanking God for the good in his life.

CHAPTER 14

At the same time, as Trevin slept, Constance performed a nightly routine in the safety and comfort of her high-rise apartment. She had held the cell phone to her ear for a while, basking in the charm of his last words. Now she had to do what she had to do.

Her two-bedroom dwelling was modest yet functional, with just the right amount of necessary furnishings to provide comfort as she "tuned in" night after night. The Berber carpeting massaged her bare feet, the silence focused her attention. She had set Trevin's key on the living room table—which was stationed at the exact center of the room—and positioned herself at its center, aligned with the aerial view of Chicago at night. The curtains were drawn open fully. She loved the floor-to-ceiling windows. One could read a book by the illumination. Constance had none of her own lights on. The dramatic grid spread like an artificial ocean of electricity. Occasionally, an airplane entered the picture in the black, black sky—taking off or landing from O'Hare.

She was even more sensitive than Trevin. She could've invited him up, but she needed her alone time now. Too bad she had to get up in the morning and go to her temp job. This was the work that was important. Staring out into the scene, and with all the thoughts in her head, Constance was reminded of a hymn that had moved her from a church visit upon first arriving in Chicago. A choir had been practicing, and they were singing something about "the Dark and Sacred Night"—an appropriate and perfect description of the evening.

And she remembered the church bells. She loved church bells. She knew Trevin did also. He'd told her of it once in a sweet memory.

Wonderful things could occur in the wee hours, she thought, *in the Dark and Sacred Night.*

Before she started, she needed to wash off the humidity from the evening. A shower was in order. It had been an outing of great energy expenditure. Disrobing, she walked into the bathroom and lit a few candles, not turning on any lights in here, either. The sherbet-orange teardrops of flame jumped to life, fluttering in sporadic rhythm.

Blasting the water full force, she stepped in the tub, letting it pound on her skin, inhaling the steam through her nose. It was so quiet... so dark... so sacred. When she was finished, she shut off the water, stepped out, toweled off, and applied generous aloe to every niche and curve until her body gleamed in the candlelight. There was fogginess in the mirror, and she cleared a path with a washcloth—circling over and over until her image reappeared—her muscles warmed.

He often called her "sweet." That was nice to hear, of course, but Constance also knew she had to be careful with her ego—it was not supposed to get in the way. Nonetheless, she touched her lips, applying the same pressure Trevin had with his mouth, imagining his strong arms wrapping around her waist.

She blew out the candles and returned to the living room, fully naked, her wet hair clinging in ropey strands. Standing at the living room table again—aligned with the matrix out there—she shook her arms and wrists, loosening fingers, setting her hips. The only audio presence she heard was the cooled forced air from the registers. Fixating on the few stars in the sky (the clouds had moved off), she raised her arms, palms up, as far they could go. Shutting her eyes, she concentrated on all-inclusive love, and the power of Trevin's memories.

Data and intent became accessible.

CHAPTER 15

Before the certain noise woke him, Trevin's dream was fantastic, supremely emotional. First, wave after wave of the most beautiful colors graced his subconscious, as if the cosmos were warming up his experience. He believed he was seeing more hues than the human eye was capable of, more luxurious than any artist's paint handed down from Heaven. Once the mega-spectrum cleared, Trevin was running freely in the strawgrass that once existed at the end of the street in front of his parents' house—"the fields" as he'd relayed to Constance. He was back in his childhood body, perhaps six or seven years of age—above it, actually—watching himself run at top speed with his grasshopper-green gym shoes of the day. With laces tied tight, his feet pounded a beaten path through the meadow.

The season was summer, probably July—the last summer his ultimate playground would remain untouched. Tall and brawny trees—those he used to climb—flanked the perimeter. Euphoria literally trailed from his movement in a wake, like colorful streamers on a bicycle. Wild flowers rushed by in tufts, white cottonwood seeds skirting his face.

Trevin stopped running, catching the sight of a strange insect perched on a plant. He remembered his young mind always appreciated the countless life forms that co-inhabited his world, and this was one of his favorites: an emerald praying mantis. He suddenly had a glass jar with him, and captured the exotic creature in it, bringing it home to show his father.

Do you think he's happy being trapped in there? his father's voice posed. *Removed from his family, his home?*

Young Trevin became ashamed at what he'd done, mired in guilt. Perspective befell him, and he returned the mantis to the fields and put it back in the uncultivated briar. The creature regained its balance, faltering in the sunshine, stunned at the turn of events. Finally, it flexed its snap-shutter wings and flew into the sapphire sky. Trevin could feel its cheerfulness.

It had really happened. It had come back in dream form to remind him.

The "scene" next transitioned to his frail grandmother—who was in her older years now and fully wheelchair bound—close to the end. Trevin immediately felt a sadness beyond definition. Nan was set against an imaginary family room of surreal drapes and furniture, a ticking grandfather clock in the corner, not yet aware of her grandson's presence. Despite the invisible tears he was already shedding, Trevin was nonetheless elated to see her. He loved her so much.

He tried to call out but didn't have a voice. He tried going to her, but his legs weren't functioning. She was by herself, staring at the floor, anxiety racking her pained expression. And then she wanted to stand. Trevin hadn't seen her on her feet in what seemed eons. Gripping the armrests, her rheumatoid-riddled hands trembling, she slowly, but indubitably began building momentum—an awful struggle to witness. All Trevin could do was mentally root her on.

She pushed with all her might, gaining comportment as had the mantis on the leaf. She succeeded—smiling like a sunbeam—dazed from escaping the iron and vinyl prison. This was a miraculous feat, given the crippling arthritis punishing her body. One after the other, she took baby steps forward, freeing from impairment and pain. The wrinkles on her skin faded, regenerating with a youthful verve. She finally looked up and connected with Trevin, and he could read her thoughts.

Do you see this, Trevin? Do you see what I'm doing? She was ecstatic.

Yes, Nan, I see you. I see what you're doing. Keep going!

Then there was a distraction. Trevin suddenly became aware of previously covered carpenter's measurements, scribbled here and there on the drywall behind her. Now he was even younger, lending assistance to the workmen completing the room. Nan was still there, but she was not in her wheelchair, and the men were making sure it was okay to let the boy help.

If he behaves, certainly, Nan said.

This had also really happened. Trevin remembered it with joy. These were grown men, huge men—nine feet tall from his vantage point—allowing him to hand over nails and screws as needed. Trevin could hear their good-natured laughter. It tickled his soul. Nan baked cookies, and she dished them out with glasses of lemonade. Trevin could smell, taste them. The men were grateful, polite—a perfect recreation of a great afternoon, sunrays dousing all in a golden sheath.

Nan had been diminutive in actuality, only five-feet-one. Now she had the heart of a giant, the picture nearing completion. The laughter faded into oblivion, the workers gone. Where had they gone? Maybe into the walls? He was left with an inner voice telling him it was okay to move forward now and hold his grandmother's hand.

Congratulate her for doing well, it said. *Vow your protection and love.*

And so he did. "You're walking, Nan, you're walking. Don't stop, I'm so proud of you." The feeling of her hand erased all sadness, his tears drying up where there was no floor. He helped guide her to the garden level window, where they could see out onto Sweet Briar Road. She was so happy to be here, holding the sill, where she hadn't been able to see out this way in so long. Emerald Lane led away to the fields from the base of the driveway. It was so green and so lush up there.

"I'll protect you, Nan," Trevin promised her. "Always."

Protect your mother and father, too, Nan communicated back.

Trevin could feel her beginning to disconnect from him, and he didn't like it. Instantly, she was out there—on the lawn—and she was preparing to walk to the fields. She turned over her shoulder and mouthed the words "'I love you'" to him. He mouthed the same back and she strolled up past the knoll, lost to the strawgrass. His heart broke but he knew she was going to a better place.

This was when he'd snapped out of his dream, still aching from sentimentality. In fact, he'd soaked the pillow with actual tears. For God sakes… he'd been sobbing!

But he'd heard a dull thump in the studio.

The acrid taste of fear replaced the emotions of the dream. He could not move. Night paralysis had set in. But night paralysis followed nightmares. He hadn't had a nightmare. The clock radio's crimson display read 2:30 a.m. and the windows were rattling. He could hear them over the a/c. He looked out into the kitchen—he always kept the bedroom door open—and saw how exceptionally dark it was. Except… there was a breeze sweeping through the apartment. Napkins were blowing off the kitchen table. Somewhere, something was open. The octagonal window?

Like his grandmother's effort from the wheelchair, Trevin jerked himself free, forcing himself out of bed—bed springs pinging—and dropped silently on the floor next to the door. Crouching, he adjusted his knotting shorts and slipped on a tank top, wiping away the leftover tears He put on sneakers just in case, never taking his eyes off the kitchen tiles, where he could maybe detect movement reflecting there.

He ventured a peek around the corner. The problem—as always—was that from this perspective, he couldn't see around the half wall at midpoint into the studio. He crept out to the kitchen table, eyes trained on the unknown.

What he saw made his blood freeze.

The octagonal window was fully open... its screen appeared to have been kicked out... and the fucking streetlight was out again!

The tree branches were bouncing wildly out there. Quite a windstorm had kicked up during his sleep. No wonder it was so dark in his apartment. Maybe it had been the blowing around that had awakened him, but whatever the case, his make-up went into survival mode. Suddenly, he wondered—hoped—that he'd locked the front door.

He heard the most imperceptible tick (or click) behind the half wall, and thought he saw shadowy movement on the hardwood floor at its corner. All moisture dried in his mouth, and he started grinding his teeth. The kitchen light would be blinding. He had to keep it dark. Needing a weapon, he went back to the bedroom and grabbed the nightstand lamp, struggling to pull the plug from the outlet. Once he had it, he rose to full height, adrenaline spurring him on. Trevin embarked on his vigilant skulk toward the studio.

There was nothing to his left in the bathroom. But the shower curtain was moving slightly from the roving breeze. There was nothing to his right. The closet doors were shut. Terror was injecting into his veins. Only a few feet more now. He raised the lamp to striking position, sensing something was about to happen.

Something was squatting at the base of the half wall, near the stereo there—human-sized, retreating.

Trevin took another step ...

Immediately, a figure exploded at him in a vicious leap, bony hands grabbing his throat. Trevin would have screamed, but no sound emerged. He dropped the lamp, breaking into shards, as desperate fingers tore at his skin, sending him back—smashing into the other half wall. Pain ripped up his spine from the impact. And just that quickly, he was in a mad fight for his life.

There was no way to assess who exactly his assailant was. Everything was happening in a blur. The crackling shards made it nearly impossible to keep balance. This was a male, taller than himself, sinewy—with puffing nostrils and a grunting mouth—thumbs grinding at Trevin's Adam's apple. The television set went next, toppling to its side, sending sparks spitting and smoke rising all over the studio. If he went down, Trevin knew he was a dead man.

So the beast-instinct kicked in.

Trevin managed to gain footing while locking down on the attacker's forearms, stopping the wild side-to-side thrashing. Using his significant leg and core strength, he braced one foot against the half wall and broke the death-grip. A pummeling of fists followed, and Trevin blocked many of them. Trevin exploded back, driving a sharp elbow to the raging face, rocking the head backward, drawing a yelp of pain. He shoved the maniac to the middle of the room and almost went down again tripping on his art chair's rollers. They came together again like two rams, knocking the drafting table, sending the sketchpads toppling.

Trevin delivered a punishing knee to the attacker's thigh, crushing muscle on bone, folding him over. Then he slipped to the side, sweeping the man's legs out from under him while simultaneously lifting him, then slammed his body onto the floor, rocking the foundation like an earthquake. Bits of shards pulverized flesh. The intruder screamed in agony.

That's when Trevin lost all rationality—the animal in him taking over. Releasing all frustrations and anger, Trevin dropped to the floor and put his own death-grip on the skinnier man's throat, squeezing and squeezing. At that moment, Trevin wished to destroy everything bad that was happening in the world, everything that was happening to *him*—the man in his clutches just a focus for all that rage and outrage.

"P-pl-ease!" a thin, raspy voice hacked out—the first intelligible line. "S-stop!"

The vaguest suspicion that this might be the intruder who'd attacked Mrs. Dombrowski also crossed Trevin's wrath. The skylight above them gave way to the moon's light—the knotty clouds here also momentarily breaking—and the darkness in the room changed to a silvery-azure glow. For the first time, Trevin saw the mug under him. This was a young man—20 at best—with a shaved head and gaunt cheekbones, a scraggly moustache and partially grown goatee. The eyes rolled back… mouth sucking in gasps. "Y-you're… killing… m-me," "it" said.

Somewhere in his frenzy, Trevin comprehended himself committing an atrocious act. The broken television—a gift from his loving parents—smoked in fits, like the life he was extinguishing. Trevin regained a modicum of humanity and released his chokehold.

He jumped to his feet, stunned at what he'd nearly done, but continued to lord over the beaten shape. The kid clutched his throat and rolled over to the side, gagging, saliva oozing out in globs. Trevin saw the serpentine tattoo on the neck. *Gangbanger*, he surmised. *How dare you attack an elderly person.* "It" continued to apologize, hacking away, hands reaching up in pleas.

"Didn't… k-know anybody was home… p-please …"

"You didn't know *I* was here?" Trevin asked, sweating like a pig. "Who the hell are you?"

"… I'm hurt… b-bad …"

"You broke into my home! You attacked *me*!" Trevin stomped at the last word, sending the intruder cowering. "This is *my* home!" He kicked the man's thigh.

"Stop! Didn't think n-nobody lived here …"

"Why would you think that?" But Trevin knew the answer—the look of the house on the dark corner—but he stabbed a finger at his possessions anyway. "With all this? You didn't think anyone lived here with all this? *I* live here!"

The fool started blubbering, trying to get the jabbing shards out from under him. "Honest to Jesus, man, I-I'm scared. There's n-nothing downstairs… I gots habits, man …"

"I'm asking again—" said Trevin. "—who *are* you? You've been breaking into houses here, I know it."

"Man… I need h-help …"

Trevin flashed on the next bit of reality: a hospital visit was in order for the mewling worm. He was going to call 911 for an emergency, but he was momentarily thrown by the wetness on his neck. He felt for it, coming back with a stain of dark liquid—blood! Probably his own. In an unguarded lapse, Trevin moved for his cell, left on the coffee table. "I'm going to—"

The gangbanger saw his moment and hurled a handful of shards straight at Trevin's face, causing Trevin to jerk sideways. He shot up using the last vestige of strength and shoved Trevin into the coffee table, causing him to pitch over it, crashing by the octagonal window and injuring his coccyx. The punk tore at the doorknob lock.

"Hey!!" Trevin yelled, unable to move.

The heavy wooden door rocketed open, punching a hole in the studio's drywall, and the intruder kicked out the screen next, clearing his last obstacle. He bolted like a jackrabbit—toes instantly meeting the quartz crystal chunk in its bag—carrying him into the railing, where the already-loose balusters gave way, and he was sent careening over the edge to the sidewalk below.

Trevin heard a sickening thud.

There was no sound other than the rushing wind and the banging, damaged screen door. Trevin worked through the agony and limped to the balcony, where he looked down through the break, everything grinding to slow motion. His hair was whipping in a stinging tangle.

The intruder was there, mangled at the edge of the lawn. There were shrill, sucking sounds coming from him—attempts at air. He was still alive! Fury turned to horror, and Trevin became sickened. "Don't move!" he shouted. "Stay there! I'll get help!"

The broken being continued to struggle, blood evident on the cement. Trevin looked at the houses around him. *Has anybody seen this?* he thought wildly. Normal people slept at this hour. The situation worsened. The gangbanger finally made it to his feet and started lumbering toward the street, trying to negotiate the tight spacing between Trevin's Blazer and the next parked vehicle. At that same time, the faint roar of a charging automobile could be heard, turning the corner at the far end, beginning to race up. Trevin could see it was another muscle car—maybe the same Mustang.

On some level, Trevin saw what was going to happen—precognition to reality. The headlights were seconds away, woofer bass pounding over the wind torrent, loud enough to wake anybody. The bloodied thug glanced over his shoulder to see if Trevin was chasing him.

"Watch out!" Trevin shouted.

Balance was lost on the bumpers and the guy tumbled onto Munnison. An awful screech followed—an infernal noise Trevin subliminally compared to the grinding of the el train. The impact between flesh and iron was twice as bad as the meeting on the sidewalk. Trevin saw the body thrown like a bale of hay, landing ahead of the skidding Mustang, which skidded to a stop after sideswiping several cars, then nearly ran over the body.

The intersection of Salmon and Munnison was now a compilation of human and mechanical misery, right at the base of the cement factory's entrance. The hood was crumpled in a V-shape, smoke rising from every connection point, and blood was everywhere. There came a ghastly scream from a woman a few houses down—a neighbor who'd seen it—the sound tearing into Trevin's core, marrying together with it the sound of the screeching brakes seconds ago.

Residents poured like hornets from their shaken nests, shouts for help splitting the night. Trevin ran down the staircase—the objective to save *someone*—passing over the impact spot on the sidewalk to reach the grotesquely wrecked shape still breathing in a jelly spill on the asphalt. The woman he didn't recognize was also there, in a nightgown, hands clamped in revulsion. The god-damned streetlight suddenly spit back to life, showcasing everything.

CHAPTER 16

⋖ — ⋗

"Wasn't my fault… wasn't my fault …"

Trevin muttered the line over and over, voice weak, nobody hearing.

Loose papers and blowing twigs periodically tagged him like wasp stings. His angle on the assailant was now obscured, the gawking neighbors having rushed in, blocking his view. He'd seen much to make him say it— the abundance of blood amassing under the torso, a life slipping away.

"It wasn't my fault …" he said again, to anyone and no one.

"Christ, don't move him!" somebody shouted. "He's still breathing."

They were talking about the person who'd been attacking him minutes ago. Now the person was a poor soul, dying in the street.

It was the bastards in the speeding car, Trevin knew instead. The three or four occupants, including the driver, had survived the crash—all unconscious from the sounds of things. Trevin heard the word "teenagers" applied to the idiots. Where did all these neighbors come from? They had mostly blocked Trevin's view from the curb, where he was rooted in a daze. Somebody shouted that an ambulance was on its way. So were the police. No one knew Trevin was also a victim. This was happening whether he liked it or not. He could hear the kid pleading for God's help, even while being face down on the cruel asphalt.

It was all Trevin could do to keep himself from throwing up.

Someone was bellowing in anger, upset that his car had been sideswiped. People swore, and block party ribbon tumbled by in wads, entangling around some neighbors' legs.

Who am I trying to convince? Trevin thought through a haze. *Aren't these my neighbors? No one will pin this on me—I've already had my problems.*

How dare you think that way!

As if punishing him for even considering such thoughts, Trevin heard something that curdled his blood: "The artist's house! We heard shouting from there!"

Trevin turned and looked with the handful of strangers who were curious, terrified at the sight of his tell-tale broken railing, begging for publicity. This made him panic. He thought of his parents, Constance. This would destroy them. The pressure built and built until he couldn't handle it anymore.

"I didn't do it!!" he screamed.

That drew the attention. The same strangers blistered him with scowls, perhaps recognizing him from the block party. He thought if he turned his head they'd see the blood trickling down his neck from the fight—sure evidence of culpability.

Mars lights from hell lit up Munnison in alarming fashion, a strobing ruby and sapphire warning sending people to the curbs, shielding their eyes. Sirens pierced the night, and a megaphone voice commanded everyone to clear a path. If any neighbors had still been asleep, they weren't now. Car doors slammed. Officers in uniforms stepped through with clackety-tack hard shoes, shouting orders. A female officer lost her temper, scolding a harping shrew who demanded to know what happened. The ambulance was trying to back in. More flashers seared the retinas. Paramedics jumped out and took to the whimpering body, launching into every emergency procedure possible. Other first-responders from another ambulance went at the teenagers in their demonic heap, which was still belching fumes.

Trevin wished to blip out of existence. He'd been raised to stand up to responsibility, but all this was too much. The screeching brakes and the scream from the woman still haunted his brain, reverberating around in his skull.

Don't worry, he almost said to an officer, *I'm not running.*

He now recognized a few of the neighbors. Those were the ones interrogating Constance in the circle. They were talking to the police. He was pointed at. Two officers approached—all badges and holsters—asking if he was involved. They saw the strain of his expression… the back of his shirt, drenched. Trevin admitted his involvement, and didn't even know he'd moved his lips.

"Stay here," was the order. The paramedics were calling for body boards.

Then something extraordinary and hideously ironic happened. As Trevin turned back to the suffering antagonist on Munnison, still gasping and gurgling—the one who'd invaded *his* life, tried to snuff *it* out—a pool of blood worked its way from under him, lengthening away in a thin rivulet toward a manhole cover, feet away.

Isn't there someone who can vouch for me? Trevin cried in his mind. Two faces in the crowd caught his attention—Peter Bebziak and his wife, Ruth.

They walked toward him, spotting him at the same time. The Mars lights obscured their features, the wind whipping their hair and clothes in such a way to give them an illusion of being a warlock and witch, coming to cast a spell. They wore matching tee-shirts: Epcot Center, Disneyworld. Peter had on absurd, tartan boxers; Ruth—dingy pajama bottoms. Peter reached for his shoulder, Trevin deflected his hand. Reflexively.

They asked what happened. Trevin answered as cogently as possible, fumbling through the surreal set of circumstances. Peter asked who the attacker was. Trevin had no fucking idea.

"Jesus, your neck," Ruth exclaimed. "You're bleeding."

"The police want to talk to you," said Peter.

"I know."

"What can we do?"

"Stick up for me, this isn't my doing."

Peter was too close again, his face annoying. Trevin wanted to slap him. "Is that the …" he tried, pointing to the attacker, "… Mrs. Dombrowski asshole?"

"I don't know," Trevin answered. "Could be."

"We believe you," Ruth said. She was allowed to touch him.

"Serves him right," Peter said, almost under his breath.

Serves him right?

The rivulet of blood was about to drop into the manhole.

"Trevin," Ruth said, "they're asking for witnesses."

Trevin thought of Constance's crystal gift still up there. How could a loving memento turn into something so devastating? There came a scream of pain.

The experts in white gloves were gingerly turning the kid over to get him onto the hard plastic gurney. One moron from the sidelines took a picture with his phone camera. The police had a fit at this.

This was sickening. Trevin saw skin scraped off bone, and the assailant's milky eyes were now fixed at the thickening sky—the eerie clouds rolling back in. There came a final arch of the throat, head tilting back, and the victim stopped breathing forever. The paramedics tried resuscitation, but it was futile. Time of death was called—a flat note above the menacing wind. Husbands lead wives away, some breaking into sobs. Peter and Ruth turned to address other neighbors. Only Trevin saw what happened next.

A semi-translucent orb of light—the color of the day sky and no more than an inch in diameter—rose from the corpse's mouth, hesitating just above the palate, giving the appearance of it being under intelligent control. It seemed to be working through a dilemma: Should it stay or go.

Trevin's mouth fell open. "Oh my God," he said, but no one heard him.

The orb glowed more brightly, generating energy. Reaching a decision, it shot straight up at an impossible rate of speed, disappearing into the magic carpet of clouds up there, tumbling across the black sky in a circular motion. A satchel of medical gear dropped, sending instruments flying. Trevin was startled, and returned attention to the paramedics, loading the body on board. The last thing he saw was the intruder's face before the sheet went over it: an empty shell. Whoever that person was—he was gone.

What… have I just seen?

The ambulance swallowed the cadaver like a morbid prize, metal doors slamming shut. The horrid siren came back on and the vehicle slowly peeled from the mob like dry skin. Peter was catching up to Ruth, who was comforting another neighbor, grabbing her face in sorrow and stumbling erratically. Trevin's hands slammed to his ears, preventing a feral scream, locking in on the cop who'd ordered him not to move.

The cop was looking his way.

CHAPTER 17

Trevin was taken to the station. For questions. For an official report. He felt like a criminal, even as he knew he hadn't done anything. Already, what was emblazoned in his psyche was the awful smell of the government-issued, deep upholstery sanitizer in the backseat of the squad car he'd been escorted in. It had made him check under himself for signs of long-dried bodily fluid stains. Who knew who'd been incarcerated there before him.

Try as he did, Trevin was never able to grasp that one golden great memory to take the horror away—he was too discombobulated. He was in this for keeps.

Physical pain had set in. He was given aspirin when he asked for it. The water had an acidic taste, not the pain medicine. He downed it prior to the interrogation. Trevin's head was hammering him, not only from the fight but from his landlord's loud and terribly cruel voice—blasting long and loud over Munnison—accusing him of bringing disgrace and misery to the house. It had been mortifying. Neighbors had overheard, shaken their heads. How had Louie Fovos—the stocky and belligerent asshole with black, tussled hair—shown up so quickly?

The police worked fast …

Peter Bebziak had never come to Trevin's defense, and had disappeared when Fovos—not even out of his nightwear—went off explosively, getting up in his sole tenant's face, screaming at him. Officers had to separate them. Louie's thick dialect hadn't made matters easy, Fovos was a difficult man to understand anyway. There'd been no calm questioning, no concern for Trevin's mental or physical well-being. Trevin was guilty—whatever the story. The broken balustrades and blood all over the sidewalk had proved it.

The police needed Fovos at the station, too.

"Sir!" an officer barked when Louie didn't agree. "A violent crime has been committed on your property. Procedure dictates recorded statements. One from Mr. Lambrose, one from you. There's going to be a consultation between our department and the district attorney. These taped statements would be used if the deceased's estate were to ever sue the homeowner. Most likely, this is an open and shut case. This is to protect you, Mr. Fovos. Do you understand?"

"Fuck!" Fovos had yelled. "There'd better not be more trouble as the result of this!"

"*What?!*" Trevin couldn't believe the man's insensitivity.

"Animals take revenge!"

A news truck arrived. Trevin and Fovos exchanged one last glare. Trevin had graduated from welcomed neighbor to demonized pariah overnight, bringing unparalleled violence to people's doorsteps. At least he'd been allowed to go upstairs and put away the quartz crystal gift—now a symbol of lost hope. He also couldn't get out of his head the last view of Munnison Street as he was driven off—the rabble judging him… that blue orb… whatever the hell it was …

Trevin had found out from the police radio his assailant's name: Brian Annarez.

Brian Annarez, he'd thought. *Now there's a name attached …*

Annarez had lived only a mile away, gangbanging confirmed. Long record of previous arrests. Burglary, theft. 21 years old. Other family members thieves, too. All had records.

Figured …

How was Trevin going to tell Constance? Would she stay with him now?

* * *

The interrogation had to be interrupted several times while Trevin ran out of the room and vomited in the precinct bathroom. He'd failed at gathering any good thoughts—past or present—anything that existed in his memories and dreams. Not even that green mantis in the fields, flying free and cleared of strife, could help.

Fovos had given his statement and was gone already. Detective MacDrenner had kept them separate. Trevin had exchanged only glares with his landlord in the hallways. Fovos had been filled with disgust and utter contempt. A surveillance camera was trained on them from a high corner.

MacDrenner turned the microcassette recorder back on. The axles on the recording device began slowly rotating—around and around, in a circular motion. "Tell me about this rock the perpetrator tripped over."

He had the steely eyes of an eagle, concentration resolute.

"A quartz crystal," Trevin corrected. "My girlfriend—" (that surreal term) "—had just bought it for me. We'd gone to a bookstore, it was open late. I left it on the balcony, when I was running in to grab the phone."

"What bookstore?"

Did it matter? "A New Age one." MacDrenner finally got the name out of Trevin.

"They carry unique gifts?" MacDrenner asked.

"I don't know what you mean."

"The perpetrator tripped over a gift meant for healing. I was just thinking of the irony."

Trevin took a moment. "Yes, that is ironic. I guess."

"Coincidence or fate? Think about it."

"Detective," Trevin said. "I'm not sure what you're driving at …"

"I like that shop," said the detective. "I've been there. What's your girlfriend's name?"

"Constance Summerlin."

"Pretty name. Sounds like summer. Any guess why this Annarez character hit your home?"

Trevin took a deep breath and sighed. "We went over this, sir. When I had him on the floor, he told me he didn't think anyone was home. He was crying. Louie Fovos has to understand that—I hope your men reinforced that to him. He has to know, he's being a jerk. The house looks deserted with the streetlight constantly going out …"

"The streetlight was out? In front of the house?"

"It's always out," Trevin said. "Well, it comes and goes."

MacDrenner leaned back in his chair, eyeing Trevin's scratches. "Unfortunately for the dead guy, you can take care of yourself."

"Yeah." *Was that blue orb a part of him?*

"There's a couple on your street: Peter and Ruth Bebziak. They said you're a stand-up guy, told us about Mrs. Dombrowski. Tough break. Said you've recently become unemployed."

"Uh-huh."

"Story for many. You have a family?"

Trevin laid it out. Yes, he had a family—a mother and father in Rochester, New York. He wasn't sure if he was ever going to tell them about this.

MacDrenner turned off the recorder, folded his arms. Trevin assumed the interview was over. The detective took on the demeanor of a counselor rather than a law enforcement officer. "In my view," he said, "you don't need crystals or incense. You need time with them. We'll give you a ride back home. I'm sorry this happened."

"Detective, I have to ask, coming from someone who sees what they do—is it getting worse out there? On the grand scale?"

MacDrenner probably appreciated the question. He leaned forward, giving the idea serious consideration. "It is," he finally said. "Off the record I'll say this, Mr. Lambrose: Put your faith in God, or something righteous. Something's coming. My wife's been having the most incredible dreams. Dreams of memories. I know that's an oxymoron. Says they're gearing us up for something. We talk about it with our pastor."

Trevin dared a frank impression. "A coping mechanism?"

"Maybe," the detective said, standing, offering a handshake. "But she's preparing."

Trevin also stood. "I've told you nothing but the truth tonight, sir."

"Good," said MacDrenner, putting his duty face back on. "The truth shall set you free." Taking a card from his wallet: "This is a support group if you need it. Standard procedure. Your insurance or your landlord's should pay for the damages to your possessions. Try not mixing it up with him, he's under stress. He's been cited for code violations. That staircase …" Then he added, "You'll get a copy of the report. We'll be in touch if anything comes up that you should know about."

Trevin glanced at the card, put it away, and walked off with an assisting officer, approaching his ride, noting the dawn breaking out there through the bullet-proof glass at the end of the hallway. As Trevin stepped onto the sidewalk, he almost drew tears at the sight of the incredible daybreak sky that was forming overhead. *Amidst horror,* he thought, *beauty reigns in Creation.*

CHAPTER 18

◄ ►

Constance cried by the time Trevin was through telling her everything that afternoon. On her own, she'd decided to stop over—after work—feeling that something was wrong. She'd taken the el. She was going to use his key if she had to, but he was already on the balcony, sitting on a lawn chair staring off into space, a broken railing in front of him.

That's what started the conversation.

The smell of cleaning agents was also overpowering. He'd cleaned everything, vacuuming all sorts of broken debris, even using a mop and broom for micro glass shards that had riddled the floorboards. The coffee table had seen its best days. Constance couldn't have been more despondent. Just after they'd parted, too.

"And there's nothing that can be done about it now," he'd concluded.

Once he'd opened up, the information poured like a leaking barrel—yet another catharsis—especially after sleeping only an hour upon returning from the station.

The mixers and day laborers were toiling away in the cement factory yard. The late afternoon heat burned.

"Why don't you go inside and run the air?" she asked. "You're broiling out here."

"The place has to air out first," he answered, not telling her about the blood stains. He'd even tried cleaning the splotch on the sidewalk. He almost broke down, again panicking that he'd corroded his soul, done something morally irreversible. She comforted him.

Her face was beautiful. Silky hair hanging in his face, eyes wide to him, glistening. He'd never seen an expression like it—unadulterated, caring. Ocean-sized waves of sympathy washed into him from her. He could almost feel her spirit entering. Beads of sweat slinked down her bare arms, collecting on her summer dress, dampening it. She said, intensely: "Listen to me. Most people wouldn't… couldn't… have handled themselves better."

She touched the nape of his neck. "How bad does this hurt?"

"It'll go away," he said, wincing.

She managed to coax him inside, treating his scrapes and bruises. She knew where the supplies were in the bathroom. She had him drink ice water, hydrating him. His body continued to ache and his head still throbbed. After the sun dipped, he told her about the orb. In detail.

"I don't know what it was for sure," he concluded, "but I've guessed. I'm positive no one else saw." Forming a quarter-sized circumference with forefinger and thumb: "It was this big, Constance. I saw the life go out of the man. This thing shot straight up and disappeared. I was meant to witness it."

None of the story seemed to surprise her. The acceptance… the calm… on her face…

She covered him with a menu of kisses. "Let's go for a walk. It's cooled some."

* * *

Damage had been wrought from the windstorm. Downed tree limbs and branches were everywhere, leaves and garbage strewn about the street. Lawns were sprinkled with shingles that had been ripped from some rooftops. The city was about to go overtime picking up everything, Trevin believed, examining the traitorous neighbors' houses, wondering who was seeing him through the closed curtains and who was still judging him. He didn't tell Constance about the ugly looks he'd received.

Twilight had set, shrouding the two in a yawning coat of blue shade. He imagined the dark as a shield, still not enough to completely cover the blood stain where Brian Annarez had hit the sidewalk. They were back, and Trevin was glancing, trying to remove the horror.

"What are you looking at?" she asked.

He kicked the edge of the grass with his shoe, spreading dried blood. "That."

With trepidation, she asked, "Is that his blood?"

"Yup."

She took a deep breath, blew it out. "The rain will wash it away."

"What rain?" he asked, squaring to her and taking her hand. "When's rain ever coming? We have windstorms, but no rain."

"Soon." She looked up into the brooding sky. "I hope."

He relived the attack all over again, mentally. Post-traumatic stress. The shock was incredible, having the same impact as one of the powerful memories she'd extracted from him. But this one was evil. Sinister. She knew what was happening, and told him it was normal to respond to the presence of hateful violence this way.

"It might be hard for me to maintain that quest," he said. "I'll forever link our great night to this madness now."

She huffed. "I personally don't buy what your jerk landlord said. I don't think any repercussions will result from this. You've had too much happen to you."

"That's why I'm not so sure."

"I have your key," she joked, trying to lighten his mood. "I'll be the first responder if anything does happen." She tried one of her stunning smiles, but only managed a bizarre smirk. He laughed, loving her for it.

Life was too short. He saw that plainly. "I don't think I'll ever tell my parents," he said, looking off to the street.

One of the neighbor's cars drove past them, coming from Salmon—no one inside waving— parking at the far end. As the occupants got out, Constance strained to see in the dim light, and held up a friendly hand. Again, nothing. Trevin recognized them from the block party, but did not know their names. He didn't even try a greeting.

"Let's go up," he said, fighting the disgust rising in his stomach.

He led her back up "the legendary staircase," just wanting Constance to be with him. "I've been thinking," he said. "I think I've hit that sign telling me to go home to Rochester."

"I knew you were going to say that," she said quietly. "And, yes, you have."

* * *

The following week, as they said their goodbyes at the station, Trevin led Constance away from standing directly under the el tracks. He'd heard too many stories, perhaps urban legends, of trains rattling bolts loose from the underside of the tracks, dropping them down on pedestrians. He didn't know how true that was, but he wasn't to going risk the chance finding out.

Constance was sad. She hated the thought of being without him, but was delighted he was going. In her estimations, it was critical for him to see his parents to decompress. She had been the great cheerleader all through the online ticket-purchase and up to this moment, but now that he was actually leaving to get on an airplane, she'd grown ferociously morose.

"I wish you were coming with me," Trevin said, looking up from the sidewalk—shielding his eyes from the blazing afternoon sun—sizing up the danger of the foundation overhead. The fortified framework and gargantuan stanchions dwarfed them, but offered some privacy.

Constance grew excited. "You do? You could have told me that earlier."

"Maybe next time," he followed, trying to calm his own nerves. He'd confessed on the cab ride over that he didn't like flying and he also hated the thought of being separated from her. She'd been his staunchest ally.

Trevin had with him a rolling suitcase for traveling, and he had to keep moving it this way and that to avoid getting it entangled in the busy pedestrian traffic. The base scratched on the gritty sidewalk. "Just forget about me," he said. "Try to have a good time. Work hard."

"It'll be hard to fully relax," she told him.

Here by the gate fence, they stood away from the stampede herding up and down the terminal steps. Trevin saw nothing but disconnection: iPods clamped to heads, no commuter making eye contact with another. To his cynical mind, the squeeze into the turnstiles reminded him of what humanity had become: a grind. The world had come to this.

Constance kicked aside debris, trying to think of something to say. "Still think you'll be gone a couple of weeks?"

"Maybe," he answered. "We'll see."

"Trevin, look at me," she said, turning him toward her, unable to handle his apprehension. "I'm not trying to rush you. When you figure it out, let me know."

To his view, her summery blouse symbolized the freedom he felt when being with her. "I'll miss you so much," he confessed, momentarily falling into her gaze.

"And smile," she reminded him. "You're looking unbelievably melancholy."

Trevin laughed. "I'm sorry."

He hadn't been in slacks, a button shirt and dress shoes in a long time, and it felt good, made him feel like a man again. "Where is this train?" he fidgeted. "Can't one thing in this city work on-time?"

He was suffering inside, pining with a cadre of insecure thoughts—wondering if she would leave him in his absence. He couldn't become unglued now. It was critical for her to see him off with as positive a demeanor as possible. "I better get up there," he said, checking the time on his cell phone, seeing an opening in the flow. "What're you doing when you get home, babe?"

"Well …" she began, putting on a humorous tone, "firstly, I'm going to fall apart being without you. Secondly, I'm going to have a nice bath—with candles—and stare out over the city at night, figuring out what I need to do with you."

He stared. "What? That second part almost sounded like you were serious."

She leaned close, seeing straight into his pupils. "Wouldn't you like to know?" She had one eyebrow raised wryly.

An understated rumbling was heard, plundering in from afar. Neither could tell from which direction. Whines torqued from metal-on-metal contact. Trevin unexpectedly flashed on the screeching brakes and the screaming neighbor from the night of horror. The psychological effects started to come back.

"Oh—shit!" he said, letting go of the suitcase, bringing his hands up to his ears.

Constance grew alarmed. "What's wrong?"

Piercing, prolonged decibels followed. It was the train—traveling inbound, toward downtown—the opposite direction from the airport. The pitch grew violent-sounding, strafing Trevin's sensibilities like a knife, recreating the awfulness, burrowing spikes into his mind.

Constance saw what was happening and tugged him away. "Come on!" she shouted. "We shouldn't stand here!"

But it was too late. The train was overhead. The "non-stopper"—as people called it—had reached maximum velocity. Trevin's clamped hands were pressing, his angular face turning red. He was squeezing his eyes shut, hoping to dam the revulsion out. He cursed at himself for not anticipating this! The quaking rattled their joints, making skin itch. Other pedestrians grimaced, dealing with it as best they could. Some kept to their business, some plugged their ears. This was torture. Trevin's teeth gritted, veins bulging at the neck. Constance threw her arms around him. He screamed, sound lost in the thunder.

Brian Annarez was flying through the air, about to hit the pavement. After the dreadful contact, there came human shrieking as the body ceased sliding, blood smearing over the asphalt. As the sound of the el faded, so did the jolt—but Trevin again saw the blue sphere shooting up into the aurora borealis.

Slowly, Trevin regained his wits. He opened his eyes, dropped his hands. Constance was squeezing him tight, protecting him. No bolts rained down on them. Some were ogling, wondering what the freak show was about.

"What was *that*?" Constance demanded.

"The… noise. Reminded me of… the incident. It all came rushing on. He's dead, he's dead. I'm… not that guy, Constance… I'm not that guy."

Constance led him to the token booth. "Baby, you're human. Remember—it's about intent. You didn't mean to hurt anybody. You didn't mean for anyone to end up dead. He attacked *you*."

"He did, but …" Thinking: *I knew what was in my shameful heart for that moment.*

"Then accept it. The ordeal's over."

She almost had to push him through the turnstile, the constant interplay of commuters never ceasing. His CTA card was in his wallet. He almost didn't find it. It was bent and dog-eared when he pulled it out. He also checked for his airline tickets, finding them stashed in his front pocket, folded clumsily. When he was ready to go, she pulled him back, kissing him passionately.

An outbound train was approaching—the one he needed to get on. This time, he launched into action before the screeching ratcheted up, jamming the card through while muscling the suitcase over his shoulder, joining the human chain hustling up the concrete steps, turning back to call to her over the crowd: "I'll call when I get in tonight! I love you!"

This reminded him of a fenced-in bullpen, filled with cattle.

Breaking onto the upstairs platform, he stole a look down again. He could barely see her, but she was a vision amongst the many, a representation of goodness against the urban milieu.

When the new train pulled in, he shot aboard and grabbed a seat in the back by a window, making sure he wasn't blocking the aisle with his suitcase. Commuters filled every last seat, bobbing and weaving with frowns on their faces. The air conditioning was not working. Already people began fanning themselves with magazines and newspapers. One guy strained to open a window—the only behavior different from the uniformity around him. The doors closed and the train lurched forward, causing those standing to grab the poles.

Already, Trevin felt empty without Constance.

They passed the new batch of commuters waiting for the next train, then cleared the platform altogether. And then Trevin saw Constance. She was standing alone in front of a red brick building on the opposite side of the avenue, desperately peering up, trying to locate him!

Trevin stood from his seat, annoying the person next to him, and waved frantically. He almost shouted, but that would've been ludicrous. The train's movement created a strobing effect with the sunlight cutting in and out between all the structures—like the light-and-flicker show of an old zoetrope movie machine—streetlights and billboards periodically blocking his view. *She'd better look here and quick!* he thought, craving one last contact with her. A reflection must have gleaned off the metal, finally catching her attention.

The last thing he saw, before an abandoned warehouse blocked everything, might have existed only in his imagination. Constance seemed to catch sight of him, and she raised her arms as high as they could go, moving her hands in a circular motion—around and around and around.

CHAPTER 19

The drive home from the Rochester International Airport with his parents was moodily hushed. His mother and father knew just as well that their son hated to fly. Just being off that damn airplane was a relief. When Trevin had been up there, looking down at the weirdly fantastic cloud formations, a returning theme persisted: *Maybe everyone's right. Mother Earth is concocting some kind of statement.*

But it was time to relax. Mom and dad were so glad to have him home. The crushing hugs had proven the resolve of their welcome, but there was still unvoiced concern, he just knew it.

Trevin stared out from the passenger seat, mesmerized by the hard lines of the houses along the highway, jaggedly cutting up, down and diagonally across his vision, then radically changing to the soft shapes of the foliage, then back again. The light and flicker show had continued here—a hypnotizing remembrance of his past.

He got out his cell phone and made sure it had automatically reset. He'd lost an hour traveling east. He turned around to his mother in the back seat. She smiled at him. He smiled back. Dad was a competent driver. He had his eyes fixed on the road.

Something's not quite right. "Everyone's so quiet," Trevin said, trying to brew up conversation.

"We're just enjoying the view," his mother said.

There was the array of familiar landmarks out there. The memories were already rampaging. But they were out of sorts, thanks to the strife he'd been through during the last half of the year. The same highway signs impended, the same ball fields beckoned, but there was an invisible barrier now keeping him from fully savoring their charms. The car passed companies that had employed his friends' fathers before the big layoffs. He remembered toiling on one such rooftop—the huge factory off to his right, with the smoke stacks and gleaming metal ductwork. He'd earned much-needed college money there doing roofing for the two summers they hired him. It was a different time back then. Where were those jobs now? Hadn't he labored at those gigs so he could focus on his career at his current age?

"Shame," he mumbled, unaware he could be heard. His dad looked over at him.

"What?"

"Nothing." Trevin adjusted the belt cutting on his pectoral muscles. The aches from the fight were still throbbing. He hadn't gotten over all the pains. "Just going down Memory Lane."

"What did you do to your neck?" his mother asked, finally seeing whatever remnant there was back there, on his nape. He reflexively reached for it, covering.

"Scraped it moving stuff," he answered, feeling guilty already about his first fib. How many more times was he going to hide the truth from them about the attack? They knew nothing of it, but certainly did know how long he'd been out of work. "The back stairwell of my apartment has some tricky corners when I do laundry."

"Oaf," joked his father. This is what pops did. "I'd expect as much from you."

This brought a chuckle out of Trevin. He lightly punched his father in the shoulder.

"Don't make me pull over," dad returned. "You won't like the results."

Trevin chuckled even harder. "Try it."

Mom rolled her eyes.

In terms of the driving arrangements, this is also how it was—dad at the wheel, mom in the back, son in the passenger seat. It would do no good for Trevin to offer driving. And, as Trevin hated airplane travel, mom disliked highway traversing, preferring to stay in the back where she wouldn't be frightened by the big trucks closing in around her.

He was thinking about them, his parents. He could see where people said he was the perfect blend of the two. Trevin had his father's strong face, but his mother's soft eyes. Mom had always been the sentimental one to dad's stoicism, and both were fairly athletic, still looking good for their age. Trevin thought of the exercise regimen his father kept himself and his wife on. Something to be proud of. Trevin was so glad to be with them. He loved them so much.

"Thanks for cranking the air, dad," he said. "It's a hot one."

"It's been real hot," his father responded. "Unusually so, and we're not even into the dog days of August. What's the weather been like in Chicago?"

"Hot," Trevin answered. "And muggy, like everywhere."

Trevin made sure his mother was okay again. "I think I'm looking more like the two of you every year."

"You do, huh?" mom said.

"But you'll always look up to me," added dad, a jape from way back—from high school days.

"Because you're taller, I know," said Trevin. "Funny, dad. How old is that one?"

Dad laughed. Mom reprimanded him. "Carl …"

Dad looked in the rear view mirror. "What? April? Can't I joke with my son?"

Mom rolled her eyes again, looking out sideways. This was all in good fun.

"How's the garden, dad?"

"We had a better run last year," he answered. "We need that rain."

"And work? You never tell me how the factory's going. Everything all right?"

"Oh… sure."

"Worrying about something else besides me?" Trevin asked.

"Don't be absurd."

Yep, thought Trevin. *Absolutely something's going on.* "'Don't be absurd'" could mean his parents were continuing to stave off what the media reported as being a brink of local economic disaster. It was common knowledge that—like everywhere else in the country—the area was suffering steep cuts in the workforce, a decline of sustainability. Trevin thought about bringing up the threat, but this was not the place or the time.

"Doing fine back there, babe?" dad asked agreeably.

"Just enjoying being with the two most important men in my life," she said.

April Lambrose, Trevin thought. *Always the congenial one.*

They traversed the entire local highway, heading north toward Lake Ontario. There'd be time to think, long and hard, Trevin supposed to himself, being here in the comforting womb of his home, all those fresh memories coming back to help make him center himself. There was a beautiful sky taking place above them, and he suddenly wished he could escape up into it—taking both his parents with him—allowing them to also purge the worries and troubles of the Earth below. They were two of the greatest people he knew. And thinking of Constance, he knew he was forming great, new memories—right here, right at this time. He'd share them with her when they spoke.

Over an approaching bridge, Trevin saw an old, rival high school coming into view. As they passed over it, he briefly caught the entrance road leading up to the main building. He remembered riding in the buses on his way there, his teammates shoulder to shoulder with him in their football uniforms, hearts pounding in anticipation of going to battle against their fellow athletes. The pine trees had grown much taller, he saw, blocking most of his view. His heart ached for those times, and he wished he could go back and do it all over again—no mistakes this time, taking all the proper paths in life. But of course that was impossible… and defeating to even entertain. When he turned back, he was missing his pals, hoping they were all doing well.

"Thinking of your 40-yard touchdown there?" his dad asked, perhaps reading his son's thoughts.

Trevin laughed, shaking off the foolish nostalgia. "Maybe."

"That was one of your best games."

"There weren't many. We didn't have a good team."

"But you guys tried," offered mom. "And you never quit on your teammates."

"Hmm," Trevin muttered, thinking of the concept of loyalty, and how much he valued it. Loyalty was a virtue, he thought. Constance would agree. Constance was big on virtues. She was always pointing them out to him.

"I learned perseverance from you two," Trevin continued. "Remember how we used to go on the roof, dad, during meteor showers, and stay up late—waiting to see the sky shows? That was perseverance. Mom, you'd go to bed. You weren't climbing up."

"I remember that," mom said. "All too well. I thought you guys were crazy. I was nervous as hell you'd fall off. Was Tommy Porch involved in that? Seems like something he'd do with you fellows."

"Tommy wasn't involved," Trevin answered. "And speaking of him—have you two seen him? I was just telling Constance about him, sharing all the crazy stories."

"We haven't seen him, he hasn't been around the neighborhood," dad answered. "You can call him while you're home."

"Maybe," said Trevin, thinking about his old pal. "I'd like to see him. He's so busy, teaching at school, raising two hellion boys, not trying to drive his wife nuts."

"For all his wildness," his mother said, "I give him a lot of credit. He was always a great friend to you, kid."

"I know that, mom, trust me."

Dad grew annoyed at a slowpoke driving in front of him, so he stepped on the gas and motored around him, making Trevin explode in hysterics. But Trevin reacted sharply when they also raced by their normal exit. "Hey! What are you doing, dad? That was our exit!"

"You're on vacation," his father responded calmly. "Relax."

Trevin turned to his mother. "Where we going?"

"Your father had this planned. He thinks we need a little diversion first before going home."

"A diversion? From what?"

"Just sit back, keep your mouth shut, and enjoy the ride," concluded his father, turning on the car radio to his favorite preset station—classical jazz from one of the local universities. A crisp saxophone filled the air, smoothing over the gloomy overtones.

Trevin had a pretty good idea of where they were going.

* * *

They went to Ontario Beach Park, along the lakefront, a favorite spot for locals since the early 1900s—at the mouth of the Genesee River. A place all three had been to a million times—a place with thousands of memories for each of them.

"Of course," Trevin said, reacting to the splendor of the sight. "I should have known. We gonna get some frozen custard, ruin our appetites for dinner?"

"Well, we're getting custard," said dad, parking in the nearest lot. "But we're not spoiling our dinner appetites. Your mom would kill us. Right, April?"

"I'm not getting any, Carl," she said. "I told you that."

"You made dinner, mom?"

"All we have to do is heat it up," she said. "You better *not* spoil your appetite. I'll kill ya."

"Meatloaf and mashed potatoes?"

"Of course."

"Thanks, mom."

"You're welcome," she said.

The corner lot here at the intersection overlooked the beachfront and a strip of shops. Dad and Trevin got out. Mom stayed inside. "Leave the air on, would you, please?" she asked, and saw them off on their merry way. "And you're not eating in the car," she said after them, powering down the window. "I won't have a mess all over the seats."

Trevin and his father stood in line along the sidewalk, waiting their turn at the famous frozen custard stand—soft ice cream by another term. Trevin let his soul bask in this familiar area, watching waders and volleyball players frolic out there on the sand—a vision in contrast to the world's headlines. A posse of motorcycle aficionados throttled by, making most cover their ears. Nothing like the screeching el tracks in Chicago. The sound reminded him of summer nights spent listening to them way off in the distance while in bed, stirring with imagination of where the bikers might be going: to exciting far-off lands and destinations. Trevin thought about subjectivity, weighing his problems against the masses, but knew he was still in need of a dramatic change.

After the two got their treats, they walked with mom to the jetty—the pier as the locals called it—and began the mile-long saunter to the end of it, where they felt the need to wallow in the fully encompassing view of Lake Ontario, engulfed by its peace and beauty. The men had to eat fast. The sun was setting already, but it was still amazingly hot. The strong breeze was the only thing keeping them halfway cool.

Rollerbladers, families and couples were coming off the boardwalk, pretty much leaving the Lambroses to themselves. It was the perfect setting for deep ponderings, except for the fishy odor.

Trevin reacted. "Whew. Still haven't fixed the problem with the smell down here, huh? Never got a foothold on the algae problem."

"It's the western edge of this thing," dad said, meaning the jetty. "Cuts down on the flow of the water. It's always been this way, even when I was a kid coming here."

The odor was offset by the charming sound of calliope music from the old Dentzel menagerie carousel in the lawn area. The ride was surrounded by parents watching their children having the time of their lives on it. Trevin grinned in a melancholy fashion. "The carousel's still operational. I remember doing a painting of that in high school."

"I remember that," said his mother. "Whatever happened to that painting?"

"I sold it to a teacher who asked for it. She thought she was getting a deal. Thought it'd be worth something some day. She thought she was investing in an early Picasso."

"There's still time, Trevin," encouraged his father. "Keep positive."

Trevin smiled at the kids, screaming in joy on the antique horses and swans. He thought about how their futures were still wide open. They hadn't screwed up like he had. "Good to know some things will never change."

The areas along the shoreline—the residential areas—were a little worn in Trevin's view. The paint on many of the Cape Cod-style houses there needed a fresh coat, and the defunct Port of Rochester terminal represented a remnant of a better past, a future that never took root. A massive ferry boat used to shuttle passengers from there to downtown Toronto and back. Not anymore.

"How long's the ferry been gone now?"

"A while," his father answered. Mom hooked her husband's arm. "Rochester lost a ton of money on that boondoggle. An Australian company bought it and sailed away with it one day. There went that business."

"So …" said Trevin. "You can now tell me why you've been so quiet. Both of you. I know something's up. I read it on your faces at the airport."

"We're dealing with things, Trevin," said his mother, looking down at the concrete quay beneath them. "You losing your job didn't help."

"Don't want to get into it?"

"There's nothing to get into, Trevin," she said. "That's why we wanted this diversion. We thought you'd appreciate it. You always loved coming down here."

About a half mile out, the breeze turned to a strong wind, cutting out all sound from shore. This created the illusion of being even more isolated. Trevin saw the small lighthouse tower at journey's end, and when they reached it, mom and dad sat on benches to enjoy the setting, and Trevin put his hand along the old and rusted shipping beacon, using it to chart a path straight up into the sky from ground level. It was an interesting perspective.

Exotic arrangements were forming out of the clouds all around them, from horizon to horizon, definitely giving the impression of being on a different planet altogether. Trevin said as much, commenting on the reddening, elegiac-looking alto and cirro-cumulus clouds looking like an alien creation from his imagination. Huge clouds were being born, drooping lazily down in clumps, meeting at the water's edge and cutting off. The sun—what they could see of it—was drunk with the most intense ginger color they had ever seen, radiating with wildfire, making the undulating waves seem all the more mystical. Only a few sailboats interrupted the dream-like scene. Mom and dad were shielding their eyes.

"What's all that sparkling around the clouds?" asked Trevin.

"Been like that for months," answered his mother. "Carl and I came out here just last week, after you told us you were coming home. We saw the same thing. The sky is getting very, very strange. It makes me think."

"About what, mom?"

Dad looked at her, shrugging his shoulders. "Tell him."

"Something's… calling to us," she said with some trepidation. "I've been having these dreams. I see the same clouds and skies in them. I don't mean it's telling us something in the literal sense, but… something's going on. I suppose that's the craziest thing you've ever heard?"

"Not really, mom," said Trevin, experiencing an eerie shudder. He again thought of Father Garren and his mentioning of Prophecy—or End Times. Maybe the theories were far-reaching? Maybe everyone was starting to think this way?

"I think it's important we're together now," she added. "We're very glad you're home, dear."

"I am, too."

"Or it might all be the result of abnormal weather conditions," said dad, continuing to stare off due west. "All this humidity sure hasn't produced rain. Maybe it's screwing up the ionosphere. I know one thing—you two are two peas in a pod."

But Trevin was seeing the prescient expression on his mother's face, and tended to lean more toward her way of thinking. He'd seen too much. And she continued …

"It's been making me savor my happy memories," she said, growing more passionate. "I mean, really cherish them, like never before. They've been coming in droves, it's bizarre, and they aren't in dreams—they're in my waking hours. I haven't thought of some of these memories in years. They're just all popping in from out of nowhere, at random times. But especially when I take the time to look into the sky like this one. It makes me relive our happy times together as a family. Maybe it's God's wake-up call."

"That's… beautiful, mom. I knew I could count on you to crystallize it."

Suddenly, something splashed in the water—hard—way off to their right, due north, where they hadn't been concentrating. It caught their attention, and the three snapped heads to see what it was. What they saw was the aftermath: a great plume of spray subsiding back into Lake Ontario, sending a rowdy disturbance ripple away from the impact point in all directions. They waited a half a minute as the wake worked its way to them, turning into a slightly less frolic lapping along the barrier. It was quite a shock. There had been absolutely nothing around it.

After catching his senses, dad spoke up first. "What was that?"

He and his wife stood, putting their arms around each other, as if in protection.

Trevin let go of the lighthouse tower, amazed. "That… couldn't… have been a fish."

"A meteorite?" asked his father.

"Who knows?" said Trevin, still awed, as were both his folks.

Any trace of the wake diminished along the jetty. They continued to stare at the spot, seeing nothing but the striking and shiny sparkles returning to its normal rhythm and pattern.

After a lull, with no additional activity, his mother said, "I think we should go. Let's start this happy time together with that meatloaf I have for you fellows."

As they walked away toward shore, Trevin said, "If you guys had a computer with the Internet, you could look up this stuff."

This earned an acerbic glare from dad. "Don't get started. Like we've said—that's an expense we don't need."

"I'm just saying, maybe it's time to get into the 21st century."

"We prefer the Stone Age, thank you very much."

Trevin's heart strengthened. If he could move the universe for them, he would. "I just want you two to know I'd do anything for you. I love you guys—I wish nothing but the happiest moments on you."

"Thank you, Trevin," his mother said. "We love you, too, and we feel the same."

The clouds continued to sparkle away at the edges, as if giant, cosmic generators had patched into them to create a heavenly showcase of nectarine and gold intentions.

* * *

Trevin imagined the camera in his head snapping away at the waterfront properties on the ride home, lamps springing to life in the living rooms. He saw Miller moths flitting from lawns in the finally cooling temperatures of the day, and winced when he turned to see more, injuries from his fight still zinging him. In the world of photography, he was thinking, there is a time of day known as the "magic hour"—the precious minutes bridging evening to nightfall—where one could still shoot subjects without incidental light, everything having a cool, blue look to it. That time was now. The trio had hung around Ontario Beach Park longer than anticipated, and it was now twilight.

They reached his homeland territory, his old neighborhood, and the functioning streetlights finally showcased the words he'd longed to read: Sweet Briar Road.

Accept no substitute, he said to himself.

The brick red, split-level colonial with the off-white trim around the doors and windows was another visual respite, a breath of fresh air. They climbed out, and Trevin looked up Emerald Lane, the dead-end street extending away from his parents' driveway, where his beloved fields-of-yesterday once existed. Now there were only the more expensive homes in the new tract—many already in foreclosure. His precious, loop-shaped neighborhood was now indistinguishable from a million others.

Dad and Trevin got the luggage as mom waited on the front porch.

"Staying out here all night?" she asked jokingly, watching them argue over who was going to grab what.

"Actually, you know what?" said Trevin. "Dad, you go in. I want to stay here a minute longer."

"I'm heating dinner up now," she said. "Don't mess with my cooking already."

"I won't, mom."

After he was alone, Trevin continued to look around. A lot of the homes surrounding them were much like theirs. Some were ranches, a few were Garrisons. The sidewalks were still maintained, the roads fairly well kept up, and all those tall trees he showed off to Constance, planted in the mid-'60s, provided even more shade now that they were larger.

Presently, all was quiet. No riotous block parties, no cars ripping by at treacherous speeds. It was nice. But Trevin still had the lingering nightmares floating around in his mind from his recent calamities, preventing him from fully enjoying being home. He hoped there might've been at least one recognizable local to wave at—someone from the old days—but sadly, many of memorable neighbors had made the exodus over the years. They'd moved away in favor of being close to their children and grandchildren, or they'd died.

From his kitty-corner angle, Trevin spotted a FOR SALE sign in Mr. Tavalier's yard. He could just see into the driveway, past the supremely high hedges still mostly quarantining the property from the rest of the block. Surprising. *Not his, too.* The lonely realty sign swung from a wooden post, its glossy finish catching the last light.

When he entered the house, Trevin asked them about it.

"Yep," dad said, running his son's suitcase up the stairs to the second floor, where Trevin's old bedroom was. Mom was in the kitchen, pulling out plates and silverware. "We just saw it the other day. The sign's been there about a week."

"Do you know why Mr. Tavalier's selling?"

Dad came back down. His face changed to a solemn façade. "He just lost his wife."

Trevin reeled. "Oh, no. When did *that* happen?"

"We read it in the paper, didn't say what she died of. What's it been, April—five, six weeks now?"

"Sounds about right," she said from the kitchen.

"At our age, son," said dad, "we find out a lot of things in the obituaries."

Suddenly, Trevin felt very accountable, wondering how the poor man was holding up. It was so dark over there. No lamps, no sign of life— like the homes on the drive here. There'd been no car in the driveway, either. Trevin remembered how Mr. and Mrs. Tavalier never parked in the driveway.

He murmured, "He's alone now …"

"What?" said his dad, going into the kitchen to help his wife.

"Nothing."

* * *

Before the meal, Trevin had a little time to himself to clean up. His hands were still sticky from the frozen custard, and he felt bad about his dad hauling his suitcase up to his old room. At least he could put some stuff away. When he entered his room, a million memories hit all at once. And normally, he would have dwelled on a few of them, but his thoughts were still drifting across the street, where Mr. Tavalier was probably by himself, suffering in silence.

I'd just been talking about him, he thought, shaking his head at the mystery and unfairness of life.

Dad had set the suitcase on the bed and opened it, and Trevin began to take a few items out. He stopped as he looked out the window, the blinds only halfway open as his mother liked it. She thought it looked neater from the outside that way. He went to his old study desk and stared out, where he could see over the hedges across the street, catching a better view of theTavalier house.

Trevin sat on his bed, feeling mournful, the trophies and favorite books from years past long since removed from the shelves around the room. The smell of meatloaf was the only thing keeping him in the moment. Dad was checking stocks on the television—Trevin could hear it. Another appalling day: war atrocities in the Middle East, the global market tanking.

Even without the overhead on, Trevin recognized his wall color: his adored, sea foam blue-green—chosen when he was eight—suggestive of the vast oceans with their incredible life forms. The only thing different was his sliding closet. It was now packed with his father's clothes.

"He's alone now …"

By the time Trevin was called, dad and mom were waiting at the kitchen table, filling plates. Dad had prepared a fresh salad from the garden. "Eat the greens and love it," he warned. "No choice."

* * *

The food was delicious, just as he'd expected. Trevin swooned over his mother's culinary talents, and she thanked him for being so kind. He still couldn't shake his bad mood. "I never even knew her," he said of Mrs. Tavalier. "Mr. Tavalier's probably saying 'good riddance' to the street. We disregarded them—like wet paper toweling just thrown away."

"That's a bit severe, don't you think, Trevin?" asked his mother.

"Is it? None of my friends alerted me, either. They must not have known."

"I know how you've mentioned over the years how you never knew the Tavaliers."

"Mom—no one did. So no one knows what happened?"

"We don't, God rest her soul," said mom. "The obituary didn't get into it. They were married a long time."

"I'm not proud of the fact that I've lived across the street from them for 35 years and I never knew her name was Emily," dad interjected, mid-chew. "I read that, too."

Trevin put the fork down. "That is depressing. Emily Tavalier. I didn't know that was her name."

"See?" dad said. "Don't be so hard on yourself."

Trevin repeated her name. "And what's Mr. Tavalier's name? Isn't it 'Cecil?'"

"Cecil, yes."

Trevin thought of his partner-in-crime, Mr. Porch and him, calling the man Nutty George. They should be ashamed. "Tommy and I discovered his real name from a dropped letter on the sidewalk. In seventh grade."

"Did you return it?" dad asked.

Trevin shot his father a droll look and said, "Of course"—leaving out the part about stuffing it folded a dozen times over in the screen door. Then he couldn't think of what the inside of the Tavalier household looked like. He'd never been in it. That had always been of great curiosity to him, especially as of late. It was strange how he'd been thinking about his long-estranged neighbor lately. He wondered why.

"Tell me what you remember from inside his house," Trevin asked. "I remember you telling me that when you and mom were newlyweds, you had to go there when it was a model home for the neighborhood. That's where the closing took place."

Dad had to think about it. "That's before anyone lived there. Gosh, I haven't thought of that in years. Yeah, that was there before any of the others. This was all a briar patch. The developers used it for closings. I don't remember much of the interior. My nerves were jangling, I remember that. I do recall the stairs when you first walked in. You had to go up a few steps to get to the living room. Strange layout."

"Why do you want to know?" asked mom.

"I don't know. My past is coming back to haunt me."

"Now don't *you* start," said dad. "Can't we please enjoy a nice dinner without turning this into a 'Twilight Zone' episode?"

"Sorry," said Trevin.

"You and your mom. I can't hold a candle to your imaginations."

Then his mother was also bothered. "Yeah, let's drop it. It's not polite to talk about people this way. But we did send flowers and a card."

"Did he receive them?"

"Who knows?" she said. "We never heard back. But we didn't expect to."

Mom offered seconds. Dad and Trevin partook. What was supplanted now in Trevin's mind was the thought of dead flowers and a card or two at Cecil's house, sitting alone atop a kitchen table or a living room table. Not a good thought.

After the table was cleaned and the dishes were chugging away in the dishwasher, it was time for another Lambrose pastime: catching up face-to-face in the living room. The three gathered this way, sharing all the things they couldn't over a crackling cell phone with drop-outs and poor connections. Everyone had been looking forward to it.

Dad closed the venetian blinds—a certain rite after dark. Each sat in their favorite fixture—dad in the recliner, mom on one of the two corner sofas, Trevin on the other—after-dinner drink of choice perched on coasters next to them all. Mom kept the remote from her husband. She didn't like his tendency of turning on the TV and disrupting the attention.

"Your father's close to being laid off," she suddenly announced, christening the chat. Trevin's jaw dropped.

"What?"

"That's what you were picking up on at the airport. It's been on our minds, in addition to what we said—you losing your job."

"Holy sh—"

Dad cut Trevin off. "Well, now, April, let's not jump the gun. It's been a rumor, just like everything else. Let's not get worked up." Carl looked long and hard at his son, folding his hands together. "But we did want to make you aware. We wanted to tell you in person."

Trevin waited, taking in the spectacle that was his wonderful father and mother. They'd always been so truthful. Now they were vulnerable. Deep down, none of this surprised him. His suspicions had proven correct. Again.

Mom said, "We make a fine team, don't we? Bad news all around. Sorry." She sighed heavily, and Trevin saw her almost start to cry.

"Dad. Mom. Look at me. You have nothing to be sorry for. I'm here for you. Whatever happens, I'm here for you, no matter what. I know exactly what you're going through."

Trevin stood, strode to his father, and shook his hand. He next went to his mother and hugged her tightly, sending all the loving energy he could into them, half believing something could come of it. When he came apart from them, he stood in the center of the living room, hands on hips. "So …" he said. "What now?"

"What do you mean, 'what now'?" said dad.

"What do we do? As a family?"

"I don't know. Nothing's definite yet. The whole country's tanking."

Mom said, "The whole world."

"I hate to ask this," said Trevin, "but… are you two holding up? I mean… financially?"

"We won't get into that, Trevin," said his father, "that's a little alarmist. Let's just say it wouldn't be easy. We don't have as much as we did—we've lost tons in the stock market—and we've already dipped into our retirement. April can't get any more hours at the library—*they're* cutting. We still have a mortgage on this house. No use getting into it; the division's moving overseas."

"I'm trying to pick up a second job," said mom.

Trevin pursed his lips. "They're not going to beat us."

Mom stared at the floor. "Tell us about your lady. We haven't heard much about Constance. We hope that's going well."

"That reminds me. I have to call her. It's going well, mom, I miss her already."

"That means we like her already," she said. "Obviously, she's a very special person."

Trevin smiled. "You should see her. She has this natural ability to light up a room. She's like a freckled sunset, people flock to her. I hope you guys meet her some day. She'd love your theory at the lake, mom, she's a freak about memories—"

The front doorbell rang, cutting Trevin off and making his mother jump. Dad straightened from his slumped position. "Who's that?" he said.

A series of hard raps followed. With the blinds drawn, it was impossible to see who was on the porch. None had seen or heard anyone. Trevin went on guard. "Expecting company?"

They weren't. Dad checked the time. It wasn't late, but it was officially nighttime.

Trevin went to the foyer and snapped on the porch light, peering through the door's windows. He groaned agreeably. "Unreal."

Grabbing the doorknob and opening it, he said to his parents, "Speaking of the devil …"

Standing tall on the porch was… Tommy Porch! The infamous father was sporting a mischievous grin, tightly gripping the hands of two very young boys, who were already trying to wrench free. Trevin saw the minivan was in the driveway, behind dad's car.

"Tommy Porch!" Mr. Lambrose exclaimed brightly, joining his son. Mrs. Lambrose jumped up, reaching for her hair and smoothing out the wrinkles on her blouse.

"Oh my Lord …" she said, coming round, somewhat discomfited by the unexpected surprise. "Tommy Porch? What is he doing here?"

"And his gene pool," Trevin inserted, opening wider.

"Get in here, get in here," Mrs. Lambrose said. "And he's brought his little men."

It was a happy reunion. Tommy dragged his kids in as they continued to fight. Obviously, they didn't want to be here. The two childhood friends got through the machismo handshakes and bear hugs, backslapping and shoulder punching. Tommy's children hid behind their daddy in fear of the noisy strangers. Trevin winced at some of the injured spots.

"What's wrong?" Tommy asked. "Turning into a wimp in Chicago?"

Tommy had to turn and yell at his sons to behave. Mr. Lambrose shook Tommy's hand and Mrs. Lambrose gave the old neighbor a big squeeze. "To what do we owe the pleasure of this visit?" she asked.

"We were in the neighborhood visiting mom," said Tommy. "Saw you pulling in earlier with Trevin, decided to stop by. I'm not crashing a private party or anything, am I?"

He certainly wasn't crashing anything, they assured. There was more over-talk. Tommy said he had to get the hellions out of his mother's house—they were destroying it. "As you know, mom can only handle so much."

"So you brought them here," mom shot back with a wry tone.

She went to tweak the younger of the two, who turned his head as if avoiding the plague. Tommy scolded him. But this was all right—Mr. and Mrs. Lambrose were used to this. This had been the routine of these kids for years. A quick catch-up unfolded, and Tommy asked Mr. Lambrose about his company, hearing about its potential bad news—all gossip at this point.

They caught up on Tommy's wife, Jenna. She was doing well. Her position as a social worker, spending long hours helping abused women and children, had her busier than ever.

"Business is booming," Tommy said. "Unfortunately."

"You tell her we said hello. Does she know you have the little ones out?"

"Of course," Tommy answered. "She's grateful to have the house to herself."

Tommy reintroduced Kevin and Mark, forcing them to act sociably. But of course they had no interest in anything other than having a wrestle. He had to pull them apart, dragging them around to his front. The youngest grabbed the hair on the inside of Tommy's thigh—under the shorts—and Tommy swore like a sailor, then apologized.

Mrs. Lambrose got down to their level. "If you boys behave," she said composedly, "there's a bowl of sugar-free candy on the coffee table."

Wrong choice of words. The children bolted straight for the living room, ripping the candy apart. Tommy had to grab them back—they weren't in grandma's house anymore. "Some things haven't changed. They're a chip off the old block."

"I'll say," said Trevin.

"How long you home for?"

Trevin didn't know.

"Earning the big bucks in Chicago. See, Mr. and Mrs. Lambrose? We all knew your son would be rich and famous someday. Saw you staring at the Tavaliers. Heard about his wife?"

"Yeah, uh, mom and dad just told me."

"It's terrible. Mom told me."

Tommy was many things, Trevin knew, but his friend always had a big heart.

The Tasmanian Devils were still acting up. They took to running around the dining room. Tommy admitted he'd better get them to the restaurant. Mrs. Lambrose couldn't believe they still hadn't been fed. "What kind of a father are you?" she chided, kiddingly.

"They won't eat at grandma's," said Tommy. "They want fast food."

"Get something in their stomach. I'll report you to Jenna."

Tommy was going to Schammer's, another staple, just like the custard stand. He asked if Trevin wanted to join them.

"Schammer's?" Trevin said. "We just ate, but I'll accompany you."

Tommy turned to his folks. "Can Trevy come out and play? I promise to have him home at a decent hour." Everyone laughed. It was obvious Tommy needed a little adult company.

Trevin was going to drive separately. He asked to borrow the keys from dad, just like he used to. Jokes were made. Trevin was sixteen again—taking old dad's car out for a spin.

The six-foot, green-eyed father of two hugged his favorite neighbors again, said goodbye, and left, dragging his progeny out with him. Once outside, he held his kids upside down—turning their protests into hysterics—jamming them into the minivan, shackling them with seatbelts. He got kicked in the jaw. When Tommy was behind the wheel, he was hit in the head with thrown toys.

Trevin turned to check the status of his mother and father's patience. These visits had become almost wearisome. "They're adorable," mom said, "but I wanted them out of the house."

"Sure you guys don't want me to stay here tonight? We can talk more about things."

"Go," dad answered. "We're going to bed soon, anyway. Got a house key?"

Trevin displayed the one he always had on his Chicago keychain. "Never been without it."

Dad asked if he needed money. Trevin didn't. He wouldn't have taken any anyhow.

"Good luck," his mother said. "You'll need it."

Dad shoved his son out the door. "If you don't return, we'll know what happened."

CHAPTER 20

Trevin texted Constance in the parking lot of the restaurant, wanting to know if he could call late. It would take some nerve to go in and sit with Tommy and his brood. He could see through the window that Tommy's children were already acting up at the counter while their dad tried to order.

Trevin was reconsidering if this was a good idea or not, but it was too late now. A catch-up with his childhood pal would be good for the soul—and hopefully vice versa.

By the time he joined the trio inside, they were already into their hamburgers, fried onion rings and sugary malts at a booth. The smell in the restaurant was as intoxicating as ever, and it was a good thing Trevin had eaten, otherwise he would have launched into the unhealthy yet delicious indulgence.

Trevin let them eat. It was like the family had not had food in a week. Trevin noted the crescent-shaped scar on Tommy's forehead. That was a bad memory. Trevin had caused it when the two were both Tommy's sons' age. They'd been swing set-hopping in strangers' backyards without permission. When an adult yelled from a window, Trevin had jumped off, leaving his metal seat swinging wildly. Tommy jumped next, catching Trevin's seat in the forehead on the return, causing a geyser of blood to erupt from Tommy's forehead. Trevin had run home in tears, thinking he'd killed his mate. His mother discovered—with great relief—that it had only been a flesh wound, and little Tommy would recover fully. Mrs. Lambrose then treated the laceration with a butterfly bandage and Tommy walked home to explain to his mother. Trevin remembered it taking some time to mentally work off the guilt having abandoned his friend like he had. From that point on, Trevin had vowed never to be cowardly again.

"It's a badge of honor," Tommy said, seeing Trevin staring at it. "Don't bring up the swing set story again. It's ancient history, and I don't want to give these guys any ideas."

"I see," said Trevin. "Good."

"Besides," Tommy went on. "Jenna's always thought it was sexy. She says it turns her on, makes her think her husband is something out of an old Clint Eastwood movie."

"Well, that's a relief to hear."

Just being in the famous diner brought back a thousand warm sentiments. This was Schammer's—a celebrated hangout since the '50s, nestled at the curve of a marshy lagoon abutting the shores of Lake Ontario, not far from where he'd been earlier with his folks. Trevin had often reflected on this place, remembering many happy times here. He figured Constance must've done a number on him. He was growing more nostalgic by the second, wishing to return to any or all innocent times. "Practically every other classmate in school worked here at one time or another," he said wistfully.

"Speaking of high school," Tommy said, stopping eating for a moment, "you should go over to Galileo. They got a new grandstand at the football stadium. Wish we had it while we were playing."

This got Trevin's mind swirling. High school. More of the best days of his life. Was it unhealthy to stew over them? "New grandstand, huh?"

"I helped build it. All the dads did. We volunteered on weekends. Drive by on the way home. Better yet—go diving off the press box like we used to."

Trevin laughed. That particular detail had been forgotten. Or suppressed. *What a recklessly dangerous stunt to pull,* Trevin thought, and grew amused at the memory. "Did we want to die? What was it—twenty feet in the air?"

"Probably thirty now," Tommy answered, entertaining his boys by puffing up his cheeks with pickles, pretending to be a hamster. "Eighth grade, right before freshman year. If I didn't have these guys with me, I'd do it with you."

"You're not serious."

Tommy lifted one eyebrow. "Do you know me?"

But Trevin's wheels were turning anyway. As he had fun relishing the details, suddenly he was jarred by the image of Brian Annarez's fall off his balcony. That was *without* mats. He had to shake the horror away and force the repulsiveness from his head.

"We'd make sure no cops were around," Trevin said.

Tommy covered the littlest's ears until his hands were knocked away. "Used paper clips to get into the booster stand. Remember all the track mats we'd pull out? Too bad we never had broads with us."

"Uh, we were a little young for that," Trevin replied, concernedly checking the response of the boys. "It was a rush, though, great for clearing your mind. It was liberating."

"Yeah it was."

Talking about it, Trevin brought back the experience. He remembered sailing off into space, the sense of euphoria, all-embracing for those brief seconds. Physics could be a high. "Think the stuff's still in there?"

"When we were building the grandstand it was. I was only kidding!"

This time Tommy ordered his boys to cover their ears. They did, giggling.

Tommy leaned forward across the table, snapping at his friend in a near-whisper. "You home 'cause you lose your fucking job?"

Trevin was shocked. "What? Why do you ask that?"

Tommy cocked his head. "Because I know you. You have that look in your eye. You actually thought about jumping off the grandstand for a minute. You do crazy shit like that when something's happened to you. It's how you deal with things. We know your business is cutthroat—especially these days."

Trevin took a deep breath, let it out slowly. "You have a way with words, Tommy. Yeah, I've been going through things."

"Uh, man, I'm sorry. Want to talk about it?"

"Not really. Eat."

Kevin and Mark finished their meal, then begged their dad to let them go to the arcade room. Tommy gave them a handful of change and saw them off. Then it was serious time. He wanted to talk more to Trevin. "How about the Bettys on Michigan Avenue? That's gotta be worth it."

"I have a lady," Trevin answered.

"No kidding. 'Bout time. The guys were beginning to wonder if you went gay on us."

Ignoring the remark, Trevin did the best he could to define Constance, realizing she was still mostly an enigma. And she hadn't texted or called back. When he was through, Tommy chastised him. "Why didn't you bring her with you? You wad!"

Trevin had a hard time placing his thoughts, not knowing where he wanted to take the discussion. He did his best by deferring—asking Tommy all about his life. Tommy was sidetracked watching his kids take turns on the machines. While one played, the other was wadding up spitballs and firing them through straws at the walls. The manager intervened, asking them to stop, then waved Tommy over to take them out of the arcade room. Trevin rid the table of the empty trays, throwing what he could in the trash, then accompanied the three to the separate kiddies' room, where they'd be no bother to anyone—hopefully.

They were now penned in by unbreakable Plexiglas. A few other children were—behaving nicely—their parents at the sidelines, eating their meals. There was a small slide and a drawing table here, with sketching utensils and a couple of plastic punching clowns to burn the energy off any hyper child. Little Kevin and Mark grabbed some crayons and got scribbling on the paper table cloth, joining another boy on the floor.

"Can you believe it?" Tommy decried. "Banished to the kiddy section?"

"That's a first?" inquired Trevin sarcastically, not expecting an answer.

Once more they fired up the dialogue, but it was hard for Trevin to concentrate. Tommy talked of grout, the high price of gasoline, and how the inner-city schools he taught at were nothing but "on deck circles for future felons." The windows vibrated, and another flotilla of motorcycles blapped by in a double row of headlights, causing Trevin to think.

That sound again. Where are they going? Where is their destination?

Within minutes, a howl split the air.

Kevin and Mark had ambushed the boy and crayoned his face, purple and green streaks running across the lad's crying cheeks. The parents were on it, pulling Tommy's goons off. Once more, Tommy had a skirmish on his hands—and he ran in—the manager again joining to make peace. Jaws motored like pistons and voices elevated to arguments, most of it drowned by the insipid cartoon music now blaring from an antique speaker system in the corners.

By this point Trevin was pining for forgiveness from the universe. Brian Annarez. His ghost had followed the artist home.

An executive decision was made. Tommy and his brats were told to leave altogether. In all his years, the former tight end had never been thrown out of Schammer's. This was a proud first. Trevin was mortified, commenting on the way out: "There's always a first time for everything."

The four were now tactically isolated in the front lot, not far from the "S" curve where the motorcyclists had blasted by. The manager—and others—were glaring from the windows. Tommy mock-waved to them. "Hello everyone! How are you? We're fine!" Then, to his boys, "I'm never taking you here again!"

Kevin and Mark threw their heads back and laughed to the night. Trevin took it all in.

Tommy leaned on one of four picnic tables there. "It's that screwing around they've been doing when they're supposed to be sleeping. Waking from dreams like they're possessed, whipping their arms in circles. They're freaks—they've been nuts!"

"What's this?" Trevin asked, his attention grabbed.

"Jenna first noticed it. I have no idea what the hell they're doing. Maybe it's payback for bombing Nutty George's house with cookies—speaking of nuts."

"Whoa, Tommy. We shouldn't call him that. I mean… think about what just happened. And that wasn't even Mr. Tavalier's name."

"Sorry—*Mr.* Tavalier!" Tommy was frustrated. "What, are you feeling bad now for the stupid shit we did to that guy?"

"Yeah."

"So after you jump off the grandstand, go up to his door, knock on it and apologize."

Trevin was staring. "That's funny. Constance suggested the same thing. Actually, Tommy, it's not such a bad idea."

"How'd he get that nick-name anyway? You named him Nutty George, didn't you?"

Trevin shook his head. "Wasn't me. Probably one of the older kids on Sweet Briar. Stupid kids do stupid things. Like when we threw the cookies at his house. Remember that, Tommy?"

"How could I forget?"

"We also Trick-or-Treated at his house. And we jumped in his bushes, messing them up. You in your Batman costume, me in that dumb spaceman suit."

This drew a laugh from Tommy. "You kept having to look down at the ground to see through that dome on your helmet. That was a lousy design."

"Yeah, I remember his driveway. There were cracks in the asphalt, all the way to the porch. Looked like an aerial map of the Amazon with its rivers."

"We smashed apples on his sidewalk."

"He didn't deserve that," said Trevin. "His wife didn't deserve it."

Tommy ran a hand through his hair and got ready to leave. "I'm not equipped to reflect on this shit like you. But that's why we're such good friends—even if you don't write or call."

"That was sharp," said Trevin. "However, we're buddies, even as I haven't stayed in contact enough. I'm sorry, Tommy. You're the closest I have to a brother. I'm glad I came tonight."

"Yeah, well, better not dodge out of town before seeing me again. Jenna would love to see you."

Just then, a car was rounding the bend like the choppers had to, slowing to negotiate the curve. Kevin and Mark had found an unfinished box of cookies on another picnic table, racing to get it. With handfuls of chocolate chips, they ran at the road—Tommy suddenly seeing, running after them. The boys had their arms raised in cocked readiness. Both threw as hard as they could, anticipating the car's speed. The cookies exploded in dust off the passenger side door. Brakes locked as the sedan skidded to a halt.

"Son-of-a-bitch!" Tommy squawked, grabbing them and tugging them away.

For another second, Trevin heard the horror screech and scream on Munnison. It was like fingernails down a chalkboard. A man of about 70, sporting the temper of a caged lion, leapt out of the sedan and launched into a non-stop tirade of obscenities. The manager came out. He'd seen it. The parents of the defiled youngster did also.

Tommy turned to his friend and simply said, "I'll see you later, man."

Trevin wanted to help, but there was nothing to do. All he'd be is a referee to a shouting match. A lesson had to be learned here for somebody. Besides, it didn't look too uncivil, not too uncontrolled. Tommy's boys once more lifted their heads to the night and laughed like hyenas, reveling in the prank. Trevin turned from the tussle and walked to his father's car, locking in on the beautifully poignant sound of the crickets and bullfrogs in the marsh behind Schammer's, harbor lights gently sparkling off the water's rippling surface. It was enchanting.

CHAPTER 21

———— ◄ ► ————

Despite the time nearing eleven at night, and the fact that jet lag had fully kicked in, making him weary, Trevin had felt the compulsion to roam somewhat before driving home. It had already been a couple of hours since leaving Tommy and the brats at the diner. Trevin had been in a contemplative mood, and had decided to revisit many familiar streets and avenues, concentrating on the various neighborhoods with all his rich memories associated with them.

Laughter. Camaraderie. Friendships. Adventure.

The moon had risen against the dark, still sky in the east—a crescent, like Tommy's scar—lifting over the apple orchards and old farmhouses on the outskirts, few other nocturnal travelers occupying the roads. The smoothness of them had lulled Trevin into a steady train of deliberation,

Still no feedback from Constance. Was she falling into her old ways?

He considered if he was subconsciously conducting a test, waiting to see if she really missed him. It was a childish concept, passive-aggressive bullshit—and he quickly admonished himself for even thinking it.

But Tommy had been right about Trevin being over-sensitive. He remembered that label following him like a crutch throughout his formative years. One such example glared like the beacon on the jetty.

Trevin remembered a classmate in first grade catching the flu and being out for that entire week. On Saturday, young Trevin found that parents' number in the phone book and called, speaking to the boy's mother, making sure everything was okay with her son. Trevin was assured all would be fine, and was thanked for the concern. Later, at a parent-teacher's conference, that same mother talked to April Lambrose, recounting her son's thoughtful act. Mrs. Lambrose didn't know a thing about it, but was uplifted anyhow at hearing the news. She immediately came home and praised Trevin for being naturally sympathetic. "It's a virtue," she had said.

The female teacher had concluded: "On the outside, he might be a toughie, but Trevy's a softie on the inside."

But where had it gotten him? Trevin wondered. He was searching for ghosts amongst the living, a pathway to a time that would never return. How his heart was breaking for so much more—for the stars! Surely that type of dreamy-eyed sappiness wasn't healthy. Presently, his dreams were getting crazy and his musings were intensifying. There had to be a reason—a reason that would shape him for the better… transform him.

Certainly the skies helped light the fuse.

Galileo was coming up on the left, his old high school. He hadn't seen it in years. Maybe Tommy's words had led him here, still echoing in his head.

He first passed it—barely slowing—then did a U-turn and came back, gathering wits as the building's stark silhouette loomed against the dark expanse.

Timidly, he turned into the front lot, making sure there were no police around. Everything looked identifiable from what he could make out: the same ochre-brick and gray stone citadels, three stories of the windows he used to stare out, the stately entrance where they posed for annual pictures, and the vast athletic fields behind it all—taking him back to quite a few glory days. He'd enjoyed his years here. Some hated high school. He let his mind wander for a minute, bringing back some of the more memorable events—the parties, teachers he was inspired by, topics that had engaged him. Jumping off the press box with Tommy was just the dawn of those years.

Was the risk worth a chance to recapture that high?

Yes, and he continued forward, rounding the access road that took him alongside the building to the back parking lot. He was trespassing, he knew. If he was caught he could go to jail. Wouldn't his parents be proud? Killing the headlights, his pulse began skyrocketing. It was even darker back here, like black onyx, the same old speed bumps forcing him to take it easy. Houses adjacent to the access road were another caution. No lights there, either. Good.

He remembered approaching a new school year from this direction, first in rides from friends' parents, then on his own. He could almost see everyone hanging out in the student parking area, some smoking. This was where guys and girls used to come to make out after hours. Sometimes the police chased them out. As the back lot fully opened to him, it was quite a sight. The moon was illuminating the grounds with a gothic-like glow of blue azure, the stars twinkling above it all. He kept going to the lawn's edge, where he stopped the car, staring longingly at the extended march to the football field, spread before him like a specter from the past. To his right was the hearty fleet of district school buses, still housed behind the noteworthy security fences. Only a few, barely effective emergency lights lit the area.

He couldn't have painted a more tranquil panorama.

It wasn't much of a stadium, Galileo's football field, and the grandstand on the home side wasn't as grand as Tommy had made it out to be. The visitors' was even worse—nothing but exposed bleachers. How it was so cold here, he remembered, exposed to the elements during the last games of the year.

The electronic scoreboard was still here. It faced away from his perspective, at what would be the crowd looking at it. It abutted the graveled oval encircling the field, used for track meets. But the grand woods, behind everything, used to set the real magic. In autumn, its majesty and the changing colors used to create an idyllic, almost mythical backdrop for athletic events. Trevin remembered staring at them on the rare occasions he was on the sideline.

There goes that sensitive shit again …

Trevin shut off the engine and searched the glove compartment for his father's multipurpose pocketknife. Now he could hear the crickets even better, a slight breeze mixing with it like nature's orchestra. Nice. He felt the coolness by the grass, a taste of summer tang in the air. The ground crew had mowed relatively recently. Even better. That freshly cut scent gave him the strength to override any remaining nervousness he had.

Finding the tool, he got out, giving another careful scan around. He spotted the steeple of his childhood church—still standing high on the hill behind him—presiding over the high school from afar. The glowing clock face was just as charming as the one in Chicago. Its effect soothed his soul somewhat.

"This is for me," he said to it, then stealthily stepped over the cable separating the lot from the lawn, remembering the time when he caught his shoe on his way to the baseball diamond, doing a face plant in the sod. Not a proud moment.

He embarked on the long trudge toward the football stadium.

What kept his mind off the consequences of getting caught was distant music playing somewhere—perhaps from an open window in the next neighborhood over, wafting through the woods. It was Celtic Electronica, melodic, haunting. The augmented female voice seemed to be calling to him like the mythic sirens on the rocks, to sailors.

By the time he arrived at the booster club at the base of the stadium, his father's car looked a mile away. He turned to the building and addressed it, touching its cold cement and steel doors, groping along until he found the simple padlock. It was still in the clasp, still constituting "tight" security measures. He tried the padlock twice. Locked tight. He went to town with the multipurpose tool, using the tiniest Allen wrench to jimmy it back and forth, the Celtic music goading him on, his heart rate leaping in jolts. The mechanism dropped open with ease.

Way to go, ace, he told himself. *Breaking and entering. How are you any different from Brian Annarez?*

Removing the padlock, he slid one half of the large metal doors to the side, revealing the great inside maw, which was even darker than the night around him. He could feel the sweat trickling down his face. Using his cell phone as a flashlight, he stepped inside, being careful, and saw all the old track and field equipment just like he'd always remembered. This was such a head rush. The booster club was still used as a storage facility.

Good.

He moved aside the bulky and cumbersome gear until he found what he came for: the giant foam crash pads against the far wall, securely encased inside cargo nets. Pay dirt!

Before he began, he urinated outside from the anxiety.

Ten minutes later he was atop the press box, looking down at the world, the assemblage of crash pads directly below him on the ground. He'd scaled the grandstand in leaps and bounds, despite still hurting from his injuries. Now that he was at the apex of the structure, he thought defiantly of Tommy's challenge, and decided he was definitely going to go through with this. He had to jump to his destiny, even if the result was purely metaphorical. There he was, he thought—no longer a ninth grader, but a 36-year old man—the ancient memories of childhood flooding back.

Trevin inched to the rim, hanging over. At this hour, with the surreal setting surrounding him, he grasped the possibility that the terrestrial world could overlap with the spiritual. The more he stared into the great openness, the more sacred and ethereal the moment became. For a moment, panic grabbed him, threatening to pull him back.

This is also for Brian Annarez, wherever he is.

Trevin wished all those who had died well—all those who'd moved on before him: victims of the terrible times… the countless masses who'd left life with unfinished business… deceased neighbors.

He focused on the stars making up the Big Dipper. Curiously, the pinpoints seemed to brighten, as if someone was turning up the switches. Trevin felt this was a 'go' sign and launched himself—falling through the air in one rotation—a fractional release from earthbound strife.

FLOOM!

He landed squarely on the crash mats, his back and neck stinging for a minute. He didn't move, wondering if he'd paralyzed himself. The intensity of the Big Dipper stars dialed back down to their originality. Slowly, he realized he was okay. The Milky Way had communicated to him he had atoned for his sins. Almost.

When he heard a police siren in the distance, he jumped up and kicked into overdrive—amazed at his own recovery rate—returning the crap to the storage room as fast as possible. Putting the padlock back on, he fastened it snugly, then sprinted like hell to his getaway-mobile.

* * *

No, he really had screwed himself up. But not badly. Trevin smarted like never before from the stupid jump—wondering why on Earth he had just done that. He was not going to tell Tommy. He stood in the driveway back on Sweet Briar—in his parents' driveway—listening to the sound of the car engine cooling. The few ticks and clicks mixed with the crickets, which still hadn't given up their music for the night.

He looked at the house. There it was: the light on inside the foyer. The closet light. The only one on in the house. The only one on in the neighborhood. It was excessively dark tonight. Leaving the foyer light on was something his parents always did, ever since Trevin was a teenager and had been out late.

A good end to the first night back. Except poor Mr. Tavalier across the street, in the house kitty-corner to him. When Trevin's attention once more drifted to it—as if on cue—a light came on in the second-floor window at the right corner. Mr. Tavalier was awake. Trevin wondered what room it was. Could be the bedroom, probably *the* bedroom. The curtains were drawn. If the man looked out, he'd have a perfect view of Trevin staring at him.

He imagined the neighbor's unbelievable grief, enduring insufferable loss alone, with no one to comfort him. It had to be awful. "God bless you, Mr. Tavalier. Wish I could help."

Sending one last wave of positive energy across the way, Trevin went in, careful not to make noise as he locked the door behind him and removed his shoes.

The house was even quieter. The ticking of the cuckoo clock in the pitch black family room reminding him of Nan. He hadn't noticed until now. The clock was a memento from the old country, one of her favorites. It was here, without her. Within seconds, Trevin became racked with sorrow, longing to see her again. In case he could detect any impression left from her—perhaps a kind word or the calling of his name—he crept downstairs for a visit.

None came. Trevin was only able to see the clock's dark, irregular shape on the far wall. Immediately to his right was the sporadic winking of highlights off her chrome wheelchair, caused from the streetlight's rays slipping in through the partially closed curtains. The curtains never closed fully. The golden flickers were dancing like miniature ballerinas, remnants of Nan's inner energy—diametrically different from her crumbling body. Trevin's mother was never able to part with the wheelchair.

This was the floor Nan had lived in for the majority of his childhood. Trevin thought long and hard about it, not believing he was finally here again. Nan had everything here she'd wanted. Dad had seen to it. A bedroom, a private bathroom, and what was referred to as the "little kitchen." Trevin wondered if, maybe, parts of her soul—"leave-behinds"— were infused into the very molecules of the house. Maybe that happened with all good people in good homes. Their souls were somewhat engrained into wherever they were happy. Into the walls, floors, ceilings—forever keeping watch over the living inhabitants.

Trevin went over to the wheelchair and sagged to the floor, holding the seat for support. Touching the armrests, he thought: *This was where she relaxed her tired arms, she was comfortable here.*

His eyes started to blur. The clock struck a dozen times. Maybe he had landed wrong on the mats after all, maybe he was really hurt. He let the highlights ride over his skin. Each sputter and twinkle connected him to a holy place. He could remember Nan shuffling to her room using the walker, smiling goodnight to him as he waited to make sure she was okay.

"I love you, Nan," he said to the air, wishing to make the unreal real.

Trevin slept right there at the foot of Nan's wheelchair. The last thing he was aware of before fading out was the light leaking through the curtains, attempting to connect with him.

CHAPTER 22

It was sometime at dawn that Trevin's father woke him up, finding his son dead asleep on the carpeted family room floor. Realizing where he was, Trevin grew embarrassed. At least his pains were gone.

"You all right?" dad asked gently.

"What happened?"

"Nothing. Everything's okay. I'm going up to bed for a couple more hours."

"Okay."

Carl helped his son up.

* * *

By the time Trevin got up for good, he felt like a ramshackle silo had toppled on him. It was noon. The banging pots and pans down in the kitchen oriented him. He told himself he'd have to behave responsibly from here on out. No more ignorant stunts—for himself or any ghost. Making sure he could balance, he crawled out of bed. Slowly, he dressed in gym ware with no shoes, and went downstairs to see what his parents were doing. They glanced at him as they wiped the table and washed their lunch dishes. He thought maybe they sensed what he'd done at his old high school.

"I'll make eggs," Trevin said, waiting on their humor.

His mother looked at the time, raising her eyebrows. "Yeah, kid, you needed the sleep. Do you feel better?"

Trevin looked at his dad. Dad shook his head no. Good ol' pops. He hadn't said anything about crashing by the wheelchair. "I do feel better, mom. Thanks. How are you two today?"

They were fine. His mother asked, "How'd things go with Tommy and his terrors?"

"Good," he reported, feeling coherence circulating back into his being. "Schammer's is still standing."

Trevin accidentally saw his zombie-like reflection in the oven door, and asked if they'd been kind enough to save some coffee. His mother served him a cup, nuking it in the microwave. He told her she didn't have to do that. Trevin nearly asked about work, but realized it was Saturday—his parents were both in tee-shirts and jeans. He sat at the table, testing the steaming liquid with his lips. Mom asked how it was waking up in his old bed.

"Great," was his heartfelt answer.

"Did you get a hold of Constance?" was her next question.

"No. She never got back with me." Trevin remembered how upsetting that was. "I texted her."

"Oh," said his mother with a frown, at the cabinets, putting glasses away. "I hope nothing's wrong."

"Nothing's wrong." Trevin wasn't so sure.

"Texting …" dad griped, tackling the silverware. "Doesn't anyone talk anymore?"

Trevin smirked. The man was kidding, at it already. Carl and April sat with their son as he opted for cereal, telling the account of the night before, minus the swan dive into oblivion. This, too, was customary. Trevin never minded it—regaling stories of the homefront. Once again it showed how much his folks cared.

Trevin had a great view out the kitchen window. A thermometer was mounted there under the awning of the back porch. "85-degrees already?" he exclaimed. "Do we know the forecast today?"

"Another scorcher, what else?" answered dad. "The dog days have arrived early. Pretty soon we'll be rationing water."

"Been in the garden yet this morning?"

"Long before your sorry ass got up."

"Carl …" warned his wife.

Dad asked if he still wanted eggs.

"No thanks. But thank you."

The day felt sloggy. Trevin didn't know why, but he had a feeling things were going to be very strange today. Dad got up and got into his fresh vegetables, washing them at the sink, cutting them, storing them in Baggies. Mom followed suit, checking the refrigerator for what she was going to prepare for dinner. Trevin just sat there, eating and sipping coffee, trying to figure out what the weird feeling in the air was. He made a pact with himself. Their peace of mind meant everything. He'd do whatever it took to help them.

"So what are your plans while you're here?" asked mom.

Trevin barely answered. "Figure out a way to reinvent myself, I guess. I won't be a burden."

"You're never a burden," she retorted. "I was just asking."

"That's all I can do, right?"

"Any ideas?" dad asked, his back turned.

"No good ones at present. Divine inspiration might strike."

"Might."

"So," Trevin asked. "How is the neighborhood? Despite the obvious across the street."

Mom answered. "What little we see of the neighbors, it's fine. Quiet. People stick to themselves now. We don't know three-quarters of them anymore. Things have changed since you were a kid, kid."

"Everybody out for themselves. Yeah, same in Chicago." Trevin thought of the Bebziaks, then dismissed them out of hand. *Lame-o's.* "Hey," he said. "We could look at old home movies. Anyone up for that? They're still in the basement, right?"

The enthusiasm wasn't shared. They didn't want to bother. Trevin sighed.

"Just a thought. What do you two have planned?"

Dad said, "Disney World. This afternoon."

"We could try one of your hikes, dad. Who cares if it's broiling?"

"We could try a little silence."

"Carl!" mom yelled.

Dad and son looked at one another, laughing, breaking the weird apprehension in the air. It was always good to be on the same biting note as his father. Mom shook her head. They didn't get far into alternate plans when the front doorbell rang, interrupting them.

"What—?" said mom. "Again? Who is that, Tommy?"

"I don't know," said Trevin, who could only shrug his shoulders.

"Are you expecting someone?" she asked.

"No," he answered, getting up. "Maybe it's a delivery."

As Trevin strode out of the kitchen to answer the door, his mother said, "If it is Tommy, I don't want his kids coming in."

"Mom, can you give me a minute?"

Mr. and Mrs. Lambrose remained in the kitchen. As Trevin entered the dining room, he immediately saw the new car in the driveway behind his father's. The blinds had been opened. It wasn't Tommy's minivan. He couldn't see the person standing at the door—he or she was too short to be seen through the diminutive, squared windows. The notion of Girl Scouts selling cookies was briefly entertained, but that was just too ridiculous. Trevin gripped the doorknob and opened, his jaw unhinging.

"Constance!" he almost shouted. "What—?" Opening the screen door, looking down on her from the slightly raised level. "What are you doing here?"

From in the kitchen, a flurry of activity erupted. Mr. and Mrs. Lambrose heard. It was a shock into action. They cleaned what didn't need cleaning. April even checked her hair in the same oven door.

All Trevin could do was to stare at the face as sweet as sugar beets, beaming at him, hands folded in humbleness. Constance Summerlin had never looked so adorable. Her eyes were wide as she grinned—awaiting acceptance or rejection—teeth pearlescent, freckles as cute as ever, sunglasses clipping back her brunette locks. She wore shorts and a light blue halter top, matching the sky behind her. Assorted baubles and bracelets jingled from around her neck and each wrist, toes wiggling in sandals. The first thing she uttered sounded like an high-pitched question: "Hi?"

His eyes traveled again to the car. He knew she didn't own one. "Is that a rental?"

"It is."

"Did you just drive here from Chicago?"

"Yes."

"All night?"

"Yes."

"Is that why you didn't answer my text?"

"Yes. Are you mad?"

"No," Trevin answered.

Trevin concentrated on the commotion in the kitchen. It was obvious his parents were reacting to the sudden appearance of their son's girlfriend, and knew not what to do. Should they come out or stay put? He grabbed for eloquence, squinting against the sky. "How could I be mad?"

Constance squeaked, "Because this is nutty?"

"It is… but I'm not mad."

She said, "Drove all night—*through* the night—to be with you. I wanted to be with you."

He stared at her. "I prayed for this very thing. Are you really here?"

She curtsied, proof positive. "In the flesh, on your parents' porch, suitcase in trunk. A small one!"

Utter disbelief held them both. The couple didn't know what to do. From the nook, dad finally raised his voice. "You going to invite her in, you clod, or do we have to hide in the kitchen all day?"

That broke the ice. Everyone laughed. Constance the hardest—releasing a night's journey of pent-up fretfulness. Trevin had never heard a sound like it; almost musical, tonal. He opened the screen, angering the rusty springs, and ushered her in. She almost spilled her purse as she did so, throwing her arms around him, kissing his lips. Trevin squeezed like his life depended on it. Maybe it did. "I couldn't handle it," she said between smacks. "I tried… but as soon as you left on the el… I went crazy. Went straight to the rental company… stopped home to grab a few items… and hit the road. I couldn't answer on the road. No texting while driving, you know."

He was unable to believe his good fortune. He couldn't take his eyes off her. She smelled like roses and French vanilla. "What about your job?"

"I called in. That's the beauty of temping—you make your own schedule."

Mr. and Mrs. Lambrose, having run out of things to occupy themselves with, made the grand entrance, Trevin releasing Constance to allow full view. She was such a lovely creature, he thought. "Mom, dad—drum roll. Meet the indefinable Constance Summerlin."

Constance broke free, bursting with ebullience, rushing into their realm with greetings, handshakes and… a smile that could demolish castles. This caused them pause. Good will flowed like a natural spring, soaking the homeowners.

"So—" mom started happily, "—Constance! This is a surprise, but a pleasant one. Welcome to Rochester."

"Thank you!"

"You drove all the way from Chicago?"

"I'm so sorry to just show up like this."

"Don't worry about it," said dad. "What's important is that you got here safely."

In their shared excitement, the four began speaking over each other like emcees battling for the microphone. The guest was made to feel as welcome as Carl and April's own daughter-in-law. Trevin was trying to calm everyone down. Mom asked if Constance wanted something to eat, dad scuttling outside to nab the suitcase, snatching the keys from her. Trevin was worried she hadn't gotten any sleep. He asked her.

"A little," she answered in a tizzy. "At a truck stop."

"At a truck stop?" Trevin said. "Are you crazy? Babe, that's dangerous."

"Oh, I can handle myself."

Carl returned with the not-so-light charcoal gray valise, jogging downstairs with it, putting it into Nan's old room—the guest room. Trevin asked if it was okay if she stayed, launching more hilarity. April described Trevin's lady with one word: radiant. Of course it was. Constance was incredibly thankful. "I don't know what to say," she concluded.

What you'll say is what you want to drink," Trevin's mother said, "You must be parched."

"I'll have water, please, Mrs. Lambrose."

"April," she corrected. "And my husband's Carl."

Off went mom, leaving the two alone. Again, they kissed. Trevin felt like he'd won the lottery. Dad returned, and there was more chit-chat, Constance slaking her thirst with the water from April. After several minutes of storytelling, Constance had to excuse herself; she had to freshen up. Trevin instructed her to where the downstairs bathroom was, and they watched her descend the staircase. The family Lambrose was left in a daze. Dad put a hand on his son's shoulder.

"Looks like your stay just got a whole lot better, son."

"Agreed," said Trevin, holding back the joy.

When Constance returned, she was like a little kid—clapping her hands wildly, so excited to be here—and to be accepted into the household. She eyed her new acquaintances with awe and respect, thanking them again and apologizing more for her boldness, then she compared Trevin's features to theirs. "You're the perfect cross between your mom and dad, Trevin. I see both resemblances."

The next fifteen minutes consisted of ancestry banter, what Carl and April knew of theirs.

When Trevin thought to ask how Constance found her way across five states, she replied: "MapQuest." She'd remembered the address from the

Fourth of July night when they went through the photo albums. "Sweet Briar Road's tough to forget."

"See, guys?" Trevin then challenged his folks. "Owning a computer *can* be useful."

"There's no computer in the house?" Constance asked, surprised.

"Apparently," said Mr. Lambrose, "this was a frequent source of contention with our boy."

"I can't do without one," Constance admitted.

"No one can anymore," Trevin followed.

"We can," dad emphasized.

Time to break up the summit. Again, April and Carl welcomed Constance, telling her how great it was to finally meet her—no matter how surprising the means—and excused themselves, going upstairs to catch up on chores. When they were gone, Constance snuggled close to Trevin, whispering, "I have gifts for them. I knew I couldn't just drop in."

"Babe, you didn't have to buy anything. They're genuinely glad you're here. This is incredible."

"It's just coffee mugs. Touristy stuff. No big deal."

"That's great, that's great."

Trevin kissed her passionately, hands grabbing her head, fingers raking her tresses. He could smell the wind from the highway still fresh on her neck and face. It was intoxicating. He asked how she *really* was, and when he pulled back, he was shocked to see she was crying.

"Honey! What's wrong?"

She wiped the tears away, embarrassed, trying to keep her voice low. "I'm… I'm just so happy. With you, with them. I love them so much already."

Trevin chuckled. "You have instant links with new people, don't you?"

"People I'm supposed to be with."

"You think you're supposed to be with us?"

Tapping her chest, where her heart was. "It's hard. I have to be careful. I'm stretching things."

He grew confused. "What does that mean? 'Stretching things'?"

"Forget it. I'm just making a fool of myself. I am a little tired."

"You're totally baffling me again," Trevin said, stroking her shoulders. "Driving all night was crazy—and dangerous. I'm glad I didn't know about it. Come on, let's go get you situated."

With his arm around her, they walked downstairs. He told her he'd been thinking of her every second, and told her he mentioned her to Tommy Porch—his wild friend from the photos.

She ate it up.

As they put her belongings and clothes away in Nan's closet, Trevin explained the family room amenities, giving the nickel tour the same way he had in his apartment in Chicago. He showed her the little kitchen, and she opened the refrigerator to see what was inside it. She was hungry, too. Trevin fetched her a turkey sandwich from upstairs. She had yogurt with it and washed it down with another tall glass of water. Trevin stared the whole time, not believing she was actually in front of him—in his childhood house. Her face was that of an angel. He distracted himself from thinking roguish thoughts by going into detail of his father's garden in the backyard, and how it needed rain.

"Dad's out several times a day, watering it."

She must have strong feelings for me, he deduced. Why else would she pull such a passionate feat—driving all night from Chicago to ring the doorbell of a house she'd never been to? The comment of her "stretching things" was still puzzling. There'd be time to quiz, though. Repentant for believing he'd banished his own parents, Trevin asked if it was okay if they both went back upstairs. He called them down as they entered the living room. It was time to celebrate.

* * *

Constance couldn't get enough of Trevin's parents' stories. She begged for more, asking Carl and April all about their memories of the house and how they came to choose this neighborhood. She wanted to know everything about their background and how they'd brought Trevin into the world.

Eventually Mr. and Mrs. Lambrose tried turning the tables. They wanted to know about her. All Constance really gave them was her impressions of the Windy City and how she mostly loved it. Constance did, however, harbor some grievances with the traffic and the high cost of everything, but she knew her landmarks. She said that anyone who didn't know the Magnificent Mile didn't deserve to be called a Chicagoan. She loved the lakefront, where she and Trevin spent valuable time, formulating hopes and dreams.

Carl and April were elated with the gift mugs. They thanked her, said the same thing Trevin did: "You didn't have to."

They killed most of the afternoon this way. It was intense, and the session exhausted everybody. Trevin was as proud as he'd ever been, showing her off to his family. Everyone was in their favorite spots, Trevin with Constance parked next to him. The feeling in the living room was that of a grand high, the vigor contagious. He had his arm around her, protecting everything about her. Everyone had glasses of water. They'd all become dehydrated.

As the sun moved to the western side of the house, the four ended up resettling on the back porch, where they could enjoy the beautiful sky and light, and see first-hand Carl's pride and joy in the backyard. They aimed floor fans at themselves. It had heated up greatly. But they'd hardly noticed with all the fervor. The overlooking view of the garden was wonderful. Constance loved it and the trees, saying how'd they'd been soaking up love from the owners for a long time—that's why it looked so good. She asked how the circular plot where the garden was came to be. April didn't mind retelling how their above-ground pool burst years ago, washing everything out—including the neighbor's raspberry bushes against the fence. "So that's where we put the garden," she said.

It wouldn't be hard for anybody to figure out: All three Lambroses were staring at Constance. Their distressed son, so locked in, smiled and laughed with ease in her presence, and that was a good thing. April said that any time Trevin could laugh at his father's bad jokes was a reason to celebrate. Everyone knew what he'd been going through, but he had yet to tell them about the break-in. Trevin certainly trusted Constance not to broach the subject.

Suddenly, all concentration snapped to a hummingbird, arriving outside at the center window, just below the awning. The delicate animal bounced lightly off it, perhaps excited at its reflection. Mr. Lambrose remarked how they never saw hummingbirds around here. It didn't fly away. It hadn't occurred to them until now, but this was the best Trevin and his parents had felt all day. The conversation turned to dinner. Constance wanted to show her graciousness firsthand.

"Why don't we go out to a restaurant?" she suggested. "I'll treat."

Mrs. Lambrose shot the idea down. "Save your money."

Constance insisted. "But you cook all the time, April. Why not take a break?"

"Some other time, dear," April said. "I had something going for tonight anyway."

"Okay," said Constance. "Another night."

Mom went to the kitchen, setting about the preparation. Trevin left the room for a pit stop, leaving Constance with dad. Carl looked down at the tiled floor, then back at the hummingbird. "Thank you for showing up for our son."

"It's my pleasure," Constance replied. When there was an awkward pause, she said, "One good storm from that beautiful sky and your garden will be the lushest anyone's ever seen."

Carl chortled. "Wouldn't that be something?"

"Your wife is lovely."

"Thank you."

"Your son's very special to me."

"That's so good to hear," he said.

Constance used subtle questioning to draw the memories out again. "So… technically, Carl—this is April's porch?"

"Technically." Carl rattled the ice in his glass of water. "My uncle was a carpenter. Volunteered on weekends to help put this together. I helped. Nice thing for a newly married couple, overreaching on their mortgage. April now has the pleasure of watching me at work from here as she reads. She loves reading. And she loves watching me—ha ha."

Constance giggled.

Dad flushed with good will. "What pleases her pleases me."

"What was it like when you built it?"

"What do you mean?"

"Describe what you were thinking when you constructed this porch with your uncle. Please."

Carl shifted, trying to think how to begin. He drummed up what he could, wanting to do the memory justice. "For one thing …" he began, "April was so thoughtful. She made us steaks almost every night. We listened to the Red Wings on the radio."

"The Red Wings?"

"Our minor league baseball team. Used to be the farm club for the Baltimore Orioles. Had some big stars come through Rochester. We had great times building this, Constance. Some of the best."

"So your uncle liked baseball? I know Trevin does."

"Yes, my uncle was a catcher. He's long gone. He was a good man, went bald in the Navy."

"How did that happen?" A tilt of the head meant acute interest.

"That's what he claimed. I don't know if it's possible, but Uncle Bill believed it was. He spent five months at sea. Said that happened to sailors under stress. The man had a talent with a hammer and nail. April probably doesn't remember this, but she wanted a room only half this size. I knew this would make her happier. It was a birthday gift, two months later. She cried when she walked out for the first time. Her toes kept feeling for where the house used to end. Furniture came later." As he told the story, Constance was rapt, watching the man transform with happiness.

"You've been a typically reticent man," she said. "Not used to relating personal experiences."

"Eventually, I come out of it," he responded. "Once you concentrate… you really get going."

"Yes, Carl, yes."

Carl shared the story of how they had Thanksgiving dinner on the back porch one freakishly tepid November. Trevin's grandmother was alive then. It wasn't easy for her being in a wheelchair. The men, including some close neighbors, carried her up the stairs in it, putting her at the head of the table. There'd been about fifteen neighbors—all good friends—who'd made the Lambrose Thanksgiving an annual event. Nan made the turkey, getting up at four in the morning to put the bird in.

"She was a considerate woman," Carl said, ending the report.

"Trevin misses her," Constance said.

"Yes, he does. We all do."

"I'm sure she was happy living here. That was kind of you and April."

"That's what decent people do, Constance. You help people who need it. Especially family. Betty—that was Nan's real name—made some mean pies, too. Linda Deltoran brought her killer green bean casserole and Betty made the pies."

"I bet you can taste them now."

"I can," Carl said, snickering to himself. "Blueberry was my favorite." Then he laughed harder. "Listen to me—I expect music to swell up under my description."

At that, Constance belted out a single note: A-flat major. Pitch-perfect, loud and sharp. It almost didn't sound natural. There was a reverberation.

Carl stopped cold. "Wow! Are you a singer, too?"

Trevin darted back. So did April, both equally impressed. "Babe …" Trevin demanded, dumbfounded. "Was that you?"

"It was, Trevin," dad answered for Constance. She was just blushing.

"I didn't mean for that to come out," she said.

"It was beautiful," mom praised, wanting to know if she sang professionally.

The answer was no. By now there were several more hummingbirds at the window. Trevin didn't know what to do. That woman was a thousand mysteries. Constance sank into her seat, unable to maintain eye contact with them. The Lambroses were held in discovery.

"Trevin," his mother said. "Set the silverware out, will you?"

* * *

Constance offered to help clean up after the plentiful meal, but was turned down. She was told to relax; she was the guest. She hadn't tasted so many varieties of food since the block party. Trevin filled his parents in about that. Constance then excused herself and went downstairs to put away more traveling articles, hearing the sound of the dishwasher chugging away—exactly as Trevin described it from his childhood stories. She loved the sound of the three chatting away up there.

In Nan's room, her suitcase had been left on the ottoman at the foot of the bed. She stood in her solitude and absorbed the nuances, wishing she could have met the lady who meant so much to her Trevin. Constance wondered if she had been like Gladys Embery. There were the toiletries to be put away in the guest bathroom. She took care of that, methodically spacing apart each item, honoring the motions, considering the invisible spaces between them.

It occurred to Constance that she was also wondering what it would be like to have a family of her own—an absurd notion …

Trevin came down. "A shocker: Mom and dad think you're great. I didn't expect anything different."

Constance smiled, but didn't say anything, walking past him back into the bedroom, where she gently sank on the edge of the bed. "Thank you," she said. "My heart's growing giant-sized."

"You're comfortable here?"

"Yes. Very. Trevin—when are you going to tell them about what happened to you in Chicago? And I don't mean Lightning Strikes."

"When they need to know… *If* they need to know."

A night-light popped on at floor level, plugged into an outlet by the bed. Constance looked at Trevin oddly. "Nan's," he said. "Programmed to come on around this time. Guess mom forgot to turn it off."

Constance stared at the glow. She was fascinated by it. "The orange light," she said. "It's warm, meek… comforting."

Trevin turned on the overhead. "Yes it is. You don't mind sleeping in here, do you?"

"No. Should I?"

"I mean, with all my talks."

"I'm sure I'll sleep very well in here. Thank you for the concern."

"The bed's new," Trevin said. "They've only had it a year." He nodded toward the empty ledge running the length of two of the walls, beneath the two garden-level windows. One window faced the backyard, the other the side yard, level with the neighbor's lawn. "She used to have a ton of knick-knacks there. She collected them. We donated them to the church, too."

Trevin stared at the single bed, the dresser with the oval mirror, and the dressing bench tucked under it. He smiled when he cited the vintage rotary phone atop the nightstand.

"Does it work?" Constance asked, following his sight line.

"No, it's just for show. Hasn't worked in years."

"She used to work for the phone company?"

"That's right," he said. "You remember."

Then his eyes went back to the orange night-light. He shut off the overhead again, sending them back into dimness. "I see what you mean. It is comforting, the glow." By now he was wistful, and he mentioned, "I wanted her to see me do something great."

"Your grandmother? She did. She saw you grow into a fine young man. She took the memories with her. We're mnemonic repositories."

Trevin looked at her, amused. "'Mnemonic repositories.' Let's see— mnemon is Greek for 'of the mind'. Repository is a storage place …"

"Very good," she giggled. "You get an A-plus. There's magic in memories, Trevin."

"Maybe that's your fixation about them."

She ran her hand along the ledge. "Was she happy living here?"

"Yes she was. She liked it better than living alone. That's why mom and dad let her move in shortly after they were married. Nan lived in their old house in the city, where mom grew up. The neighborhood was already going downhill, and Nan had lost her husband a long time before that. Mom was her only child, remember. Nan hated being in that house by herself."

Constance asked, "Do you ever feel bad, not having family of your own?"

Trevin replied as optimistically as he could. "This is probably how I was meant to function. What about you? All those foster homes you lived in …"

"I appreciate things," she answered. "Maybe I wouldn't have if things had been different."

Trevin rubbed his jaw. He couldn't help but notice the freckles on her great legs. "I can't get enough of you," he said, seeing how she'd react to it.

Gently, she said, "Good," then observed the light outside. "There's not much daylight left."

"Sweet Briar's trickling away twilight," he said. "I can give you a tour of the neighborhood tomorrow, if you'd like. Add that to your mnemonic repository."

She smiled. "Great! When we're refreshed."

He cocked his head. "You okay?"

"I have to change into evening attire."

His mother called from the top of the stairs, wanting to know if they wanted pie. They'd be up in a minute, and thanked her in unison. Trevin stepped far enough back to where he could observe Constance in her entirety. His eyes were smoldering with a passion he had yet to know. A confidence washed over him. That's when she shooed him away. "Trevin, go upstairs."

"Will you be long, madam?"

She sighed. "No."

"Don't keep us waiting," he said with a wink, leaving her. "There's pie."

CHAPTER 23

Constance came to Trevin in a dream that night. In it, she walked into his bedroom—his childhood bedroom—sat on the edge of his bed, and placed a flat, open palm on his forehead. He wasn't quite awake, but semi-conscious, and he was aware of her alluring form, and the tremendous power hidden inside her. With a few words, she began extracting his memories through her palm into her being. Literally. One after the other, in an ever-quickening stream, they began to leave his soul, floating like tufts of cotton blown to the wind. She took everything—who he'd been, who he was currently and who he'd ever be.

When he woke up… all was a shock. She was not with him, but he could hear the sound of her voice laughing heartily with his parents down in the kitchen. The window was open next to the bed and he could also hear the sound of a lawn mower outside from some distant territory, just like he remembered from childhood. But this wasn't childhood, this was present day, and he checked the damn time—*noon* again!

The shade was *tap-tap-tapping* the sill. Again, just like he remembered from youth. The periodic sunlight struck his shirtless body, and he jerked out of bed, grabbing for the shade drawstrings. They got away from him, sending the vinyl roll snapping wildly up to the brace bar, the severe sunlight blasting into his bedroom, blinding him.

What the hell was going on in the kitchen? he wondered. It sounded like they were having a party.

As the fog cleared his head and he could see, Trevin suddenly landed sight on Cecil Tavalier—the actual man himself—outside on his lawn, pacing the side of the house that was facing Sweet Briar. Trevin had that great fortuitous angle over the hedges, and could see the man obviously looking for something. There was a garden there—not as accomplished as dad's—but one with small bushes and flowers.

The poor, wifeless neighbor, thought Trevin, instantly feeling sorry for him.

The sun gleamed off Mr. Tavalier's head. Over the years, the goofy-looking soul had lost nearly all his hair. He was much older looking, with a turtle-shell gut sticking out from under a paisley button shirt. His Bermuda shorts betrayed bony, chicken-like legs. Trevin was fascinated.

"Hey sleeping beauty, you awake?" shouted his father from downstairs.

Trevin backed away from the window to answer. "Yeah, dad, I'm awake. I'm coming down."

"You're going to sleep half your life away."

"Give me a minute, please."

Mr. Tavalier appeared to be in a tizzy. He'd really lost something, and he was closely examining the area of his property, poking the soil bed with flip flops, pushing flowers aside. Just when it seemed he'd come up with something, he'd moved on. What was he looking for?

Trevin's father's voice boomed again. "Your mother and I are going to church. You have to get moving if you'd like to come. Constance says she's waiting to see what you're doing."

He'd forgotten it was Sunday. There was always a 12:30 Mass. Mom and dad never missed it if they couldn't get to the earlier one. "I don't know," Trevin replied. "Constance and I were supposed to go on a tour of the neighborhood."

"It's your choice, but get dressed and get down here. You have a guest!"

Mr. Tavalier continued to search and poke, search and poke.

Strange …

* * *

Trevin and Constance were at the living room window, waving to the churchgoers as they backed out the driveway and drove off down Sweet Briar. When they were out of sight, she turned to him.

"I would have gone."

"There'll be other occasions," Trevin said, feeling somewhat guilty. "Figured we'd go for that tour before the day heats up."

She paused. "Okay," she said, and began staring at him. "Your parents told me about Emily Tavalier. That's so sad. I'm sorry for his loss. You must have been upset when you heard."

"I was."

* * *

The tour kicked off at the end of the driveway. Constance was at Trevin's side, wearing sandals, sunglasses, a shear blouse and comfortable shorts. Trevin had on a loose-fitting tee and also wore shorts. Both had two water bottles for the trek, hanging from fanny packs. Their skin was slathered with sun block. She was awaiting his cue.

He gathered nerve, figuring out the minutiae of where they were to go. This was going to be a rush. He surveyed Sweet Briar, looking left, then right—Mr. Tavalier had gone in. There was not a soul around. "It's dead around here," Trevin said. "Like how Munnison's become."

"Don't concentrate on that, honey, this is going to be a glorious outing."

He swept an arm in grand fashion, pretending he was a carnival barker. "Step right up, miss. Sweet Briar Road—that away and that away. Straight ahead, Emerald Lane. What do you fancy?"

"I don't care."

"You're taking the fun out."

"Sorry. Let's start straight ahead. You always talked of this dead end and the fields."

"I like the sounds of that," said Trevin. "Let's go."

With a fist bump (something Constance didn't know how to do), they headed off, walking diagonally across the street—opposite from the Tavalier house—toward the NO OUTLET sign on the southwest corner. Right away, Trevin was quick with the information: "In the old days, that sign read "Dead End." Even signs now have to be politically sensitive."

He looked at her. She was energized, like a tot on Christmas morning. "Maybe that was too morbid."

"Tell me everything," she said, not taking her eyes from the object of his anecdote. "Tell me all your memories. Even the emotions."

"Okay, a happy customer. See that guardrail at the end?" About 100 yards farther, the lane curved gently, ending at a grassy knoll. A metal rail marked where the street officially stopped. Reflector decals caught the sunlight, glimmering like rubies. "That's where the fun all started. The houses you see weren't there. It was all tall strawgrass and trees."

"Perfect for a child."

"We loved it. A pageantry of majestic-looking trees lined both sides of the knoll, extending behind the houses on both sides of Emerald."

"The trees that are still there look old," she said.

"Those are the originals, what's left. They've grown over the years—sentinels of the old place of wonder. We'd climb them, look back this way. The church mom and dad are at could easily be seen from up there. Turn around—see the steeple?" She did. "I love that."

She started to tingle, and had to stop. She was really getting excited, like a chill was coming over her. It was quite remarkable, and Trevin halted. "Constance. What's the matter?"

"Nothing," she said, having a physical response to the descriptions. "I'm just imagining the joy. It's vivid. Let's keep moving."

"Shit."

"I told you I had a sheltered life." Now Constance was embarrassed, but they did move on.

It was great to reminisce, Trevin thought. It was a catharsis, after all the crap he'd been through. Apparently, it was even more so for his girlfriend. And he wanted to please. He oriented her, giving her the north, west and east directions. They were heading south.

She reached out to hold his hand.

He had to sip from his bottle already. The sun was hot. "Not many people drive up Emerald. It's for locals only. Maybe that's why I chose Munnison in Chicago—I was looking for something like this."

"A return to the happiness," Constance said.

"You're making fun."

"No, sweetie, I'm not. I'm commenting."

"Sweetie." This is perfect. "We were blessed. Now every parent is terrified to just have their child in their front yard. It was never like that. Before any of these homes were here, this was called a "briar patch." Just look at the street names: Glen Briar, Blue Briar, Larch Briar."

Passing the No Outlet sign, they first came to the colonial on the corner. Mentally, Trevin was returning in time to those old days, the specifics bubbling up from his subconscious like a natural spring, making him feel better, lighter. He was reminded of catching snakes with Tommy and then letting them go… running free with friends… admiring praying mantises… sitting on this white picket fence …

Constance seemed to be sensing this.

"See this fence? It's been here forever. Mr. and Mrs. Eason used to live here. The neighborhood kids would lean on it, eat frozen treats from the ice cream truck. We'd hear the music and wait as it rounded Sweet Briar. We'd pay with the money we earned from chores. Sometimes a parent would spring for the gang."

"Tell me about the Easons."

He told her what he remembered of the family, their pleasantness bringing him joy. He called them a "super nice family," and didn't know who lived here now. "I don't know if my parents do either," he said. "I'll always remember the Eason twins—two adorable little girls, years younger than us. They were always running in this yard, squealing with laughter, golden curls bouncing. They literally looked like baby dolls. I can still hear their laughter—like cherubs. Everyone loved them. They must be married now."

Constance was closing her eyes, imagining the girls' freedom. She obviously loved this.

Trevin smiled. "Wherever you are, Eason twins, Godspeed. Don't even know if you ended up in Rochester. We looked out for those girls. Nothing bad was ever going to happen to them as long as we were around. As long as *I* was around."

"That's so nice to hear, Trevin."

Her telling him that gave him inspiration. It was as if he was seeing the little girls running around the house, not a care in the world. He was so glad to be able to share these special moments with such an alluring and sensual woman, craving to hear about his silly past. He could walk on air.

The next house was a ranch.

"This was the Driscolls'. I think they may still be here—we'll keep our voices down. Their kids moved away, I know that. Two boys, two girls. Used to have a crush on the youngest daughter."

Constance's eyebrows spiked. "Oh?"

"A childhood crush. You must've had them. She was a year older. All the guys thought she was hot. I just admired her from afar. She was actually pretty quiet."

"A quiet woman. You like that?"

"I'm just saying she didn't communicate much. That might've added to the attraction. She was always wrapped up with schoolwork—she didn't care about us."

"How do you know? She might have liked you back."

Trevin led her by the house. "We were never very close with the Driscolls. The oldest boy was a hothead. One of the fathers—can't remember who—scolded him for cursing when we were out playing street hockey. Mr. and Mrs. Driscoll didn't appreciate their son being called out in front of the neighborhood, and they developed a bad attitude from that moment on. Once in a while Ms. Hottie joined us at a pool, but she kept to herself. We didn't bring up her brother and she didn't either."

"What happened to Ms. Hottie?"

"We went to the same high school—Galileo. We said hi in a hallway, but that was it. Over time we faded into oblivion."

"Fade away into oblivion?" she asked. "You'd want to do that?"

He stopped. "Now what does that mean?"

"Into the west? Into your sunset? With all your good memories?"

"I have no idea what to say to that. It's a figure of speech. Are you kidding?"

"I'm just asking. This is so… romantic." A smirk—gentle, not smug—grew at the corner of her mouth.

"Now this house," Trevin said, arriving at the last house on the right before the knoll. "We had great fondness for." It was another two-story colonial, fortified by mammoth shade trees on the sides and behind it. "This was a major player on the block. We had tons of fun here. This was the Morneaus'. Spent a lot of time here. Sadly, Mrs. Morneau passed away a decade ago."

"What happened?"

"Cancer. She died young, I think in her mid-40s. Mr. Morneau then sold the house and moved away, I have no idea where. They had two boys—William and Christopher—very good childhood friends. And Cathy, the youngest. None of them came back after college, haven't heard from them since."

"If you were such good friends, why'd you lose touch?"

"Excellent question. That life-thing again. Good ones get away, it sucks. We were constantly eating apples in those trees. We'd play sports in the backyard. And swim. There was a built-in swimming pool back there—the only one around. Wonder if it's still there …"

When they got to the knoll, they could see into the backyard. The pool was still there.

"Well I'll be …" he said. "After all these years. That was one cool pool. The Morneaus threw the best backyard parties, birthday bashes, late-night swims. Summer was great here. All that splashing and hollering. I loved swimming here at night with the stars over my head. Mr. Morneau was an amateur astronomer. He'd pull out his telescope and set it up at the darkest part of the yard. By eleven at night we could see the entire Milky Way Galaxy. The crickets were loud. We'd put on bug spray—reek of repellent—neighbors would come round, join in. The universe—brought down to our wide eyes. Mystifying." Trevin had gone away, returning to those great times.

Constance read his body language like a chart. When he "returned" to Earth, they crossed Emerald to the other side, past the guardrail and the knoll, warm emotions flooding his system. "People once loved and cared for each other around here," he said.

"Embrace those memories," she said.

The first house on the east side was a modest split-level with oaks and maples in the front yard, secluding it. The facade appeared less kept up then the others, paint faded and chipped in sections. Shabby Adirondack chairs sat dormant on the porch.

Trevin was careful not to make it look like they were staring at the house. "This was the Buccinis', very decent but ancient couple. The place looks as old now as it did then. Agnes and Milo—living fossils. They must've been in their 80s then. I don't think they had children. If they had they would've been fully grown when we were kids. The trees always kept this private, like now."

She half-laughed. "I hope they didn't know you called them living fossils."

"Forty was old back then. They were straight from the old country, thick dialects. They had an American and Italian flag in their window. They also kept to themselves, but that was understandable—they were elderly. My parents talked with them. I'd rake their lawn and shovel their driveway. The Morneaus got a snow blower one winter and William and Christopher went nuts, taking over. We had a lame-brained idea to build a tree house in that first tree, just outside their property. They said a bunch of things, we had no idea what. Years later, we found out Milo was offering his help. He was a construction worker. It was his way of reaching out. Another example of how stupid we were."

Trevin looked at Constance, trying to read her. The sunglasses made it impossible. "The sound of nothingness."

"You've called yourself stupid a lot. You were just growing up."

"Moving on …"

Trevin's fascination was on the upcoming house, another modest ranch. He was locked in on the driveway, comparing it to how he remembered. "The blacktop's been paved recently. There *is* life here."

Constance was eager to learn. "Whose place was this?"

Again, he kept his voice low. "This is the Arcarisis'. Now here's a seminal memory: Danny Arcarisi—the son—was much older than me. I was only in second grade when he was in high school. I was standing right here on my bike when he helped launch my artistic future. He knew who I was because our parents were friends. He shared with me—at this exact spot—a collection of bubble gum trading cards from a science fiction TV series—one of my favorites."

"Bubble gum trading cards?"

"It's not important, but they were real geek material. And we were geeks, as we found out. We bonded over those dumb things. I loved the stick of gum in each package."

"Sugary treats for young, healthy teeth," she wisecracked, unleashing a full-fledged smile.

It almost knocked him back. She gestured for him to go on. "Not everyone can have choppers like you—come on." But he kept explaining— "The show had space aliens, monsters, mutants, great stuff to send my imagination roaring. Apparently, Danny Arcarisi also loved the show. He showed a punk kid like me a little kindness, trusting me to go through his treasured cards with all those cool creatures. He spoke to me as an equal during that talk, no condescension. His girlfriend called him away. I gave the cards back and that was that. It was the only thing I can remember talking to him about at length."

"What happened to him?"

"He's been married with a family for years, lives in Pittsburgh, works for the City Hall there. Some high position in planning and budgeting. Hopefully, he's doing right by everyone there. I'm sure he is. I think his folks are still here."

"You want to go knock on the door?"

"No, no. I wouldn't dare." He laughed. "These incidents are resetting my mood."

"That's exactly what I want them to do," she said. "It's poetry to my life, too."

"You sure you're enjoying this?"

"Every second."

"I'm relieved I've engaged or amused you. Man, the sun's hot. Where did the weird clouds go? There haven't been any in a while …"

"What's this next house?" Constance asked, moving his concentration along. It was a split-level, with an extremely well-maintained yard, and many potted plants. Theatrical flowers sprouted from them across the window sills.

"Here… was the Laneskes," Trevin said. "Party central for adults, right next to the Tavaliers. These people tore the roof off the neighborhood. They threw clambakes, organized the block parties. They were bombastic, fun, loud—that's why everyone loved them. Their kids were older—older than Danny Arcarisi—one boy, one girl. I remember the smell of the ribeye steaks always over here. Seafood, corn roasts, lots of alcohol and lots of cigarettes. People got hammered here."

"Lovely. The responsible neighbors," said Constance, unable not to notice the next house—the Tavaliers. They had a different view here—the hedges less obtrusive, lower. The house could better be seen in all its two-story, New England colonial glory. "Cecil and his wife must've been vexed with all that festivity right next door, outside their windows."

"Honey, I feel bad enough," Trevin said, going back to the current story. "I snuck out once and hid behind that bush there to see what went on here. Mr. Laneske used tin garbage cans to steam clams in. I couldn't believe it. They were brand new, of course, it wasn't gross. I can still see the steam rising from them. Tiki Torches hanging from those trees, canopy tent pitched over everyone, Sinatra and Herb Alpert blasting from a hi-fi stereo. Adults falling out of chairs!"

But she was still on the Tavalier house.

He said, "I wonder if those still alive still think about those days like I'm doing?"

"I can assure you they are," said Constance.

"Mr. Laneske… lost his wife like Mr. Morneau. Then he did the exodus like so many others. I have no idea who lives here now but the house still looks good. That's a positive thing."

"So your mother and father are among the last originals."

"They are." Then Trevin keyed in on the next house. "And then, of course …"

Mr. Tavalier's province. Trevin and Constance crept along the wall of hedges. Doing so created an intimidating impression.

"Let's be extra quiet," he whispered. "I know he's home." He swiped a loose outcropping, the slightest infraction of an otherwise faultless monument. "Man, this foliage has grown a hundred feet. We got baseballs stuck in these shrubs. Goes all the way around as you can see, except at the Weber's—on the back side."

The substantial foliage looked impenetrable. "This couldn't have helped their reputation," she muttered.

"Exactly."

When they had passed the driveway (barely glancing up), and were on the corner of Emerald and Sweet Briar, they stopped. "Did you see the "For Sale" sign?"

"Yes, I saw it."

He was almost panting. Sweat was trickling. "Man, we screwed with this guy."

"But that's over and done with, babe."

"We were afraid he'd kill us. He wanted to."

"No, he didn't," Constance argued.

"It's so weird being close again …"

"Honey," she said. "Lighten up."

Trevin couldn't help it. His blood pressure had shot up, guilt roiling his guts. "Let's go."

He tugged her away, rounding Emerald back onto Sweet Briar, where they ventured east, to the next house. The high hedges still dwarfed them. The next house was a flat ranch. An out-of-place RV camper was on the side of its garage, hidden among tall pines, a gravel spread underneath—giving quite the bucolic impression. Mr. Tavalier's yard, as Trevin mentioned, was opposite it.

Constance reacted to the RV. "They can park that there? It needs a campground."

Trevin whispered again, covering his mouth. "Mr. Tavalier hates that RV. He and Mr. Weber exchanged words about it years ago. The Webers are great. I think that's why Mr. Weber grew those pines. His family always loved camping. It has always been here. Mr. Weber lost his wife, too."

The two-car garage was open. Trevin and Constance could see into it—to the many shelves of tools, fertilizer and old tires. An SUV hugged the right side. They could also see through the rear door leading to the backyard. There was a hose being drawn taut back there. Someone was out. A figure came into view wearing garden gloves, coiling the hose.

"Mr. Weber!" Trevin bellowed, recognizing the septuagenarian—getting the man's attention.

"Who's that?" Mr. Weber bellowed back. He was sporting a bare and furry chest, bristling with perspiration. The man was in good shape for his age.

Trevin waved enthusiastically. "It's Trevin Lambrose. How ya doing, Mr. Weber?"

"Trevin?"

The man dropped the gear, entered the shadowed garage and then exited onto the driveway, re-entering the sunshine, swaggering fully into view. When he drew within feet of his visitors at the sidewalk, he took on an expression of pleased incredulity. "Well I'll be dipped in chicken fat. It *is* Trevin Lambrose—in the flesh."

He took off his shopworn gloves. They shook hands, years melting away in an instant. The grip was as strong as ever. Mr. Weber was a sinewy chap with a chiseled face and white hair twirling in a question mark on his forehead. He was older than Trevin's dad. "What are you up to, young man?"

"Standing face-to-face with one of the last of the unicorns," Trevin responded.

"Unicorns?"

"One of the last of the original neighbors."

"Oh, I see. Yeah—I'm still here."

"It's good to see someone from my past."

"Good seeing you. Home on a visit?" Nodding at Constance. "Hello, miss."

"Home on a visit. Mr. Weber—this is Constance Summerlin, my girlfriend from Chicago."

Constance greeted the gentleman, sunglasses coming off to blast him with the full effect of her effervescent smile-blast. Mr. Weber's crow's feet un-creased. "Uh… welcome to Rochester, young lady."

Constance responded with a curtsey. "Thank you."

"That's her rental in our driveway," Trevin explained. "I flew."

"That doesn't make sense," said Mr. Weber. "But it'll do."

Trevin explained how he was showing off the neighborhood in all its glory, rekindling special memories from years gone by. The widower listened intently, folding his arms over his burly chest, as if trying to cover up now. There was much to retrace, Mr. Weber agreed: many great moments to recall. Trevin said things were much better in the past.

"Constance," Mr. Weber started, "I thank God every day for Trevin's folks. They've been good neighbors all these years. They were great to me when my Doris died."

Mr. Weber had lost his wife five years back. Constance learned the details, hearing how Trevin's parents were there for him in his mourning—offering food, comfort and support. It was obvious the sadness was still heavy in the man's heart, but Mr. Weber stood proudly and courageously, apologizing for keeping the young folks in the hot sun.

"You're not keeping us, Mr. Weber," said Trevin.

"Enough of the 'Mr. Weber' nonsense. It's Matthew, Trevin. You're old enough."

"It's what I'm used to," Trevin chuckled. "Matthew sounds disrespectful."

"My son's 43, for Christ's sake—your old buddy."

"How is Mark?"

"He's going through a hard time. He was laid off down in Corning. Good thing his wife's working."

Trevin and Constance looked at each other. They were very empathetic.

Mr. Weber addressed Constance, asking about her story. As usual, the young lady dodged the specifics, drinking her bottled water, telling the man how sorry she was for his son's hardships. The brief rap session was colorful and rich, making all three feel uplifted. Constance smiled and smiled, encouraging the two to talk of as many emotions as they could. Trevin knew what she was doing, Mr. Weber didn't. Constance shuddered with intensity again. Trevin didn't think Mr. Weber noticed—he was busy finding happiness in stories he hadn't thought of in years, much less recited. Trevin asked if Mr. Tavalier had ever made more of the RV.

"Naw," Mr. Weber shook it off, titillated from the chat. "That was a long time ago. The poor man's had enough to deal with lately. I'm sure you heard …"

"Emily's gone. Yes, we know," said Trevin. "Terrible. Mom and dad sent him flowers and a card."

Mr. Weber said, "Looked for the wake, but couldn't find it in the paper."

"I don't think there was one," said Trevin, bothered by its implications. Then he shook his head proudly beholding his bronzed neighbor. "Gosh, it's good to see you, Mr. Weber."

"Matthew!"

"Matthew. You look great. Still have that basketball net over the garage, I see." To Constance: "His son Mark was a heck of a player. We shot hoops here all the time."

"And I'm sure you have great memories of it. Tell me—"

The telephone rang in Mr. Weber's house.

Mr. Weber had to grab it. "That's probably Mark now, excuse me." He pumped hands with Trevin and Constance one more time and waved as he headed back up the driveway. "Great to meet you, young lady, enjoy your visit. Trevin—tell your parents to stop over sometime."

"I will—*Matthew!*"

They watched as Mr. Weber disappeared into the kitchen through the garage. They turned to walk away, Trevin wiping his hand on his own shirt, offering the same to Constance. There had been a lot of perspiration.

Mr. Weber stuck his head out. "Trevin—it *is* Mark! He can't believe I'm talking to you. He says to connect with him on Facebook."

Trevin laughed. "I will, tell him I said hello. Tell him I'm thinking of dunking a basketball in the net right now and hoping it doesn't carom into Mr. Tavalier's window."

Mr. Weber pointed, a signal that read: *Don't even bring that up.* Then he threw a thumbs-up, shutting the door. Trevin's exuberance remained. Constance saw the thrill on his face. "What was that about?" she asked.

Trevin led Constance away, throwing a quick glance over his shoulder, making sure no one was hearing. "Mark, William, Christopher, Tommy. We were playing really rough one day—pulling the ball away from each other, slamming it down on the driveway. The ball struck the edge—where it used to be irregular—and took this wicked bounce, blasting right into Mr. Tavalier's back door window, smashing it."

"Ouch."

"Yeah, ouch. We scattered like flies, never did get the ball back. That's also a reason for the pines going in. We always thought Mr. Tavalier took it and kept it along with all the other crap sailing into his yard. Mr. Weber apologized on our behalf, and made his son pay for the damages. Then we all paid Mark our share, but we never ended up apologizing to Mr. Tavalier. Time marched on. That incident helped seal their icy relationship."

"Boy, Mr. Tavalier's stories are relentless."

"Told you."

"I've noticed the wives have mostly died first. Statistics usually have it the other way around."

"I've heard that," said Trevin. "I don't know what to say to that."

Constance took his hand. Firmly. "Well—everyone will end up together again."

"I wish I could be so confident about the afterlife. I just pray it exists."

"I know there must be an interesting story behind this next house," Constance said, moving them along. "This lime-green monstrosity. Boy, that paint color's audacious."

Trevin, still amused from his encounter with Mr. Weber, lit up with a lion's share of memories, starting with the "lime-green monstrosity." The Bolians lived here. Good neighbors. Constance learned the house had always been that way. They had iguanas as pets, hence the paint color. Mr. and Mrs. Bolian decided it fitting, given they loved the "fat and sassy things." The reptiles ate out of their laps like cats. Salads and strawberries. The Bolian kids bathed them in the tub. Mr. Bolian owned a toy store.

On to the next house. Constance was exhilarated. His fascination became her fascination.

The DiFrancos lived here. They had lots of children. Many birthday parties were attended to here. Giant cakes and party streamers. Teddy and Brad built an ice-skating rink in their backyard. During the winter months, girls on the block pretended to be Olympic champions, figure skating around the boys checking themselves like hockey thugs. A fence was broken.

Tommy Porch had a paper route on Sweet Briar. Tommy broke his leg, Trevin took over: a great way to get to know the neighbors. Gave Trevin and Tommy a sense of responsibility and accountability, contribute positively to the community.

The church's message emphasized the importance of doing things larger than oneself. The local kids used to go on donation-gathering extravaganzas for a Muscular Dystrophy Telethon on Labor Day weekends. Every Labor Day weekend. Constance learned that it was still a nationally televised fundraiser.

"We went door to door," said Trevin, lost in the nostalgia. "We raised lots of money. Got on TV every year, dumping the proceeds into a big tank, waving at the camera. Called ourselves "The Sweet Briar Bunch." Our parents would throw pizza parties when it was over—at the Morneaus."

Constance heard the dumb jokes his friends told each other. She heard of floods on the block after bad rains—Trevin got an eye infection playing in it—and how mothers used to yell at everyone for running from yard to yard with reckless abandon.

"Yes, Constance—" he said, lost in joy at the recalls, laughing, "—there was no better day than when all of that was happening."

FLASH!!

A blinding light—stronger than the evening at the Chicago lakefront, again not damaging to the eye—zapped their world, lighting up the day, cutting his attention off. Trevin covered up!

"What was that?!" he said, freaked out and shocked. "Did you see that?!"

She had. Constance had seen it, but she didn't seem stunned. She was calmly looking around. Trevin was dazed. "Man! That was like the night in Chicago. Remember? Son of a bitch!"

Her nonchalant behavior merely had her looking in the sky, sunglasses down from the bridge of her nose. There was nothing up there, only a clear blue sky.

"I've never heard of day lightning!" he said. No neighbors were out, frantically waving their arms in panic.

"You were… far away in your memories," Constance reminded him.

"I know. Damn. My eyes aren't burning. There's no after-image, thankfully."

A jet airliner was banking in a turn, no doubt coming in for a landing at the local airport. The fuselage was metallic, stripes of red and blue along the sides. Flares glinted off the wings as the sun struck it, manifesting lesser flashes.

"Maybe it was the plane," he said, chugging his water.

"Who knows?"

"Was it a good tour?" he asked.

"First rate," she answered.

They closed their circuitous route on Sweet Briar, returning home, only a few cars passing by—no one he recognized.

* * *

Trevin and Constance sat on lawn chairs on the porch, cooling off after their tour. Trevin was still making sure his eyes were okay after the super-flash. He was pretty sure he was in the clear, but he didn't want to chance it. He was staring at the patches of dark, blobby clouds appearing way beyond the newfangled housing tract at the end of Emerald.

"How about that?" he said. "First sign of an impending shower. We might actually get some rain. It'll have to work its way up—that's far south. Those are alto cumulous, I think. I remember from my days at earth science class."

Constance turned to him. "Impressive. Keep up on that, Mr. Scholar."

She turned back to make out what she could of them. He loved her. He really, really loved her. She had made all the difference in his life, he knew. He was also happy that his parents were pretty damn fond of her, as well. They had said as much to him in private.

"What a saint you are," he said to her, "encouraging me to go on about my useless, happy times of years gone by."

"Stop it. What do you want, Trevin?"

"To make future memories. With you."

She turned a second time to look at him. She was still wearing her sunglasses, so he didn't know what she was thinking. Perhaps she was finally going to unload her own feelings—he had taken a big risk saying what he did.

"I still don't know where we are," he said. "In your opinion."

She opened her mouth to speak, and his parents pulled into the driveway.

They climbed out of the car, mom fanning herself with a church bulletin. Dad also checked out the potential downpour. "That looks promising," he said. "Hello everyone."

Trevin asked how church was. It very interesting, it seemed. The sermon was actually scary. "The Coming Storm, it was called," mom reported. "They usually don't get as apocalyptic at our church. I don't know what got into them. I actually was uncomfortable with it."

"Mom," said Trevin. "It's all over. I had a pretty disconcerting conversation with a priest on the street a while ago. I'm not sure if I believed him, either."

"Made me think of my weird dreams," she said, stepping up on the porch. "The bad parts."

"You're having bad dreams, April?"

"A few, Constance. Nothing that is a concern."

"Hmm," Constance said. "I hope not."

"A carryover from the old Catholic days," Carl said, joining them, then inquired into the walk. The report was favorable. Trevin told them he saw Mr. Weber. "Matthew," as he requested to be addressed.

Dad sighed, put his hands in his pants pocket. "We should get together with him soon. You two having dinner with us tonight?"

Constance interjected, insisting on that restaurant.

"Oh, honey," said Mrs. Lambrose. "I've already started making something again, sorry. Unless you two prefer going out by yourselves?"

"We'll stick around, mom."

Trevin asked if they'd seen anything during the service, like through the stained-glass windows.

"Like what?" dad asked.

"Um… lightning?"

"It was a clear blue sky before that started rolling in—" pointing at the horizon. "Better stay out of the sun, son."

Mom said she was going indoors. She was turning the air on—the heck with the bill. No one had problems with that. So maybe it was going to be a casual Sunday afternoon. They were again alone, Trevin grabbed Constance's hand and kissed it. "For dessert, though, I'm buying them a computer."

* * *

After one of April's tantalizing chicken dinners, served in loving portions, Trevin and Constance drove in a downpour to the mall. It was finally, mercifully, raining. The windshield wipers beat furiously, working overtime to keep Trevin's line of vision clear. They'd taken her rental. Constance was staring up through the sunroof, mesmerized by the mini-explosions of never-ending droplets on the tempered glass, emphasized when they were stopped at a light. They hadn't told his parents where they were going.

With the dwindling money to his name, Trevin decided on a PC, not a laptop. It would be a total surprise. He knew just what he was looking for. Nothing that would keep dad away from trying e-mail communication or surfing the web every now and again. Mom would fare better. He explained to Constance how she'd been accustomed to the machines in the libraries.

On the way home, stopped at yet another light, Trevin was filled with good will. He couldn't wait to see the expression on his parents' faces when he presented them the gift. So moved, he pulled over to the side of the road and told Constance that he loved her.

"I really, really do," he said, staring into her eyes. He found himself holding his breath when she diverted hers. Then she reconnected with him.

"I love you, too," she declared.

He could have leapt to the moon, which was just now clearing through the ebbing storm.

* * *

His parents hated it. They hated that their son—so strapped for cash and in such a precarious life situation—had spent his money to buy them a gift. It was the exact opposite reaction than the one Trevin was seeking. Upon presentation, mom fell to her sofa and cried. Dad shuffled out of the living room into the kitchen and sat silent as a graveyard. The PC remained on the coffee table. Constance remained standing by Trevin's side, dumbfounded. Trevin felt like an idiot.

"Mom, please… you don't have to cry."

Mrs. Lambrose could hardly speak. She snatched tissues from the box next to her and blew her nose, wiped her eyes. She apologized to Constance for putting on a display in front of her. Constance told her not to worry, and stuck up for her man, explaining how Trevin bought it as a gesture of his love, and how he wanted them to have better access to their son—via e-mail—and to be able to take advantage of job-seeking opportunities, should they come along.

"I know all that, Constance," April said, "but Trevin doesn't have the money. We're so worried about him."

Constance and Trevin looked at each other, exasperated. What a disaster this had been!

Dad returned, assuming the role as spokesperson. "Trevin …" he said, voice controlled like a steady motor, "we can't keep this."

"Dad," Trevin retorted, "it's only money. We've talked about this for a long time now."

"But we don't need a computer. How many times do we have to say this? How are you paying your rent?"

"Dad, I'm managing. I have a savings account."—drawing groans from Carl.

"What's left of it," said his father. "That's exactly what we didn't need to hear."

Trevin put his arm around Constance's waist. He also felt embarrassed.

"*We're* struggling. We would have bought this if we could have."

"I know, dad… but… life's too short to worry about this."

Carl scoffed. "Uh, that's not a good reason—that's why we have to watch it."

"That's exactly why I'm not!" Trevin insisted. "I don't care what you two say. I love you guys and I wanted to do this. Now accept it! It *is* the 21ˢᵗ century!"

The Lambroses looked at each other, acknowledging how headstrong their son was.

"We care so much about your future," said mom.

"Mom! You've been caring your whole life. It's such a gift to me, I'm blessed. But I'm sick of circumstances controlling me. It's time I controlled *it*. This is my revenge! Look at it that way!"

"Trevin …"

"Enough, mom! Stop. Dad, tell her to knock it off. I got a great deal on the damn machine."

"Like that makes us feel better," dad quipped.

The three were at a standstill. There was no denying it… Trevin meant business!

Constance sat down next to April on the sofa and put her arm around the woman, consoling her. "It'll be all right, April, everything will be all right."

Mr. Lambrose returned to his recliner and rubbed his face.

Trevin put his hands on his hips. "Don't make this a buzz kill," he scolded.

"What about your health insurance?" dad pressed.

"My unemployment benefits help. Don't worry, I'm going to work again—geez."

Constance did have a soothing effect on Mrs. Lambrose. But the woman was still worried. "Carl, I could show you how to e-mail."

"That's the spirit, mom. Make the sour puss do it. Or I'll punch him."

Miraculously, dad snickered. The bad moods were starting to wear off.

April sniffled, said to Constance, "We don't bicker like this in front of others."

Constance smiled, almost laughed, and she joked: "Hey, we're all hummingbirds tonight."

No one knew what to say. The three burst into laughter, having no idea what their guest meant. "What?" said Trevin, shaking his head.

"Just a stupid line I thought I'd try," Constance said, rolling with it all.

And everyone came to their senses. Things were much better in the room. Constance went on to explain that April could look up recipes on the Internet, Carl could get gardening tips, and everyone would feel better connected with each other. Trevin couldn't have said it better.

"If we keep the computer," dad said, resigned. "We're paying for the Internet service."

"Well, of course you are, I'm not doing that," Trevin said, and they all laughed more.

Trevin broke from the newfound solidarity, carrying the computer down to the family room, setting it on the round card table by the wheelchair. "This is also for you, Nan," he whispered. "Feel free to contact me any time."

While he heard the laughter upstairs, Trevin put a hand on the armrest, standing in silence. The high emotions mixed with the heated debate had sapped his energy. Topic-changing talk of the weather began, and they were all glad it had finally rained.

"Trevin get up here," his father's voice demanded. "Your mother would like a group hug."

CHAPTER 24

Monday afternoon, Constance was curled on the sofa in the family room, the one she'd grown fond of sharing with Trevin. Her nose was buried in a book, something she'd plucked from the Lambrose bookcase: an encyclopedia volume on ocean life. She studied as many species as she could, learning as much as she could. Her now-confirmed love and his mother were both down in the family room, avidly becoming familiar with the new computer. Occasionally, Constance would overhear their discussion. Mrs. Lambrose was asking about storage devices—a term Constance could relate to.

Carl Lambrose walked in from the office, setting his folder on the vestibule bench. Constance put the encyclopedia down. "Hello, Carl. How was work?"

"Fine," he answered, taking off his tie in the mirror. "How are you, Constance?"

She thought the patriarch a bit tense. "I'm fine," she answered.

"How are our computer aficionados down there?"

"They're doing well from the sounds of it. They've been at it a while."

Yes, there was something in his body language, she thought. A weightiness, a strain. Carl stuck his head into the stairwell. "Hello, you two."

April and Trevin greeted in unison, then April said, "You're next, Carl. Your son's a marvelous teacher."

"Ha. Not today."

"Why are you home early?"

Carl checked the time, dismissed the hour. "It's not that early, April. Can't I use some of my personal time to be home with my family?"

"We'll be up," said April, tapping away.

"You don't have to stop." Carl went back to the mirror, again rubbing his face as before. Rather hard. He asked Constance, "Having a good day?"

"It's been relaxing," she said, trying to figure the situation out.

"You and Trevin go for another stroll down Memory Lane?"

"Not today."

"Listen." He turned, faced her. "About that dinner you've offered: I've been thinking, maybe April needs a break."

"Sure, sure. Oh, that's a great idea. Yes, let's do it. It's about time I return the favor around here. Where would you like to go?"

The distinguished yet exhausted-looking man shut the door, sealing out the heat. Constance lost sight of him around the bookcase as he blankly stared at Sweet Briar. "Let's let them decide."

* * *

Constance observed Carl at the restaurant. The man's face was still overwrought, but he was hiding it well. Constance didn't think his son or wife noticed—this was too nuanced of a dining experience. The group had settled on Thai, Trevin's suggestion. The interior was exotic and dark, shielded from the late-afternoon sun by bamboo plants and partitions with fantastic Oriental paintings water-colored on rice paper. Trevin was identifying the fish in the aquarium they were seated near. His mother was commenting on their lovely colors. Mr. Lambrose had insisted on driving, taking his car.

Admittedly, Thai cuisine was a bold choice for Carl and April. They had never treated themselves to such a place, but they'd been up for a challenge. Trevin, of course, boasted of the fine eateries of this ilk where he'd taken Constance in Chicago. Comments flew—all positive—when the starter soup arrived, and they savored the hot, lemony taste titillating the back of their throats.

When the next appetizer arrived, Carl eyed it like it was from another planet. "I'm not using the chopsticks," he made clear when his wife handed him a pair.

Mrs. Lambrose thanked Constance again for giving her a break from cooking.

"Oh, it's my pleasure, April. Thank you for finally letting me take you all out. Why did we have to bring our walking shoes, Carl?"

"I have a surprise afterwards," Mr. Lambrose answered.

Trevin took a break from devouring. "Not the jetty again, or frozen custard. That's too far away—we're in the city."

"No, we're going the other way," Carl replied. "I have dessert planned, so to speak. And we won't have to worry about these calories."

"What, are we running a marathon?" Trevin snapped.

"Quiet and eat."

The waitress left a pitcher of water at their request as the main courses were brought out, hot and steaming. When each plate was generously filled, Carl, April and Trevin were about to dig in when Constance asked for a pause. "Before this—" she said. "—Would you mind if I said grace? I should have done it before the appetizers."

No one minded. They set their utensils down and grew still. In the dimness, the flames from the table's votive candles flickered off their eyes.

"I was just inspired," said Constance. "Thank you." She cast a sideways glance at Trevin, winking at him. "Let's hold hands." He smiled.

Constance placed her elbows on the table, holding her hands out. They joined as one. A few patrons discreetly looked over, but went back to their meals.

"Let this be a prayer to our futures," she began, taking time to meet each person's eyes. Then she bent her head, going formal. "We acknowledge You and everything You have made in Creation. We are thankful for everything You have given us. I am deeply appreciative for having been placed in this family's grace. Bless those of us here at the table, and those without families. We are all on individual paths, guided by the love You provide, but are destined to a single location. We also pray for those who have passed on before us. May they be forever in Your light, and may You allow them to watch over us until we can be together again, at last leaving our Earthly concerns. We'll never forget this day. We'll never forget creating these new memories. Let us make more so that we may travel far. Let our memories—our great treasures—help transport us to Your realm."

Constance was done.

She broke hands, setting hers in her lap. The others followed suit. Constance waited, slightly unsure if she had made a scene. Her smile brought closure. "Thanks for the indulgence," she said, and started heaping rice onto her plate.

Apparently, she hadn't upset anyone.

"Well …" the patriarch said, breaking the awe. "I'm saying 'Amen.'"

Carl performed the sign of the cross as April broke out of her stupor, handing her husband the largest entrée on the table. "Constance," she said. "That… was… amazing. Thank *you*."

"Spur of the moment," Constance chirped back, shrugging. She then made sure everyone had the rice, passing it around until all the plates were filled.

Trevin was staring at her.

"What?" she pressed.

"Nothing," Trevin answered. "Just looking at you."

"Well stop it and eat up."

The mood lightened. As the four dug in, sampling to their hearts' content, they sensed the bond growing deeper among them. Their waitress sauntered up, this time without food. "I just want to say—" she bent at the waist, whispering, "—that was nice, all of you holding hands. I don't see it ever." Straightening, "Is there anything more I can get for you?"

"No, thank you," said April. "We're fine for now."

The waitress nodded and walked away. Mrs. Lambrose filled everyone's glasses with ice water from the decanter, asking what food everyone enjoyed the most.

* * *

Mr. Lambrose was again behind the wheel. He was on one of his missions again, having informed the group before they left from home to bring their hiking shoes, but as of yet he had not disclosed their destination. He wanted another surprise. Everyone cooperated fully, not pressing for answers, not wanting to dash the man's fun. Constance was now the front-seat passenger.

They drove much farther out than expected, motoring well into the countryside, far away from downtown Rochester. The ride had taken on a magical, dreamlike quality, hypnotically relaxing. Dad's jazz played. The windows were down, and at this cruising speed, the remaining heat of the day wasn't an issue. There was no one else on the road. The car's interior had become a wind tunnel, whipping the occupant's hair with unmatched freedom. Constance's mane was swatting in flapping locks. Tires dipped, compressed and rose as they traversed the less-traveled lanes, momentary weightlessness coming in fits and starts. Leftover rainwater from the storm splashed upward in periodic bursts. An unsullied fragrance permeated the air, the open fields retaining all things fresh and sweet.

Trevin drew the personal metaphor that they were headed to a new horizon, and they were happy about it.

After an excessively large spray surprised them, blasting higher than the vehicle itself, Mrs. Lambrose told her husband to slow down. Mr. Lambrose eased back, bringing them to a more conscientious speed. "You've already given me a bad hair day," she joked.

Constance caught a passing glimpse of an amazing horse farm, turning her head to see as much of it as she could. It disappeared quickly. Her eyes landed next on the side-view mirror, where Trevin was again staring at her from the back seat. His smile communicated the deepest of loves.

Constance commented—to no one in particular—just how beautiful the area was. "I had no idea New York State could be so rural."

This may or may not have been the right thing to say. Dad opened up, giving her a history lesson on what he knew of the region. And that was a lot. He grew up out here. Constance became relieved Carl was lightening up.

Trevin looked over at his mother next to him. She had her head reclined, preoccupied with the sky straight up through the back windshield. "What are you looking at?" he asked, checking with her. He saw right away the same startling sight: very bizarre clouds.

April muttered, "They're back. I really wish I knew what was going on."

These were fantastic yet eerie-looking, the most unusual so far. Maybe it was the precipitation and the humidity that had formed them: a series of lens-shaped disks, radiating with concentrated light, aglow with firelight even before the sun began to set. To Trevin's flair for science fiction, they gave an appearance of flying saucers.

"It's as if they're following us," April added, asking her son if he knew what kind they were.

"Actually I do," he answered. "They're lenticular clouds, but I've never actually seen them in person. They form at high altitudes, I know that. And they're rare."

Dad couldn't take his eyes from the road, but Constance checked them in the rear view mirror. "They go as far as the eye can see, like a fleet approaching," she said.

"They're strictly meteorological, babe," said Trevin, "nothing supernatural." He told his mother to stop straining her neck.

"It's definitely a pattern—" April said pensively, ending the attention. "—getting my mind in order. I'm crazy, I know."

Constance crooked her head to talk to her. "You're not crazy. There's no reason to censor yourself, April. Just let it come."

Trevin thought of Gladys at the Lakebreeze Healthcare Campus. He thought of her similar talk and of the renderings of circles she'd been performing in her sketchbook. He almost brought it up, but decided to keep it to himself. This wasn't about him. This was about his family.

"You're all going to love where I'm taking you," said dad. "It'll really open you up."

Twenty minutes later, they turned into a state forest preserve, only a small sign on the side of the road announcing its entrance. Again, they were the only ones around. The puddles here in the parking lot weren't as heavy. Maybe the storm hadn't been as robust this far out. As dad climbed out, he ordered everyone to switch into their hiking shoes. They cooperated, everyone now knowing they were going for one of Carl's power-walks.

"Are we going through the woods or just around it?" April asked.

"Are you kidding? Through them," Carl squawked, growing even more cheerful.

Trevin admired the dark greens of the shadowed woods ahead, ready to embrace them at the entrance to the path. "Why here, dad?"

"I have something I want to share. Everyone's been talking like they're in an episode of 'The Twilight Zone.' I was inspired. All this talk of memories and circles and meaningful places. You three aren't the only mystics. Let's get hoofing, no complaining."

As the quartet began their journey, dad led the charge. After the pavement ended, and the topography of the path went from somewhat beaten to rapidly earthen, mom warned: "Nobody goes in the house after this with these shoes on."

They headed west, into the sunlight—which was now finally starting to become long in the day—and the spacing between them became increasingly harder to cover shoulder to shoulder. So they walked single file—dad in front, Trevin in the rear. Trevin formed a new, primitive impression that they were an ancient tribe, and the men were configured this way to protect the women. The foliage became dense. The canopy of trees took on a cathedral quality—vaulted ceilings made of nature—a swaying masterpiece of holiness, aglow with auburn and jade. The light that did sneak in tickled their forms, and mom, behind Constance, reacted to the dramatic luster of the young woman's mane.

"My gosh, Constance. What color is your hair, exactly? The way the light is dancing on it… There are so many subtleties. First it looks opaque, then it's translucent at the contour."

"It's brunette, I think," said Constance, flattered. "I don't color it."

"I'd almost say it's indescribable. It might be the light, but I can almost see a prism of Earth colors. But it's beautiful."

Trevin warned, "Don't break the march, mom—dad'll shoot us."

Farther and farther they hiked into the depths. It was much cooler here, the greens pregnant in each leaf, veins alive with the rich photosynthesis, process, countless berries acting as accents. Personal thoughts became easier to access. Eventually, after ten minutes of no one talking, Mrs. Lambrose saw a particularly interesting twig coming up—an aberrant one—one that demanded attention. "Look at this," she said as they came up to it, stopping the group. The three had to readjust—they'd been so absorbed.

The twig drooped at nearly eye-level, dangling by fibers. It had been half-severed from a small and anemic tree. As the draft whipped up, it spun crazily in a loop, pantomiming a pinwheel. None of the other intact twigs were that affected. It was impossible not to note the irony, given the musings over circles and circular motion. They gathered around, watching it as if hypnotized.

"There's your theory, mom," said Trevin. "It's all around us, in nature."

"That's why I stopped," she replied.

They tried to determine which direction the breeze was blowing from. It was omnipresent, gusting this way and that. Mom touched the twig. "It's talking …"

"Well, that's not exactly what I had in mind," said dad, "but that is interesting. Come on, we have to be watchful of what sunlight we have left."

Dad's army training pulled them in his wake. Despite the hustle, this was an enjoyable experience. Spiritual, too, if they'd been asked to vocalize it. This was a chance to put aside worry and outside influence. Other than their crunching feet, the noise was reduced to near-zero. They fell into single file again as the path narrowed even more, ending at a hillock marking the *real* woods.

Was this ancestral memory at play? Trevin wondered. Had people of the Stone Age cherished their memories, too? Did Cave Man Sammy and Cave Woman Sue reminisce?

"Carl," April said, a dawning awareness taking over her, "didn't you plant trees out here when you were a kid?"

"Bingo," Carl said.

"So that's why we're here?"

"Sort of. I came out here with my dad and my granddad. This is my cradle. Constance, I grew up in a little hick town five miles over. My back story's in these parts."

"Very cool," said Constance. "I love it. I don't mind walking out here at all."

"Don't worry about getting lost: I know this area like the back of my hand."

"I wasn't worried," she said.

Numerous dead trees had toppled from years of lightning hits. Occasionally, one blocked the way, forcing them to step over, careful not to slip on moss or ferns. They sweated. The cardio was growing intense, but the three were fueled by Carl's excitement. He told of riding horses and picking apples here when he was no older than eight. The sunlight tapped the crowns of their heads in shifting lanterns of illumination. No way could Trevin have imagined—discussing his parents' hikes with Constance—that they'd actually be doing one on the outskirts of Monroe County.

"These preserves close at sunset, don't they?" he asked.

"We're almost there: The reveal is everything. There's a center point up here. That's where we're going."

Constance turned around to Trevin. "A man on a quest. Like you."

"I remember," Trevin retorted.

As promised, the trail widened as the trees cleared. They stepped through the last thicket and once more filed side by side. "Ta-da," dad sang, presenting the endgame.

There was an enormous open meadow here, wild strawgrass making up most of it, bramble and brush peppering the edges where the tall trees continued in a great arc, hugging it all. The four gave themselves room to take in the wonder. Dad waited for them to catch on to the visual coincidence. They were all impressed, providing their own exclamations of approval.

"Wow," said mom.

"Yeah, wow," followed Constance.

"This is your 'fields,' dad," Trevin said.

"In a way it is," Mr. Lambrose replied. "And—don't you see it? It's one, big circle. A giant circle."

Mrs. Lambrose put her hands to her face, finally realizing. "So this is it! Oh yeah, you've told me about this place, I'm finally seeing it first-hand. This is fantastic. Look, you can follow its radius. It must be—what—a hundred yards in diameter?"

"Almost perfect," dad said as the other two followed suit. "If we could see this from the sky, it would look like it's been designed."

"Like those crop circles we've heard of," said Trevin. "Are we in England? Feels as far."

"This is natural," dad responded, putting hands on hips proudly: the trademark. "It's always been here. Been thinking of it. Guess we're all on the same crazy train. Not many know this is here. I used to come in from the other side." Pointing: "We planted the trees there, where the pines are shorter. A creek runs straight through the middle, come on."

Taking his wife's hand, dad next guided them through the strawgrass in high steps, cutting a line to the center, 50 yards in—arriving at an equally dramatic core: an incongruous babbling creek. Here, the water was snappish and pure, sparkling like a natural spring. Trevin measured its distance to the circumference, scratching his head.

"Dead middle," he assessed. "Amazing. What are the chances?"

"Slim," dad said immediately.

At its embankment, polished pebbles had long collected from the current. In the center of the stream, a swirling eddy sucked water in a circle where others had gathered. A puckish funnel was gurgling like it was alive. The flow surged at its apex, where the force was strongest.

Dad looked around, happy with his choice. "Does everybody like?" he asked.

They did. They said as much and stared at its peacefulness. Trevin turned to his girlfriend, who dipped her eyes and shook her head.

"It *is* everywhere," she said.

Then Carl made a stunning confession. "I wanted all of you to see this. This was where my dad first told me he loved me. I'll never forget that moment, after we planted the trees. Talk about a memory. How could I forget this spot? I promised him I'd do the same for my future family: Make the best life possible for them. I needed to bring you here. It's a great place to tell you that I love you. All of you."

The words impacted, April, Constance and Trevin becoming moved. Very moved. April fell into tears and hugged her husband, kissing him on the cheek. "We love you, too, dear. If we're all on this train together, let's try to get off at the same destination. I don't want to be without my family."

For the second time in the visit, the family unit became as one.

CHAPTER 25

By the time they found themselves ("found" being the operative term) back on Sweet Briar, there was a collective impression of having traveled to the moon—everything but the American flag having been planted. It was a superb finale to a superb outing. The four were emotionally and physically drained, and another histrionic sunset was blasting in full bloom. Stepping out of the car and stretching, they couldn't help but admire each other's appearance as well as the look of the neighborhood—all bathed and awash in a reddish-orange radiance. They lingered there, feeling the solidness under their shoes from the driveway. If they could put a term on it, all felt as if they'd been spiritually refreshed.

It was April who spoke first. "Remember the shoes. Leave them outside, we'll clean them tomorrow."

The next minute brought an even more effective celestial tour de force. Less than half of the sun was observable, swollen at the sides, sucking up all the nuclear fusion it could. The saucer-like lenticular clouds had gathered in clumps around it, smoldering in vermilions and pinks, canary and citrine gold. Trevin talked his parents into sticking around. He wanted to enjoy the peak of the sunset with them; not wanting the magic to end. April wanted to go in and gather some lemonades, but Trevin stopped her.

"Just sit," he asked, and gathered lawn chairs from the porch, setting them in a row by the sidewalk, facing due west. He had each one sit as if preparing for some grand orchestra to start. A stronger breeze than in the preserve soothed them as they gave in to Trevin's wishes. "This is dessert," he said, settling in.

Constance sat to Trevin's left, his precious mother and father to his right. Trevin snapped away at their profiles, capturing mental pictures. He somehow believed they'd forged a bond, destined to carry them all to a yet-unachieved greatness. They had a grand view over the housetops.

Hollywood couldn't create such a vision. The longer they stared into the sky, the more the colors appeared to shimmer, shifting and pulsating in ever-expanding rhythms. Emanating rays shot to the firmament in shards, dissipating in the east. The first evening stars had appeared behind them in the cobalt and plum purple.

And the memories began to flow. Flow and flow and flow. First Trevin, then his mother. Then Carl Lambrose joined in, bringing up nuggets from their past that pleased them and made them smile. They almost couldn't stop—the good will was flowing like melted butter.

"I remember skies like this at the drive-in," Trevin mentioned, his mind far off.

This made his dad chuckle. "The Winking Moon?"

"The Winking Moon," Trevin parroted. "The very one." Constance didn't know what they were referring to. "The Winking Moon Drive-In Movie Theater. It's not there anymore, babe. It was a staple in this community for years. I worked there as a teenager."

"That's a whimsical name," Constance said. "You love moon imagery."

"I do. I was 17, I loved it. It was a great summer job. I was outdoors all night. Used to go way in the back before the first movie started and stare at the sunset like this. It set the stage."

"That goes back a few years," mom weighed in.

"A few."

"I used to wish on them like stars. Wished my friends would show up, provide me with some laughs. It usually happened." He pointed. "Look where the greatest amounts of those lenticular clouds are collecting. They're turning cumulu-nimbus. Makes it look like a giant valley in the sky, doesn't it? Complete with shining rivers of gold. Streams, mountains, hills. Don't all of you see it? It's all there. There's a whole landscape up there."

"I do see it," said his mother. "It looks like heaven."

"Dad?"

"I've finished with my indulgence for the night."

"Hon?"

Constance squinted, really trying to see what everyone else saw. "Um… if I look at it like a negative photograph, yes I see it. The streams are those squiggly lines, working downward, right?"

Trevin nodded affirmatively. "Yup. It's like the Finger Lakes, made of light. The mountains roll all the way back until you can't see the sky anymore. The houses block them. It's Arcadia—the playground of the gods in Greek mythology." He traced over the ridges and dales, tinted with saffron, hills of mandarin. "Sinking into the west, kissing Sweet Briar …"

"I want to go into it," Mrs. Lambrose said. "I want all of us to go into it. No harm can come to us there."

"That's a great idea, mom," said Trevin, hazily. "A phantasmagoric delight. Everything good is to the west. My friends lived west of here… my schools… the ball diamonds. Let's drive up into it and disappear."

"Not with my car you're not," dad said, shattering the atmosphere, drawing laughs. He got up, folded his chair. "I'm going in. I need a shower."

"I'm going in, too," said Mrs. Lambrose, joining her husband. As they strolled to the porch, slight kinks working their way out in their tired legs, a car rounded the bend by Tommy's mother's house (in the west). For some reason, they all stopped to look at it. It stuck out, moving slowly their way.

There was recognition. "Could that be …?" said Trevin.

The headlights sprang on like two leopard eyes at dusk, surveying for food. Trevin recognized the fedora hat as the driver came into view. "Mr. Tavalier! Speaking of mysteries."

"Trevin, shh!" his mother scolded.

Constance sat up, reacting like this was something to get excited about. "Is that him?"

"Act normal everyone!" Mrs. Lambrose insisted. "For crying out loud, don't stare!"

But it was hard not to. This was a rare appearance. Trevin figured, from Mr. Tavalier's perspective, this must have seemed like an odd scene—four neighbors sitting out in their driveway like four parade attendees, awaiting the first float. The car reached Emerald Street at the No Outlet corner—sluggish as molasses—beginning its slow turn with no signal. The lone occupant glanced over, Coke-bottle eyeglasses catching the last firelight raging in front of them all, eradicating the opportunity to connect directly with his eyes. Trevin waved—a neighborly gesture.

Mr. Tavalier executed something shocking: He waved back! The man's hand rose and fell in a single motion. By the time Trevin registered the unexpected shock, the car was already pulling into his driveway, disappearing behind the cursed hedges.

Acknowledgment? Trevin asked himself.

They heard the automatic garage open and close, then … stillness. Only the loud cicadas and starlings broke the silence.

Trevin turned to his parents. "He waved."

"He did," responded his dad, removing shoes, clapping them. "Don't make a federal case of it." Carl opened the door for his wife. "See you guys inside." And they went in and closed the door.

Trevin turned to Constance. "He may have smiled," she said.

"He may have …" Trevin was flabbergasted. This may have been some kind of breakthrough, he explained. Constance held his hands, happy for him. An avalanche of pity then took over, consuming him as before, changing the mood, spreading throughout his body as ruthless as a virus. The lonely widower had just made first contact.

"I finally saw him," Constance said.

Trevin checked the top left window of Mr. Tavalier's house. It, too, was reflecting the stunning sundown. The squares faded in glowing embers.

"What are you thinking?" she asked.

"I see a light go on in that window in the upper right at night. I think of him waking, no one to talk to." He rutted his forehead. "Let me show you dad's garden before it gets completely dark. I have to shake this off."

They also put their chairs on the porch where they belonged and rounded the house from the garage side, passing through a metal gate into the backyard, where Trevin presented his father's creation for the first time. Their feet sunk in a tad. The grass was still damp from the rain.

"It's much more impressive from back here," Constance beamed, still checking Trevin's face when he wasn't looking.

The neighbors' houses threw large shadows over most of the lawn. White moths flitted up from the cooling soil into the nightfall, blinking like flecks of cotton. Constance saw the fence surrounding the property. All the neighbors had fences.

Trevin tested the garden soil like he was going to excavate, prodding about like Mr. Tavalier had with his garden. "He was searching for something …"

"What?" Constance didn't know what he was talking about.

"Nothing. These plants are still drooping. Even after the storm. Apparently, it wasn't enough."

"You have to add yourself to the mix," she said. "Don't be afraid. Come." She led him to the middle of the soggy garden, the wet and floppy vegetation skirting their sides, clinging to their clothes. She started asking the vegetables and greens how they were doing—if they hadn't received enough rainwater. Trevin was amused. Distracted, but amused.

"You're trying to be goofy," he said, brushing the hair from her freckled face.

"I hear that mayonnaise is good for the leaves."

Trevin smirked. "Gladys said the same thing."

"I miss Gladys," said Constance, caressing the stalks. "We have to make a difference now, you know—while we can. Maybe you should make a difference with Mr. Tavalier."

Constance crouched, whispering to the tomatoes. Trevin was behind her, and couldn't help but be struck at the sexiness of her well-toned, insanely freckled lower back. The blouse had pulled up, revealing a peek. Her skin looked wraithlike in the dimness.

Checking to make sure his parents weren't watching from the back porch, he felt like he was in junior high all over again. He considered the physical aspect to their relationship, or lack thereof—wondering if she thought of it. He almost asked, but the strongest breeze yet picked up, knocking him off it. He told her once more how beautiful he thought she was.

She stood, brushing off her hands, twinkles darting her eyes. Debating what to say, she moved to within inches of him, positioning his hands firmly on her hips—reminding him of the night at the block party. There were many good memories from *that* night. After a stilted instant, she said, "*You…* are beautiful. You made me ride into the sunset tonight."

* * *

They climbed up to the rooftop that night, well after midnight. His parents were asleep in their bedroom and had verbally allowed for it earlier. Perhaps they weren't totally asleep now—Trevin's dad had yelled once already at them for making noise, snickering and chortling their way out the upstairs bathroom window to the top.

The Milky Way was in all its glory—a beautiful, clear night. The chorus of crickets and the lulling traffic on Mt. Read Boulevard sang to them. They could even hear the slight sucking sounds from all the above-ground swimming pools in the area.

Trevin and Constance took the best seat in the house, literally—overlooking Sweet Briar and Emerald. They had taken beach towels with them to soften the texture of the shingled rooftop.

All of it brought back his childhood memories. His better times.

More than once Constance had to suppress the giggles, acting like a schoolgirl on her first prom date. Whispering, she said, "Don't let me roll off."

"Stay by my side. Don't stray."

"We're right over your parents."

"Dad and I used to do this all the time to see the meteor shower. Just be cool."

Their sandals adjusted to the gritty surface. Constance dropped her full water bottle and it rolled all the way off the gutter, vanishing into the blackness with a thump in the yard. She let go a cackle. The infectious noise caught Trevin by surprise, and he laughed, unable to remember the last time he felt so clear-headed. They were six feet from the chimney, maybe 10 from the eave. The new housing tract sparkled like diamonds in the dark. "We're going to have dimples on our asses when we're done here," he said, causing another round of explosive hysterics.

Then she cooed, cozying up next to him, settling in. "This… is exquisite. What meteor shower is this again?"

The incandescent moon was rising in the east above the houses there. A blazing sliver streaked across the heavens, burning out in seconds. All of creation loomed above, striking awe into his heart. "Surely this is a portal to the sublime," he said, then, answering, "The Perseid meteor shower. It appears to come from the constellation Perseus—right there. Dad and I did this each summer. Mom didn't climb the roof. You can see up to 80 shooting stars an hour at its peak."

"When's the peak?"

"Around three or four in the morning."

"We're not staying out that late …"

"We could try," he kidded, then looked back to his street. "There may be a thousand Sweet Briars out there… but this one is mine."

There were no lights of any kind in any of the homes. Everyone must have been asleep. The glowing clock face of the church steeple a mile or so behind them was the only noticeable beacon. Trevin reflected on his recent, stupid dive from the press box. As he contemplated the fact that he could have killed himself—robbing himself of this moment with the beautiful Constance—he again burned with questions plaguing him since their dating became official. Her background and caginess when he delved into it had not been resolved. He wanted an answer to each mystery, especially now. He didn't know what to do. When he was set to dare, she jumped his moment, surprising him by saying, "You're helping me, Trevin."

"Helping you? How am I doing that?"

It was obvious she chose her words carefully. "I've been on my own a long time."

"And?"

"And you have a past. I guess I'm having mine through you."

"Babe, have you ever thought of looking up your birth parents?"

"I don't think about that," she answered. "It would sidetrack me."

"From what?"

"My purpose."

"You're talking in riddles again. Your life is not a job."

"It sort of is," she replied.

Just when he was about to flat-out ask what exactly she meant—no haziness—a different light snapped on at Mr. Tavalier's house. Not the top right window, but one on the first floor, parallel to the porch. The living room? It went off again after a minute.

Constance saw it, too. "My heart is also breaking, thinking of your neighbor suffering."

The next light popped on where it should: second floor, top right. "My soul was shattered in Chicago," he said, staring at it. "I hope he hasn't had that happen to him."

"Compassion is a virtue," she said.

"It is, I think."

She sighed. "Love never dies."

She's managed to skate the issue once again, Trevin thought, watching several blazers streak a path across the black sky. He thought of the blue orb he saw rising out of Brian Annarez, and compared it to the activity they were now witnessing. Constance yawned and started to get up. "And my tushy's sore," she said.

"I knew it would be," he said, springing up with her, helping her. He checked the time on the clock face, just now registering how long they'd been up here already. Both agreed it was time to go in. They flapped the towel, sending residual granules scattering to the winds. Some caught the streetlight, sparkling like stardust.

"Philosophy under the stars," he said, guiding her down. They crawled back in through the bathroom window on the second floor, locking it behind them.

As Trevin kissed her passionately goodnight in the dark at the guest-room door, they heard the cuckoo clock strike one—damn late. He'd make progress soon, in many regards.

CHAPTER 26

Two more steamy days and nights passed; a total of seven since Constance's arrival. Trevin was formulating a good time to return to Chicago, but there were a couple of things he wanted to do first. One was pushing his parents every day to familiarize themselves with the computer. The few times the TV had been on, nothing but war, corruption, murder and mayhem assaulted their senses. Mom said it first: "The world is definitely on its last legs." Trevin treated Constance to the wine valleys in the Southern Tier of New York State, and powered through a few more high-octane walks with his folks. Anything for diversion. They didn't yet have the Internet, but soon would, thanks to a special deal offered in hopes of helping to jumpstart the economy. Somehow, Trevin felt complete knowing it was coming.

Trevin couldn't sleep on the seventh night. Jamming his fists into the mattress and pushing up, he moaned at another late hour: 2:07 in the morning. What kept him up was a pulse-pounding urge to act. On something! Life had taken him in directions he'd never wanted, and his soul ached to find meaning. He had to get his mojo back, make a difference, be a hero for his own self as well as for Constance and his parents. He'd be his own fucking momentum.

A clarifying memory from childhood came to his aid. He remembered a friend of his parents—a priest—a young and resolute man who was invited to dinner occasionally. After the meals and bottles of wine, the holy man paced each room, reciting supplication to bless the house. Trevin remembered the Rosary dangling from his hands. "The house is now sanctified," he'd say. Mom and dad were always grateful.

This led Trevin to think about a personal theory of his, mixing science with religion—formed in his days of physics classes. There was actual physical spaces existing between atoms, mystery components holding them together. *Maybe that's where Nan is,* he'd wondered. Scientists were in pursuit of these "yet-unknowns," this God-energy, this divine magnetism. Maybe the "nice" deceased people were part of this equation. Perhaps their retained essences could only resurface when the proper forces were in alignment—when love aided in summoning them.

Slipping into his faithful jeans and a tee-shirt, Trevin crept into the lightless hallway, honing in on the soft breathing in his parents' room. *How many times had I been comforted by that sound?* he asked himself, momentarily placing himself back in the days of yore, when he was just a tot. They'd always left their door half open. He remembered how whenever he'd awakened from a nightmare, he would hear the breathing, sometimes snoring, and he knew he was safe. *If they weren't scared of the dark,* he knew, *why should I be?*

He wordlessly wished them good dreams and tip-toed downstairs. The entire house was dark, the only illumination being the tiny glows from power outlets and appliances, and from the streetlight in front of the house squeaking through the Levelor blinds.

First, he went to the living room, drawing within reach of the floor-to-ceiling bookcase, where the shelves of medical manuals, dictionaries, encyclopedias and old novels smelled as slightly musty as ever. He put his nose to them and reflected. *And how many times did I sit on the floor here and read?* He'd always loved that.

His parents' photo albums were in repose, held by sturdy book-ends. He plucked one and went through a few pages, angling the book to the streetlight after adjusting the blinds. He had a particularly old one, long before he was born. Mom and dad were full of smiles, donned in clothes and hairstyles of the time, younger than Trevin was now. The realization was staggering to him. He'd forgotten how bare the neighborhood had been, before the build-out and "Incubator Alley." The coupé in the driveway was classic. Sentiment leapt from each crinkly page.

He put the album back and tried another, the dried cellophane threatening to lose the pictures. Page after page revealed impossibly young faces of the neighbors from the tour, full of the life that was ahead of them. Permutations and flights of homesickness ensued, unleashing a tide of emotions. Sweet Briar, itself, was slowing down. Like him. Like everyone. It was time to be intentional. Trevin wished them all well.

Continuing into the family room, Trevin had to be careful not to stumble in the stairwell. He didn't need to be waking anyone. The streetlight still cut narrow paths down here, still igniting living highlights on the wheelchair—flaring great and small, communicating in hushes.

Knowing nothing of Constance's slumbering breaths, he visited her closed door and listened in, placing temple to wood. There was no noise. Considering what he was doing to be intrusive, he backed away, returning to the wheelchair—the focal point of the house, by his perspective.

"I miss you, Nan …" he communicated, becoming sad. "I was always afraid of this day. Wish we could have one more conversation. You came to me in a dream. It was a dream, wasn't it?"

He parted the curtains and left them that way. The top half of Mr. Tavalier's house was observable from over the hedges. The facade was, of course, dark. Grabbing the wheelchair, he unfolded it and gently sat, positioning to the viewpoint his grandmother had when she tried to look out. He thought he had the angle right. He was even lower now. The metal was cold to the touch, highlights riding his hands.

"This was how you saw Sweet Briar, remember? I'd put the kettle on for us. Are you still here? Any part of you? Was I right about the spaces between atoms? Have you been watching over mom and dad, protecting them?"

Something then raised the hairs on his forearms. Not in a frightening way, but as if prompting him to shuck off the glumness and check out the little kitchen. He followed the impulse, as if guided by an omnipresent and masterful puppeteer. Another one of his precious nightlights, plugged into a high outlet, faintly illuminated the room with its familiar, carroty glow. Trevin could make out Nan's favorite stool, one of the four tucked neatly under the bar table.

So many happy memories …

There the kettle was, on the gas stove—a squat, ivory thing with its shiny surface and heat-proof black handle. The stove's electric clock was frozen in time, reading 3:50 a.m., the time he was born. Was that a coincidence? He'd never know. He imagined the kettle boiling with hot water, steam rising. Nan would have him ready the teabags—two fresh ones, tabs draped over the mugs. Tea was their special indulgence. He never bothered with the stuff after she passed away. Every time he now smelled the drink …

There was nothing in the old refrigerator but bottled water his parents used for their walks. He checked the cabinets. With the exception of the mugs, old plates, an empty ice tray and a case of jarred olives, there was no longer any sign of Nan. No more tea would be prepared from this station.

There wasn't even a bottle of liquor anymore.

You had a lot of fun here with your retiree friends, usually when mom and dad were gone. Beer mostly, sometimes the hard stuff. You'd mix it on the counter. I can still hear the laughter.

As Trevin drifted out of the little kitchen and once more returned to the wheelchair, he saw the light in Mr. Tavalier's top right window pop.

Enough was enough. Trevin had finally had it with the signs. "Okay, Nan… time to take that step."

❊ ❊ ❊

Trevin stood outside on his parents' porch, as still as a lion, staring determinedly at the light across the street, drawing the necessary strength to do what he was about to do. He now had his gym shoes on, the ones he'd scrubbed after the hike. He double-checked the neighborhood, making sure no one was watching him. The night air was filled with pine, permeating his nostrils, so redolent during these hours. The moon was gone. Few stars. No strange weather patterns up there. Shooting stars surfed the ionosphere. One blazed out in a fireball.

He also checked to make sure he had his house key with him—he'd locked the door behind him! What an effort it had been keeping quiet as he crept out from the foyer.

Talking himself into moving forward, he embarked on his journey, walking off the porch and down the driveway, stopping at the curb where the sewer grate ran under his feet. Mom and dad's house was hushed behind him, triggering an unbelievable memory from sixth grade. He'd snuck out at two in the morning and met up with his buddies, gorging on junk food at an all-night convenience store. Returning home, he discovered his dad had waited up for him—striking a pose as an imposing silhouette in the living-room window. Trevin had paid deeply for that stunt. It was like "they" said: "It's funny now."

He only made it half-way across Sweet Briar when he halted at the Eason's white picket fence, wondering if he even had the right to do what he was about to do. Sweat trickled down his neck even as the rustling wind kept him from broiling. It was plenty humid out here. Now that he was in the clear, the airstream could be heard competing with the crickets.

Before knocking on Mr. Tavalier's door, the only way for Trevin to fully draw enough courage was to make a quick retrace of the path on Emerald he had with Constance—a refresher course on how important the neighbors had been to him in the first place. Even he wasn't making complete sense to himself. Trevin figured he still was being encouraged by that master puppeteer.

He continued walking all the way to the Morneaus, where he stalled again at the sight of that famous backyard pool. A couple of security lamps went on at the side of the house, startling him. That was new. The Morneaus never had security lights! Times had changed.

"Thanks for the pool parties, Mr. and Mrs. Morneau, I heard your kids did well for themselves. Good for them. How is everybody? I'm here, talking to your old house in the dead of night, acting like a loon. See where my life's gone to?"

He crossed to the other side of Emerald, past the berm with the dented guardrail—the start of the old fields—ending up in front of Mr. and Mrs. Buccini's old place. He had no concept of how long it had been since they died. They *must* have died. "Sorry we didn't build that fort together, Mr. Buccini. God rest your soul. And your wife's."

The reverse view down Emerald Lane was dramatic, just as he'd remembered from childhood. His bedroom window was an impassive black square like the others on his parents' house, and the clock steeple poked up from behind the roof right where the garage was. He could have been the last man on Earth. It looked like the block had been totally abandoned.

A car drove by! Trevin shot behind a tree. Couldn't he be out for a night-walk in his old neighborhood? Not when he was going to be trespassing in a minute, he told himself. This was going to be a greater flirt with danger than jumping off the press box.

After rummaging more morsels of his mind, making his way past the other homes of his yearnings, he finally landed in front of the mystery man himself—Mr. Tavalier's driveway—free and clear of the damn shrubs. This was a great shot straight up to the alien porch. If Nutty George (damn Tommy Porch) had been looking out of any of his front windows, he would have seen a startling sight: a lone figure, staring back. Trevin asked himself one final time if he had the testicular fortitude to carry through with his resolve.

Yes!

He cracked his neck, limbered up, and let the great puppeteer push him up the driveway, head down, thudding all the way to the porch, recalling this angle from trick-or-treating with Tommy. *That ridiculous monster-astronaut costume!* The ineptly designed helmet only allowed this view. This time, however, there were no cracks in the pavement. *But there are cracks in my head!*

This was a return trip from Mars for Trevin, back from what seemed a trillion years.

CHAPTER 27

‹ ——— ›

At that moment in Trevin's parents' house, Constance snapped awake, an intuition alerting her that her man had stepped out of the house, and that something monumental was going to happen.

Monumental.

She sat up, the thin sheet sliding off her shoulders, exposing her to the coolness of the room. She zeroed in on the nightlight under the dresser, loving its halo. It was as comforting as one of Trevin's warm memories. It wasn't quite time. Not yet.

She needed to get out there.

❊ ❊ ❊

Trevin was holding one of the pillars for support. The overhang above him cloaked him in shadows, even though the same streetlight that bled into his family room, shedding light on his grandmother's wheelchair, shone here as well. Blood was pumping, temples pounded. He was treading on sacred ground here, almost literally. If the precinct experience in Chicago had been nerve-jangling, he didn't want to imagine how this would be if Mr. Tavalier had the cops haul him away.

How do I know that both barrels of a shotgun won't come telescoping from the door?

I don't.

This isn't stalking—it's compassion. Unlike those bastards Glen, Solorio and the neighbors on Munnison.

Let it go, Trevin, let it go …

Knurling his fingers, Trevin went for it, moving at the outside screen, raising his fist, fighting the impulse to flee. He gnashed his teeth as his irises widened to take in more light.

Rap! Rap! Rap! The synthetic glass rattled louder than expected, reverberating around the open space, nearly scaring the shit out of Trevin—sounding like a cannon to his ears. This was the middle of the night, in an ultra-quiet neighborhood. He waited for dogs to start going crazy. That didn't happen. Did he just scare the hell out of poor Mr. Tavalier? For all Trevin knew, the man was stuck to the ceiling now—having erupted from the bed.

Or maybe Mr. Tavalier wouldn't answer. He could've self-medicated himself into a coma.

Trevin went at it again, head down, nostrils flaring: *Bam! Bam! Bam!* A fourth for good measure. He thought he heard something. Standing on his toes, he dared a peek into the door's window. The streetlight allowed some view into the foyer. He saw steps leading up to a first floor, as dad had recalled. He stepped back, diminishing the threatening position. A doorbell was to his right: an orange, glowing thing, like a Cyclops eye. *Why do doorbells always glow orange?* he wondered. His finger depressed it, launching a convulsion of chimes within: a multi-toned oeuvre loud enough to wake the dead.

A weak thump could be heard inside, originating somewhere higher up, possibly the top floor. Someone began descending stairs—an ominous *clump-clump-clump* growing louder. All moisture dried in Trevin's throat. Part of a figure materialized at the top landing, enough to identify a pair of slippers attached to hairy, spindly legs under a shabby robe. Time and space folded over.

"Who's there?" the stern voice called out. It was sobering.

What did Trevin expect? He had trouble releasing the first syllables. "Mr. Tavalier? T-Trevin Lambrose… from the across the street." He didn't know if he was heard.

"What's wrong?"

"N-nothing, sir."

No movement from the ridiculous slippers. "Trevin Lambrose?" The tone was still angry, but maybe it had mellowed a click.

"T-that's right, Mr. Tavalier—Trevin Lambrose."

Another protracted pause. "What are you doing?"

"Nothing… I—" Trevin was cut off.

"Is there an emergency?!"

"No! No emergency."

"What do you want then?" There should've been a "the hell" thrown in.

Trevin stammered, unable to recall the voice from any personal registry. Like an idiot, he'd prepared no speech. "I… I know this must seem bizarre—it's terribly late. I-I'm sorry to bother you at this hour—"

"What do you *want?!*"

"Um… don't be alarmed, sir. I'm visiting my folks… I've seen your light on at night… I've been worried about you. You waved to us in the driveway."

"So I waved to you in the driveway. I'll say it again: *What do you want?!*" The hair seemed to thicken on those skeleton legs.

"Mr. Tavalier—my folks told me of your loss. I'm terribly sorry. I've been thinking of you."

A longer cessation. "We've never talked."

Ouch. That hurt. Trevin hung in there, saying, "Um, that's why I'm here, Mr. Tavalier—I know we've never talked." He couldn't have been more sincere.

The figure stepped all the way down into the foyer, reaching the door. Undoing the inside lock, it opened ajar. "Is it really you, Trevin?" The tone was now sane.

"Yes, sir, it's really me. I'm sorry about your wife. I wanted to apologize before returning to Chicago."

The inside door swung open further, revealing more of the stranger. The first thing Trevin noticed was the excessive pot belly parting the middle of the outdated bathrobe. Boxer briefs under that. Striped. No face yet. "Chicago?" the paunch asked.

"Yes, sir. That's where I live now."

The lamp above the door burst into being, both startling and blinding Trevin. He hadn't seen the man's arm go for a switch. Squinting through raised arms, Trevin heard the inside door opening. Distorted through faux-glass, Trevin noted a haggard and ancient-looking face coming into view, older than even the Buccinis would be if they were still alive. The streetlight garishly refracted in the square-ish, Coke-bottle eyeglasses, obliterating the actual eyeballs. There was a fierce scowl (what Trevin dubbed a "subway face" in Chicago), carved lines dropping to below the lips and flappy jowls that stopped at a bony jaw line. Trevin's artist-self would have dubbed the image: "Elderly Turkey in a Bathrobe."

He waited for the gun blast.

Knock that shit off.

Slowly, Trevin lowered his hands. The Prodigal Neighbor had returned all these years later to stand before his former target of ridicule.

"Doorbell scared me silly," grumbled Mr. Tavalier.

Nervously, Trevin said, "I'm sure it did. Sorry."

"Stop apologizing."

"Sorry."

"Nobody's rung our doorbell at 1:30 in the morning in the 40 years I've been here."

"I-I went through photo albums," Trevin confessed, thinking quickly. "You were in the background in some, when I was a kid. I wanted to reach out—I'm a changed man."

"From what?"

"Um …" Trevin half-turned, gesturing at the realty sign in the lawn. "You're… leaving."

Mr. Tavalier's voice dropped low. "My brother's selling it for me."

"Brother? I didn't know you had a brother."

"Why would you?"

"Good point," said Trevin, peeling his back from the half-wall, wincing. That's all he needed to do, he thought: reinjure himself. "You might not believe this, sir, but we've been thinking of you. My parents and I both have."

"I got their card and flowers."

Trevin nodded. "Good." Clearing his throat, "They uh… don't know I'm here. I came up with this idea myself."

"And?" Mr. Tavalier was boring a hole in him.

"Maybe I shouldn't have done this …"

After a long, awkward lull, the porch light snapped back off, bringing the night in again. Mr. Tavalier's grumble said, "I'm dealing with things, young man."

"I know you are. That's why… that's …"

Suddenly, Trevin heard the metal twangs springing from the outside screen door. Trevin backed up again. Mr. Tavalier was opening it, and stepping into full entirety—taller than his younger counterpart remembered. The downtrodden-looking man edged his head out, craning his neck in such an uncomfortable position that it looked like it was going to snap. He was apparently trying to see up beyond the eave into the sky. Trevin couldn't help but think of a soft-shelled turtle extending its head as far as it could go. "The stars are lustrous," Mr. Tavalier said.

"Yes, they are."

"We need more rain. I saw shooting stars earlier."

"You did? Constance and I also—"

"So how's life as an artist?" Mr. Tavalier suddenly said.

Trevin was stunned. "How did you know I was an artist?"

He studied what he could: the senior's bulging Adam's apple, the balding dome (no fedora), remaining strands pancaked on the crown. Grief had taken its toll. Also, there may have been a track of recent tears there, staining the old man's cheeks. Mr. Tavalier receded back into the dark.

"You always were," he answered. "Your mother and father were proud of it."

This was crazy, Trevin thought. He was having a conversation with Nutty Geo—Mr. Tavalier—about his art career standing on his porch in the fullness of night. "As of recently... it's been quite the stressful vocation."

"I see. Your mother still works at the library?"

"Part-time. They've cut her hours."

"Haven't checked out a book in years."

Another pause. Trevin felt stymied, nowhere to go. Maybe it was time to go. "I didn't mean to bother you, I'll leave you be ..." He started to walk away, but Mr. Tavalier slumped in the doorway, halting Trevin. "Whoa, you all right there?" He almost reached out for the man.

"Thank you for being kind," Mr. Tavalier answered, brushing it off.

An icy feeling crawled up Trevin's spine. Was the man really fine? "You sure you're okay?"

Mr. Tavalier answered, "I say prayers for her—my Emily."

Trevin heard quiet sobs, then sniffling. Mr. Tavalier wiped his eyes with his bony forearm. When he took a deep breath of air, he exhaled sharply, and almost collapsed. Trevin had to rush in this time, opening the door with his shoulder, placing hands on the man. "Easy, easy. I got you."

This was serious. Trevin was in rescue mode, supporting the fellow like a bag of brittle sticks. Mr. Tavalier uttered a few sounds, then spoke to the ground. "She was beautiful... my Emily... beautiful like the shooting stars ..."

They were half in and half out of the doorway. Trevin got them both indoors, in the foyer. The screen door banged shut, echoing throughout the neighborhood. "Put your arm around me," he said, leading Mr. Tavalier up the strange steps. "You're going to sit."

The same, familiar odor as in the Lakebreeze Healthcare Campus hit Trevin's nostrils. *Same rug sanitizer?* Continuing into the completely hushed living room, realization hit: *I'm inside the house of mystery!* It was a total head rush. The curtains were drawn open, allowing the streetlight's beams to rake in the enormous bay window, sharply cutting heavy shadows everywhere. Where it was dark, the light was cool blue. Where it was illuminated, it was orange radiance—once again.

Trevin had never heard such a silence.

"Put me here, put me here," Mr. Tavalier wheezed, directing them to the lone chair by the foyer steps, its back to the window. There was a Demi-lune table next to it, coasters and magazines piled high.

Trevin set him in it. He'd done this with Nan many times toward the end. "When were you here last, Trevin?" was the odd question.

"I've never been here, Mr. Tavalier."

"Oh."

"Only on your porch—at Halloween. Ages ago."

"That's a shame."

As the man relaxed, Trevin stared around, snagging a last look before he split. This was amazing. Mental pictures clicked away. *Wait until I tell Constance,* he thought, and went for the steps. Again, the frail man stopped him. "Trevin! Can we… talk for a few minutes?" Trevin couldn't believe what was going on: sheer candor from a most unlikely source. "Do you have the time?"

This was unreal. What were the chances of this? Trevin's instincts screamed at him that Cecil needed someone to talk to; that this was its own form of reaching out. But safety first.

"Mr. Tavalier, do you want me to call 911? You're out of breath."

"No, no, no—that's unnecessary." Cheekbones caught the streetlight. Indeed, there were glistening paths, glossy highlights from wetness, filling Trevin with volumes of sympathy.

Trevin's quest had taken him here, he believed. Constance had more or less led him here. And himself. Maybe this was providence. Few breakthroughs came in a lifetime. This could be his. He answered softly, but firmly. "I'll stay, sir. For a while."

"It wouldn't be an imposition to end all impositions?"

Trevin shook his head as surely as he could. "Certainly not."

Mr. Tavalier's neck looked like it was going to snap off, weak muscles holding it up.

CHAPTER 28

⊰ — ⊱

Constance had strayed far beyond the familiar territory she knew as Sweet Briar Road. Now she was outside. She had selected the proper clothing, put them on in haste, and crept out of the house through the front door—the same way Trevin had. But she did not have a key with her. This was blind faith she was going on. And knowledge.

The new streets were as still and quiet as an open desert, no sign of anyone awake anywhere. She had a fairly good idea where her Trevin might be, but there was a need to drift, to explore, to touch the magic of the night. Better to grant the space, she knew, than to intrude. This was way too important of a moment for him. She'd be there when he was through.

Needless to say, she didn't know anything of this new suburban locality. She was pleasantly surprised to see the looping and enigmatic aurora borealis-thing up there slipping through an opening in the night sky, which was filling in with storm clouds. The iridescence sated her with all matters of good and soothing thoughts.

She thought: *But I don't want him taking his eyes off the prize.*

She closed her eyes, taking slow breaths, expanding her lungs. It was a good time to just be. There'd be less opportunity soon.

❄ ❄ ❄

Mr. Tavalier told Trevin not to turn on any lights: He always kept incidentals off when he could. He explained that he was a night owl (like Trevin), and appreciated the ethereal mood the night cast in his house. The streetlight had been put there to do what it was now doing: shining in.

Even the staircase leading upstairs—which Trevin had an angle on sitting on the adjacent sofa—was shrouded in moodily engulfing darkness.

They faced each other. Trevin's mind was spinning, processing everything—the inner sanctum of a suffering soul. He offered to take his shoes off. That wasn't required. The carpeting under Mr. Tavalier's feet was worn. Forty years of slippered feet rubbing the same spot had done a lot of damage. Realizing his belly had been on display, the old man suddenly tightened the belt around his waistline. "My turn to apologize."

"No problem," said Trevin, still trying to convince himself this was real.

"Forgive the dust, too. I haven't cleaned."

What dust? How could Trevin see it? "I wouldn't have known. Your place looks great."

"I need water. Want some?"

This'll be one for the ol' mnemonic repository. "Um, yes, sir."

Mr. Tavalier wobbled to his feet. Trevin went to help, but was ordered to sit by Mr. Tavalier's flapping hand. "I'll be back."

Keeping his head down and wiping his eyes, Mr. Tavalier shuffled around the corner of the wall that blocked Trevin's view into whatever was there—presumably the kitchen. He adjusted the cushions under his lumbar region, perceiving a low, electrical buzz from what had to be the refrigerator. The tension was at an all-time high, different from the fear he'd faced waiting to see what would pop out at him from his apartment that night in Chicago. The clinking of ice in glasses was next, followed by the water filtration system being activated.

Sitting there alone, reality shifting, Trevin believed he could discern the slightest warmth from the streetlight outside. That was probably impossible, but he turned his face to it anyway, closing his eyes, turning his cheeks this way and that—testing it out.

There was *something* there, *some* sensation.

Above him, a ceiling fan hung motionless. Any minute, it could come alive and begin whirling like the loony twig in dad's woods.

The branches were starting to sway out there, out the window.

He thought of his parents and Constance asleep across Sweet Briar, unaware any of this craziness was happening. What would they think of him?—bathed in a crispy ginger glow, waiting on a glass of water from Mr. Tavalier—surely one of the most unusual episodes in his recent, quixotic life. Imagination ran wild.

But there was something in the air. An… attendance.

In the same room, an old piano against the wall to his left was utterly charming. So was the antique mirror above it. There were matching bureaus on each side of the piano, cluttered with ceramic pots. Were they Emily's? Had she thrown them in some ceramic class taken in compensation for not having children? Who were their namesakes, if anyone? Who knew? He had to stop thinking that way.

There was a framed photo of the married couple on the end table to his right. Even in the dark, Trevin could distinguish the happiness exuding from it. Perhaps it was a church photo. Mom and dad had one just like it. Congregations did that.

When Trevin looked the other way, he noticed the grandfather clock. He had not seen it until now with all the overflow. He gasped. Grandfather clocks had always been treasured objects from his past—like he had confessed to Constance at the block party. The paradox was astounding. He remembered many of the old neighbors having them. It had, of course, been there the whole time, standing like a sentinel between the stairs going up and the one's going down into… who knew where? There was a 19th century, Old World illustration of a full moon etched on its face, plated with brass, begging to be studied. Highlights pinged off the metallic surfaces like Nan's wheelchair.

Trevin traipsed over to it and saw that it wasn't working. The pendulum was motionless in its locked-glass base, as lifeless as a dead tree. No ticking. The woodwork was resplendent, ornate carvings from top to bottom. Mr. Tavalier surprised him with the water.

"Like my clock?"

Trevin took the water and backed off, not that he had to. He wanted to chug the first offering, but sipped, his body dehydrated. "It's wonderful. I love grandfather clocks."

"I'm sitting."

Trevin did also, obliging back to his rightful place on the sofa—facing Mr. Tavalier—who motioned at one of the coasters on the coffee table. Trevin snagged one, setting his glass on it.

The mysterious neighbor was again a silhouette, coronas flaring at the rims of his bifocals from the streetlight behind him. "Night—" the shape said, "—brings my only solace."

"I understand the sentiment, sir."

"You can drop the 'sir.' Call me 'Cecil.'"

"Okay… Cecil." Trevin felt awkward saying it, but saluted with his glass and took another sip, ice jingling.

"So …" Cecil initiated, setting his glass down, folding hands. "You're here."

"I am—sir. Cecil, I mean."

"My slipper caught the door."

"The slip earlier?" asked Trevin. "No, it's fine, that didn't worry me. I appreciate you trusting me enough to invite me in."

"I assumed your parents raised a decent person."

No comment. Trevin was already thinking of the mean things he'd done to the man. *Nutty George…* Disgraceful.

"You took a big risk coming over," said the shape.

"I know."

"That young woman in your driveway. Your special lady?"

"Yes. That was Constance Summerlin, my girlfriend. Heh, it's official. I should make up business cards."

No laugh was generated. The shape said, "Been a long time since I've seen someone other than your parents there."

"A trip direly needed."

"That sounded weighted."

Trevin cleared his throat. "Enough of me. Again—Cecil—I can't tell you how sorry I am about your wife."

"Not enough of you. You're an artist in Chicago."

Obviously, the man wanted to steer the chat. "Well," said Trevin, "Chicago has its ups and downs. The city itself is great."

"When you were in high school—at Galileo—there were articles about you in the paper. You won awards."

"You read those?"

"Emily and I always read the papers. Earlier you said your career had become a 'stressful vocation.'"

"The economy, businesses going overseas, technology taking over. It's had a big impact on what I do. I work for advertising agencies—well, *did*. I was laid off."

"Gosh, I'm sorry. Times are hard." Whether he knew it or not, Cecil had crossed his legs, assuming the appearance of a psychiatrist. Or a patient. How could Trevin talk of his woes given what his host had gone through?

"Thank you," Trevin said. "I'll bounce back."

At that, the shape took off his spectacles and set them on the Demi-lune. As he next spoke, the emotional seal started to crack. "It's… been difficult to rest."

"I'm sure."

"Most neighbors never bother to wave. Your parents do." The wind rattled the windows and Cecil shrugged. "We never went out of our way to make that happen. She was agoraphobic, my Emily. She was afraid to go out. It's a legitimate medical condition."

"I know," said Trevin, listening intently.

"She became anxious when venturing out. I had to be right there."

"We didn't think you wanted to be bothered," injected Trevin, suddenly wondering why he'd never thought of that diagnosis—agoraphobia. *What an ass I was.*

Cecil chuckled weakly. "Of course."

"I hope that wasn't harsh."

"It wasn't. I'm sure it was true." Cecil's slippers began sliding back and forth on the carpeting. "We were two square pegs in a round hole—the round hole being the neighborhood. We didn't have children. We tried."

"You don't have to talk about that."

"That's why you're giving me your precious time, right?"

"It's not an effort, Cecil."

And so the exchange of communication flowed. Mostly from Cecil, melting away years of friction and distrust. Trevin learned of Cecil's brother—that he was the only living member of Cecil's family—and that he resided on the other side of town. They were mostly estranged, no reason given. Cecil's parents had been dead for 30 years. Emily's, 20. Emily was also an only child. "God decided for Emily and me to be each other's family," he admitted, infusing extreme melancholy into the information.

Cecil worked for the local brewery for 39 years. Shipping and receiving. His hands kept going to his face, tears filling his eyes again.

Trevin's heart began shattering into a million pieces, the big picture becoming so crushing. A widower was withering before his eyes, turning to an empty husk. Obviously, Cecil's tortured mind kept falling back to his loss.

"We ran out of time, Emily and me," Cecil sobbed. "We thought we had all the time in the world." He excavated a handkerchief from his robe pocket and blew his nose.

Trevin tried changing subjects so he wouldn't choke up. "What about your hedges, Cecil? What are they about? I've always wondered …"

"They're so high, huh?"

"They kind of sent a signal, to be honest."

Sniffle, whimper. "They were for her. I tried to make her feel better. Protected, shielded. There were so many families around, so many children. It was a reminder we couldn't have them. I shouldn't have put them in. Emily eventually told me she thought them rude. Were they rude, Trevin?"

"Um, I don't know. To some, yeah."

The wind was now howling. Trevin was thinking storm. The trees didn't just sway now—they shook—and every mirrored and crystalline object in the room glittered with the streetlight blinking in and out. Cecil leaned forward, burying face in hands. Things were growing precarious.

Trevin couldn't bear seeing this, and he got up and went to the grandfather clock again, keeping his attention off the slow breakdown.

"When did this stop working?" he asked.

"Oh, my… clock. That… was our first anniversary gift to each other. First as husband and wife. The night we bought it, a storm was threatening, pouring by the time we got to the store. Would you believe the damn thing stopped working the very day Emily was diagnosed with cancer?"

Trevin turned, his stomach dropping. "Cancer? Is that what it was? We didn't know. The papers didn't say."

Cecil thumbed tears away. "I've stood there like you, witnessing the clock's power in the middle of the night. The highlights on the metal? The streetlight feeds it. Makes it alive."

"It's… beautiful." *Incredible he'd mention it …*

"I've watched it many times—life is in those pulses. At night it comes alive, if I leave the curtains open. There's communication."

As Trevin focused on the ever-so-gracefully revolving hands moving against the Old Roman numeral clock face, his mind wanted to embrace any happier time. This made him feel guilty he was emotionally abandoning Cecil. Above the time was a half dome. A whimsical, nautical representation, like something out of a fairy tale, spoke to him. The illustration was of the man-in-the-moon smiling down on an antique sea vessel—a schooner—sailing to far horizons. Utterly soothing.

"That changes to a day scene in the daylight hours," Cecil said, fighting back the tears, seeing his guest losing himself to it. "The ship comes our way during the day, the moon becomes the sun. That was our destiny, Emily and me: guided by the heavens." The man's breathing was different. It was now labored.

"Your words are perfect," said Trevin. "I could fall into it. Can't explain why, but an instrument like this makes me yearn for my past."

"There are reasons we collect good memories, throw out the bad ones. The moon's blessing the memories of the sailors. Many of the good neighbors around here are dead."

Trevin felt the beveled wood and shallow indentations, praying he would come out of this night okay. "I know," he said, "I think of them often."

Trevin sat back on the sofa. "Sir, should I call your brother?"

"I miss the originals," said Cecil, putting his hands back to his face again. "Do you remember the Laneskes, next door? They threw those wild clambakes. Everyone seemed to enjoy themselves. There was a lot of drinking. We got invitations a couple of times."

"Why didn't you go?" Trevin dared asking.

"We knew people made fun of us."

Now Trevin felt especially guilty. He and Tommy …

"Marry that woman of yours," Cecil said. "Don't miss out. Marriage is one of life's greatest joys."

"So I've heard."

"How long have you two been dating?"

"Since spring."

"Tell me about her."

This caused Trevin to balk. The man had just lost the love of his life and now he wanted to hear about Trevin's relationship—which was hopefully just taking off. *How could he want to hear about a love so accessible?* But turnabout was fair play, the adage went. "She's about my age," Trevin began. "Five-feet-five, brown hair, freckles all over …"

"No, you're an artist," Cecil asserted. "Do something different. Describe what you feel when you see her coming to you. That's what a true artist would do." One last sniffle and Cecil was locked in.

A twig hit the bay window dead center, raindrops slapped the glass. Definitely, a storm was moving in, and fast. Trevin found his example.

"Well… I remember watching her this past spring, walking toward me in Grant Park. That's in Chicago. We arranged a meeting in the evening, by the lake. I couldn't take my eyes off her, the city in the background. I knew in that instant, that my life was going to become macroscopically better as she entered it. Already, I couldn't imagine days without her. She has this… luminosity, radiating. Unmatched. I feel it most when she smiles at me. They're mini-suns. The way you were looking at the sky earlier, sir? She makes me believe she can take me to them."

The shape must have been impressed. For a moment, he said nothing. Trevin recomposed himself, surprised at how easily the description came. There was a sniff, and Cecil said, "That's the single greatest description of love I've heard outside of the letters my Emily wrote to me."

Trevin abruptly missed Constance, badly. Where was she? *Wait—she's close,* he sensed, *not asleep.* Was she outside? In this approaching storm? He couldn't understand why he now had these notions. But yes, she was… around.

"I didn't mean to get mawkish," he said.

"There's no such thing when you're talking love," said Cecil, slowly rising from his chair. He collected his glass and Trevin's, and shuffled away again the same as before. "I'm in need of a little bite to eat," he said. "Care to join me in the dining room? Just some cookies. I nibble late sometimes. Emily teased me about it."

"Cookies?" Again, ironic with Tommy's talk of cookie-throwing. Trevin walked around the blind corner, seeing the table for two. Yes, only two chairs. He saw his parents' sympathy card. It was atop the hutch beside the table, flowers long wilted in the vase.

That's where they sat. Wonder if that's where they were sitting when Tommy and I nailed their house with our cookies?

Indeed, the kitchen was to the right, behind the living-room wall. Trevin guessed correctly. Cecil was collecting fresh glasses from a cupboard. "Have a seat," he said, back turned. The man again hadn't bothered to turn on a light. A nightlight by the toaster created the sole illumination.

Compelled to push the experience further, Trevin took a chair, facing Cecil. Cecil came back with a handful: the two glasses, a gallon of milk from the refrigerator and a re-sealable package of disc-shaped ginger cookies, distributing them. As he sat, he said, "Shall we? I have a sweet tooth." The labored breathing was worsening.

"Maybe just one," Trevin allowed himself.

Cecil had a hard time opening the bag. Trevin did it for him. Cecil doled out napkins—from the hutch—not referencing the Lambrose flowers. Trevin had a take on the back door, where Mr. Weber's RV was parked not far from there—where the basketball smashed the glass.

Must have been quite the scare. I'm a dick.

Trevin concentrated on the bizarre development. There they were— two neighbors—having lived across the street from each other for years, never knowing one another, now noshing cookies and nipping milk in the dead of night. The sound of crunching became exaggerated, the electric buzz underlying the ridiculous cadence. Poor Cecil was pitiable. His cheeks were puffed out like a hording chipmunk, jowls wobbling.

And the trembling hands …

Into the top drawer of the hutch Cecil went, rummaging through spare batteries and flashlights until he exhumed a bulge of legal-sized envelopes. Letters. Trevin could see handwritten cursive on the fronts. Female. Some were dog-eared. It looked like they'd been in there for some time. "From my Emily," Cecil said, holding them dear, then putting some on the table between them. "I saved them. She wrote many over the years. Closest I have to her still being with me."

Oh, no, thought Trevin with dawning alarm, *he's not going to …*

"Would you like to hear one? To hear what a wonderful person she was?"

Trevin's heart pitted. He wasn't sure if he was ready for this. "Mr. Tavalier, that's personal. You don't have to—"

Cecil removed the brittle rubber bands holding them, choosing one after a shuffle. He let the others slide into a loosened stack on the tabletop. "Please, allow me …"

"That's between the two of you. It's sacred."

The man's droopy eyes bored into Trevin's. Their eyes had adjusted sufficiently to allow for this. "It'll make it more real," Cecil insisted.

Trevin prepared himself. "Okay. I understand."

Cecil went to the next drawer, retrieving a candle and holder, and set it up by his right side, lighting the wick with a match from a matchbook. The flame checkered their faces in orange and red flickers, imitating whatever mystery Trevin held with the nightlights and the doorbells. (All he could think of was light). More sticks, sloppy leaves drummed the windows.

Removing the epistle from the crisp envelope, Cecil said, "Even though we were married, she liked writing me letters. I'd come home, find an envelope at this table. My Em was a hopeless romantic."

Trevin shifted in his chair, already uncomfortable.

Cecil adjusted his bifocals, glazing the first lines. Then, he read aloud: *"My Dear Sweet Cecil. I want to thank you for our lovely evening last night. It was so thoughtful of you to take me to dinner at my restaurant of choice. You remembered I wanted to try it out. I felt like we were on our first date again. In fact, I pretended we were."*

No, this wasn't right. Trevin bristled, "On second thought, Mr. Tavalier—"

A placid hand went up. "Trevin. Again. Please." Trevin ground his molars.

"I never let on, my love, but I pretended it was years ago, when we were young. Do you remember how nervous we were then? I wanted every detail of that first date to come back. And it did, sweetie. We had our whole lives in front of us. Even though we're both shy, we found happiness together in this cold world. I never told you this, but on that first outing so many moons ago, half-way through dinner, I prayed we'd end up together—as husband and wife. I didn't want to scare you off so I didn't say anything at the time. No matter what was to come, if we were together, I knew everything would be fine. And you know what? It is! Cecil, I want to make our happy memories live forever so that we can live in them forever. It will be our Heaven. I want you to know, my darling husband, that my love for you will never die, even when we no longer are in physical form. If our happiest moments together is what the Afterlife is like, that'll be perfect. Your loving wife, Em."

Cecil folded the letter, placed it back in its envelope, and set it with the stack, tapping it for good measure. Tears were threatening to burst again as he lowered forehead to knuckles, clasping hands as if in prayer.

"That was a lot to share, Cecil." Then, thinking perhaps a touch of humor might be in order, Trevin tagged on, "That must've been some restaurant."

It worked. Guffaws erupted—half crying, half laughing. But that was okay. Cecil lifted his head as the tears tumbled, and he became delighted at his guest's wit. "Good one, young man."

Trevin handed over napkins. Cecil balled them to his face as the mirth turned to blubbering. "M-make the m-most of it… while you can …" He put away the envelopes, then the cookies and milk. Rinsing out the glasses in the sink, Cecil carefully went to dry each one. This was when Trevin had had enough, and he thumped the table top lightly.

"Mr. Tavalier, I have a confession to make, and it paradoxically involves cookies."

Cecil turned, dishtowel in hands. "What in the world are you talking about?"

"This is going to sound silly, but hear me out. Tommy Porch and I threw cookies at your house—like the ones we just ate. I can't believe how things are overlapping."

"You… you threw c-cookies at my house?"

"Chocolate chips. I've wanted to apologize for that for years. Both of us threw them, at the same time so it would be even. We did it a couple times. It was something to do, we were bored. I apologize from the bottom of my heart."

"You threw cookies at my house?"

Trevin felt terrible. "Yes." The "nutty neighbor" wasn't so nutty. The man was registering all this, and he was mulling over its implications.

"W-why would you do that?" Cecil asked, wiping the tears away.

"Throwing was a fixation," Trevin answered sheepishly. "Remember—we were baseball freaks. I'm coming clean. We figured with you we'd never get caught; you'd never say anything. How shameful is that?"

"That's your confession?"

"Did you hear them hitting the house?"

"No, Trevin, I didn't hear them hitting the house. Not that I remember. But if it makes you feel better... I forgive you. Don't do it again."

"I won't."

"I'm trying to sell my house," Cecil said, putting the glasses back in the cupboard, rearranging the others. "I don't want cookie all over it. You can tell Mr. Porch, too. He always was a little shit."

Trevin smirked. "Next time I see him, sir."

There was the weirdest sensation coming over the scene. Trevin felt strangeness again, like someone was purifying the ambiance around them. Trevin concentrated. He was sharing a moment in time—with an important person from his past—that no other two humans could.

Was Constance out in the storm? Lightning flashed the sky. Thunder followed.

Cecil appeared to grow tired. All the crying had wiped him out. Finishing his work by the sink, he shuffled back to the table for two, where he was going to sit. Trevin wondered what they were now going to talk about. It was when Cecil reached the table, and set one hand on it to lower himself into his chair, that he slipped—and went to the floor—catching his forehead on the edge!

Smash!

"Oh my God!" Trevin rushed in, rescuing the senior in seconds, holding him, helping him. "Mr. Tavalier—are you okay? I got you! I got you!"

The poor man held his cranium, a welt already forming. The entire table had nearly come down. The candle was wobbling, flame shaking.

Trevin fretted, got the man back to his chair. He was going to call 911, and said so. Mr. Tavalier stopped him frantically, not wanting to have anything to do with that. "No, Trevin, no! For God's sake, I'm all right—I just lost my balance. Don't call 911, let go of me!"

But Trevin kept gripping, instinctually. "You might have really hurt yourself!"

"Don't call anyone, damn it! Can't a guy trip?"

"Not like that!"

Trevin blew out the candle and made sure every object was steady, moving everything out of the way. The bickering and fussing continued, the two men talking over one another. Trevin had a supportive hand around Cecil's back. That, Cecil allowed. God, what a horrible thing to see …

The huffing… the wheezing …

"Just let me sit, Trevin… Oh my Lord …"

"Mr. Tavalier, there's nothing wrong with going to the hospital. I can take you."

"What did I just say? No ambulance! No hospital! Just get me some damn water!"

Trevin obliged, leaving the man for a minute. It felt like a sin. Trevin didn't know where the paper towels were, and tore through the other cabinets until he found them. If there was blood coming, he'd be ready. Thankfully, it wasn't necessary. Cecil's slumped form was something to monitor, though. He told his elder to sip. Slowly.

"Stop coddling me, boy! What is it with people your age?"

But this didn't calm Trevin. He'd just seen an anguished gentleman pouring his guts out, then cracking his head and spilling to the floor. And earlier—at the door—Cecil was wobbly! Mr. Tavalier's skeletal shoulders jutted like craggy peaks under the dingy robe.

"How about your brother?" Trevin suggested. No way was he going to desert this man until knowing he was safe and sound. "How about if I call him?"

Another mistake. Cecil blew up, barking like he'd been asked to walk the plank. He just wanted help getting on his feet. Trevin did as ordered.

"Cecil, I'm at a loss. What do you want now? Want me to leave?"

"No," replied Cecil, voice weakening. "I need to walk this off—let's go on a tour."

CHAPTER 29

Constance was facing west when the real gusts kicked up, taking her hair for a tumble. The raindrops followed, pelting her. Through a break in the churning clouds, she caught glimpses of a few shooting stars cutting sharp paths across the night sky. She imagined being completely consumed in their beauty.

She was still blocks from her man, working her way back to him. She had been continuing the wander, soaking up more intentions from the sleeping souls around her. It's something she did. It was something she loved. It was something she had to do. The people's memories around her were currently dormant: Subconsciousness floating free; lifetimes carried as cottonwood seeds, lifted by time, emotion.

The side streets around Sweet Briar were also empty, sacrosanct. Not one traveler had been spotted. Trevin would love this if he'd been out with her now, in this environment. But she knew he had more important things to do. There wasn't even the sound of the distant traffic he'd taught her to ardently appreciate.

A car came into view from around a corner, pulling into a driveway one house away. Music could be heard wafting from the radio—alternative rock, early '90s. Constance was on the sidewalk, and stopped to watch. The second-hand clunker shut off its engine, the music following suit moments later. The storm ramped up, but a tumult had not yet fallen.

As the young man and woman stepped out—mostly likely in their early twenties—they were silhouetted in black against the block's row of functioning streetlights. Constance could make out their hair also tussling. She tried to identify with them internally, get in touch with what they were experiencing. Both had attractive, lithe bodies under their flapping and clinging light clothes, the wind making the scene all the more romantic. They had not yet seen the lone woman staring from 40 yards away. Seeing the two hang on one another at the front grill made her think of things she'd never dared before.

They must be arriving home from a date, she thought. The male slumped on the hood, wrapping his arms around the female and pulling her into him. As she fell into his embrace, she kissed him: Two lovers in a mating ritual. Constance knew that kiss. Trevin planted those on her and made her burn with strange desire. Constance longed for one right now, against her more prudent judgment. She heard the couple laugh, a sound mattering to them.

Constance took more steps. That's when the strangers saw her and froze. This made Constance hesitate further, and she heard the young woman nervously inquire into who she was. The body language was tense, the girlfriend squeezing instinctually for protection.

"I have no idea," the young man answered quietly, emphatically.

Constance considered the surprise from their perspective. All they were seeing was a sudden appearance of a lone lady, out of place in the heart of night, gawking at them like she wanted something from them. She'd better proceed with discretion.

The boyfriend spoke up, authority in his voice: "Everything all right?" The sound traveled well despite the howling wind.

Constance responded with a buttery tone. "Yes. Everything's fine." She felt the first heavy drops finally popping her, cool in temperature.

"Better get inside, ma'am," the young man suggested. "The sky's going to erupt."

This attention was met with disapproval from the girlfriend, who obviously didn't want her boyfriend running a dialogue with the stranger. Constance saw her whispering grievances, trying to get him to walk away. *Don't worry, dear,* Constance projected onto her. *He's merely showing concern.*

Again, Constance scanned the houses, their windows dark, shades sealing out the world—appreciating the portals nonetheless. She considered the fine people she'd never know, the happy memories she'd never hear. Other beneficiaries would profit from those. She called out above the window to the fused couple: "Are you happy?"

"Excuse me?" the guy called back, straightening. Now there may have been a tad of distrust.

"Are your lives filled with happiness so far?" Constance said, knowing she was stepping over a boundary. "Do you prosper from your past?" She couldn't help it. The need to know was like that of an addict needing a fix.

The girl tugged her boyfriend away, trying to start him up the driveway. She wanted to go in.

Surprisingly, the young man hung in. "Babe, she might need something—" Constance could hear him say, "—she might be in trouble."

"No," said Constance, feeling the rain hitting her face. "I'm not in trouble. I only want to tell you to make this time count. Your love together will matter."

That did it. The frightened mouse pulled him harder up the driveway, shushing him as he protested. She even reached into his pocket and pulled the keys out, the jangling sounds cutting through the racket. When they got to the porch, he said to Constance, "Better get inside, lady! Take care of yourself!"

Then they went inside, slamming the door. Constance even heard the lock engage.

"Thank you," she called out—matching his kind timbre—suddenly feeling rather bewildered, not understanding why she had done that. They weren't *her* business. She blamed it on Trevin's kisses… and unfamiliar affairs of the heart.

The real storm started. Loose twigs and leaves caught her sandaled feet, then somersaulted around them, blowing off into oblivion—like in the forest preserve, where the water in the stream rushed around the eddy. Everything was tumbling into a flux: A new history was approaching.

CHAPTER 30

———◄ ►———

"Keep moving your feet."

"I'm not an invalid, Trevin, you don't have to hold me."

Cecil was peeved, and removed his flabby bicep from the young man's guard. They'd gone on the tour of the first floor and were now at the precipice of the stairwell, preparing to descend into the darkness of whatever came next. Trevin considered they were standing at the mystical "heart" of the house—much like his parents' at the same, general area. As overly dramatic as it was, he was up for the adventure.

"Sure you don't want to turn on a light?" Trevin asked.

"We'll do that down there," Cecil wheezed. "Please, she's nearest me in the dark. Let's keep going."

Cecil reached for the hand railing. Trevin braced, holding the man's arm again, only at the elbow. This time Cecil allowed it. They found their way down, one step at a time. This wasn't a basement, but an entertainment room. The overhead snapped on, filling the half-underground lair containing dated furniture with dazzling light, blinding them both. Cecil groaned, covering his eyes. Trevin had to squint painfully through the back of his fingers. Slowly, the ceiling dome—the source of the light—came into view. The light in the ceiling radiated spires in all directions, hitting the four walls in spikes. The wood paneling surrounding them was the same 1970s leftover as in his parents' family room. There was a front-screen projection television in an enormous shelving unit, taking up nearly the entire wall on one side.

"Wow," exclaimed Trevin, beholding it. "How old is that thing?"

"Old enough." Cecil pointed around, catching his breath, doling out the verbal specifics. "That's the laundry room back there. I also have a storage room to the right, and the steps going up to that door lead to the garage."

The room had a musty odor. The hand-cranked windows probably hadn't been opened in some time. Trevin looked at the strange steps. *So that's how they sneaked in and out all those years without anyone seeing,* he deduced sneakily, punishing himself for thinking so callously. *Odd design. Their secret entrance.* "Looks like you have everything down here," he said aloud.

"This was where I enjoyed my shows," Cecil retorted. "There's nothing to enjoy anymore. Mostly it was me in this room, except when Emily did laundry. She also did the cooking. Italian, French, good old American meatloaf. Tried my hand at it, but she made me stick to my lawn work."

"Speaking of such… Have you been eating?"

"I do okay. She had some recipe books."

Trevin felt extreme sorrow destroying him again. He couldn't believe he was experiencing this first-hand. To keep his mind off his heart breaking, he looked around, and spotted a framed photo by the television that looked intriguing. "May I?"

Cecil gestured him over. Trevin got closer.

It was another portrait: The married couple in a vastly earlier stage of life—a cliché pose from that period—its color faded with age. Both were in a three-quarter stance, looking off-frame into space. Cecil was standing—wearing a suit with enormous lapels, tie as wide as a bus—hair dark as were the ridiculous mutton chop sideburns. Below him sat his beloved Emily. She was smiling under a bouffant hairdo, plaid dress and cat-eye glasses glaring. Cecil had one hand on her shoulder as she held it back with the hand closest to it.

Trevin was ashamed to think it almost cartoonish. "Lovely," he said instead, turning to see Mr. Tavalier removing his bifocals, rubbing his eyes—lids as thick as chopped liver.

"It comes at moments like this …" Cecil said quietly, mind venturing off. Trevin didn't know if he was being addressed directly. But he listened. "I was sitting on this sofa—years ago—when Emily raced home from her errands. I'd been off, taking care of taxes. Something was strange in her voice when she called from that payphone. By the time she got home, she was a wreck. I asked what happened. She was getting over a cold, you see, she'd been weak. At the shopping plaza, she'd started crying uncontrollably behind the wheel of the car after experiencing a sudden daydream—a flash. Remember, she didn't go out by herself often. She flew home to make sure I was safe. She said she suddenly saw us lost in a wooded place, a dense forest. We'd become separated and wandered off on different paths, we couldn't find each another. She was calling me over and over. I couldn't hear. She panicked. That's when the poor girl snapped out of it, made the call from the payphone and refused to tell me what was going on until my arms were around her. She burst into tears as I jumped up from this sofa. I was confused, but held her tight until all the fear was gone. I played it off to her pills. That was one of the most important moments I had with her: making sure she was calmed that day, protecting her, wiping away those tears."

Cecil's voice trailed off, and he stared at the rough carpeting under them, the recollection still alive and vivid. "Later we laughed. That was the kind of girl she was—always caring for me."

Trevin was stunned into silence. Cecil left the room, shuffling toward the steps leading up to the garage door, past the laundry and storage room. Trevin eventually caught up as the man's hand was on the door knob. What in the world was he doing?

"Mr. Tavalier?"

Cecil unlocked the door and stepped into the hot, muggy and very dark garage, wandering around the mystery sedan and making his way to the garage windows, where he stared out into the beleaguered street. The smell of gasoline and insecticide immediately hit Trevin's nose as he followed after him, beginning to worry. The howling was much louder here, rattling the thin panes. Sharp, shivering shadows cut about the tight spacing. Once again, it was the streetlight providing the sole source of illumination. Trevin became aware of the gallons of used house paint, the toolboxes, the weed killer, rakes, ladders, shovels, a lawn sprayer and a snow blower. A workbench was in the rear, household clutter everywhere.

"Mr. Tavalier? Why are we out here?" He bumped into the car.

Cecil stared at the storm like he wanted to merge with it. "Do you… believe we'll be with our loved ones again?"

Trevin thought it over. In his view, the poor man had become like a vulnerable child, seeking validation of a most treasured fairy tale. "Well… Constance certainly believes that. We've had that discussion. I certainly hope it's true—it's the unknown."

The sky bundled and swelled. The rain hammered in sweeping sheets. Cecil backed up, then turned and crouched, looking into the passenger side of his sedan, where a passenger would sit. Trevin caught soft whispering. What was this? The man was talking as if someone was there. His inflection was super-congenial.

"Cecil?"

"Right where? Oh, I see. Of course. I will, dear… thank you for telling me. Take your time, take your time …"

This was not promising. Trevin couldn't forget that this was a predicament he'd gotten himself into. Was it time to involve the medical authorities—or his brother—after all? What mattered was the safety of his misinterpreted acquaintance. He got no more than two steps closer when Cecil straightened to him. "Did you lose a basketball here?"

Trevin halted. "What?"

"When you were a teenager. Did you lose a basketball? It broke our window."

A chill ran up Trevin's spine. "As a matter of fact… we did."

Cecil muttered a final something into the passenger window, hooked a forefinger Trevin's way—indicating he wanted the young man to follow him—and they returned to the sanctity of the house, turning on extra lights as they made their way to a broom closet inside the laundry room.

There was a special box behind the usual brooms, mops and buckets. Cecil asked for Trevin's help moving things aside to get at it. In Trevin's hands, something clunked inside the box. He dismissed what he thought it could be as Cecil practically yanked it from him, setting it atop the washing machine to start stripping back the stubborn cellophane tape holding the lids closed.

Cecil boldly presented his sympathetic new ally the dimpled and deflated orange rubber sphere from childhood—the basketball in question. The elderly man stared with newfound attention as Trevin's stunned face folded over, turning the object slowly, reading the signatures in black marker: the Morneau boys, Mark Weber, Tommy Porch, himself.

"Holy shit …"

Cecil went to chuckle, but coughed, spilling into wheezes again. "S-she… reminded me… I had that."

"Who?"

"Emily. She told me to give it to you."

Trevin had to sit. There was a wooden footstool by the dryer. He plopped onto it, basketball in hands, dropping head and shoulders. Did Cecil really speak to her in the car? Whatever the case, he doubted things could get more fantastic. "Come morning," Trevin offered, "I'm going to be permanently altered."

Cecil was proud of his accomplishment. But he couldn't stop coughing, and he said he had to return to the living room; the tour was over. Trevin set the ball into the box and escorted him, feeling his brain slinking more and more into the surreal. When they got back to the original setting, Cecil now stared into the grandfather clock's enigmatic face—keeping his nose an inch from the man-in-the-moon illustration.

"Was that really Emily, Cecil?" Trevin asked from behind him. "I haven't seen that ball in 28 years."

In front of his eyes, Cecil was transforming—metaphorically speaking—into a poor imitation of Fred Astaire: loosening hands and feet, shaking legs, swinging waist from side to side, limbering up. Despite the forehead knock, he appeared to be willing himself into a really good mood. "Placing" his thin arms around a phantom dance partner, he paused for dramatic effect, and announced: "Women are creators, Trevin. Nurturers. They make the universe spin on its axis."

"Spin? Like circles?"

Cecil began waltzing about the living room to imaginary music, careful to avoid the obstacles in his path. Where the hell did this sudden athleticism and energy come from? Trevin tried to distract him. "About that basketball, sir. Let me again apologize. We got carried away at the Webers. Yes, it was us who broke your window. Mr. Weber paid for it. Do you remember?" But Cecil was somewhere else—graceful, coordinated, happy. "Mr. Tavalier, maybe you shouldn't do that; you could get dizzy. Did you ever consider a bereavement group? I volunteer at this nursing home in Chicago. Lots of seniors—"

"We'd dance—" Cecil said, interrupting, "—in this room. She loved to. In the dark. We used the record player."

Trevin thought of Constance (who was nearing), and how she took advantage of moments like this; going with the flow, coaxing information out of people spiraling off on flights of fancy. What else could he do? "Tell me about it then, Cecil. Tell me about your dance memories."

The waltzer sashayed around the room, continuing to avoid furniture—no easy task. The streetlight's radiance juxtaposed with the otherwise cool blue veil made Cecil look like a dream image. Thunder boomed, lightning flashed up the room. The old man was unaware of any of it. This was getting tricky.

"I'd dip her. Like this …" Cecil pantomimed the move. "We had the windows open. We loved the sounds of the neighborhood before the neighbors: The crickets, the distant traffic on Mt. Read Boulevard. Don't get us wrong, Trevin, Emily and I cared about our neighbors—we did. We wished them well in our own right. We prayed for them. I wonder if they see us now?"

"What's got you wondering, Cecil?"

"They're in our memories… staying with us, influencing our days…"

Again, Mr. Tavalier nearly stumbled. Again, Trevin nearly shot in. The "music" ceased, and so did Mr. Tavalier's inducement. Finishing the engagement, he bowed in appreciation—with a hand across his heart to his "partner"—and sunk back into his solemn self. Trevin stood by. The labored breathing returned, and it was apparent Cecil's knock on the forehead bothered him again. He quietly declared: "My bed calls me …"

Trevin moved in. "Of course, Cecil, sure. We'll get you into bed, then I'll leave."

He expected an argument, but there was none. Cecil nodded, made the move toward the upstairs stairwell. "Nice to have met you, Trevin."

CHAPTER 31

———◄   ►———

Squinting against the storm, Constance was making her way to the Tavalier house, using the hedges as a navigational device, staying on them to guide her in.

* * *

As Trevin discovered, the light that came on most nights was indeed the bedroom—Cecil's bedroom. Top floor, right side (from the perspective of his parents' house). Shepherding Cecil in after the man widened the already ajar door and hit the switch; he couldn't believe what he saw next. Cecil had created a shrine to his deceased wife using photographs of the two of them throughout their lives, starting from before they were married through what looked to be only recently. Scarcely a square inch of space was available. Stripped photo albums were sprawled on the carpeting, their ringlets gaping open like baby robins waiting to be fed. Hardly a snapshot was left on the observable pages. Cores of used tape had been discarded throughout the room, a dispenser tipped on its side. The memorial took up all four walls, from floor to ceiling. Trevin saw the step-ladder used to reach the high spots.

Cecil made no attempt to soften the impact. Disengaging from Trevin's proximity, he shuffled to his queen-sized bed in the center of the room, turned, and dropped onto it, sitting. The covers were pulled back already. "Thank you for your assistance," he said.

"No… problem."

To Trevin's right, as he faced them, were the oldest photographs— ancient black-and-white similes of the boy Cecil and the little girl Emily.

Separate snaps. Obviously, these were taken before they knew each other. Some were their teenage years, or barely twenty. Trevin saw their families, what little there was. Turning clockwise like a slow-moving carousel, the images grew newer in chronology until the couple appeared in the same frames together: probably their mid-twenties. A closet broke the mosaic, returning to show the Tavalier's marriage years. Trevin saw the house being built in the early briar patch, and eventually, the hair turned white—ending back at square one.

"Life-wallpaper," Trevin mumbled to himself: the perfect analogy.

Only then could he appreciate the rest of the décor: the mark of a woman's touch. This was a big bedroom with feminine furniture. The frilly curtains hid the brewing storm. No loose clothes, no television. The bed was flanked by his-and-her end tables, matching lamps on each. Two cedar dressers were opposite the bed, both with slickly carved facades matching the clock downstairs. The only thing offsetting the symmetry was Emily's elegant dressing table and make-up bench on her side of the room. Doilies and perfume bottles still sat atop it, its ovoid mirror no longer reflecting her likeness. Suddenly, Trevin became self-conscious at his fascination.

"Sorry for staring," he said.

"I let you in here."

"How long… have you been at this, sir?"

"A long time," Cecil answered after a long pause. "Since after the funeral. I'm leaving it like this, even though people will come in to look at the house."

Trevin was going to question the wisdom of doing that, but who was he to comment?

Cecil removed the ridiculous slippers, and turned on the lamp on his nightstand. "You c-can shut that overhead," he said, voice cracking.

Trevin did as ordered. Now only the lamp lit the room, embracing them both in somberness. Trevin felt like he was violating a consecration, as if by staying too long he'd threatened the state of Cecil's delicate soul, perhaps interfering with whatever connection he had with the beyond. After all, his amazing collage was crafted with the deepest of emotions, the most personal of intentions. Trevin did not wish to dishonor that.

"I wake up …" Cecil said, massaging his head knot, wattle under his chin jiggling, "… in the middle of the night. I work on this."

"Is it finished?"

"Maybe."

"You've surrounding yourself with her," Trevin conceded. "That's understandable." Then, not knowing what else to say: "Is there anything else I can get for you, Mr. Tavalier?"

Cecil shook his head. "No, thank you."

The newly appointed caregiver stayed on the diorama, processing the workload one last time. "Does it help?" he chanced.

Cecil said, "I don't know. Yet."

Yet? What did that mean? The building sadness was crushing Trevin's chest, watching and listening to all this, tears threatening in his own eyes. His throat was certainly burning. "Thank you for letting me see it, Cecil."

Cecil removed his bifocals—set them on the nightstand, on top of a Bible—his naked eyes revealing sockets so sunken that they seemed to go on forever. "I miss her so."

Trevin was still waiting for that break to leave. "You try sleeping now. No more scares hitting your head."

"I gave the kids a scare. On the block. They hated me."

"They didn't hate you, Cecil."

The elder wiggled his toes on the carpeting, alerting Trevin to the fact he never took his own shoes off—this whole time! He looked down, making sure he hadn't tracked any mud or dirt into the room. Thankfully, he hadn't. Trevin took a deep breath and sighed. "Any ideas of where you're going, Cecil, after you sell the house?"

"Anywhere."

"Offers?"

"No. Market's terrible."

"I'll miss you," Trevin said.

Cecil shook his head in doubt. "No, you won't."

"Cecil!" Thinking of the right joke: "We shared cookies and milk together tonight, come on." But there was no laugh.

Instead, Cecil pulled the album closest to him using his feet, picked it up, and thumbed through the pages where a few untouched snaps remained. There was a loose photograph, and Cecil took it out, looked at it. He held his hand out for his young guest to snag it. "Look at this one. You'll find it interesting."

Tentatively, Trevin once more took something too sacred to abuse. The photograph was jarring. It must have been decades old, taken no doubt by Emily. She'd been standing in the living room, aiming the camera out the large bay window into the front yard, where her husband was striding by proudly with the lawnmower, cutting the grass. Cecil was waving to her. In the background—through the much-shorter hedges at the end of the driveway and into Emerald Lane—was an extremely young Trevin Lambrose and Tommy Porch, both with baseball gloves and caps, ready for dad to hit the baseball to them! And both were unaware they'd been captured on film.

"Unbelievable," exclaimed Trevin, recording the irony. "I've told Constance about these days playing ball with dad. You caught us …"

Cecil was getting ready to cry.

Trevin handed the photo back with tender loving care. "That was a long time ago. So close, yet so far away."

"That'll do."

Cecil returned the piece to the album, set it delicately on the floor, and climbed into bed, adjusting the sheet loosely over his bony legs. Trevin was accustomed to seniors doing this: It happened all the time at Lakebreeze. Trevin said, "I can check on you tomorrow. I'll leave my cell number in case—"

"You should go, Trevin, I'm all right. Don't worry about me. I'm a clumsy fool."

"I still—" Trevin never finished his sentence.

Cecil brought his hands up and covered his face. Then, there was a scary eruption of tears, the hardest yet. The poor man mewled, crunching his face, gritting teeth. The sound was terrible and fierce, and it certainly gutted Trevin to witness it. There was a fresh box of tissues on Emily's dresser. Trevin ran for it, catching a glimpse of the hairbrush by the mirror.

Emily's hair was still in the bristles!

"Here!" Trevin said, handing the box over, watching the man pull a half dozen out, flooding them with sobs. Trevin didn't know what to do. He fixated on the clownish cowlick sticking up from Cecil's hair as the pathetic man brought his hands down from his head. The pity Trevin was imploding with was equivalent to an avalanche. He tried shushing Mr. Tavalier, letting him know everything would be okay—to just go to sleep. What more could be done?

Trevin would keep his word and return the following morning, regardless of what his parents or Constance would ask, insisting on getting the brother involved. That's the way it had to be! This was stark reality, straight across the jaw.

"R-reach in her drawer," Cecil blubbered, sucking breath. "There's a letter."

"I'm not going to reach in—"

"Do it! Please! I need it! She wrote it after she knew she was dying."

This was insane! Again, Trevin did as ordered. Perfect penmanship on the envelope. Cecil blew his nose, trembled to get his bifocals back on. He almost knocked the nightstand lamp over adjusting the light. Nonetheless… *My sweetheart, I love you with my whole heart,* he read through weeping. *"Aside from my disease—which we've discussed at length—there's something else vital to share with you."*

"Mr. Tavalier, stop! Please."

"When I'm gone from physical form, I want you to understand that I will still be with you. I wish I had clearer information—I just know this to be true. You'll be seeing me, my dear, I promise."

Cecil was soaking the sheets around him. He strained looking at Trevin, the letter dropping to his heaving chest. "She never lied to me, Trevin, she never lied. I have to believe this! I have to!" His face had contorted in anguish.

Trevin was simultaneously touched beyond words, and terrified. "You honor her, sir. Nothing you've told me will leave this room. She's not suffering now. Hold onto that."

"Want to know how I honored her? I bought a gold ring for our 50th anniversary and lost it before I gave it to her!"

"Sleep, Cecil. Don't talk." This was getting frightening.

"It would've meant the world to her. I searched high and low, but couldn't find it. I even searched the garage, the lawn, the garden."

"Wait—the *garden*?" That must have been what Cecil was looking for that day, when Trevin looked out his bedroom window and saw him digging in the soil with the toe of his shoe. The gold ring.

"On the side of my house! Thought I'd dropped it watering the flowers. Always kept it on me so it would be a surprise." Cecil dug the nails on his free hand into the mattress, emotionally beating himself up; crying, crying. "I was so afraid to lose it. I did anyway! Even called Streets and Sanitation—asked if it turned up in the garbage. I never had the heart to tell her …"

Talk about memories! Trevin was witnessing what explosive ones could do. "It's all right, Cecil, she forgives you. She—"

"She never did anything to deserve her suffering."

"I'm sure she didn't, sir."

"She saw the ring in the store and fell in love with it. She never suspected I would buy it. She never knew I had it. People run and gun, leaving a wake of disaster everywhere they go. I lost it, I lost it. I kept looking for it!" Cecil rolled on his side, away from Trevin, building to inconsolable moans and fits.

Trevin tarried at the doorway. "I must be leaving," he was saying, overloading at the network of frozen moments cocooning him in. He willed good thoughts Cecil's way; hating the fact he was abandoning the senior. He ripped himself into the hallway, eyes demanding to reset to the dark. He couldn't see downstairs. All he could hear was the relentless weeping; Emily's name being warbling over and over. It was dreadful. Trevin couldn't imagine losing someone so close. The drive to cherish inflated his mind, and he placed both hands to the walls for balance, going to take his first step into the stairwell. Suddenly the lamp went off—plunging in a greater abyss—and Trevin almost toppled down, grabbing the handrails, almost pulling them out of the drywall.

Son of a …!

There was something there! At the bottom of the landing, in the living room. Inert and massive, blocking his path at the juncture. The storm was really knocking around the streetlight, creating that zoetrope, light-and-flicker effect again. It was extremely disorienting.

Trevin's heart was in his throat. He risked another step, scrutinizing.

It was the grandfather clock!

What the hell?

Somehow, it had moved—or been moved—several feet from where it was, confronting him with its broad backside, daring him to squeeze by. Trevin's brain flip-flopped in a tailspin, grasping for sanity. Who was down there, and why had they done this? He could barely see past its bulk into the living room, where it was difficult to see. Vibrating shadows made ice creep through his veins. Instinctively, he looked back, called out. "Cecil?" Nothing but the tortured sounds of the sobbing. "There's no one in the house, is there? Does your brother have a key?"

Nothing.

Ultimately, the crying ebbed. Rattled breathing indicated Cecil might be passing out. Trevin had terror pulsing his being, reminded of the night Brian Annarez jumped him. Now he had to protect his newfound friend. An interminable hush fell over everything, the smell of the clock's cedar breaching his nostrils. He crouched, seeing past. Both the sofa he'd been sitting in and Cecil's favorite chair had been pulled a couple of feet from the wall. So had the piano at the far end. And the bureaus.

Whatever this was, Trevin prayed it was benevolent.

A riotous clap of thunder caused him to jump, falling onto his posterior, sliding him down to the back of the grandfather clock, where it stopped him flat. The hammering on the overhang outside from the rain sounded like a thousand pelting sticks.

He got up, warily inching around the unknown, ears on hyper-alert, listening for anything that would tip him off. His abdominal muscles tightened like cables, making sure no one was going to leap out at him. Once he made it around safely—to the "lit" side—Trevin examined the clock's grained surface for fingerprints, using the lightning sparking up the house to see by. He didn't find any. He checked the kitchen. Nothing. Downstairs in the entertainment room. Zilch.

The grandfather clock held the answer. Trevin stood with his back to the living room, hands on hips (like his dad), scrutinizing every square inch of its façade—the illustration, the schooner, the man-in-the-moon. Trevin looked at the carpeting. No drag marks. The indentations remained where the giant object had pressed for decades. Each reflective household object was giving off highlights—jewels shouting for attention. The buzz from the refrigerator sounded louder than before.

The real moon broke through the storm and blasted in through the bay window, brightening the clock face to an unnatural degree, an azure glow of eerie iridescence shifting reality.

Trevin got his face closer to it, the highlights branding his soul with meaning. There was a sensation of things beginning to fit together, an arrival of a transcendental truth. He became acutely aware that someone was behind him who hadn't been there a second ago. A rush of serenity replaced the fear, calming his terror. He rotated from the cosmorama, ready to encounter whoever—or whatever—was there.

Emily Tavalier.

Trevin's world would never be the same.

Emily, appearing as flesh-and-blood, solid as the walls containing her, was as Trevin had viewed her in the church photograph with her husband—impossibly young, wearing dated clothing from those times, outlandish and passé eyewear on the bridge of her nose as Cecil still wore. She stood motionless in the center of the room, poised—petite hands clasped at her waist, one high-heeled shoe in front of the other—staring at Trevin (or through him) toward the ascending staircase.

There seemed to be nothing but extraordinary kindness in that relaxed face.

The gargantuan shock in Trevin's brain was replaced by a shattering calm. Every abstract concept and notion of God sprang to mind. Whatever she was—she was saintly. Truth be told, he half-expected this turning. This was a deliberate unveiling, an event, meant to be witnessed. An alignment had been made. Seconds seemed like hours. There was nothing to do but reach out in thought.

Mrs. Tavalier, he communicated to her without moving his lips; the thunder and lightning booming all around them. *You couldn't have arrived at a better time.*

Hello, Trevin Lambrose, came back an inner understanding, no movement anywhere on her person.

His senses began folding inward, into a realm where no living person had before treaded, knowing the returned greeting originated from far beyond any boundary of space and time. A thousand questions, insecurities, fears and hopes fired across his synapses, but he dared not ask one. Emily was immaculate, now shining from within, skin becoming so superlative there was not a hint of a wrinkle or imperfection. Nor did she have a single shadow anywhere on her body, even as the wildly fluctuating lighting in the house took on an ominous atmosphere.

But again… Trevin was not afraid.

When she took a step forward, he stepped back. But it was more from reflex he did so.

Trevin conveyed gratitude. Emily did not communicate back. Yes, she was seeing past him to the staircase. Trevin turned briefly, getting his bearings on the grandfather clock. He did not want to bang into it. When he turned back, she'd instantly closed the distance, like a jump cut in film. He flinched. She was a foot away, just to his side. Now she was disconnected, exuding an impression of complete, ethereal concentration. Maybe she *was* ethereal concentration.

Had she heard her husband's crying?

For the first time in what Trevin had been told was years, the pendulum in the base of the clock started up, its ticking palpable, building momentum. Whatever was about to commence, Trevin did not want to impose on it. He could literally feel the vibration of her love for her husband flying off her. He stepped aside, taking in her profile. She was taller than him, even without the heels, alive with effulgence. Splendor and infinity were externalized here. What would it be like to touch her? Perhaps it would be a sin to try.

Emily glided past the clock, moving around it as he had, and started to climb, holding the handrail for support. Was that even necessary? Trevin was watching her, back to the living room, but then he sensed something additional, and turned back—seeing 15 or so more deceased neighbors, occupying the spaces where the furniture had been pulled from the walls.

Thank you… came the final hint.

Tears broke from Trevin's eyes, overpowered by emotions long since dormant. He attempted consolation in their all-encompassing love, even as it wasn't aimed at him. In this moment, he wanted to make the biggest difference in the world. It was so good to see them.

Most were neighbors Constance had been told about: Mrs. Morneau, Mrs. Weber, Mr. and Mrs. Buccini, Mrs. Laneske, the Deltorans and others—prim and proper, wearing outdated clothing from the last time Trevin remembered seeing them. And, like Emily, they were all glowing with an inner power and divine resolve, not concentrated on him. He did know they knew he was there, but they were "assisting" Emily, with fixation and purpose.

Turn to your family now, a different voice said in Trevin's head. It hadn't come from any of the neighbors. It seemed to have come from somewhere out there… in the storm.

* * *

Outside, Constance was drenched and uncomfortable, but she didn't care. She could see what she could see over the high hedges. She would be waiting for him.

CHAPTER 32

The screen door almost blew off its hinges as Trevin stumbled from the house, the porch having become a rain and wind tunnel. He didn't know how he got here; he was in a near-catatonic state. The rocking streetlights zigzagged, disorienting him. There'd been a tremendous fall-off in temperature. Somewhere deep in his psyche, the scientific notion of a "persistence of vision"—the phenomenon where continued ocular movement was necessary to produce sight—stayed with him. When his attention fixed at any one point, the periphery dwindled like mist rolling in from the moors. The riotous storm made deafening machine gun-like fire on the eaves, water cascading off in sheets, drenching everything. Somehow grabbing the bricked half-wall for support, Trevin powered his way off the porch and down the driveway, exposed to the worst of it, rain pattering like mallets, drenching what the tears hadn't. The driveway heaved like it was made of black rubber, asphalt emitting an ion-charged scent.

But all that was immaterial.

His mind operated only by motor skills. Whatever was taking place in there was not to be tampered with. Not even the violent lightning could stop him from distancing himself. It hadn't been *his* time—all that was improper for *his* eyes. Trevin's shoes slapped gullied puddles. He nearly wiped out on the slick sidewalk. The hedges were convulsing. He pivoted right to see Constance, and slammed on the brakes.

She was looming in the middle of Sweet Briar Road, soaked to the marrow. Trevin shielded his eyes, and saw that she was waiting for him. He *knew* she'd been out here, another kink from the Great Beyond. A single thought came to him: *I can't live without that woman.*

He sprinted the remaining distance, collapsing full as he reached her. She caught him strong—very strong. "I've got you!" she shouted above the noise. "You're safe!"

She hooked his arm around her shoulder and led him back to his parents' house. "Let it soak in!" she coached. "Let it soak in!"

She led him not inside, but around the garage and into the backyard, to dad's garden—to the edge of it. Their feet nearly sunk in the marsh-like conditions. This was crazy! Trevin was baffled, teetering, trying to see her face. It was so dark back here! Only the flashes from the lightning allowed him to see her features. She dragged him to the center of the circle, amid the shaking, slapping stalks and sinking mud. She took his hands and made them wrap around her as she'd grown fond of doing.

She forced him to concentrate, and with her free hand, she dug into the pocket of her shorts—never breaking eye contact, never blinking (even in the cruel rain!)—and removed a small object, round and metallic. At the next lightning crack, it was revealed: Emily Tavalier's lost anniversary ring!

Trevin wanted to pass out, right there and then. How the hell could this be happening? Cecil had just been crying over it.

Drops popped off the thing, and Constance's delicate hands. The ring was gold-plated; a tiny diamond embedded in the band, fitting for any anniversary—much less a 50th. She let him take it, not letting him drop it. As he examined it, she bellowed, "I found it! I know it's important!"

There was pleasure in her voice.

"Trevin, your new friend! This was his!"

As the next wallop lit up the world, Trevin discerned the engraved inscription on the backside: DEAREST EMILY- I LOVE YOU. CECIL. Trevin's logic couldn't possibly function anymore. He lowered the gift, clenched.

"A good visit?!" she queried, smiling large, water cascading down her face. "Come on!"

She scurried them inside, leaving their shoes by the garage.

* * *

In the dark, Trevin was led to the guest room, having found himself wrapped in towels. His body shook, and the cuckoo clock gently matched what he'd barely remembered from over there—providing some grounding.

Constance was a gravitational force, commingling with his own soul, replete with warm memories of his own family, strings of joy and affection overloading his system. She went in first, too narrow for both passing through simultaneously. The night light was on—orange and inviting—like the doorbell. Every indiscretion he'd ever been guilty of also sprang to mind, competing for dominance: the wrongs he'd done. He wanted to make up for them.

Constance closed the door, sealing them in. Outside, the storm was lessening, its ferocity easing. Their rogue droplets sprinkled the carpeting. She knelt on the mattress, lifting the shades halfway, seeing what it looked like out there. The morning was just around the proverbial corner, yawning, changing the brightness in the east just over the house next door. The color was that of velvety blue-plum. "Join me at this," she whispered.

Trevin almost fell into her again. She cradled him.

This was the most radiant and diverse sky yet, settling the trauma that had been threatening to displace every cell in Trevin's body. He could not remember witnessing such an empyrean. Virtually every category of cloud was up there: nimbo stratus, cumulus, cirro stratus, cirro cumulus, scrolling at different rates of speed. Some were exceedingly high, others so low they might scrape the rooftops. They were expanding, contracting, breaking apart, congealing; glowing as if astral candles were lit inside, separation congruent and in accord. Morning stars winked alive through magenta and blue mists. Way out, he could see a few funnels, like the one in his Chicago alley.

He dared looking at her. Indeed, she was waiting. The downpour had put a natural curl in her locks. She smiled only for him. "Yes," she whispered. "It happened. It *was* real."

Kneeling upright on the mattress, Constance guided his face toward hers, tilting her rose petal lips to kiss him. All sensation became electricity. They wriggled their clothes off, throwing them aside. Trevin's hands worked up the middle of her back, an untested awakening stirring within her like a motor. There'd be no holding back. He fell on top of her, and they entwined on the sheets. He explored more of her lips, then launched at her neck. The air left her mouth. She closed her eyes. He caressed her as a master sculptor figured his starting marble block.

She took one final inventory of Trevin, and let go of her own fear, succumbing to utter bliss, reasoning that this was perhaps her bequest for the hard work she'd put in so far. She would never exactly know. With each pant, blood turned to lava. In psychotropic fashion, the walls disbanded, revealing the entire galaxy above, below and all around them. That was fitting. They became one. Fear and love, terror and peace, all entwined. This was right. She'd been waiting for this a lifetime, and she was his Alpha and Omega. Their sweat dripped onto the stars of gold.

CHAPTER 33

Mr. Tavalier had died.

Trevin found out when there'd been commotion at the poor man's house, around 8 a.m. or so. Mom and dad had been on a walk, seen the ambulance, police, and a stranger's car at the house, and talked with Mr. Weber, who'd also been out, raking downed branches and leaves. Mr. Weber had spoken with the unfamiliar man there, who looked astoundingly like a slightly younger version of Cecil Tavalier—discovered it *was* his brother— and asked if there was anything he could do. Mr. Weber ("Matthew!") was cordially turned down. Mr. and Mrs. Lambrose immediately awakened their son, alarming him with the terrible news.

"What's his name—Cecil's brother?" Trevin had asked, head swimming, heart plummeting at the same time.

"None was given," his dad had answered, walking out of the bedroom.

"Do we know what happened?" Trevin yelled out the door.

"Mr. Weber said natural causes, probably. Apparently, Cecil had a history of heart trouble. Who knew that?"

In his father's absence, alone, Trevin murmured, "No one …"

Then his mind began melting down.

* * *

The delirium of the night before mostly came back as Trevin stood on the porch with his parents and Constance, trying hard not to break down at the scene taking place across the street.

On Emerald Lane, nosey neighbors were gathering. This is what had brought them out. *Figured,* grumbled Trevin, so angry he wanted to scream at them. A combination of fury, fright and complete stupefaction was taking root. He was trying to hide all of it from his parents.

And through her own tears, learning of the tragedy, Constance was checking on Trevin, and held his hand. A certain power surged through them, an acknowledgment of what they'd done, and where Trevin had been.

Yes, Trevin knew somewhere down deep. *Last night had been for real.*

Dad collected and folded the lawn chairs that had blown into the yard during the storm. Mom was trying to distract her thoughts, saying she'd never seen so many standing puddles. Dad said they should go in; it wasn't right to gawk.

Trevin thought of the anniversary ring. It was still upstairs in his pants pocket. The damp, still-soaked pants pocket. *She had come for him,* he thought. *And they'd left together.*

The back end of the police car was jutting from behind the hedges. The brother's car was on the street. The storm had knocked down an entire tree at the end of Emerald, by the old entrance to the ghost fields. It looked like it was making a statement: "Don't come in here anymore."

There wasn't a cloud from horizon to horizon.

Cecil's brother appeared at the sidewalk, cell phone to ear, madly rubbing his equally balding head. Trevin watched. An officer was right behind him, there for support. The brother had the same pot belly and beaked face. Amazing and sad. The cop steadied him as he collapsed onto the hood of his car. Some of the insufferable neighbors returned to their homes.

I was the last person to see him alive, Trevin realized, then had to suppress a sudden wave of panic. He had to get the ring. This was his chance to give it back. Trevin wouldn't be held accountable for anything—Cecil and Emily would have seen to it and protected him. He broke from the three, running upstairs and obtaining what he had to get. Constance knew what he was doing. Mom and dad freaked out, tried to stop him, when Trevin stormed by them, making a bee-line for the poor man crying over the death of his brother.

* * *

Trevin was stopped by the officer, who saw him approaching. Cecil's brother sprang from the hood, glaring suspiciously, pain and agony having drained his face.

"What are you doing?" the officer demanded.

Trevin almost couldn't feel sensation in his feet. He was driven here as if by yet another unseen conductor. "I'm not trying to intrude, officer—I have something for this man here. I'm so sorry for your loss, sir. I'm from right there—" Trevin pointed, mortifying his parents into going inside. Constance remained. "I'm visiting my parents. I found something."

"You're not family," the officer warned. "Get out of here."

"You're Cecil's brother," Trevin said to the unknown gentleman, stunned at the uncanny likeness to the departed, and still imagining a mighty God who'd allowed him to see what he had last night. The brother demanded to know what Trevin wanted.

"I found something that belongs to Cecil. I know his name. I know it belonged to him."

The officer was set to physically remove Trevin when the brother interceded; stopping the lawman—saying it was all right. The officer had to get official documentation anyway. He begrudgingly left the two men to their business. He'd be back in a few minutes. Cecil's brother told Trevin to step to the side with him, blowing his nose with a handkerchief (like Cecil), and stopping tears from falling. This close, Trevin matched the droopy eyes to the amazing soul he'd only gotten to know the night before.

Trevin introduced himself, apologizing rapidly, as he'd done with Cecil. "I have no right being here, but we all care—my family and I. I just wanted to say—"

"What do you have of my brother's?" was the interruption.

Trevin presented the ring. The brother took it, scrutinized it, judged the young man visually, and demanded to know more.

"There's an inscription," said Trevin.

The man held the ring up to the sunshine—which was growing bright and hot again—and found the engraved words. A helio sparkled off the jewel as it caught the light. Squinting through thick glasses, he brought it down, gazing *through* Trevin. "Where'd you get it?"

Stress and cloudiness was debilitating Trevin's ability to communicate properly. He hated lying—really hated it—but he had to. He'd lied to his parents about what really happened in his apartment that night in Chicago, withholding the truth, and he was about to repeat the behavior. What else was his choice? He had a thousand mysteries rushing his head, threatening to give him a nervous breakdown. "In the hedges," he answered. "Could've been there for years."

The man looked at the monstrosity, grew glummer, and said, "I always hated those hedges."

"I recently learned your brother's wife's name was 'Emily'."

Things softened. Trevin learned the man's name was "Gavin." "Gavin Tavalier." Another unique one. The man cupped a hand to his mouth. "I… came to check on him. He hadn't returned my calls… Hadn't seen Cecil since her funeral… Went in with my key… It was supposed to be a surprise: I was going to take him to breakfast. He passed in his sleep. I think he may have fallen—he had a bump on his head."

Trevin balked, swallowed hard. *Oh, shit.* "A… bump, sir?"

Gavin looked directly at him. "Never mind. Thank you. Thank you for returning the ring. And thank you for caring."

Inside, Trevin breathed a sigh of relief. "I knew he was by himself." But he also felt illicit, low. Whatever the grandfather clock had been about, should he dare inquire? "Was… anything out of place that he could have hit his head on? Furniture?"

"No. No, but—"

The officer called from the driveway. "Mr. Tavalier? I need you to sign these forms."

"Excuse me," Gavin said, then walked away, briefly touching Trevin on the shoulder—a gesture letting the youngster know his efforts were sincerely appreciated.

That was it. Gavin was gone. A paramedic came out of the house, rummaged the ambulance, and went back inside. Trevin briefly saw a gurney in the back. It was empty. So far. His parents had to be staring from the living-room window. He could not see into them; there was too much reflection. Making the exodus from the premises, he put his head down and rejoined Constance, who was still waiting for him.

"Feel better?" she asked.

He couldn't answer.

Within the next half-hour, the police car, the ambulance with dear Cecil's corpse and Gavin's automobile, drove away with no fanfare. No need to light up Sweet Briar with lights and sirens. In their wake and stillness, Trevin only conveyed the basics to his folks; nothing about a ring, a grandfather clock or the souls of the deceased neighbors from yesteryear manifesting themselves, proving there is an afterlife.

In the dining room, everyone sat in separate chairs around the table, trying to make sense of the awful turn of events. Trevin stared at Constance, replaying in his mind everything that had happened. He stared until his corneas no longer recorded, persistence of vision fizzing out, everything going gray at the edges. He should have been ecstatic. After all, the lovemaking had been fantastic, but his very foundation had been rocked by an experience beyond description. It felt like his world had flipped upside down and been shattered with a hammer. When Carl and April excused themselves to process things out on the back porch, Constance got up, joining them.

Something was wrong. Maybe the sexual mojo hadn't been enough to eradicate the sadness in her, either. He'd seen her shut down to a certain extent—psychologically speaking—as the four had gathered. Moments later, Mrs. Lambrose called to her son.

"Trevin, come out here, will you?"

As he arrived by their side, they were all staring out the window at dad's garden. Despite nearly being flooded, the plot was more robust than ever—impossibly so—the most verdant greens one could imagine.

"Are those… plants taller?" Trevin ventured to ask.

"I think they are," answered his mother, amazed. "And there's more tomatoes than before, I know it."

"Dad, what is this?"

"I don't know," his father answered, putting hands in his shorts pockets. "I have no idea." As one checked the other yards, theirs was easily the exception—a botanical miracle. Trevin shared another look with Constance, who remained mum. There was a lengthy moment of silence.

Carl gently said, "If there's a service for Cecil, I'm going."

* * *

That afternoon, the four were sitting in their usual spots in the living room. They still had not shaken the funk, and had only moved to a different location. It was the most awkward and uncomfortable atmosphere Trevin had experienced at home. April asked Constance if she was all right. Constance said she was. Magazines and newspapers were set aside. No subject or story mattered. On two occasions, Trevin stood and gaped out the window, half hoping to see Cecil waving to him from behind the hedges, letting him know things were as they should be.

But, of course, that didn't happen.

It was imperative to do something—anything—to stave off the melancholy. April caved first, trying her hand at another computer tutorial. She suggested Carl join her. Instead, Carl inspected the garden first-hand, sloshing through the muck, examining the incredibly rich vegetation. April lasted only minutes, then went to be with her husband.

"What do you know about this?" Trevin asked Constance, breaking the ice. "What do you know about any of this?"

"Nothing," she said.

"I don't believe you."

"I know," she said, then fidgeted. "Are we going back to Chicago?"

"I think so," he replied.

She tried a half-smile. It fizzled. How utterly uncharacteristic. But she remained cheerful. "I think that would be best. I think we should start moving forward. That would honor Mr. Tavalier."

"What about us together? Last night! What about that?"

She had no hesitation replying. "It was fantastic. It was beyond my dreams. That's the problem." Then she shrugged, confounded. "My focus has been compromised."

Trevin pulled back, not knowing how to counter. "You and mom and dad are all I have," he emphasized. "I don't want to lose that."

"Yes," said Constance. "I know that, too."

CHAPTER 34

There was a service for Mr. Tavalier. It happened quickly after his passing—in only a couple of days. The Lambroses had learned of it from a personal invitation—delivered priority mail—direct from Gavin Tavalier himself. In it, the sole relative again thanked Trevin for reaching out. Trevin and Constance held off returning to Chicago to attend. The four not only attended the church service, but were granted permission to also stand at the gravesite funeral, where a pleasant priest gave the eulogy. Gavin had written the words. They were beautiful. Emily's name was mentioned a dozen times. The priest was certain she and Cecil were together now. Carl, April, Constance and Trevin learned plenty. No one knew Cecil had been a plant manager of the local brewery for as long as he had. Other than the groundskeepers… they'd been the only ones in attendance.

Trevin cried in private afterward before getting back in the car and driving home with his family.

That was the last anyone saw of Gavin.

* * *

When it did come time to leave for Chicago, the four hugged tightly. It had turned into a melancholy morning where no one really had slept well the night before. Parting with family was awful, it was heart-breaking: there'd been so much of that recently. Since Trevin had an open arrangement with the airlines, he'd cancelled his seat, and opted to accompany Constance in the rental. There was no way he was going to let her drive back alone.

Constance had withdrawn almost fully by now, gone off somewhere. It was obvious to everyone that something—other than Cecil's death—had interrupted her usual, upbeat train of thought. That, in itself, made the day all the more difficult.

Mom had stocked the vehicle with a cooler full of sandwiches, granola bars and bottled water, easily accessible during the drive. Earlier, dad had pulled one of his stunts: absconding with the keys and running the rental to the gas station, filling up the tank on his dime. This had caused a row. Trevin said he was going to knock his father's block off. Dad had dared him to try.

"Boys …" his mother warned, putting an end to it.

To complicate the doldrums even more, incredibly sad activity started taking place over at the Tavalier household. Burly men with moving company tee-shirts had pulled a huge truck into the driveway, and were coming and going from the inside of the household, emptying its contents. The upper quarter of the damn thing could be seen over the hedges, sounds of orders heard barked. Gavin had to have arranged this.

Dad's clichés sailed: "The time has come;" "No sense delaying the inevitable;" "Get going and get at it," and all that other jazz. Trevin hated hearing them. He was weary of the world forcing him into disagreeable circumstances, but he knew there were millions of Americans just like him right now, suffering equally. As the four hugged a final time, tears erupting from mom, Trevin secretly declared that only he had the power to make change truly happen. And perhaps Constance. She seemed to have the power to do a lot of things.

"To change," dad threw in as Trevin and Constance got in the car. "Positive change."

Constance sat in the passenger seat. She didn't say much. Carl and April picked up on it, and thought it was as if a jewel had lost some of its luster. They encouraged them both to drive carefully and to work hard. Cutting the emotional umbilical cord, Trevin promised to call from the road. But he had one more story, and leaned over Constance to tell it out the open window.

"If it's short," dad joked.

It was a dream he'd had the night before the funeral. He wanted to share it. "We were at the Dentzel Carousel at Ontario Beach Park. It was nighttime, mom, you and I were the only ones riding it. We were the age we are now. No one was commandeering it—it was operating strictly by our will. You were watching from the lawn, dad. There wasn't a soul in sight. We saw harbor lights way off in the distance, like we used to love to watch. They sparkled like diamonds on the water, communicating, telling us—if we stayed together, and helped one another out through thick and thin—everything would be okay."

His parents were speechless. Constance had closed her eyes during the words, melting them in, drawing them into private mental quarters. Mom finally said, "That's a good dream."

Trevin smiled. He and Constance strapped themselves in.

April crouched to see the taciturn beauty. "Honey, you sure you're okay?"

Constance said, "I'm just a little blue, April. I've grown to care for you two so much."

April touched Constance's hair. "It's been great having you, dear. You feel like family to us."

"You take care, young lady," dad offered, nodding at her.

"Thank you, Carl."

Trevin's hand went to turn the ignition over and he stopped, noticing the sky. "Look."

They all followed his gaze, even though his appeal had been nearly a whisper.

There were legions of the lenticular clouds up there—in the horizon—huge and flat-disked, breaking the otherwise pristine blue sky. They were drifting slowly their way. If the four stared long enough, they could discern the spectacle's slow movements. The shapes were most noticeable to the north; over the church steeple on the hill.

"Don't start with a meteorological lesson," dad said, "just get out of here."

Trevin addressed Constance directly. "Do you see them?"

She looked at him. "Of course." There was aloofness in her tone.

Trevin started the car, backed it onto Sweet Briar, and squared the vehicle westward, ready for takeoff. He saw his parents sauntering down to the curb after them, and took a mental picture. This painting would be called: *Modern Norman Rockwell Sending Son and Girlfriend Off to Uncharted Territories.* He was trying to keep his mind off Constance, who'd freaked him out.

"Give it a real 'go'," mom called out, waving to them. "Love you guys."

"Love you, too," said Trevin as Constance blew a kiss." He took his foot off the brake. "Use that computer! E-mail! Especially you, dad."

"Yeah, yeah," dad dismissed.

Trevin accelerated. They were all waving. His parents grew smaller in the rear-view mirror. Constance had turned to watch them. As they neared Tommy's mother's house, just at the bend of Sweet Briar, Trevin's attention was diverted to the movers in the Tavalier driveway. The grandfather clock was being hoisted into the back of the truck. The men were struggling.

It was a final punch to the stomach.

At first, Trevin didn't see Tommy Porch coming the other way in the minivan. Tommy jerked the wheel at him. Consequently, Trevin jerked the rental the other way, slamming on the brakes and skidding to a halt, almost barreling into a lawn. Constance's eyes bugged out of her head as the seatbelt snapped her delicate chest, throwing her forward. Tommy also arrived at an abrupt stop, throwing the minivan into reverse. By the time the father of two aligned with them, Trevin's eyes were boring a hole through his childhood friend, anger flushing every cell. Constance was all right; she was just shaken up. The cooler had flipped forward, almost launching its contents.

Tommy had done a number. He was grinning like a fool.

The two beastie boys were in the backseat, hollering away as usual, acting up.

"Did I scare you?" the court jester asked.

Trevin gave it a long, sarcastic beat. "No …"

"I was just coming to see you, ya schmuck—where're you going?" Spotting the stunned but beautiful woman in the passenger seat: "Oh. Didn't know you had someone with you. Sorry."

"Tommy, this is Constance, my girlfriend from Chicago. Constance, this is Tommy Porch, maniac personified."

"Hi," said Tommy. "Nice to meet you."

Constance couldn't verbally respond. She nodded.

"Tommy," scolded Trevin. "You have your kids with you."

Tommy told them to shut up. Little Kevin and Mark just kept cackling, excited by the scare. "Where you going now? Thanks for stopping over, you dick."

The melancholy was temporarily put on hold. Trevin felt gutless, and stupid, and apologized, explaining that Constance had just shown up in the car they were driving. And time got away.

"A likely story," said Tommy, assessing the situation.

Trevin stepped out, leaving the door open, and sidled up to the minivan, explaining why they had to get back to the Windy City. Tommy ordered his kids to behave, figuring out the truth of the conversation.

He jumped out, pushing his former partner in crime. It wasn't a serious attack. "You asshole. You were just going to leave? Without calling or saying anything?"

"Tommy, it's not like that." Trevin ran a hand through his hair. There was hurt in his friend's face, and he felt awful. He re-introduced Constance, said they had many things to do.

Tommy addressed her frankly. "I'm just meeting you now and you're already stealing him back to Chicago?" To Trevin: "We didn't even have a chance to get together again after Schammer's."

Constance showed her first sign of "normalness" again. Massaging her pectorals, she said, "We didn't plan it this way, Tommy. I'm really sorry."

"Trevin's said nice things about you. He's a chooch, though!" Tommy popped Trevin in the shoulder.

"I've heard a lot of nice thing about you, too, Tommy," Constance said, diffusing him.

Then Tommy laughed it off. "She's gorgeous, Trevy, she's a keeper. Constance, this guy is something else."

"I know" she said.

Trevin was embarrassed. None of his excuses sounded reasonable. He apologized for his lack of correspondence. Things had gotten crazy, really crazy.

Tommy lifted his arms, let them drop. "Yeah, well, buddy—you always were a lone wolf, doing things your way. Jenna's gonna to be pissed. She was planning on cooking you dinner."

"That makes me feel worse. I just said goodbye to my parents."

"Your parents, huh?" Leaning into Trevin's ear, referring to Constance, "You take her to the press box? If you know what I mean."

Trevin shoved Tommy back. "No. Wad!" Constance looked at them strangely.

"Wuss," Tommy retorted, cackling like his kids. Tommy was nothing if not consistent. "I wanted to see your mom and dad again. Did you have a good visit with them at least?"

"Yeah," answered Trevin. "Yeah, I did."

Kevin and Mark began the toy-throwing. It quickly got out of hand. Tommy said to Constance, "What'd you think of Mr. and Mrs. Lambrose? Great people, huh?"

"They're terrific," she answered. "I love them."

"Everyone loves them," Tommy said.

"Tommy, I'm sorry. We better be going."

"Yeah, Trevy."

Constance said, "It was nice meeting you, cookie man."

"*Cookie* man?" Tommy looked at his pal. "Is that some reference about Nutty George? Did you tell her what we did?"

"Tommy. Did you hear about him? Mr. Tavalier?"

"No, what?"

Trevin laid it out. Tommy went ashen. Trevin divulged what he could, leaving out the paranormal, mind-shattering crescendo. When he got around to saying how they'd gone to the funeral, Tommy was vexed.

"You should've called, dude," he exclaimed. "What the fuck? I would've gone. I don't think my mom knows."

"It wasn't in the papers. They're emptying his house now. You'll see the truck."

Tommy shook his head. "Nutty George …"

"His real name was 'Cecil,' Tommy."

A pause. "I'll say some prayers, shit." Then, figuring something out in his mind, Tommy suddenly came up with a bright plan. "I have an idea. Let's send the man off properly."

"What are you talking about?"

Something was going to be grossly inappropriate.

Tommy went to the minivan, took the box of animal cookies from his kids—they screamed angrily—and returned, reaching into it and taking out a handful. After getting his fist around a bunch, Tommy shoved the box at his chum. "For Cecil. For old time's sake."

It took a moment, but Trevin caught on. "For Cecil," he echoed, taking a bunch for himself. They set facing the direction Trevin had come from, positioned a cookie between their thumbs and forefingers, and cocked their arms, waiting for each other's cue.

"Ready?" Tommy asked devilishly.

"By the way, Tommy," Trevin said. "Cecil forgives us. But he said: 'no more.'"

"What?"

"Never mind. Let 'em fly."

Together, they launched the cookies, sailing them high into the air like bakery Frisbees, watching them twist and turn above Sweet Briar, arcing over the bend 50 yards away. They hit and exploded in the street, two puffs of dust. A final cackle erupted from all of them—except Constance, who was staring. Back slaps and handshakes smacked, crushing hugs hurt, last words were exchanged. The "two T's" returned to their designated vehicles.

"Constance," Tommy shouted climbing back in. "Too bad you didn't spend time around me—you would've loved me."

"I'm sure, Tommy," she responded in kind.

To Trevin, "Love ya like a brother, cock."

"Like a ball sack, like a dirty sock. Love ya, too, man. Tell your mom I said hello. Bye boys."

Tommy floored it, heavy metal blasting from the stereo, making his trolls howl with insane joy. Trevin watched them go. Trevin would miss Tommy. He said to himself he'd call him from Chicago sometime.

"You two are odd," Constance quipped.

Rolling the wheels and jutting his chin, Trevin said, "At least I got you talking again."

CHAPTER 35

—◄━►—

Constance was drowning in preoccupation. She knew she hadn't been—and still wasn't—very good company. Too many issues had risen to the top lately, thick as silt deposits. And with the hours and miles ticking away on the return trip to Chicago, her thoughts had become increasingly stiff, as had her back and legs. She was afraid she'd taken personal pleasures too selfishly; concerned how a pull-back would affect the big picture.

They turned on the radio, caught the latest world headlines of horrid turmoil. An unprecedented terrorist bombing had taken place in the Middle East, disease continued to spread rampantly in undeveloped countries, and threats of nuclear war were ramping up from rogue nations. Trevin snapped it off as they described how a U.S. gunman had opened fire on his former employees after being let go from a manufacturing company. Dozens were killed.

"Music?" Trevin asked, again trying to make conversation.

"No thanks," Constance answered, starting to feel antsy. *Focus,* she said to herself. *No matter what.*

The tires scraped the rutted shoulder, startling her. Trevin recorrected the wheel. He'd strayed off the road and back.

"Be careful! Please!" she implored.

"I am!"

Her tone was sharp, curt, unbecoming. He seemed flustered with her. He used the adrenaline jar to ask the question: "Are you still with me? I mean—are you *still* with me?"

"Yes, Trevin, I'm still with you," she answered. "I'm just trying to figure some things out." "You've hardly said anything the whole trip so far."

Such a lovely man, Constance considered. Respond to him gently. "Trevin, don't get frustrated."

"Yeah, well, what's there to figure out? I need you, especially now. That means mentally, too. I'd like to think you need me. We have a long ride ahead of us—figuratively and literally. I can't stand this riding here in silence; I don't know what to think."

"Please… don't yell at me."

"I'm not yelling at you. Something's going on. I've noticed it. Mom and dad noticed it. We didn't talk about it, but we didn't have to. Ever since that night. That… unbelievable night." He sighed heavily. "You know and I know we've experienced something extraordinary. You kept so much from me, for a long time. There's still a shit-load I don't know about you."

"Trevin, don't be crass."

"Don't you think about me? In all kinds of ways?"

She ran her fingers through her brown locks, awash with volumes of inner empathy and understanding. "Trevin, I derived everything from you the other night."

"What does that mean? You're talking in code again. I've told you everything—you've told me nothing. You never did say how you knew I was at Mr. Tavalier's house."

"A hunch, Trevin. I knew you'd gone out."

"Oh, please, you're going to have to give me a little more than tha—"

On cue, his words were cut out as a downpour erupted out of nowhere, hitting the windshield like a giant squeegee slapping water down at the road. It didn't let up. Trevin fumbled for the windshield wipers, panicking that he couldn't find them. He barked at Constance to tell him. She didn't know. He found them a few seconds later, turning them on high, gripping the steering wheel like an iron vise. He could now see. He also turned the headlights on.

He got everything under control. "Holy shi—" Looking at her, "You okay?"

She had shot up in the seat, fully alert. "I'm okay."

"Where did *that* come from? Must've been a cloudburst …"

The skies had suddenly crammed in above them with rain clouds. The horizons were clear, filled with more of those strange lenticular clouds. Thank goodness there weren't other cars around. Constance stared sideways out her window, at the landscape. Re-gathering her wits, she relaxed her vision, seeing the foreground zipping by at a faster rate of speed, the background crawling like molasses; terrain alternating from suburban milieu to cornfields.

"Don't shut down again," Trevin beseeched. "We'll get off the road. I'll stop. It should blow over soon; there's light on the horizon."

"Okay."

A few miles up, they mercifully found a roadside rest stop. They ran from the car to the overhang leading into the diner area, watching the rain barreling in. There were other travelers who'd joined them, fascinated. The sky had turned the most curious mix of dark plums and azures, and nobody really knew what to make of the outlandish cloud formations that collided, swelled apart, broke up and dissipated, then reconvened at other areas as if out of thin air.

Huddling together, it was physically the closest Trevin and Constance had been since the night after Mr. Tavalier. Constance held back from throwing her arms around him, kissing him fiercely. Trevin maneuvered them to get out of the way of people going in to eat. He would have admitted that it felt wonderful to feel her body against his again.

From their relative high locale in the bucolic valley region, they watched as conditions worsened, overpowering the interstate. Truckers and vehicles were pulling off in droves. The splendor of the storm, combined with the fantastic colors and light, staggered the imagination, creating profound psychology. Over a farmland across the thruway, there came rolling in a giant, cylinder-shaped cloud—perhaps only 500 feet up and hundreds of yards across—like an eerie, pregnant dirigible. It was dark and bloated at its bottom, and unleashed its own walls of water in sporadic bursts, raking the land as it pleased. No one had ever seen anything like it. Comments could be heard, some rife with fear. Beneath the tube, horses galloped into the barn for protection.

Constance said, "I have to go in. I'm going to the bathroom."

Trevin stayed put at the spectacle, along with others. When Constance returned, the "blimp-cloud" had long passed, like a sky submarine aiming for shore, moving to where the sun was breaking. Constance had to nudge Trevin out of his trance. "Ready?" she asked.

"Uh… yeah …" he said, and she jogged him back to the rental.

Knock off the passive-aggression, she demanded of herself. *He hasn't done anything to deserve that.*

Yes, corporal pleasures had trumped her.

* * *

There was a family on the shoulder of the road, miles ahead, midway into a bend of the same interstate they'd been on for half the day. Constance lifted her sunglasses to see better. The man—presumably the father—was battling a blown back tire on the danger side of the road, where the traffic was flying by. The jack supporting the wheel frame had the SUV up high. Anyone could see the man was having a hell of a time loosening the nuts. On the other side—on the embankment side, sloping down to the median—waited a woman and two small children. Trevin and Constance were relieved they were away from the menace of the thoroughfare.

Trevin, bringing both hands back to the wheel, making sure no eminent threat was around, shot by them.

At first.

He took his foot off the accelerator, slowing down on the safe shoulder zone, making sure he wasn't going to cause an accident. The shudder and bounce was pronounced as they rode the coarse gravel to a stop. Constance now had him in her sights like a hawk.

"What are you doing?" she asked.

"Helping."

"Oh."

He searched for state troopers. None were seen. Putting the transmission in reverse, Trevin turned around, throwing his right arm over her seat, and accelerated, staring out through the rear window. The car made a whining sound as it backed up to meet the stranded souls. He stopped the rental 20 feet away, making sure he wasn't scaring them. Then he idled. The A/C continued to push loudly through the vents. "Want to stay here? I'll keep the air running."

Constance knit her hair up into a ponytail. "I'll come out."

"Powerful memory," he felt the need to explain. "Family vacation. Vermont. I was the age of those kids. Same thing happened to us. I remember dad fighting like mad to get the lug nuts off. I tried to help. Took forever, but we did it. We would've been grateful if somebody helped us. I remember mom's stress and anxiety. She thought we were both going to get sun stroke."

Constance assessed the people through the rear window. "I'd say they're a family."

"And soaked to the bone with sweat. It's really become hot."

"The children must be four and five. Boy and a girl."

"And no hats," said Trevin, opening the door and getting out, waving to them. Constance followed, grabbing four bottles of water from the cooler.

The clan were all in beachwear—flip-flops and sandals. Judging from the man's panting, it must've been a while since the tire was off. The woman was shielding her eyes.

Trevin and Constance made their way to the hapless quartet. The high temperature clung like devilish washcloths on their bodies, ubiquitous cicadas buzzing like an overall mournful sigh; summer's end approaching. The SUV sat on the edge of an unmowed knoll continuing down to a straw field—a catchment basin, marshy from the shower.

Trevin offered to help.

"That would be great; thanks a million," the man said, relieved. "See, hon? There *are* Good Samaritans still around."

Trevin did the introductions for the two of them. The married couple reciprocated, then presented their children. Constance made sure everyone got water. The poor people had been baking for a half hour. As it was, the family was returning from a vacation visiting relatives. Their cell phones had not charged for the road. The hotel they'd been staying at lost power, and it had been impossible to juice them up.

"No problem, let's see what you got here," said Trevin, moving in. There was a wake of rubber debris littering the concrete a quarter mile back. A blow-out.

The mom said something to the children. They cheered happily; glad to have their daddy provided with assistance.

Constance stared at them. Her heart melted.

Trevin set to the tire like a lion, up for the challenge. In less than a minute, he got the nuts off, muscles and sinews coming to the rescue. This impressed everyone.

"Wow," exclaimed dad to his family, "lucky we ran into someone who works out."

Over the next 10 minutes, the men got the spare tire on and set the remainder of the ruptured one in the SUV. Trevin had been quietly observing Constance, playing with the children under the watch of the mother. She was with them in the safe area. She'd been telling stories, making them giddy with joy. Overall, she'd elevated their moods, coming alive again. Her smile—the beam that had been missing—had them spellbound, and it didn't appear as though the heat was bothering them. Not while they were with Constance.

When Trevin was ready to get them on their way, the man handed over a rag, and Trevin wiped his hands with it. The men swapped their own good will, and shook hands like brothers meeting again after a long absence. "Don't know what we would've done without your kindness," the father concluded. "I was getting worried."

Trevin dismissed the compliments, checking for blisters. He was only too happy to be of assistance. "The spare should be good 'til your next stop," he said.

The man offered cash. Trevin refused.

"We'll always remember this," said the missus. "A good act by good people."

The little children couldn't part with Constance. It was as if they'd known her as their great aunt for years. They tugged on Constance's arms, grinning from ear to ear. "Mommy," said the little girl, "I'll always remember the pretty lady with the pretty freckles who told us funny stories."

"And how she made me think of happy things," the boy followed.

"Come on, now leave the nice lady alone," said the mother. "She has to leave."

The little girl plucked a wild flower, handed it to Constance, and Constance squatted, drawing the children together. She whispered in each of their ears. The adults weren't privy to what she said. Then the children ran to their mother and father, hugging them merrily.

There was no sign of heavy traffic anywhere. Maybe travelers had decided to wait out the storm longer. The signs were lingering in patches, leaving brilliantly hued rainbows arcing and shining all over the yawning landscape.

The teams parted ways.

As Trevin and Constance got back into the rental, the merciful air-conditioning soothed them.

"A good deed done well," said Constance, putting her seat belt back on.

As he merged onto the interstate, he'd gunned the speed to 65 miles per hour already.

* * *

That night, Constance made love to him again, in the hotel room, where they were forced to spend the night because of more inclement weather. It hadn't stopped raining since shortly after helping the family with the tire. As it turned out, neither could ignore each other, despite the attitudinal armistice. Constance burst into tears afterward, hanging off the mattress like a wilted flower, linens thrown around them. Trevin jumped up.

"Constance! For God's sake—what's the matter? This was beautiful."

"I shouldn't be doing this," she said, punishing herself. "I'm feeling this… went too far…"

"I can't take this!" Trevin protested. "If you're going to… everytime we—"

"The air conditioning's freezing," she interrupted, trying to collect herself. "Please make it less cold."

He dressed and did as asked, frustrated beyond belief. He thought she'd been "back." Apparently not. He stood staring out the hotel window through the blinds, bending them, listening to the sound of a far off locomotive train whistle. "That sound—a train," he said, venting, "used to be something I treasured. Tonight, it sounds mournful." He turned, moving to the single chair in the room, sitting down. "Sounds like the end of something great. I'm worried."

When she didn't say anything, when she merely sat up and gathered as many sheets around her as possible, he added, "Doesn't our lovemaking mean anything to you? It means everything to me."

Constance crunched up to a sitting position at the headboard, staring into the sheets. "That was a wonderful thing you did today—pulling over, helping that family. They'll have fond memories of you. They'll reminisce." When she looked up, saw he was pleading for an explanation, she said, "Trevin, this is my first time."

Trevin tried a softer approach. He sat on the bed with her. "That's great, hon. There's nothing you can't tell me."

"I'm enjoying your touch. I wanted you to be close to me."

"Whatever this is," he whispered tenderly, "I'll wait for you."

"On your parent's roof, when you and I were looking at the Perseid meteor show, I felt your memories—in each atom—the ones making you the happiest. Keep embracing them, Trevin. No one gets through life unscathed."

"I know that, Constance."

She grabbed tissues from a box, blew her nose. "Yes, Trevin, wait for me."

"For how long?"

"Not much longer." She thanked him for who he was, and they rested in each other's arms, eventually falling into dreamland.

* * *

They arrived in Chicago at noon the following day, knowing that their relationship had changed. Trevin commandeered the vehicle into the cramped rental lot where Constance had contracted the car. Trevin's depression returned almost immediately. There was a collective impression of completing an odyssey—and not for good. A busy crowd was filing in and out, most likely the spillover from the last days of summer holidays. He asked Constance to find the rental agreement. It took her some doing to dig it out of the glove compartment.

Adding to his anxiety was the sense of claustrophobia from the tall factory buildings penning them in on three sides of the property. And the fortified security fences surrounding the perimeter evoked a prison. Trevin's emotions were bubbling. He didn't know what was going to happen to their relationship now or in the near future. So much had happened. And, as with the last leg of the trip, the heat pushed mercilessly in through the windows, overpowering the a/c, making them jump out of the car once they found an available docking spot. With the motor off, the metal guts groaned; an extended effort coming to a close. The back of Trevin's shirt was soaked with sweat. Constance fared better. She dumped the garbage of power bar wrappers, banana peels and empty water bottles in a nearby receptacle.

As they waited for someone to come out of the office, the tension drove them to extreme unease. The storms had ceased a while ago, but the sun scorched here in the asphalt and concrete jungle. Sunset couldn't arrive soon enough.

"So," Trevin chanced, "how do I know when you're ready for me again?"

She couldn't make eye contact. "I'll let you know. It sounds awful saying it …"

He wanted to get the hell out of there, but he had every intention of picking up the tab without her knowledge.

"Aren't I supposed to go in and pay?" she asked, looking around.

"I'll be right back," he said, storming off to the office with the keys. Even in his disposition, his chivalrous nature couldn't be suppressed. This was his way of demonstrating—despite the bullshit—that he wasn't going to give up being a gentleman. That's just the way he was.

In Trevin's nonattendance, a friendly agent in a company shirt came at Constance after finishing with other customers, holding a clipboard, asking how everything went. She was thrown at first, her mind a thousand miles away. She read "Anthony" on the name tag. He kept the small talk to a minimum, performing the walk-around inspection.

"My… boyfriend …" A stumble came to her as she said it, "… has the keys, Anthony. He's inside."

"Great," Anthony chirped, checking items off his list.

When Trevin returned, and Constance found out he'd taken care of the bill, she almost became angry: something else she'd never experienced. Trevin knew where this was heading. He explained that he'd spend his money where he wanted—like the computer—refusing her money as she tried to pay him back. He was as stubborn as his father.

Anthony sized them up discreetly and popped the trunk—a gunshot to Trevin's ears. They unloaded the suitcases and traveling items, and things were ready to be wrapped up. The agent thrust the pen and clipboard at Trevin. "Sign here, please. You keep the bottom copy. The keys are inside?"

"Yes."

The two men shook hands. Anthony thanked them for their business as another employee ran out with the keys again, jumped in the car, and whisked it off to an open washing bay. Constance stared at Trevin, trying to understand him.

Trevin ignored her, looking at the people on the street, immersed in their private deportments. Some surely were ending their day, he figured, others just beginning. "Noise," he said aloud, to himself.

"Are you taking the el?" Constance asked.

"Yep."

"I'll walk you to it. I am, too."

"You don't have to."

"I want to," she stressed, tilting her head.

He paused. "All right."

Feeling like garbage, Trevin telescoped the handles of their traveling suitcases and gave Constance hers, and they both started hoofing it.

On the sidewalk, the rolling wheels ground on the abrasive cement. The din and chaos around them worked on his nerves. Trevin kept his head down as a crow flies, aiming to where he knew the nearest station to be.

"Slow down," she said. "You're dehydrated."

He didn't respond.

"Don't get insecure."

"No, of course not," he shot back, then cringed at a shrill police whistle.

"There's nothing I wouldn't do for you," she said.

"It's like you're walking right out of my life."

"I'm not. We can both catch up on things; concentrate on ourselves for a bit."

"I was going to do that anyway," he said, taking a diagonal across a busy street—almost losing her.

She caught up after him, a cop chastising them for jay-walking. Two cabbies were going at it, swearing at each other over a near mishap. They made it to the other side and Trevin accidentally impeded the progress of a pedestrian who was in an extreme hurry. The man gave a nasty look, swearing something at Trevin under his breath. The hostility around them was an oppressive swelter. Constance reached for his shoulder. "Baby, trust me."

"I love you."

"And I love you."

They reached the terminal, a different one from before. Here at sidewalk level, the same hordes of humanity pushed and shoved in and out of the turnstiles, triggering a mental defense mechanism that had Trevin falling back into replay of all the pleasant moments leading up to him meeting Constance for the first time in the book store. It had been such a happy time. Constance seemed to perceive this, and closed her eyes in a rhapsody, as if plugging into his thoughts.

"Don't stand waving at me this time," he said, getting out his CTA card.

Constance became upset, hurt.

They were forced to move again to a shadowed underbelly of the elevated platform—and again—they readjusted their belongings. Community flyers and cheap advertisements fluttered like dying butterflies around them, taped and stapled to rusty stanchions and telephone poles. Trash blew against them, banality and bad news lit up the headlines in the dirty free weekly dispensers. Trevin wished he had aspirin. The sinful shrieking of the train started to strike.

"Relax your teeth," she coached, seeing what was building.

Sure enough, a train was making its violent turn, its wail becoming high-pitched. To Trevin, it sounded like the neighbor who'd screamed on Munnison Street. He let go of his suitcase, keeping it at his side. The thundering became a herd of robot buffalo, shuddering the underpinning, sending trash churning in a dusty whirlpool at their faces.

"Yah!" he yelled rebelliously, clamping hands over his ears.

It was overhead before they knew it—cutting into bones, proverbial spikes working up his head, stealing breath. Constance grabbed him. She remembered.

Trevin's brain unleashed a tsunami of negative memories. The el's screeching fully became the scream of the neighbor, and the braking car, and the impact. Then the smell of the attack itself, Brian Annarez's raging face in the dark, the ripping claws at Trevin's skin, the fragmentation of murderous thoughts …

My murderous thoughts!

Constance wanted to save him. This was an assault, channeled brutality. She couldn't cover her ears—her hands *had* to be on him.

Trevin was ready to scream. The son of a bitch was trying to kill him! Then, Trevin began tipping the scales, craving to destroy his assailant! With his own hands! There was no virtue in this. The body hit the sidewalk—a sickening "thwap"—blood seeping from the body …

The blue orb.

Constance forced him to look at her. Into her irises. There came a blessed disconnect, a current of calm. Trevin lost sensation. Sound cut, nothingness replacing it; shocking in its dissimilarity. That persistence of vision fuzzed out again, fading everything to gray. Intuition said this wasn't Constance—this was something else: a haven coming to rescue him.

A familiar and loving sound doppled in from an audible horizon. Trevin knew this, too. A view into the past "drew the curtains back," revealing his grandmother's tea kettle in the little kitchen. It was her, Nan, sitting on the stool with her back to him, tending to it. She knew her grandson was there. She was exuding an aura of tenderness. He'd seen this angle so many times—two cups on the countertop, teabags and lemon slices, waiting to be dunked. Nan was alone, yet not lonely, the wheelchair in the other room (he also knew that). So joyful was he to see her, born anew from the best of times! The screeching metal had been replaced by the whistling. He could feel the steam, smell the aroma, taste the sharp, delectable flavor. He saw warm colors and the blue flame from the range's pilot light. She lifted the kettle with ease—no arthritis impeding her—and set it on the cozy to her right, extinguishing the flame.

The el was gone; a gentler din returning like well-behaved pupils to a classroom. Constance was hugging him, inches from his face. The sight produced more than a few looks from strangers eyeballing them.

"Better?" she asked, eyebrows arched, anticipating good news.

"Nan wanted to share tea," he said, knowing she already knew.

"Good."

Constance was definitely part of the equation—he *could* trust her. This had been her way of proving it. The suitcase, when picked back up, felt real in his hand. Another train would come. It was time to go. Before shuffling solo through the turnstile, he stopped, turned around, looked at her. There was an air of foreshadowing.

"Have your parents come for a visit," she urged. "Soon."

That was the last thing he'd hear from her for a while.

CHAPTER 36

Trevin recalled the adage: "Everyone returns."

The first thing he noticed—to his chagrin—upon opening the door to his stuffy apartment, was the box of crap delivered from his old Lightning Strikes, courtesy messenger service. Solorio had made good on his threat/ promise, returning it all. But who'd been in here to leave the box inside? Judging from the fixed balustrades on the balcony, and the patch of repaired drywall behind the door from the gouge (minus a paint job); it must've been Trevin's "pal" and landlord, Louie Fovos. At least the ogre hadn't touched Constance's quartz crystal rock, which still sat atop the drafting table in the studio. Trevin tried staving off the instant cheerlessness of being back alone by staring into the sparkles, created by the late sunlight straining in from the skylight above it.

It was no use. Trevin wasn't going to "grow" happy.

He set the suitcase aside, and immediately turned on the air conditioning, concerned it would take a long time to clear out the mustiness caused from the apartment being sealed up all this time.

The octagonal window was still shawl-free. An awareness of extreme isolation hit.

How could this have happened with Constance? *What* had happened?

Trevin went straight for the kitchen and slammed three glasses of water from the faucet. She'd been right, of course: He was dehydrated.

What was he going to do?

He'd unpack later.

Better call mom and dad, let them know I arrived safe and sound. Well…safe.

* * *

There was a low-grade hum in Trevin's temples over the course of the next few days, heard mostly when it was disturbingly quiet. He'd prayed it wasn't the onset of tinnitus. The most striking case was when he stood on the balcony, (examining the repairs Fovos had made). Trevin had developed a headache after seeing a TV report about the latest war breaking out overseas. Munnison Street had been empty, no friendly neighbors inquiring about his well-being. The tone remained strumming Trevin's cranium until he looked into the sunset and it wore down. He'd hopped aboard an el afterward, embarking on an aimless trek around the city—nowhere to go, with all the desire in the world to arrive someplace else.

Trevin was lost. And he was fearful for his future.

When his parents had asked about Constance in a phone call, he'd lied to them, telling them everything was fine; they were both just really busy getting things back in order.

Another lie. Great way to begin anew—prevaricating to the people who mattered most.

Mom and dad told him Mr. Tavalier's house was still up for sale. They'd never seen Gavin again. For some uplifting news, Trevin told them about an upcoming job fair he was going to attend. Also he was planning on contacting placement agencies, seeing if he could initiate anything there. It was worth a shot. The economy was getting worse. What dwindling manufacturing there was in the country was crumbling. Hell, it was a depression! And it was a cycle of madness—the whole world was in the toilet.

Am I joking? Did I say there was some uplifting news?

Still, the Lambroses cheered on their son, encouraging him to remain tough; he had so much talent. Trevin laid into them for not e-mailing, especially dad. Now there was no excuse.

"Keep an eye out for that special day, son," dad had sarcastically rejoined.

Trevin went to bed that night, the hum having returned, the concept of critical world-change screaming in his head.

* * *

True to his word, Trevin sat before the executive recruiter, gussied up in an ironed shirt and tie (first time worn), listening to her pat speeches on the depressed and oversaturated market. The unemployment rate was at its highest in 80 years. He didn't need to hear that. Her hair was a distraction, woven ultra-intricately in a power braid. This was the second time she asked the question: "Are you willing to take a contract position?"

Trevin snapped out of it. "Yes, ma'am. If that's my way back to the art world—I'll do what it takes."

The recruiter turned to the monitor, scrolling for relevant information in her database. "We've seen nothing full-time in this crisis. You do have great experience."

He was tempted to say: "Tell me something new," but settled for "Thank you."

Entering his statistics, she tossed in, "We have Ph.D.s in for work. That's how bad things are."

Trevin was waiting for it—the knockout punch ("We'll be in touch."). He'd visualized this nightmare scenario: sitting in a featureless cubicle, begging for a future. She had to repeat herself when he zoned out, worrying about everything.

"I said: Where have you been looking?"

"Um, the major search engines on the Internet," he answered. "The classifieds. Even tried cold calling. It worked for me in the past."

"Ever think about sales?"

"I'd rather stick to what I …" Last word fading, "… love."

"You're being proactive," she said. "That's good. So many have dropped out altogether." To her credit, the woman was supportive, even as it was part of her job.

"I'm not a quitter."

Trevin wanted to sink into the chair, literally. It had taken a Herculean effort to face this. He was back in the West Loop, Lightning Strikes only a couple of blocks away. Constance was near. He knew that. Not like he had known she was out in the storm that night at Mr. Tavalier's house, but she worked these parts. He had no idea where, of course—she still hadn't called—but the realization gave him a weird sense of solace. He certainly wasn't going to play Joe Stalker and hunt her down. He had his pride.

The recruiter was staring at him again. "Do you have any contacts in your field? Favors to cash in?"

Thinking of his ex-boss Solorio, he shook his head. "Not really."

"Well, I have everything I need," she said, wrapping up. "Resume on file, contact info …" She minimized her screen, set her hands on the desk. "Mr. Lambrose, this process might take time."

His eyelids twitched. "I'm best at face-to-face interviews."

This merited a pause. "Are you?" the look read. Trevin reflected on how he'd conducted himself. "We'll try to get some," she said, then stood, reaching over the desk to shake hands. "We'll be in touch."

There it is, he thought: *the capper.*

He got a take-home package of the employment agency's history in the Chicago marketplace. There was an added pen as a special gift. He never looked at it again.

* * *

At the Navy Pier job fair, Trevin likened himself to a hermit crab, hunting for that special shell to crawl into. It wasn't going well. His confidence was shot, he was completely demoralized, and that nagging desire for a bigger destination—greater than any he'd find roaming this crowded banquet hall, bleary-eyed representatives sitting at fold-out tables, barely listening to his pitches, throwing CVs into a pile—had returned with a vengeance.

He'd snagged freelance gigs here and there from Craigslist, but this nightmare had to end, this ceaseless realm of uncertainty and hopelessness. He'd spent days wondering, pondering and praying. Something *had* to give. He could almost taste change in the air. His life without Constance, and whatever the hell had happened to him in Rochester, was shuffling him away to nothingness. Staring at the scuffed floors, he reminded himself to stay strong for his parents as well as himself. They were so worried about him. He was so worried about them. Every time they spoke on the phone: more disquiet.

They needed salvation.

When the cell phone rang in his pocket, strangely thrilling his groin (a tad), he couldn't identify the number, so he scrambled to find a quiet corner. The number was local: downtown business district. Maybe it was the placement agency calling with good news. He waited. A message wasn't left. He wasn't going to start the nonsense again with waiting for the perfect time to talk, so he dodged out a side door to the pier terrace—which faced the breathtaking skyline of Chicago at the lakefront.

He found himself locked out. Now he had to make the best of it. He called back.

Wrong number.

Some drowsy fool answered with slurred speech. Trevin hung up, feeling his temper rising. Why was the world going the way it was? Was there a design to any of this? Why had Constance so desperately sought for him to embrace his happy memories and cling to them like a lifeboat? Trevin pounded on the glass to let himself in. When his cell rang again, he almost didn't bother with it.

"Trevin Lambrose," he snapped, propping the door when someone opened it for him.

It was his landlord, Louie Fovos. And boy did the man have an attitude! "Where the hell have you been? I've stopped by twice. Were you out of town? Did you get the box I left inside that had your name on it?"

"Yes, Louie, I got it. Thank you."

"Where are you?"

"Excuse me?" Trevin wanted civility.

"I hear noise. You sound different. What do I hear—seagulls?"

What did Fovos care? Trevin let go of the door again, opting to go back to the terrace, letting the beauty of the skyline pacify him somewhat. He wasn't going to get worked up in a fury. "I'm at Navy Pier, Louie. How can I help you?"

"What're you doing there?"

"Louie—what do you want?"

"I'll cut straight to it," said his landlord, sounding harried. "I don't have good news."

Trevin's heart sunk. He was getting used to this. "What now, Louie?"

"You've been a good tenant, but things happen."

Trevin gripped the wall, feeling stone. "Louie—what are you saying?"

"I'm afraid I'm going to have to ask you to move out of my house."

A hot, lancing sensation pierced Trevin's abdomen, rendering him immobile. Maybe he hadn't heard correctly. "What?"

"I'm sorry. It's too big a risk having a tenant in there before the house is finished."

Trevin's guts twisted. The bastard was lying, he knew. This was a scheme. The hothead bastard had never forgiven Trevin for the police episode and the violence and embarrassment he'd brought to the address. "Louie, I've been your tenant for two and a half years."

"Some of your neighbors contacted the alderman. I've had phone calls."

"That's crap, Louie, and you know it. You've never cared what anyone said."

"This involves code, Trevin. I'm not going to argue with you. You're a liability. I don't know when I can finish, I don't have the money. I shouldn't have let you in to begin with."

Trevin blistered. He wanted to reach through the phone and throttle the man. This was a ruse. "Mr. Fovos," he shared calmly, "You asked why I was here. I'm at a job fair. That means I'm looking for work. That means I no longer have my job. I never told you, but I should have. I'm in a bad way right now and I really can't afford to be kicked out of the apartment. I was out of town visiting my parents, decompressing."

"Well, you're not decompressing in my place anymore. I'm sorry, but you'll have to find a different apartment. I wish you the best."

"Louie, please. Don't… do this. Whatever differences we had that night with the police… They told you it wasn't my fault. There'll be no repercussions from what happened."

But Louie wasn't having it, calling Trevin's occupancy a "risky venture," demeaning Trevin further. Trevin lost it, going up one side of the landlord and down the other. There was no way he was going to let this creep get away with this. Trevin accused him of railroading him. It wasn't fair. It was personal. Heartless.

Now Louie lost his temper. "I said I don't want to get into this! The fucking intruder incident was too much! You made me a god damn target, Trevin! No more risks for me—you're out!"

"This is ludicrous!"

"You have until the end of the month!"

"That's not enough time!"

"Make the time! Make arrangements! Put the same effort into finding an apartment as you did making me the fool of the block; it'll work. And don't think about trashing the place, either, I have a lawyer. You'll go right back to the cops." Then the weasel hung up.

Trevin stood dumbfounded, blinded by the sunbursts off the steel and glass. Lake Michigan seemed to beg him to throw himself over the balcony. Apparently, the cosmos still wasn't through with its cruel jokes. He *was* being railroaded! A particularly powerful heliograph burst off a nearby flag pole, catching him just right—and in that moment—the ugliest of intentions erased from his mind, like a tape that had been suddenly erased.

The light is sentient, he thought abstractly. *It's listening. It's there to help us.*

* * *

Trevin awoke in his apartment that night thinking he'd heard another noise. Instantly, he was planted for attack. There was a weak breeze rattling his windows. With his heart racing and mind spinning a hundred miles per hour, he poked his head out into the kitchen, noticing the bluish glow in the studio.

It was his computer. Something had awakened the monitor from sleep mode.

Upon inspection, the troll figurine Constance purchased at the service bureau had mysteriously fallen onto the keypad, calling attention to a new e-mail message on his browser window. Just one message.

How had the figurine …?

Something told Trevin to check the message—now—this was important. Picking up the figurine and setting it aside, he sat, and clicked on his inbox. There was a reason he was jarred from sleep. The subject line read: "We're coming to visit!"

The body copy was filled with typos. It was from Carl Lambrose. Pops had written it.

"Son- My first E-mail messaGe! I hate typing. You proud? ha ha Forgive the typos. Don't know how to Fix tehm—too much work to go back. Figured we'd contact you t his way, get your attention. I even managed to turn the computer on myself. writing to announce we're comng to CHICAGO! Next week! I know, Get up off the Floor."

Trevin paused, amazed. He was struck by the irony of Constance's last counsel: "Have your parents come for a visit. Soon."

And now they were …

"We've made arrange ments already so you can't argue. We bought the airline tickes but have to save money so were staying at your place. Hate to Cramp your style but that's the way it Goes. You visiteD us\, time to reTurne the favor. Knew you were down when yu left, and knowing you're working hard finding ajob, we wanted to cheer you up, providing you can handle your parents being there. Looking forward to seeing Constance, too. Haven't heard

much about her. Talk more latER, this has taken forever to write. I don't type good... ha ha, I mean, well. Tallk soon. Over and out. M & P."

Trevin sat there in the dark, the words sinking in. His parents were coming for a visit. It'd been forever since they'd been to Chicago. And they'd never been to his current apartment.

This was great news, crazy news. He nearly pounded out a reply, but knew they were long asleep. He felt ashamed once more for not calling them each and every day. He hadn't kept them in the loop as much as they probably would have wanted since returning, but they hadn't pressed. And then his heart sank. *Constance.* They were so fond of her. What was he going to tell them? Another lie, most likely.

He heard Fovos' dire command in his head: *"You have until the end of the month."*

The asshole.

Trevin went to the octagonal window. The streetlight was working, but still shed no light on any activity there. It was as if the neighborhood had been going away since his return. Eerie. Mom and dad. Constance's figurine woke him up for this. They loved their son enough to fly their way here and be with him. He was truly blessed. They'd be together.

"Have your parents come for a visit. Soon."

It would be remedial for the soul. Maybe Constance would wish to partake.

CHAPTER 37

Roles had reversed themselves. Trevin picked his parents up at O'Hare as they had him at their airport in Rochester. And as soon as he saw them, Trevin knew something was the matter—more troubling than when he flew there. It was just a hunch, but as he'd learned, his hunches usually added up to something. They hugged just outside of the security zone, where anxious family members embraced their loved ones. Carl and April's frowns were immediately replaced by bright smiles and big hugs.

Good actors, Trevin thought.

"You made it," he exclaimed happily. "You're here."

They were staying for a week, a full week. Dad tried to shove cash at him, and the mock-fighting started. The matriarch squashed it instantly. Trevin terrified his mother by taking the Kennedy Expressway home, dodging and weaving through Chicago traffic in his trusty dark green Blazer. He was catching the artery just before rush hour, so he had to make the most of the relative freedom. She sat in the back, naturally. He got off at an earlier exit, working the side streets in hopes of entertaining them with a tour of the various neighborhoods. Dad loved the architecture—mostly bungalow. Mom was horrified by the lack of parking in nearly every residential street. All Trevin could do was make a joke of it.

"Welcome to my world."

Mom couldn't keep off the subject of Constance. "We're looking forward to seeing her. What's going on with you two? Your father and I haven't heard much about her lately. Has she snapped out of that funk she was in when you guys left?"

"She's as busy as always, mom. We'll see her."

"She knows we're here, right?"

"She does, mom." *Be proud of yourself, Trev—another little fib.*

Dad glanced over at him from the passenger seat. "But you have that look."

"What look?"

"Like something's wrong," dad said.

"I could say the same for you guys. I know it wasn't the airline meal that gave you those dour expressions. They don't serve food anymore." Then Trevin darted a quick, sarcastic glance back at his father. "*You* have that look."

Carl turned to his wife, straining against the belt. "He's going to be like this already, dear."

"No," said Trevin. "She's busy. Temping's in high demand now. You know that."

"Relationships are about sticking it out through thick and thin," countered dad. "You know *that*. She's a great lady, son."

"Dad. Chill."

"Just something to remind yourself of."

"Thanks."

Mom changed the subject. "Well, I'm glad you got a kick out of your father's e-mail. We broke down and got a free month trial to the Internet. As it turned out, we needed a vacation. It's a good time to visit before you get that new job—which we know is coming."

"You know it, mom." Trevin looked at her in the rear-view mirror. *Such a sweet soul. Such a cheerleader.* He wished he were that optimistic.

Dad was already on the look-out for Munnison, remembering the name. When Trevin turned on Salmon, Carl spotted the house instantly. "The one on the corner. There's the staircase. My God it's ugly."

Trevin sighed profoundly at the remark, rushing for the spot right in front, producing a slight yelp from his mother. After he parked and shut off the engine, his parents were still gawking at the façade. "I'm serious," followed dad, "it's a monstrosity! No other house has one. I mean, the architect should be imprisoned."

"Dad! Enough."

"You described it, Trevin," said mom, more delicately. Judging from her face, even she was aghast.

Trevin climbed out. "Lady and gentleman: Welcome to the Grand Palace."

A few neighbors were around, but far down—near Mrs. Dombrowski's house. Trevin thought about waving, but gave up as they weren't looking his way. He took care of the suitcases, avoiding the area on the sidewalk where Brian Annarez's guts had been broken from the fall.

They climbed to the top landing, mom and dad surveying the unoccupied first floor. They'd heard enough of that, too. Re-assembled at bird's-eye view, they marveled at the sights, looking around. The Metra and the el were blasting by, half a football field's distance away.

"I see why you sit out here," mom said. "It's inspirational."

"Yep," said Trevin, asking dad to hold the screen door, opening the inside lock. He didn't want them to see his fingers trembling. How much longer could he keep the apartment's secrets from them? They were at ground-zero, for God's sake. "It's not the Drake," he said.

"No, it's better," replied dad, feeling the cool air smacking them straight away. "It's a meat locker. What are your electric bills?"

Trevin pointed. "Inside."

He was nervous. Aside from his dick of a landlord, they were only the second and third people to have entered. Maybe he wasn't too old for his parents' approval. The reminder that he'd have to vacate soon—in such an unfair amount of time—made him want to vomit over the balcony.

Trevin staked claims for sleeping on the sofa. He'd put fresh sheets on his bed. They were to have his room. The second wall unit in there meant they could control the cold air as they wished. Dad fixated on Salmon Street once more, commenting on the monolithic security wall around the grounds there. "The cement yard?"

"You got it," said Trevin, shutting the door.

"You should paint a mural on that wall. Advertise yourself."

"I'll march right down and go to town, dad."

"If you two are going to snipe at each other all week," warned mom, "I'm going to scream."

"Just trying to start the vacation with a laugh, dearie."

April laugh-mocked at her husband. The sound was intentionally clownish.

But still, something's wrong, thought Trevin.

The Lambroses surveyed the studio: their son's creative center. Dad noticed the patched drywall. Trevin made up a lame excuse about damaging it with a T-square. Mom flipped over the skylight, imagining the sun playing about the room. Trevin gave the nickel tour. They loved the apartment's layout, thought it unique, finding everything quaint and fitting. Mom went gaga over the ample walk-in closet and bathroom at mid-section. This made Trevin feel moderately better. He absorbed the surreal quality of having his beloved folks in his environment. His quiet desperation for their company had been bad. Now he could enjoy it. Well—until eviction …

After freshening up, arranging and hanging personal items, the three relaxed, lounging in the chic studio. The air conditioning was lovely. Dad inquired about the quartz crystal atop the drafting table. Trevin told them the story of Constance buying it for him, which brought her name into the mix again—causing him to dodge more inquiries from mom, dreadfully wishing Ms. Sunshine and Freckles were here as part of the reunion. The topic of a meal arose.

"Let's invite her," said dad, clapping his belly.

"Constance?" said Trevin. "She won't come."

"Why not?"

"I told you—she's busy."

"Well call her, Trevin," urged mom.

Trevin side-stepped the topic, asking where they wanted to go eat. "There's everything. If you want something exotic like the Thai we had in Rochester, all we have to do is drive a bit."

"And lose your parking spot," said dad.

"So what? Do you think I'm going to let parking get in the way of enjoying this city with my mother and father?"

"Flattery will get us to buy dinner," joked mom.

As Carl and April changed clothes, Trevin tried Constance on the cell out on the balcony to please them. The sound of the air conditioner would drown out any argument he may have with her. He couldn't take it any longer anyway, but he was prepared for the same bullshit—voice mail.

A van caught his attention: a white Ford Econoline. It was traveling down Salmon toward Munnison, readying to turn. It would go right by the house. There was something about it that gave Trevin pause. The thing was sinister-looking—an evil intent about it—poor shape, dents peppering its sides, tinted glass all around, rendering it impossible to see inside. When it was gone, a female voice picked up the cell call: "Trevin?"

"Constance?" He choked on saliva. "I-I didn't think you'd …"

"Answer? Of course I would! Oh my goodness, it's so great to hear from you; it's been weeks."

To his shock, her tone was perky, not standoffish. His heart practically pushed through his chest. *You've been out of my life, shredding my heart apart.* "My parents are in town," he said.

"Your parents are in town? For real?"

"For real. We just got back from the airport."

"Oh, that's so cool! That's great! How are they? How are *you*?"

How am I? How do you think I am? I've been worried sick not knowing if I'd ever talk to or see you again. But he matched intonation: "I'm fine, everybody's fine. And you? You're well?"

"I am. Busy, but well."

"Good." Then he punched it. "What do you say you have dinner with us tonight? They want to see you. *I* want to see you, damn it."

She hesitated. More than he wanted. "You… don't need your space?"

"Space? Do I need my space? Constance, you're the one who said you needed space. And time!" *Take it easy, bro. Don't get confrontational.* Merely connecting via cell phone was elixir enough. "I'm on the balcony, they're inside. I'm thinking Thai again—for old time's sake."

God it was good to hear her alluring, husky voice …

He heard her suck in through her teeth. "Tempting… I don't know if I can make it."

"Babe!" (He hadn't said that in a long time.) "Come on. It took a lot for me to call you—I miss you—I still don't know what happened between us, but that's all right. Let's start anew. Please."

"That's sweet."

"Drop whatever you're doing. This'll become a memory you'll love."

"Trevin, I'd love to, just not tonight." There was genuine tenderness.

"I'm worried about you."

"Don't be. Plus they just got in. Don't you want to spend time with your parents alone?"

"Constance, they're here for a week."

"Good to know," she said, then there was a delay. "What are you telling them about us?"

Does it matter? "Just that we haven't had much time to spend with each other. Constance, I miss your damn freckles."

She laughed. Was that a good thing? "Trevin, darling, we'll get together soon. Very soon."

"When?" He felt the emotions unleashing now. "Constance, I love you! Completely. I'm falling apart over here, and I'm getting thrown out of my apartment."

"*What?*"

"That's right. I have less than a month."

She was devastated. She asked what happened. Trevin gave her the run-down, blamed it on his weasel landlord—who obviously had it out for him.

"He believes there's more trouble coming?" she asked, angered.

"Not exactly. He just said it. He thinks I'm a liability."

"Did you tell your parents yet about the incident?"

"No."

"Trevin, you should. Remember we talked about that in Rochester. Get it off your chest. Listen, I can't join you tonight, but everything's going to be fine, I promise. I know it's been a terrible time for you, and I'm sorry for what I've put you through, but it's not going to last much longer."

"I don't understand half the things you say."

"I asked you to trust me. Remember?"

"Constance, come on! I'm on an avalanche here!"A bicyclist heard him while pedaling by, and looked up. Trevin turned his back to the street. "Have I offended you somehow?"

She said softly, "You didn't offend me. Quite the opposite, actually."

At that moment, the Econoline van cruised past again, in the opposite direction. Trevin saw it from the corner of his eye, and stared at it again until it was gone. Constance noticed the silence. "What is it?" she asked.

"Nothing."

Dad knocked on the octagonal window, mouthing: "We're hungry."

"Constance, I thought I meant more than that."

"You do, dear, I—"

"Then don't leave me hanging," Trevin interrupted, and then hung up on her. That was bold for him. Maybe stupid. But he had to get his breath back. He felt queasy, rejected. It was time to cater to his starving folks.

His dad was at the window again, pretending to be eating his own arm.

* * *

Constance didn't show up. That wasn't a surprise. What was a shock was the news Carl had to share with his son on the way to the restaurant. He'd been laid off. They'd traveled all the way to Chicago to tell Trevin in person, keeping the terrible news at bay until they were all face to face. Half the company had been let go, his entire department exterminated.

It happened the day Carl arrived home early—back in Rochester—when he'd taken them on the hike to the sacred center in the forest preserve. It had been a pilgrimage, of sorts; a mad stab at solace. At least there'd be a severance package.

The world was spinning out of control, for the Lambroses personally as well as globally. No one knew how or why this spiral of madness had been ignited. But did it matter? The mystery behind Trevin's hunches had been unveiled. He consoled his parents all the way to the restaurant. They hadn't picked Thai. Over the meal, his father was impossibly apologetic. Maybe that's where Trevin got it from …

"Dad, it's not your fault. Don't beat yourself up. We've all been there. That's just the way it is these days. Don't forget what we talked about in your living room. I'll always be here for you guys—always. One family, one struggle. But we're together."

The universe …

Trevin had to excuse himself. He vanished to the bathroom and composed himself. He almost punched the towel dispenser off the wall. *Not them!* he seethed. *Please not them!*

Back at the table, his mother and father wondered if they should have told him earlier. When Trevin returned to the table, they didn't even get into the fact that they were in dire straits with the house mortgage, or that they didn't have enough to retire on. Nothing was clear anymore. They almost couldn't eat the hot food when it was set in front of them.

"Let's try to have some fun while we're here," mom tried.

Trevin told them about Constance, that they needed some time apart. The stress of everything had worn them both down; they needed a break. His parents were sorry for him. Very sorry. They asked how long it would be before he'd see her again. He didn't know. They were taken aback, and concerned they might not see her. Over the years, Trevin had dined in restaurants alone, noticing pairs with nothing to say, no communication between them. That wasn't the case here. Dad reached for the pitcher of water and filled his wife's glass. His hand was trembling.

Trevin became racked with emotion. The lessons in hard knocks had pushed him to the limit. He had to make another stand—they *had* to shake off the blues. "You know, I've said this before," he began passionately, "but I love both of you. A lot. You've given me everything. I'll never—ever—let anything happen to you. I'd die before that would happen."

"Trevin!" his mother reacted. "For God's sake, don't say that."

"I would. I hate this. I don't know why all of this is happening; I wanted your lives to be rich and beautiful beyond imagination."

Dad's facial muscles were clenching. "That's a tall order, Trevin. This is life. Hey, we forgot to say grace. Can we do that?" Carl bowed his head, mom followed. Trevin stayed on them, still jacked up.

"Lord," his father said, "thank You for bringing us together. We've had our trials as of late, but we know we're not the only ones. We are missing someone tonight who's made a great mark on us. We ask that You bless her, too. May this week bring happiness ahead of the struggles, and may peace come to us all. Amen." They made the sign of the cross.

"Thanks for adding Constance," Trevin said quietly.

"You're welcome."

Trevin had taken care of the bill in advance.

❊ ❊ ❊

Carl lost it in the parking lot after having found out his son paid for the meal. The stress had finally bested the patriarch, as well, and he'd blown his top. April had to step in and calm her husband. He was really upset—not the reaction Trevin had wanted. There was no pushing or shoving, but there was uncharacteristic yelling, and the man's annoyance shot up to a point Trevin had rarely seen. Carl honestly didn't appreciate his son spending any more of his money, and tried literally shoving cash back in Trevin's pocket. Trevin only took it to calm him down. April was a bundle of nerves, and lectured them both. This was not how the week was going to go! She was damn serious! "Do you both understand?" she ordered. "I won't have this! We're all under pressure! Now the both of you get a grip and stop this childishness right now!"

When mom yelled, Carl and his son listened.

On their way home, they picked up groceries for the week, mom coaching her boys back to health through reminiscing, bringing back some of the greatest memories. The "oldies" were "goodies." They served a purpose. They were good to think about. They helped everyone now. They helped to remember the love. They helped get the happiness flowing again, where its power lingered at the forefront of their brains—placating… appeasing …

They circled the neighborhood, eventually finding a spot on Salmon, north of the cement factory. They'd have to walk. It would provide an opportunity to work off the heavy dinner. It had been an exhausting first day. Jet lag had taken its toll.

Trevin expounded on Midwest Septembers. They were hit or miss, like Western New York. One year autumn would be comfortable, the next miserable with summer's leftover heat. Miraculously, tonight was the former: dry as a lint trap but pleasant, twilight swooping in like a gentle bird seeking shelter.

Mrs. Lambrose turned her attention to the first stars, shining like diamonds in the sapphire firmament, seeming like they'd popped on and not been there a minute prior. Trevin prompted her to make a wish. She did as requested. They were almost to the staircase when the streetlights came on—*all of them*. Even at Trevin's corner.

"What'd you wish for?" dad asked.

"I'm not saying," she reprimanded. "You don't say what you've wished for. It won't come true. Take it on blind faith—I've asked for plenty."

They all laughed, the good sound joining the night birds and the el and the Metra. All of it seemed to mix. Trevin suggested coffee. They'd sit and chat for another hour or so before retiring to bed. Just when they were absorbing the healthy mojo again, a box truck blasted by on Salmon—right near them—startling them crazy. Mom yelped!

"Where'd that thing come from?" asked dad.

They'd never seen it coming. It took a moment to recover. The clumsy vehicle took a mean right on Munnison, bouncing and rattling off like an angry rhinoceros. Dad grumbled something about crazy-wacko city drivers, and for a nano-second, Trevin had gone on attack-mode, prepared to counter attack. Paranoia had never quite left. It itched, teased, haunted. He developed a clammy sensation, like they were vulnerable, susceptible to some unseen evil force—like they were being studied. What the hell was this? All the same, he felt surer moving his mother to the other side of him, away from the street.

"What are you doing?" she asked.

"It was just cutting through," Trevin said of the truck, stifling the obvious comparison to the night of horror. "A lot of idiots do that here. Everyone on the street hates that."

When they were at the foot of his staircase, mom had to enjoy the sky one last time. The creepy feeling had left Trevin, for now. Dad was just glad to finally be nearing getting off his feet.

"Ready?" Trevin asked the two.

The three ascended, mom first, dad second. Trevin came up the rear, surreptitious glances thrown up and down Munnison. Another Metra bulleted by, shaking the staircase. Mom held on, reacting to it. Trevin explained this was another common occurrence. The black eyes of the first-floor windows stared with nefarious intent, even in this early twilight light. He jogged the last steps to get past them, unlocking the door, snapping on the track lighting.

As they were safely sealed inside, Trevin was secretly mourning their departure already. It was going to be awful when they had to go back. He felt he had to make the most with them while he could. Time was gold! After everyone had changed into comfortable evening apparel, they reassumed their rightful places in the studio as they did in Rochester; the same configuration as on Sweet Briar. Mom and dad were on the sofa, Trevin on his art chair. Dad immediately snatched the remote and turned on the TV to a local news broadcast. The television was one Trevin had found in the alley and lugged in. It worked perfectly. The old one had been completely trashed in the fight.

There was a morbid police drama unfolding in real time; something about a bank robbery gone awry. Six people had been killed already.

"Carl, must we?" April pleaded.

He tried other channels, bombarded with bad news, infomercials and moronic sitcoms. Carl turned it off almost immediately. It was time to just chat, not about anything grim. Light stuff, things that made them content. More memories, perhaps. They'd prosper from the gift of being with each other.

They didn't find much to talk about. Trevin asked if the air was too cold, and turned it up a notch. They were on their own, controlling the environment in the bedroom. Carl and April retired within the hour, thanking their son for picking them up at the airport. Trevin hugged them goodnight, watched them retreat to their quarters, close the door …

… feeling the need to protect them. Unease, dread, was prickling the air.

He took their place on the sofa, sentiments of all shapes and sizes roiling in his mind. Horrors were mounting; the world on the brink of destruction.

CHAPTER 38

Trevin had a memorable moment at the Museum of Science and Industry the next day, summing up how he was feeling overall; about the future of humankind, the decline of its value system. It happened at the Henry Crown Space Center, an exhibit he'd always loved—given his deep interest in the cosmos. Besides, it was a good distraction. Best to do a few, touristy things.

The Apollo Moon Landing exhibit was a life-sized replica of the module spacecraft the American astronauts used to reach Earth's satellite. Simply awe-inspiring. Terra Firma was a vivid blue sphere set against an immense black universe filled with stars, the craft having landed on the moon's surface, the American flag planted on the barren gray ground. This had always been one of Trevin's favorite displays.

He worked his way in on the side, wishing to unite with the grand achievement, and consider its significance. What made it difficult to get up close was a squadron of schoolchildren who'd commandeered the area, listening to the guide, blocking the diorama from those in back.

The capsule looked awfully minuscule and claustrophobic, given the fact that the astronauts had traveled in it for a total of six harrowing days—three going, three returning. Trevin considered the stress, the monumentally complicated procedures carried out with supreme accuracy. He squeezed in, wedging to the corner. Looking up, he pondered civilization opening to the stars with this giant step.

He inadvertently looked down.

Someone had etched the words "FUCK YOU" on a moon boulder with black marker.

Some would laugh, he knew. Some would ignore it (not the curators!). Someone might take a video with an iPhone and post it on YouTube, and the snarky comments would follow.

Maybe Trevin had lost his sense of humor, but it seemed an affront on progress itself. The defacement would remain for the next noticer. Perhaps a child.

* * *

On the Magnificent Mile, April Lambrose browsed a few of the fancier stores while her husband and son waited in a nearby food court, talking of sports and Chicago history. Dad's thoughts never strayed far from trying to figure out a way out of the crisis he'd been thrown into. Trevin's never left Constance. April almost bought a power outfit. She dreamed of landing a great new job.

When they met up, April unloaded on her men the biggest hugs the shoppers had witnessed in public that day.

* * *

That evening, they ate comfort food in Trevin's apartment: sandwiches and soup from their stockpiling at the grocery store. Afterward, to form, Carl and April set about cleaning the dishes, their son having to wrench that duty away. They next went to straightening what they'd mussed in the rooms, fussing about like badgers on steroids. Trevin told them to stop. When they pulled out the vacuum cleaner, Trevin ordered them to the studio. "Just freakin' relax! Tomorrow I'll turn you loose downstairs. Maybe you can finish the floor."

Nerves were frayed. It was difficult to put aside the worry.

She hadn't brought it up, but the tiny hairs on April's arms had been prickling since returning to Munnison. Goose bumps dimpled her skin, and it wasn't a flux from the outside temperature. Constant tension was ongoing.

And so it was for Carl, additionally. He just didn't want to say anything.

It was as if they felt they should be doing something—something in "preparation." What, exactly, eluded them. They weren't going to administer group self-therapy; they wouldn't even know where to begin. Trevin went to the octagonal window and stared out, seeing if there was anything out of the ordinary out there. The skies had been relatively quiet, the sunsets mellow.

Something was impending …

He tried to remember what it was like to hold Constance's hand.

He loosely thought of the Lakebreeze Healthcare Campus, wondering if he should call, set something up with Allison. Motivation was lacking. It was hard to come up with good ideas.

"Your mother accuses me of doing that—" dad said, sneaking up on him. "—staring at the street."

"You watch every car," Trevin chuckled.

"I do not."

"Want to enjoy the balcony before it gets dark? Maybe we'll get a good sky show."

"Actually, I don't. Let's not do that," mom answered for them, actually frightened at the idea of being so exposed. "Who's up for lemonade?"

She made it in the kitchen. They enjoyed a glass with the brownies purchased downtown.

About an hour later, when nightfall had formally arrived, all their eyelids were half closing, like leaflets fluttering in a determined breeze. The more Trevin quieted on his drafting chair, seeing his precious folks on the sofa—husband-wife, mother-father—the more devout his personal vows became. He imagined a cone of security around them, reinforced by a field of love. Soon, it felt like he was floating, a beam of intention and hope traveling from his heart to theirs. However metaphoric, he prayed God would shield them. His dear, sweet mother opened her eyes, smiled at him.

"I think we're fading, dear," she said softly. Dad broke from his daze, sat upright, and finished the last of his lemonade.

"You're right," he said, "I'm beat. I'm in that weird state where I'm tired, but know I'll have a hard time falling asleep. Maybe I'll read."

"It's been a good day," said Trevin.

They set about deciding who was going into the bathroom first. Naturally, mom won. Dad changed into his usual sleeping attire: shorts and an undershirt. Old school. Then he sat on the bed and just stared. Trevin turned off the lights in the studio and went to the kitchen, cleaning the glasses in the sink. He saw dad brooding through the doorframe and offered support. "Hang in there, pal," he said.

"If you need help paying rent, let me know."

"Dad, no."

"I can see why you're happy here. You'll be on your feet soon."

Trevin perceived time slowing; a surreal trick of his mind. The water running in the bathroom sink took on an exaggerated quality. The droning of the air conditioning became the hum returning to his head. He wiped the trickle of sweat dampening his forehead with the back of his hand, then heard the wind outside shudder the windows. Dad clapped Trevin on the shoulder as he came out of the bedroom and passed by, switching places with his wife in the bathroom. As his mother was entering the bedroom, Trevin asked how she was doing.

"I'm okay, Trevin. Too bad there isn't a Blue Flower Park around here we could go to."

The sudden and sharp memory hit both men like a shot of magic, boosting their spirits. "Blue Flower Park?" Trevin exclaimed. "The amusement park? What made you think of that?"

Mom snickered once, then answered, "Someone once told me to think of happy memories when things got gloomy."

Trevin knew exactly whom she was referring to. "Constance …"

"The very one," mom said back, sadness in her voice.

Ignoring the obvious cue to talk about the lady, Trevin asked, "How long has Blue Flower Park been gone from Rochester now?"

Dad began brushing his teeth, but did so at the doorway. "A long time," he answered, adding to the reference. "We hadn't gone there since taking you as a kid."

"Every Memorial Day Weekend," Trevin said. "That was the tradition."

The wind slapped the panes. The memory had triggered something much-needed. In the darkened domicile, the three began sharing happiness from the park. Trevin's mind reeled back to those carefree days. He stared at the light from the bedroom, cutting a path across the tile floor and partially up the wall, listening to his parents talk of that special place. He went to the refrigerator and helped himself to a second glass of lemonade, his mother reminding him of the time he was 14, and cleaned up easily at the arcade. "You won easy," she said.

Dad smiled, rinsed out his mouth. "One baseball at the plastic bottles. That's all it took. My baseball-practicing with you paid off that day."

Now Trevin smiled, blood pressure calming. "One throw. I won a toy robot."

"Tell the story again," said mom. "It'll make me laugh."

Trevin recited what he could. Truth be had, he did it for their benefit—he remembered everything! On the midway, in order to win the prize, he had to gun down a total of three fake bottles all attached to a long doll rod, using three softballs. The first pitch was thrown so hard and so accurately that three came down at once. A second toss wasn't even needed.

The three Lambroses broke into laughter. Collective harmony and bliss began to flow.

"The barker was impressed," dad said. "Said he'd never seen that happen."

"The Sky Ride was my favorite," mom interjected. "Remember? It took you over the whole park—fifty feet up. And you lost your sneaker over the lake, Trevin?"

Trevin chortled harder. "Aw—hysterical. It came right off; I was swinging my feet so violently. We watched it all the way down. I can still see it hitting the water."

"We had to buy you flip-flops after that, you brat," mom laughed. "And the carnival music? It played all day. Did I ever tell you guys how much I hate clowns?"

"A million times, April," said dad. "We know that. There were only a few there."

"A few is enough! The good ol' days came with a price."

This was cathartic, light years better than brooding over the current state of affairs. The proverbial seal had been cracked, and the joy flowed, effortlessly, urgently. The more they concentrated on the specifics, talking about them, the more real they became, each morsel building on top of the previous. Moments the trio hadn't thought of in eons were given rebirth, and through the process, their souls became intertwined and spirits grew. Blue Flower Park was there in all its glory. April won a prize—a stuffed animal. She donated it to the church bazaar. Dad remembered a child getting sick on a kiddy coaster. The mortified parents had to apologize afterward to all the riders who'd been hit by vomit. There were game booths, pinball machines and fortune tellers. The apartment lit up. Lightning was entering the picture. Their laughter stopped for a second as they checked the windows, but then went right back into the good times, enjoying each other's recollections. The euphoric feelings freed them, dislodging from their subconscious like buried treasures. Trevin happened to glance down at his hand. He was going to chug the remaining lemonade (a subtle tingle was there, not unpleasant).

He could see right through it to the floor …

CRASH! He dropped the glass, breaking it into pieces. *What the hell was that?*

The merriment ceased. Dad snapped on the light as mom grabbed paper towels, and while Trevin remained frozen in place, they wetted them, set about mopping up the shards, mom ordering her boys to watch their step.

When Trevin looked again, his hand was back to normal—solid and firm.

They asked if he was all right, what happened. Trevin didn't know. He checked his parents' hands for the same illusion. There was nothing out of the ordinary about them. He didn't know what had happened.

"And we were just talking about your hand-and-eye skills?" dad sniped.

"No-one-get-cut!" mom accentuated, tossing the wadded balls into the garbage.

Trevin turned over his shoulder to the pitch-black studio. Through the octagonal window, the streetlight out there was blinking rapidly. The power was shorting. The pole itself and the tree branches were swaying. Another storm? There hadn't been any reports …

The joy was gone from Trevin's heart.

"Crisis averted," dad said, confirming the floor was clear. "It broke in chunks."

Out there, atmospheric cruelty was flogging the trees, punishing like a hateful stepchild—in direct contrast to the jollity that had been generating in the kitchen. Trevin shut the light back off, suddenly frightened for himself and his parents.

"What are you doing?" asked dad.

Trevin was convinced he might be losing his mind. "Sorry, sorry about that, I'm okay. I just hate the sound of breaking glass. Everyone, let's go to bed. Let's get tucked in and forget about everything. Mom, dad—to your places, let's go. Forget about the storm."

They looked at him like he was crazy. He checked his hand again. Good as new. Eventually, they heeded his advice, and mom and dad made sure Trevin was jesting and went to their room, shutting the door. Trevin stayed, hearing them settling, dad groaning with relief. Then he went to the washroom and splashed cold water on his face.

Fifteen minutes later, Trevin was in the studio, surrendering to his pillow, trying to force himself to sleep. The storm was not letting up. It seemed to be rocking the house. Only the air conditioning could keep the howling at bay. Trevin's eyes kept snapping open, staring at the power button on his computer across the room—an all-seeing eye examining him for signs of madness—reminding that he was still ignoring coming clean about what had really happened here.

Micro changes in air density were touching his skin, urging him on. He couldn't take it anymore; intuition was killing him. He'd toss and turn all night if he didn't get this off his chest. He got up, shuffled to their door—and like the night at Mr. Tavalier's—he drew a breath, and knocked. "What is it?" his father demanded, intentionally sounding like a hard ass.

"You asleep?" Trevin asked.

"Does it sound like we're asleep? What do you want?"

"Got one more minute?"

His mother's voice came next: "Trevin, if you want to talk, open the door."

When he opened it, it was too dark to make out their figures. This was another portal, of sorts. Their window unit was much louder than in the studio. The blobs repositioned, propped up in bed now. Mom asked, "Is something wrong?"

He leaned in. "I need to tell you both something."

They were vague silhouettes, but now they were clutching the pillows in their hands, probably bracing. Not comforting body language.

"Sorry to disturb you," he began. "It's the main reason I came home. It wasn't me losing my job. There was an incident."

There was an incident. The sentence sounded appalling. Dad's reedy arm turned on the new lamp closest to him, the one Trevin also rummaged from the alley after the previous one had been smashed in the story he was about to unleash. Everyone was squinting now. "What happened?"

Gone was the sarcastic tone.

Now they were going to be plagued with this new horror, Trevin thought. Anger replaced nerves. He spat the story out—all of it—from soup to nuts, sans the supernatural finale with the orb. When he was finished, his mother said only one thing—

"Oh my God!"

Dad was also dumbstruck. He needed clarification. "*What?*"

Sickness settled in Trevin's stomach. "I didn't know the guy. It was totally random. I know his name: Brian Annarez. He had a criminal record. He was breaking in to steal stuff; he didn't think anyone was home. The police think he was responsible for other incidents in the neighborhood: an elderly lady. When he attacked me I went crazy."

Mom was grabbing her mouth.

"And when it was all over …" said Trevin, "yeah, he died."

A long pause followed as the significance ripped his parents like battery acid. Undoubtedly, this was the most debilitating jolt to date. Dad swung his legs to the floor, quietly asking Trevin why he hadn't divulged this before.

"How could I?" Trevin answered. "Haven't you been through enough? I've been nothing but a drain. The guy thought this was an abandoned house because of the damned first floor. My landlord blamed me, for whatever reason, and now he wants me out. I have a month."

Mom wasn't able to hold back the tears. "My God… I'm so glad you weren't …"

Dad had to be clear. "You said this man was hit by a car?"

"Yes, after I chased him out. I was trying to stop him. I saw the car flying up. Remember that box truck earlier? I told you—people race up this street all the time."

"So… you're free and clear?"

"Well, yeah, so to speak …" His parents stared at him. The insidiousness of it all …

So here I am again, Trevin screamed at himself. *Doing it again. Look at their faces. I'm delivering them nothing but more anguish. What a good son I am!*

He had never seen a scowl like the one his parents were now sporting, dad's brow a cluster of wriggling snakes. Each aspect must have been like splinters under their nails, right down to Detective MacDrenner's interrogation. The report had cleared him of any wrongdoing, yes, but mom was steepling her fingers to her head already, saying prayers. Trevin spared them the gore. Who knows what they would have thought of the blue orb rising from the corpse?

"It's been eating me like a cancer," Trevin said.

"I bet," said dad, staring at the sheets, still unable to find the sagacity in not telling them before now. "Still you should have …"

"What good would it have done?"

Mom scrambled out of bed and hugged her son, apologizing for crying. "I feel sinful saying this… but better him dead than you. Put it behind you, Trevin, you defended yourself."

Trevin relaxed his mother's grip, had dad return her to the bed, and pulled up a kitchen chair and sat on it in the door frame. He wasn't going to break down in front of them. He made a bad stab at a joke: "Trumped your lay-off news, doesn't it, pops?"

Dad rubbed his neck, unable to laugh. "How much of this does Constance know?"

"Everything. Why?"

"The question just came to mind. I'm just hoping she knows."

There was another enormous burst of lightning, and the wind felt like it was going to blow the roof off. This time it scared everyone. Dad checked the time on the clock radio.

"Near midnight," he said. "I say we leave this behind and get a good night's sleep. We can resume talking about it in the morning."

"Great idea," said Trevin. "Mom?"

Mom was good with it, although she couldn't stop the tears. Within the next half hour—purification (mostly) complete—all three found dreamland, waterways of understanding passing between them.

* * *

Trevin sat upright, the cyclopean window next to him. It was now the middle of the night. Outside, the flashing and blowing was ferocious. He leaned off the sofa, seeing a shape enter the kitchen and disappear behind the half wall. It was dad, fetching water from the sink, dipping his head under the spigot like always. Trevin heard the tell-tale slurping. *A trait of that generation,* Trevin thought amusedly. *Mr. Weber did the same with the hose.* Out of the dark came an "aah."

Trevin called out: "Still don't use a glass?"

A pause, then dad answered sharply, keeping his voice low. "Don't want to break one like you did, you clod. Go to sleep."

"Why're you up?"

"Same reason you are. I'm not sleeping."

Trevin was relieved he'd told them about the incident, but he still had that ominous tension in his gut. His mother surprised them both by also coming out of the bedroom, tying her robe belt tighter across her waist. "Nobody's sleeping with you two yakking."

She also got water. She used a mug.

Setting feet on the floor, Trevin asked, "Is it going to rain or what? This wind!"

"It hasn't made up its mind," said dad, and went back into the pitch-black bedroom with his wife. Trevin followed them to it, once more staring into its inky depths. The air blowing out at him was freezing. "Oh, goody, April, he's looming again. Not going to surprise us with anything else, are you?"

"Carl, stop," she said. "What is it, dear?"

Trevin said, "Nothing." In truth, that deep desire to protect was coming up again. He had no idea why.

"I'm still thinking of what you went through," mom said.

Dad said, "So that means him standing there, staring at us all night?"

"Maybe we can go to the Botanical Garden tomorrow," Trevin followed. "I know you'd like that, old man."

"Then we have a plan," dad said. "Now go to bed and stay there."

Trevin was going to leave, maybe do some reading, but something on the balcony caught his attention. It was through the octagonal window, from his peripheral vision. Whatever it was had momentarily blacked out the view of the streetlight across Munnison.

He backed up to get a better angle.

"What is it?" asked dad.

"Nothing," he said again, but wasn't so sure.

Within moments, part of the view became blacked out again—just the corner. Sure enough, *something* was on the balcony. Trevin's fluids froze. It could've been a figure, but he couldn't be certain. His eyes locked on the scene.

"Trevin, what?" his mother insisted.

The "blob" cleared the octagonal window to the front door. Trevin saw the crown of (a head?) in the Demi-lune window. It looked like a hood with cupped hands trying to see in. Was someone standing on his toes? It might have been looking straight at Trevin. Alarms went off in his mind, wild cannon fire alerting him to terror. Then "it" dropped from sight. There was a scramble in bed—must be his father.

"Stay here."

Trevin charged at the studio. Whatever this was, he was going to use his body as a blockade. He only got to mid-point when the screen door yanked outward and the inside door shuddered with violent, rapid kicks: *BOOM! BOOM!* His mother screamed. Trevin halted. Dad was already in the kitchen. "What is that?!" dad shouted, blocked by his son's back framing the studio.

Trevin lunged, trying to reach the door—

The next mule-kick blew the hinges off, slamming the door wide open to the night—a harsh gale sucking in like a tornado, loose papers exploding into the air, plaster chips splintering. In rushed a lone assailant with a handgun, holding it at arm's length, swearing at the top of his lungs: "*Don't fuckin' move! Nobody fuckin' move!*"

Dad bellowed for his son—"Trevin!" Mom screamed again.

The merciless voice wouldn't let up, shouting: "*Don't fuckin' move—you fucks!*"

Trevin's hands shot up, ready to block anything blasting past him. He was going to sacrifice himself. The figure proceeded further, annihilation-mode—indeed in a hooded sweatshirt—leaves, twigs following. Mr. Lambrose hit the kitchen light on impulse, blinding everybody. Mom screamed and stumbled into the kitchen, falling on her knees. Carl picked her up, put her behind him. No one knew who this maniac was.

Horrific déjà vu scalded Trevin's fried mind. The dirt bag kept the hood on, the greasy sweatshirt flapping open, revealing an emblem of an American bison. Ripped jeans, gym shoes.

Trevin regained momentum, went to bull rush. The gun indexed, aiming right between his eyes. His father's shouting wrangled back any fractured awareness he had. More foul warnings continued: "*I fuckin' mean it, mother fucker!*" The gun also pointed at Mr. Lambrose. "*I'll blow your heads off!*"

"Dad!" Trevin could finally shout. "Listen to him! Don't move! Save mom!"

"I got her, I got her!" April latched to her husband. She wasn't going to abandon her family.

The cacophony was deafening. The sky looked like it was going to rip the roof off. Trevin crab-walked sideways—arms out, hands up—attempting to dilute the intruder's ferocity. All he could act on was shielding his beloved family. Any misstep could end their lives. He had to wait for the right moment, Neanderthal instincts turning on again. This was connected to Brian Annarez, he just knew. This psychopath was taller, thinner. The asshole slammed the crippled door shut with a full extension of the heel of his boot, ceasing the windstorm, sealing the prisoners inside. Trevin heard his dad's abstract yelling, ordering mom back to the bedroom. She wouldn't go. For the love of God—the gun was real, real as sin!

"Who *are* you?!" dad raged with command.

"*Shut the fuck up!*"

"Dad! Don't—"

Carl started threatening the criminal back, warning him not to harm anyone. Vicious, conniving eyes volleyed at him. Trevin got in on the act, demanding to know if this "was payback."

"I'm doing the talkin', not you!"

This had to be what this was. "No way are you going to do this!"

That gun was a gaping death hole. *"I fuckin' will! You're dead!"*

"What is your name?"

Mr. Lambrose called for his son to join them, but Trevin didn't budge. This would have been a tactical error. He had to stay in this scum's face, distract him. His mother was crying and pleading, which really ticked off the criminal. "Shutup, lady! I've come for him!"

For Trevin.

"Mom, it's all right!" This gave the intruder unintended, valuable information.

"Mom, huh? These your folks? Fucking righteous ..." Arrogant, gloating.

The hood came off. The punk took more steps, coming into the light, and the Lambroses saw the visage of revenge. To Trevin, there was a strong resemblance to the Annarez character—this one also in his mid-twenties. Black hair hung with angst, an uneven goatee added to the wickedness.

"Who *are* you?"

"No questions! Get back like daddy says!"

Trevin had no choice. He was forced into the kitchen, in front of the table, mom and dad behind that. He bumped its edge, made it rock. The thug marched forward, weapon-arm an iron bar—spotting from one person to the next—stopping equidistant in the apartment, between the bathroom and the walk-in closet. The Lambroses were now three sitting ducks. Perfect prey. Mom was weeping. Trevin felt his father's free hand reach across the table and cup his shoulder.

Carl, to the gunman: "Don't-you-hurt-my-family, boy."

"Shutup."

"Do whatever... he... says ..." Trevin said calmly.

Lightning lit up the skies, as if reacting to the insane, tribal mentality. Trevin wondered if this was ultimate Karma, past indiscretions coming back to destroy them, and blamed himself for the dread brought down upon them. It certainly wasn't out of the realm of possibility, given how his life had gone. *I wanted to do bodily harm. Now I've brought my poor parents into it. I should die.*

He wanted to cry out to the heavens, but he had to concentrate.

"Why the surprised face?" the intruder asked him, sardonically amused. "Didn't you see this coming? You know who you killed, didn't you?"

Validation. This *was* about Brian Annarez. "Keep on me," Trevin instructed, "only at me."

"You took something of mine."

"We can talk this over, mister," dad offered. "Trevin's a good son."

"So that's your name: 'Trevin.' Good to know. I'm finding out all kinds of crazy shit."

"I don't know what you think happened," Trevin said, still trying to reason, "but you've got it wrong. If this is about Brian Annarez, you don't know the truth. Are you a relative?"

"Cousin."

"He did it to himself."

The gangster's face snarled terribly. "Bitch, no! *You* killed my blood!"

"Your 'blood'? Brian Annarez broke in *here*. Is this your retaliation?"

"My what?" The crumb didn't even know the meaning of the word.

Trevin felt urine trickling down his leg. God, he had to protect his family. "Look, I'm sorry he's dead, but I'm telling you—it was an accident. Tell me what you know of it, and I'll explain."

"Mister, if our son says it was an accident, it was an accident. Now let us go. Turn and—" "*Shutup!* I ain't talkin' to you."

"*Don't*—" Trevin snapped, matching his opponents tone, then brought it down, "—talk to them like that." His blood was lava. "That… was your van the other day, wasn't it? The white Econoline with the tinted windows. You were watching me."

"Stakin' you out, bitch, that's right. Had to make sure you were who you were. Been plannin', you haven't been around. Thought you blew town, chicken shit."

White-hot fury.

"Listen and understand. If Brian was here, he'd tell you I had nothing to do with his death. He was hit by a car after he attacked me and ran out. If anyone was the 'chicken shit'…"

"Trevin …" his father cautioned.

"Get it? I didn't kill him. You got your information wrong, however you received it."

The gun trembled. "I know he died after being here. That's what I fuckin' know."

Mrs. Lambrose started praying openly, hoping God would intervene. She offered money. The intruder wouldn't hear it. They wouldn't call the police. He laughed at that. "You be quiet, too, lady."

"I said—" Trevin growled, "don't talk to them like that. You're doing what your *cousin* did. You don't want to make that mistake."

"This ain't no mistake, mother fucker. Don't make no difference if mommy and daddy are wasted, too. This is for 'Bri.'"

"What did you hear?" Trevin dug. "Tell us. Let's clarify things."

"He had a child, you know. Baby girl. Brand new."

"How could I know that? He should've thought about her. He obviously wasn't thinking about her."

The trespasser's bloodshot eyes were watering now, nostrils flaring. "I'm gonna kill you."

"Mister, put the gun down!" Carl Lambrose ordered. "This won't bring Brian back. We love our son, like you loved your cousin."

"This evens things, pops. This—" brandishing the weapon, "—is the equalizer."

Trevin kept staring, trying to bore the energy in. "Nothing's mattered more. Humble yourself, friend. All you've had has been given to you."

The intruder distorted his face, displayed poor teeth. "Are you a fuckin' pastor, Lambose?" (Mispronouncing it) "I know your name, it's on the mailbox."

"And you're an Annarez. See how that works?"

"You killed him."

"I did not. I have the police report."

"You lie so bad."

"Want to see it?"

"No, I want to end your life."

Trevin visualized his spirit blanketing the depravity. "Mom, dad. I'm sorry for everything. I wouldn't have had you come—"

"Son," dad said. "We're here. Gladly and willingly."

Suddenly, mom gathered her lungs and screamed: *Just go! For God's sake—we've told you the truth. Just leave us be! Save yourself from your own stupidity and leave!*

This jolted everybody. Breath was held.

The attacker launched into an obscenity-laced diatribe, cutting everyone down to size—telling them who was setting the rules, who "the fucking king" was here. Revulsion reverberated against the walls, the barrel finding this one, then that one.

Trevin figured the dirt bag hadn't planned what to do once inside. "Keep that on me, fool. This is between you and me. You and me." *Mom, dad, I'm sorry. Why did I listen to Constance? Bringing you to town.*

Mr. Obscenity smirked. "It's all of us now. No choice."

"There's always choice," Trevin said. "Brian ran out because he knew he was doing wrong. Like you."

Dad tried a different tactic. "Trevin, we know this man has goodness in him. He'll tell us his name."

"Wanna know my name? It's 'Harry.' You fuckin' happy? It don't matter 'cause you ain't gonna be around."

"There's a higher order, Harry," dad said. "You'll answer to it."

"Bullshit. There ain't nothin' after this."

"I saw proof of it, Harry," said Trevin. "Twice. Once, after your cousin died."

Harry swiftly grew confused. "Huh?" Even his parents didn't know what was implied.

"Trevin?" That was dad.

The wind pounded the house. Lightning lit up the rest of the apartment. "Trust me," Trevin stressed, "the soul survives. Something better is out there."

The gunman became curious. "What'd you see?"

It was the moment Trevin had been waiting for: a brief respite of the intruder's utter hatred. Keeping his hands out, Trevin took one gentle step forward. He was going to elaborate, but at that exact moment, the wind became too much, finally pressuring the casing of the rocking streetlight across the street so much that it blew the bulb out, shattering with a disproportionately loud boom.

Everyone jumped. *Harry* jerked.

BANG!!

The automatic gun accidentally discharged, a single bullet striking Trevin in the sternum—at the heart, shirt blown open—lifting him off his feet and backward onto the table, where he crashed off it, collapsing at his parents' feet.

Two louder screams never shook the Earth. Carl and April wailed at the horror, rushing in and grabbing their son, pulling him to them— blood spraying everywhere. They toppled to the floor. Trevin was instantly paralyzed. Harry's eyes went wide. He still had the gun pointed, smoke curling out of the barrel. Harry's surprise was so sudden it might've been able to turn him into a pillar of salt. Carl and April clutched at the wound, mom shrieking: "*Oh dear God! What have you done?! What have you done?!*"

Carl lunged at the refrigerator, yanking hand towels from the handle, forcing them into the gash, April shouting for someone to call 911.

But they had no phone!

Harry blinked in leaden flaps, pathetic brain numbing as driftwood. His arm flopped, almost dropping the firearm. He stumbled backward, finishing in the studio, where he first toppled the art chair, then crumbled against the drafting table, spilling Trevin's sketchpads on the floorboards— quartz crystal rocking like a seesaw.

Trevin's eyes were fixed straight up. He was sucking for breath, red liquid and spittle bubbling from his mouth, unable to grasp what happened. April lifted his head to keep his airway open, Carl kicked the kitchen table to make more room, yelling: "Find a phone, Harry! There's one right by you! Get it, damn you!!"

But Harry couldn't comply. He had become useless, gawking at the scene like a drone, detached from the efforts of the strangers trying to keep the man he'd just shot alive. His voice attempted a weak, "Let him die." He tried again, louder this time. "Let him die!!"

"*Shut the hell up!!*" Mr. Lambrose screamed. "*Get that damn cell phone, you bastard! Behind you!* Trevin, keep breathing, keep breathing!"

Harry mechanically looked about. No real effort.

Trevin's hands began fighting his parents'. Perhaps this was mechanical, too; the flight-or-fight impulse at work. There was no doubt, however, his agony was searing. Dad held him down. Mom tore into the drawers, retrieving more of anything to soak up the gore. She slammed her knees when falling back to him; tears were cascading into the slippery blood.

"*Get that phone!*"

Actually, the "bastard"—in his sick mind—was determining whether or not to finish the job, wondering if he should put two more in the old goats' heads. There was too much noise.

Giving up on the human filth, Carl shouted at April: "Where's my phone?"

"In the bedroom!" she blubbered back. "I think! I don't know!"

"Keep your hands here!"

Carl broke away, striking the bedroom light, tearing the area apart. Couldn't find it. Came out, pointed at Harry. "I'm coming that way, asshole! I'm looking for that phone!"

Two steps, and …

BANG!!

The second shot rang out, missing Carl's head by an inch, lodging in the kitchen wall. Warning shot. Harry had lifted his arm back up, and shot on purpose. April screamed: *"Please! You're not doing this!! What is wrong with you?!"*

"I AM doing this!" Harry screeched in return.

Pure hell.

The valiant couple returned to Trevin's condition, working desperate measures. Trevin was making the sound of a broken filter sucking in a condemned swimming pool, unable to verbalize; the world blacking out. Dad's knees slid on the blood-spattered floor. "We're not losing you, Trevin, hang on!"

April went to lift her son, but Carl stopped that action. "No! Keep your hands here, dear, press down! Harry, you loathsome scum, I don't care what you do—I'm coming for that phone!"

The gun clanked as Harry pushed from the drafting table, aligning with the front door. Maybe escape was the best policy. "Don't shittin' do it …"

Carl stood like a Minotaur from Greek mythology, readying the charge.

"Carl!" pleaded his wife. "Your son needs you. Let the man go."

Harry again lifted the gun, stomping his foot for effect, breaking pencils underfoot. "Old man, say your fuckin' prayers and come get it."

Mr. Lambrose stomped his own foot, aping the aggressor, visualizing severing the object of his detestation's jugular with his own hands. "I'm going to rip your head off."

Trevin emitted a guttural cry, spiraling toward the inevitable, momentarily pausing dad's attack. Trevin tried rolling over, craving to just curl up and go to sleep. He articulated a sad and frail "M-mom …"

"Don't give up, sweetheart, stay with us—Carl!" she responded, fingers working the scarlet puncture, trying to stop the blood from jetting in pumps. Carl continued staring the devil down, debating what to do.

"Son, your mother has you."

Harry decided not to bail. He was going to end this. Just an additional pound per square inch on the trigger—performed twice—and this annoyance would be over. Vengeance would be his. He took aim. This time he was not going to miss.

Suddenly, there came an audible clunking sound. They could hear it, outside, over the rumbling thunder and heaving wind. Someone was coming up the staircase! Harry swung attention to the door, preparing to blow a hole the size of a whale into it. "Who's that? Who the fuck's comin'?"

The brave couple had no idea. Said as much.

Ears cocked to its abnormality. The person was nearly at the top landing, striding as casually as a dinner guest's arrival. Dread gripped Harry, digging like forks. They saw the figure saunter by the octagonal window to the damaged door, the crown of that person's head pausing in the Demi-lune window, like Harry's. Only this person wasn't going to break down any doors.

Harry ordered his trigger finger to pull.

Then he doubled up. Instantly. Seized in a violent, painful convulsion, disabled from doing anything. He screamed in anguish, face contorting. A key inserted into the lock, followed by a click, then the distressed entrance once more swung open—uppercuts of wind returning. The woman's long hair blew wildly against the blackness. Harry managed an ungracious, "The—fuck?"

But Carl and April knew who it was.

"Constance …" Trevin's mother gasped.

Trevin tried lifting his head at the sound of his love's name, a greater production of blood spilling from his mouth, running down his chin and neck. The great Miss Summerlin held the apartment key Trevin had given her, smiling at him, ignoring the intruder by her. She was dressed in all-white, silky summer clothes, befitting of her super lithe body. It was as though her muscle tone was even more pronounced. On her feet—the sandals they'd heard.

Mr. and Mrs. Lambrose somehow knew. Macroscopic goodness had entered the scene.

Harry decided he was going to kill Constance, and tried. Just as speedily, the smile left her face, replaced by a scowl. Harry collapsed to the floor under the control of an unseen force, incapacitating him as rigor mortis stiffens a cadaver's body. The pain was crushing.

Constance took in full diagnosis of the picture, looking at each person, then forced the door closed with her thoughts. She drew to within inches of the quivering criminal, studying him like an insect, staring into what soul he might have had. The vicious offender was being ripped apart from the inside out, cell by cell, and was too petrified to stare back. Through clenched teeth and bubbling snot, came his appeal: "W-who a-are you?"

"You'll know," Constance replied. "Someone's being assigned to you."

Her voice was stronger than usual. Ubiquitous. Ostensibly coming from all directions. Everyone knew she was here to finish something.

Or begin it.

Trevin wasn't doing well. The female enigma knew that. Time stood still. For everyone. Except Constance, who nodded once in acknowledgment at the patriarch, then the matriarch, and with those big brown eyes, warned Harry: "I'll get to you."

Constance stepped past him, setting the key on the drafting table atop the quartz crystal, and joined the fine people she'd come to know in the kitchen area. Trevin was a dying wreck at her feet. She sensed his heart reach out to her, fixating on her. She thought of just how fully she'd grown to cherish these three, and gushed with empathy.

"Mr. and Mrs. Lambrose," she began, "you came to town. That's good. Everything will be all right now. Trevin, you can hear me, my dear—I've returned the key."

Trevin tried to talk. His body felt like it was split open.

Reality was bending like putty.

The Lambroses knew they were at *some* kind of ground zero.

CHAPTER 39

—◆—

Constance studied Trevin while Carl and April were on hold, waiting for *something* to happen. The kitchen locale became the center of a completely new atmosphere, growing to embrace the Lambroses in an invisible energy bath. The artificial light in the ceiling lamp was the only unnatural contrivance. Constance was now the greatest source of dynamism. Absolutely nothing like this had ever been felt before; incomparable in all of human experience.

Quite the pathos, she saw. April was beyond despondency, supporting her Trevin's bloodied head with one hand, the other pressing the chest wound.

Carl was over them both, cupping them in shelter. Quietly, Carl pleaded first. "Please… we'll do anything… you have to help us. That— *thing*—shot our son."

Constance had blood now poking at her sandals. "I know what that person's done," she responded. "It's your time to be together as family. I've come to put your good memories to use. All of them."

They had no idea what she was talking about. In the background, Harry groaned in misery, still unable to move. April's free hand lifted, reaching to touch the forearm of the mysterious creature before them. They knew Constance was definitely not one of them. One of anything.

Trevin screamed as he also tried to move, another organ rupturing inside him, another life function failing. He coughed, and blood and regurgitated fluids sprinkling upward, spotting his face. His mother put her hand right back.

Constance stepped as close as she could, Trevin right under her. Carl's bloody hand delicately clamped her wrist. "Have mercy …"

The blood slid off Constance's skin in beads, leaving the already perfect skin still unblemished. Carl tried hard not to react to her odd skin texture, cool and utterly smooth. He let go, and more beads hit the tile. Unimaginable influence was in their midst.

"I am… mercy," Constance said.

"I'm… sorry," Carl murmured.

"Don't be. I was receiving last-minute instructions. I got here when I could."

April cried. "Can… you… help?"

"That's why I wanted you here. It was to be just Trevin, at first. After meeting his parents, I put in a special request. This is my beginning, too."

"Don't let him die …" April said.

"No one ever 'dies,' April. I have you here."

Trevin wheezed, gurgled. "Sweetheart… w-who are y-you, r-really…?"

Constance crouched. "I told you you could trust me." Then she kindly asked April to remove her hands. There was hesitation. This would prove difficult. No force on Earth could make it easy for a mother to let go of her dying child. "For what I need to do," she said to the mother.

April slowly lowered Trevin's head to the floor, Carl propping it with yet another blood-soaked towel. Constance kneeled, then escorted her own hands to the gunshot wound, where she applied her own pressure to the destroyed sternum. Her force was greater. Trevin screamed, more terribly this time. Constance's fingers disappeared into a puddle of blood, flints of flesh sticking to them. His parents were instructed to then put their hands on top of hers. In mortal fear, they complied—mom first, dad second—their tears falling and coagulating into the mess.

"Now the chain's complete," Constance said. "Don't take them off until I say."

Dad was going to ask questions, but Trevin managed a full sentence. "I… I loved you."

For a minute, Constance's face changed, stumbling with unexpected emotion. She was going to have to concentrate. She had to stave off the distracting memories of her own; the overjoyed moments she'd shared with Trevin. Moments she knew perhaps she shouldn't have had. Regaining her composure, she said, "I loved you, too, Trevin." Then she looked at all of them. "You're all so beautiful."

Again, Constance was reminded how she wasn't supposed to get involved. But to say such words felt right.

In the lapse, Harry freed from immobilization and broke free into a run at them—startling everybody—lunging at Constance and grabbing her around the throat, yanking her away, disrupting the chain. He rammed the gun against her temple.

"No! NO!!" screamed April.

"*Quiet!!*" Harry screamed back, face distorted through his own pain and bewilderment. He slipped on the blood and almost went down, giving Constance a violent wrest. Everyone started shouting over one another. Constance remained serene, continuing to coach:

"Carl, April, don't give up. Leave your hands there. We're going into the hemoglobin… the platelets."

"*Shut the fuck up!*" Harry was in control—or so he thought—fueled with hate and murder.

"You're sidetracking, Harry," said Constance. "You don't want to do this."

"*How do you know my name?!*"

"*BECAUSE I KNOW!!*" Constance yelled, her voice musical chords, equal in strength to the shuddering storm raging outside.

Astounding. Everyone stared. What the—? Musical chords?

Harry was retaken by the invisible restraint. Once more, he folded, releasing his grip. He started struggling, as if trying to exorcise demons from himself. He was not going to succumb again. Nothing in his mind was more immediate than destroying. Total annihilation. His heart was black.

Over the howling storm, the drone of the air conditioning, there came the soothing and reassuring sound of church bells, off in a distance, not far from where Trevin's apartment was located. It had been there before, but never this clear, never this sharp. They all heard it. Constance channeled it, soaking it in. Harry was hissing in pain.

"Listen …" her voice faded, going back to a human voice. This time she did not falter with Harry. "Church bells." She closed her eyes, rapturously eating it up. "Because you loved that sound, Trevin, I loved that sound. Trevin—remember ?"

He did. In his fragmented mind, Trevin recalled the steeples in the night, his favorite time, and the peace and serenity it created within him. "Yes… over the land."

"It's going to play a hymn."

Sure enough, the singular gongs segued into a holy canticle, adding layers to the experience, pealing in with crisp and clean notes; a dreamlike juxtaposition countering the hatred. Constance re-opened her eyes. "Heavenly," she whispered.

Harry's arm sagged. He staggered rearward, releasing his grip on Constance.

"GAAAAHHH!"

He lost motor function. Everything was made gummy. The weapon dropped, clattering on the floor. One final attempt was made to escape. He crooked his heels and lurched, but that wasn't enough.

"Feel what you've caused, Harry," Constance said, not looking at him, resuming her conduit position at Trevin's side. "Feel what you've done to *all of them.*"

"*Make it stop, make it stop!*" Veins spread to full expansion, sweat popping from every pore. Harry crashed into the studio, taking the drafting chair with him.

"Get the full effect."

Constance upped the throttle, and Harry was rendered unconscious, mouth open, spittle dribbling. In Carl and April's hysteria and confusion, they'd never stopped doing what they were supposed to. Constance was again free to address them.

"Now you're going to begin your part. You're going to use the other 90 percent."

"What are you talking about?" Carl demanded, melting down. "The other 90 percent?"

"Your mind. The 90 percent that stores your memories. The mnemonic repository. That's what it's for. It was impossible for you to know until now. For anyone to know—until now!"

April Lambrose wheezed in questioning noises, unable to grasp.

"Like I said: It's time," said Constance, understanding this. "Concentrate. It's time to get the operation under way. I'll help. Just start thinking of your best memories. Your reservoirs are ripe with overflow. Trust me."

She spread her fingers wide over the wound. A sucking sound rose from the meat. Grisly. Horror filled Trevin's parents. When she spoke, the unearthly chords returned. "Stick with me. You've been waiting for this."

April grasped for foundation. The melodious church hymn cut through in the background. "Y-your voice. It's… music."

"Yes …" Carl agreed.

Constance sang, "You had to be stripped, you three. Eventually, everyone will be. It's time. Hardships, emotional pain, blows to your ego. It's all for a purpose. There's humility involved. Look what you went through. It's not my doing. Pain is sacrifice. Bad memories are burned away."

Then she did the grotesque.

Constance dug her forefinger and thumb down into the wound-hole. Trevin howled and bucked. Mom and dad panicked and held him down. The pandemonium was terrible. Tears flowed and prayers spewed. Constance found what remained of the bullet and pulled it out. It was lethal looking, blunted, covered with flecks of bloodied flesh. She held it to the light, letting them see, then she tossed it aside. It pinged off the molding and came to rest in the corner.

Trevin was now practically cataleptic.

Placing her hands back on the wound, Constance continued. "You've seen the signs: the skies, the fantastic light, the circular motions. You've seen the activation start up. There are physics involved. Quite beautiful effects, wouldn't you say? Trevin, hold your parents' hands, you can do it."

The dying artist stirred, becoming as lucid as possible. As instructed, he lifted them and reached out, the crimson fluid slopping across body and floor. His parents took them, one for each.

April stared at what Constance was becoming.

"You weren't… responsible for this?" she asked. "The violence?"

Branches broke loose and pelted the house, like a hurricane roaring through. In contrast, Constance was as sweet as wine. "No," she answered, "I don't do that. Couldn't do that. That's beyond my control. It's all part of the equation. You three are among the first." Then she smirked, thinking of something personal. "I never knew I could feel this way. It's been exceptional."

Suddenly, Mr. and Mrs. Lambrose began to feel light, literally, as if their extremities were losing sensation, and they were weighing less. But that didn't matter. What mattered was their child.

"You knew something about me," Constance communicated to Trevin, brightly pleased.

Trevin tried a smile, yet he was still not out of danger. There was precious little blood left in his organs. "B-but you wouldn't s-say …"

Constance bent to Trevin's pallid cheeks, an inch from his ear. "I didn't leave you," she whispered in tones. "I was… reprimanded. Remember, intent matters."

"Intent …" Another eructation of blood had to be coughed out. Constance wiped it away, assuring his trembling parents everything was fine.

"Let go all negativity," she said to everyone. "You're going to be so happy." Back in Trevin's ear: "Thank you for your physicality. It was exquisite. I understand better now."

"I w-want to b-be with you …"

"Trevin, you'll forget me. You have better places to go."

April and Carl were sensing a major shift in consciousness, gaping like two gutted pumpkins.

To them all: "You'll all forget me. This is the way it's to be. In understandable terms: You have to commit totally. There's nothing to fear."

April murmured rapturously. "Show us what we have to do."

With that, Constance began to vibrate, white iridescence coming into being just beneath the surface of the skin. It intensified in rhythm to the continuing canticle outside, competing bravely over the storm. Its luminosity somewhat blurred her features, especially the trademark freckles. Nothing in living imagination could compare with it. The Lambroses knew they were going to being taken beyond limit. Their eyes were fixed on her.

April: "Just… please… don't separate us."

"I won't. I wouldn't. That's why I asked you to come together. Will you do what I ask?"

They both answered "Yes." Carl said, "We have… faith in you…"

Trevin had no pain now. He was hearing everything, just not seeing with his rolling, bloodshot eyes. He knew his parents were there. They weren't going to abandon him, as he'd never them. This unleashed one of Constance's stellar smiles. It manifested an arc of light that lit her head up more than any other part of her person.

"Trevin, you can see now," Constance's song went. She was more beautiful than he had ever witnessed. "You've been wondering about my fondness for discussing memories?"

He nodded, pushing blood with his tongue.

"This is the reason. This is the next step. You've been readied, and so have we. You had no idea how you've been preparing your whole life. Now everyone, bring to mind your happiest times, like you know how to do. Carl and April—you as well."

It would take a superhuman effort to assemble any in Trevin's state. His parents: not so bad. They were willing to go to any length to assure survival. Constance gave them time, tuning in, listening to the music outside. The memories were there, naturally, but not vivid. Their recollections were fragmented, deep in their mind, and they became frustrated, sputtering receptacles incapable of finding and holding the picture.

They needed a little help. Constance willed their channels to open.

"Trevin—remember the rooftop back home? The two of us together, under the stars? They gave you inspiration. Both of us, inspiration. Carl and April, you've shared many happy times with me. Think of those now. You can do it."

"M-mom? D-dad …?"

"We're here, son," said Carl in a reverie.

"They're here," Constance tutored. "They're doing fine. Don't compare. They're on their way. They're mining the glories of their lives. You have to, too. You can do it. Forget about this life; forget about the hardships, the lessons."

"They're in… no pain?" Trevin asked, also feeling the lightness.

"None whatsoever. Just the opposite."

He wanted to please Constance, to embrace the fall into forever, and he wanted to take his family with him. That is what she wanted, it was communicated. Abstractly, one after the other, bits and pieces of wonderful, recent memories came to mind.

Anything to brush off this crazy world!

That would be best. He'd have to find his way. His beloved parents were already in far-off wonder, still holding their son's hands, willing him with them.

"Dear God!" April exclaimed with absolute clarity, seeing her life like never before.

Constance was pleased. "That's right, April. Ah yes, I feel that. Those *are* good memories."

"Oh… my… Lord …" Carl came with next, Constance also complimenting him.

They were locked on.

"Trevin, the quartz crystal. Remember the night in the store?"

Okay, that worked. Trevin could solidify that perfect moment. The recall was immediate. Like a screen being projected upon, it replayed in specifics, no detail ignored. The memory was more real than when he'd actually experienced it. He could smell the store's incense, he could taste the air.

"Embrace it," Constance belted out, chords gorgeous. "Don't hold back."

Trevin's damaged eyes were staring beyond the ceiling, into his past. "You were… so great… I was… so happy. Can't be d-denied …"

"They're real, Trevin, they're real!" his father was able to say, understanding a new dimension.

Constance liked that. "See? They're with you. *We're* with you. Tell me more, Trevin. Your hand was in mine."

Trevin intensified, finding kernels, blissful like a spring bloom. "S-sweet like peaches. C-chimes over the door… like church bells."

"You humans will take yourselves. I'm the vessel. The bad memories were for contrast. Remember the church on the hill?"

Trevin tried a grin, enveloping in a womb-field of specifics, each beat more real than real—categorically transforming him. "I wondered… what it would be like to walk the aisle with you… in a church, marry you under church bells. You have a soul, too, I know. Connecting with mom and dad… like the light in the sunset …"

"Yes, the beautiful, beautiful sunsets."

Carl and April were performing great on their own. Something about Constance was allowing them to tap into the most luxuriant and loving recollections of their lives. Their physical forms were changing at the molecular level; changing for the better, evolving them. Together and separately, they were reliving the ultimate happiness in their sum totals, one after the other. Simultaneously, the bad and mediocre ones were glancing off, dissipating into showers of nothingness. There were all matters of sentiment, all erupting in grand fashion, having been dormant and almost forgotten. The simplest things were most important. Textures overlapped, near without exact proximity.

Constance had gotten things moving.

These people are brave, she considered, *worthy of this operation.*

Bold, thick strokes of golden life rushed back in streams; each touch, taste, feel, sound and sight returning. It was nourishment for the cosmos. Constance emitted soothing waves of super-consciousness moving them quicker and faster, harvesting them, cultivating them …

"Remember your garden, Carl. April: your new back porch."

Carl was the pride and joy ignited on his wife's face as he walked into the kitchen with a handful of homegrown tomatoes, soil flaking off. He was the kiss planted on her cheek as April took them under the sink to rinse them off. Carl could smell the fruit, feel the cement steps, see the sun drenching its creation. His dear wife was saying how she was looking forward to the first salad. He heard the clink of the colander, was warmed by the colors. He felt the metal gate creaking in the breeze as their parish's bells rang from the hill.

April was back to her first experience with her porch—the maiden viewing. She was its embrace of potential. The skies were gorgeous and huge as she rolled up the awnings, testing the mechanism. There was the spikiest bouquet of organic properties—mulch and cut grass—and the weeping willow extended its umbrella of shade, and cooled the lawn. She could feel the touch of each stalk, the roughness of the removed stones. Carl had gone into the basement to clean up. She could hear the basin sink running in drumming cadence. She was drunk with affection for him; a fulfilled dream. She loved him, and became the cold glass of herbal iced tea on his parched lips.

Picnics and young times together, separate incidents, actualized in multiple dimensions. Their parents, relatives, friends near and dear. Carl and April saw Trevin as a toddler, his first steps. Cheers, delights. Peripheral memories arrived obliquely, making them laugh in surprise. Space tore in slices, handing back billions of memories. There were as many as there are stars in the Milky Way.

They were supposed to break free, Carl and April. Yet, they couldn't. They were unwilling to let Trevin die. As Constance caught this …

FLASH!

The same outburst of searing light consumed the kitchen. No— *everything* became consumed! No one was harmed. Constance had physically let go of Trevin, and was standing before them once more, giving herself the most room possible. Trevin mumbled in comprehension: "Y-you… a-are… the light …"

"We're *all* light," Constance crooned, octaves changing and gliding. She was pure, pearlescent wisdom, connecting them to not only their source, but *the* Source. The first sparkles started at her contour, hugging tight, reminding Trevin of the highlights he'd become obsessed by.

Is that what they were? Notices of Constance's true identity? Candles… reflective surfaces… *the chrome in Nan's wheelchair?*

Carl gripped his wife, every underpinning cracking. "Take us," he implored. "All of us… Please…"

"You're taking yourselves. I'm just the vehicle." Constance had already reached into their atoms, but they needed to go farther. A phantasmagorical soup developed in sections, the room beginning to fade away, revealing the unfinished first floor apartment below, riddled with contractor's brooms and tool kits.

But the Lambroses did not fall. And they were not afraid to. Somehow, they were being held in safe fortune. Trevin's blood was still spreading outward, but it was going nowhere. All three of them could see past the walls to certain areas of the neighborhood. The trees were in a crazy dance, protesting with all their might. Above, clouds were churning and rolling by in circles, the city's light pollution illuminating it in eerie radiance Patches quivered, all in accord with their spirits.

The bizarre aurora borealis returned, brightly seen through the breaks in the clouds. It was forming a funnel of sorts. They could see the millions of stars inside it.

"Keep strong," Constance sang at the three. "Reach all the way in. I feel the memories. Oh, they're good. They fulfill me. It's finally time. You can do it. Many loved you. You've loved many. It's going to happen all over."

Nuances and fractions pulled the family together, binding their souls. A billion more memories arrived, re-happening, re-enriching. Now all their skin began to fade as Trevin's hand had earlier.

"You're no longer your physical selves," Constance explained, overjoyed. "Trevin, your mother said you always were sentimental. That's a good thing, for all of you. This is where we'll be taking everyone. Your world has come to a close."

The speech enabled the Lambroses to be aware that they weren't going to be around much longer. "Y-you're… an… angel …" April attempted.

"No, I'm not one of them, but they're around. You are the first to know us. This is our introduction. Think of me as… a facilitator."

"Facilitator," Trevin repeated in his delirium.

"You often wanted to know of my birth, Trevin. I had one, but not how you'd understand it. We are not in any writings, any religion, any mythology. We simply are timing."

Trevin chuckled inside, sharing their last joke. "California …"

"Where I first opened my eyes to the world, yes. At sunset, where the surf crashed. I have memories also."

"Where the sun meets the water," Trevin quoted from their past.

"Where the sun meets the water," Constance repeated, sounding like her own choir. The actual church hymn echoed her pitch. "Trevin, you were my first assignment. Then you, Carl and April, because of your grace. It wasn't expected, but that's how it evolved."

Breathing like a straining bull, Trevin managed a look back at his parents. There wasn't much left. Flesh and bone had mostly disappeared. But he could still squeeze their hands.

"The grind is behind all of you. Your trials and tribulations were to prepare you. You wonder why the world is out of control. It is, and we're here to change all that."

Trevin mouthed the words, "T-thank… you …"

"You're most welcome. I made mistakes, but my Superior is very understanding. I was forgiven for my indiscretions, and I'm to carry on with my mission. I wasn't sure for a while." As airy as Trevin's childhood meadow: "Trevin, your beautiful sketches gave me my own inspiration. You're all going to be so happy to see who's there."

And with that, sparkles began piercing the air around Constance. As she'd done throughout her history with Trevin, she lifted her arms and opened her hands, and a portal as massive as a mile high and a mile long opened behind her—so suddenly it took what was left of the Lambroses' individualities away, created disorientation and shock.

It was a mind-boggling vortex, circular in proportion, but from what the humans could see from their perspective, it was barely an arch, way up there. What was left of their eyes strained at its zenith. Constance was between them and it. The vortex had a "lip," or edge; so impactful it brought immediate, overpowering emotion. The three burst into tears.

For them, no longer did the house on Munnison exist. In fact, Chicago didn't exist. The structure was fashioned from a blue haze, rotating slowly as if it were a giant, celestial Ferris Wheel—seeming to expand and contract, its outer walls accruing more speed than the inner—clockwise closest, counter-clockwise elsewhere. The notion slammed their psyches. *This* was what it was about—*circles* and *circular patterns*. But that wasn't the best part. Trevin realized what was inside.

Constance had mentioned his sketches …

The Great Promised Land was a construct from Trevin's sketchpad: The one Constance had been smitten by the night of the block party. A giant, bucolic landscape of his design: their entrance into Paradise.

Rivers and streams of sparkling, bullion water babbled endlessly, receding back into space as far as the eye could see. This was an infinite horizon. In the middleground and background, swelling valleys and dales merged with Eden-like mountains, rising to unimaginable heights. The sky was in sunset-mode, in phase with the most celebrated any person had ever experienced in reality. A most purified reddish shine irradiated every nook and cranny that faced it, complimented by the softest purple and blue shadows where it didn't. Funnel clouds descended from the clouds of every category. There were waterfalls in the mid-hills, and cooling mists swirled from them into the air; the sun filtering like jewels of light striking rainbows above them all. They could hear and feel the pounding rumbling, alive and very real. Closest was a grove of trees, lush and vigorous, hatched in rocky hillsides of umbers and greens.

"Yes, that's right, Trevin—from your gifted imagination."

Constance began turning her wrists in twirls, palms open wide. "What's beyond is greater."

They knew this motion, this movement of her wrists. That's what she'd been working on: the symbolism of this distinct arrival. She was the orchestration. Constance's motions mimicked that of the vortex walls, and the closest layer started to "breathe."

The Lambrose family collected one final time. Carl and April crouched to their son. Trevin was smiling. They put their free hands on his shoulders, offering up their remnants. Wisps of haze broke in puffs, pulling around Constance, synchronizing to her hands, some tendrils reaching to the three. The remaining tears were eaten up, vanished. Constance was completely aglow from the inside out now.

"You are them… they are you. Your happiest memories are in use for the next stage. Trevin, you've fulfilled your quest. You wanted to protect your parents. You have. A strong virtue."

Out of Trevin's forehead, a sheathed bubble appeared—the shape and size of Brian Annarez's—made of the same blue miasma as the haze. This contained yet another memory; not the soul as first suspected. This memory was the relief the stranded family on the side of the road felt after

Trevin and Constance helped them. They'd reached their home safely, and were telling of the rescue to their relatives, regaling the "kind couple who made a difference."

Trevin's parents experienced it, too. They were part of it; shared thought, spirit. Their essences were filled with pure ecstasy. Love. Blue orbs began springing from their foreheads, one after the other. Constance thrived on each as the golden moment first passed through her and her circling hands, and continued on into Paradise. The faster her motion, the more the stratum of time and space became meaningless. Only the best fused into the sunset.

The Facilitator Constance broadened her one-in-a-million smile. Her synapses flowed with joy, like milk down a marble staircase. She transmogrified into complete light; a galvanizing beauty made entirely of cycling sparkles, ready to complete the first process.

Baseball with dad. Summer days. Going to the library to visit mom. Picking up her medicine as she needed it. How she cared for her husband when he was under the weather. April would not have wished for life without her two men. Dad provided for his family, filled with purpose. Voices from times past. Moths springing from lawns, trees undulating like poetry.

"I see the lawn chairs," came dad. "You're in one, April. The one with the blue and white strips. They sink." He smiled. "A child handed me a flower. He has a round face. I'm 25 years old."

April recalled the day of her birth. "Mother and father, looking at me for the first time. A cold February morning, like Trevin's birth. The room's warm. It's been difficult, but I'm here. My mother's holding me in her arms. Now dad. She handed me to him. His kind eyes. I see the sky for the first time. Crystal blue, not one cloud. Snow came later."

"The other 90 percent, keep going," Constance assured. "You store everything."

Carl: "Coming home. Grandfather's here with his big cigar. He won't stop talking. He didn't light up; he went outside, under the birch tree. I *am* him."

April: "My father took me to New York City. We're in Times Square. So many people, buildings so tall. Everywhere I look: possibility. We're stepping out from Grand Central Station. An ice-cream parlor. He buys me a cone. Cherry vanilla, sprinkles on top. It's huge, like everything here. Dad's got a sundae. We're on a park bench, watching the world go by. The best ice cream I've ever had. Dad's happy, showing me the city.

This is where he's from. My dear, sweet father… my dear, sweet mother. Been so long."

April heard a voice, faint and separate: "April …" Masculine, feminine—at the same time.

"Mom? Dad?" Maybe they were here. She desperately wanted to see them.

"They've always been with you, April," Constance sang. "They always will be."

"There's… a dog," Carl bantered. "Not my pet; a neighbor's. Down in the old neighborhood. Rochester, a long time ago. I'm a kid. Six, seven. He's everyone's friend. A mutt, no one knows the mix. Smokey's his name. Looks like he's been created in a laboratory. Always there for us. Walks to school with the kids, skipping alongside, wagging his tail. Has a crooked gait. Oh, he smells when it rains, that wet dog smell. My parents are arguing this day. Ran through the yards all the way to the hill. I'm sitting under a tree, crying. I'll be darned. That crazy dog's found me. He's bounding up to me. He knows when I'm down. I feel his fur in my palm, knotted in spots."

April: "Here it is! I'm taking a stroll with my best friend, Suzanne. About to start my first year of junior high. The end of summer, late August. Hate this time of year, everything's over. I'm scared, Suzanne isn't. She has the heart of a lion. She's saying to me: 'Let 'em try teaching us anything.' She makes me laugh so hard. After dinner we sneak off to the new school. She walks me around the building, teaching me to stare it down. Suzanne smokes cigarettes. Flicks a butt off the bricks, daring it. She has a story for each window: 'Here's where I'm gonna meet my boyfriend,' 'Here's where you're gonna blow up the science room,' 'Here's where we're gonna pass notes.' She tells me to think of our pranks when I get nervous. A different afternoon, and Suzanne's mother pulls me aside, secretly asks me to watch over her baby. First time I'm hearing of her vulnerability. Her mom tells me she's scared of not fitting in. We never tell Suzanne. They move to Montana of all places. I lose a friend."

Carl: "It's your birthday, sweetheart. I'm excited to take you out. I'm driving home, stopped at a light. In my rearview mirror, I see a car is going to ram me. It's not stopping. Can't get out of the way. I'm disappointed. I'm thinking how sad I'll be not having more time with you. The car skids halfway through the intersection, misses me by an inch. Trees are swaying, letting me know I'm still going to be with you."

April: "You make sure I'm with you."

Trevin was doing much better. "Bunch of us guys: Tommy, Joe, Steve. We're at the drive-in movie theater; the Winking Moon. Tommy has his dad's pickup truck. The whole summer's ahead. Packed, this night. They want to find the girls. 'I'll catch up,' I'm saying. We're in the last row, the woods lining the perimeter. I look east, and there's my moon. Full, huge. Only for me. I wish for love, ready to give it a real go. My loud friends come back. I hear the speakers—over 900 cars. Echoes everywhere."

Carl: "Ducks quacking in the pond. Strange to hear them at night. They're under the pier."

Trevin: "I meet this girl. Her name's Paulette, from Wisconsin. Her family's in town for an antique show. She tells me of the grasshoppers on her farm. I tell her of my mantids. We're laughing."

April: "I see the colors of the flowers. They're mostly white. Yellow centers, orange in the petals. They're here in our fingers."

FLASH!

One after the other, each picked up on the other's memories, making them theirs. The important moments were the building blocks. Constance was presiding over the affair, elated.

Trevin's fireflies; under the pine trees. Carl's first car; his freedom driving along the lake. April's recipes. Tortellini. Making everyone happy. Their wedding day. April in her frilly gown. Loved ones taking part in the ceremony. Friends, church personnel taking pictures, applauding. Descending concrete steps, rice sailing over their heads, church bells clanging. Gaze into the sky. Good cheer. Separate times. Together times. Reading, learning, Sunday afternoons, thinking of others, carrying out deeds for the less fortunate.

FLASH!

Carl signing mortgage papers. His father's presence with him, hovering over the many signatures, lawyer across the table. *Go ahead, son. You'll handle this fine. You have April to look after now. She needs a good home.*

Every decision and consequence ever made poured out.

Trevin's first gymnastic meet. Winter coffee and holidays. Especially Christmas. Morning dew drying. Laughter at spilled Jell-O. Poolside. The smell of wheat fields 17 years ago. Classmates taking notes. Suck-ups. Ha! Sea otters cracking shells on their tummies. Helping to clean the garbage spill at the mall, made the store manager's happy. Camaraderie between strangers. Funky music at the State Fair. One hairy guy dancing. Let go of the balloon and watch it rise to the sky. Each kind word. Cause and effect.

Sprinkles on vanilla cake with fudge frosting. The diary of the universe. Each pulse, defining who we are. The Dawn of Creation… destiny …

The "breathing" eased, and lustrous haze swam in free space. Behind Constance, the most spectacular thing of all appeared …

April's parents were waiting for her.

So were Carl's.

Carl and April wanted to be with them.

There was a distinct and swift comprehension that had been there all along. A facilitator also did this—allowed parties from both sides to converge, reunite. Carl and April were overcome, wishing their son to follow them into "the Return—"

—Constance's mission.

Trevin became further astonished. The "good" neighbors, the ones who'd materialized at Mr. Tavalier's, had returned. They were smiling at him, welcoming him, welcoming them all. These were the ones from the good ol' neighborhood: Mrs. Morneau, the Buccinis, Mr. and Mrs. Laneske, Mrs. Weber and Hank and Linda Deltoran, to name some …

And… Cecil Tavalier was there. With his wife, Emily.

Yes, the couple was holding hands, thanking Trevin without words. They were thanking him for everything he'd done for them. They were communicating this through love, as the neighbors had the night at the house. Intent mattered. Gone were the ravages of age and time. Cecil appeared youthful and complete now, too, just like Emily and all the others.

The billions of orb life experiences became cunning paths to salvation. Every gradation of life was reborn. Every passion, every thought, each decision, date, condition, location and human occurrence flew to its rightful place, ahead of their owners. Each song, each sweet whisper, every ounce of love—given and received—was there for their transport. Sorrow was no more. And when the Lambroses were reduced to mere thoughts and intentions, April communicated to her husband and son: "We had great joy, didn't we? Through the bad times and good."

"The best anyone could pray for," Carl communicated back. "I'll always love you, April."

"And I'll always love you, Carl," countered April.

Then they trained care back to their son. Trevin felt their souls merging with him. He beamed, "I'll always love you both. Always."

"As we to you, Trevin," April and Carl assured. "Forever."

There came one final recognition …

Nan appeared from the nearest hill, completely free of her dreaded wheelchair and mortal pain. She smiled at them, as vibrant as any of Constance's through the odyssey. Even though he wasn't in form any longer, Trevin's spirit cried from happiness like never before. Nan encased her grandson's soul like he'd created the world itself, erasing its quintessence with the greatest love and happiness ever known. All were in euphoria.

Trevin, was her thought, as tender as peace itself. *We'll share that cup of tea.*

Yes, Nan, I'd like that very much.

One final lift of Constance's arms, and the Lambroses were no more. All relatives and friends were with them, and they became the sunset inside the Great Landscape. No one was separated. Evening turned to nightfall, and in the nightfall there came starlight, and the stars shimmered as the vortex closed.

Her job was complete.

With *them.*

CHAPTER 40

Harry came to. He hadn't been killed, but he felt he'd come close. For the first hellish minute, he thought his neck was broken, body still in agony with spasms. A musty odor was hitting his nostrils. Something very bad had occurred.

It was damned cement. Under him.

He found himself outside the strange house with the fucking staircase, face down on the sidewalk. Like a punk-ass.

The sky was as black as death. The street was dark. A sense of dread threatened to swallow him whole. He thought he was alone, trapped in a vacuum with no other human souls. Dirt, leaves and debris had gathered around him from fierce winds howling in his ears. He dared lifting his head again, a sensations of a hundred rusty nails driving through his skull.

In the 360-degree ambit, what the hell was going on? Nothing but gloom in a neighborhood. Brooding atmosphere. Big trees were swinging. They might come down on him. This corner could be his demise.

What the fuck happened?

Struggling with elbows and wrists to sit up, he screamed in pain, and along with it came great lucidity. Rolling to his side, half on the lawn, he looked up at the façade, not quite remembering what he'd done. There was a reason he was here. If he had a case of beer and a vat of aspirin, he might be able to figure it out.

Wait! Shit. He'd done something bad …

He'd driven the van, stashed it blocks over, jogged here. He remembered that. Also, he had his piece with him. Stashed in his filthy jeans. It was gone now. Where the hell was it? Wanted that dude upstairs dead. Geezers, too. "Cuz" Brian. Come to right the wrongs.

But that ain't what went down.

Bullets. Bullets. Wait—!

He'd shot the prick …

Groped his body. Made sure he wasn't the one full of holes.

Dark windows, staring at me like dead eyes. Those were the windows of the house he'd invaded. It was coming back to him now.

Parked cars glowered like dispassionate jurors, deliberating a sentence. No traffic from the highways could be heard, no roaring commuter train, no airplanes. Only the venomous hissing of wind he had to squint against.

When he tried to crawl, pain exploded again. He was a pathetic wounded animal, waiting to die after being hit by a truck.

He'd been put through the wringer, he knew that. Maybe by rival gang members. Or police. He'd taken his knocks before, but never like this. This was the unknown. He tried thinking of family, any comforting thought that could provide solace. His mind was blocked. This had to be the god-damned suckiest situation he'd been in. He'd bred evil. Up there. Hadn't thought that going in …

Suddenly, there came a horrific realization that he was in a world of hurt. Mentally, physically—but most significantly—spiritually. He remembered shouting. And tears. Pleas for mercy. Compassion was prayed for but not given. Hate festered a rotten core. Then came a "bitch," or whatever the fuck she was. Something that cut the heart out of his chest. Would've shot her, no matter how hot she was.

Something caught his attention under the darkened recess of the first-floor landing. He was only feet away, and thought he saw movement in the shadows. Harry stared, eyes feverishly battling the blowing elements around him. There was something else. Above. On the balcony. Someone was there. Yes, a figure strode to the edge of the railing and stared down at him. He sensed that whoever it was, it was ready to launch the wrath of the universe on him.

At times, Harry had wondered if his bad dealings would catch up to him. Maybe it had.

This curled him into a fetal position, more on the sidewalk than off. Telepathically, an influence communicated into his pea brain. It said: *You're not moving until you see this. The truth.*

The thing up there wanted him to know he'd receive no clemency.

Fuck! It's not done with me!

An atrocious, acidic aftertaste came to his throat. He heard buzzing in his ears, followed by a different voice—one he recognized—like an echo of a mournful cast: *This is where I hit, Harry. Right under you.*

His eyes went to the undershadows again. There. That's where this second "voice" was coming from. A doleful-looking young man with no blink to the eyelids (even as twigs hit them), came crawling out on hands and knees, scraping himself across the sidewalk, drawing to within several frightening inches of Harry.

It's me, Harry, your cousin—Brian. His lips and mouth did not move.

Harry wanted to scream, but couldn't. He tried wrenching away, terror clawing his body, lungs permitting only gasps, but he was pinned in place. "Y-you're… not… here!" Harry wheezed. "You're d-dead! I… was at your funeral!"

"Brian" worked his way to his feet, lingering above his blood relative, no trace of bodily injury. Yet… he seemed …lost. Tapping the hallowed sidewalk with the toe of his shoe, Brian offered: *I did die. Here.*

Then, to fully crush Harry's sanity, hollow pockets began to form on his cousin's skin, particularly the facial region. They starting shifted about, like a hollow tube moving through butter, rolling up the brow, down the cheek, into the neckline… chest …

Harry could see the house and black sky punching through in patches.

It was my fault, Harry. No one else's.

"H-how, Br-ian… w-what …?"

Time for a lesson. Through some sort of psychic transference, Harry "learned" his cousin had indeed been the wrongdoer—the selfish intruder—like the asshole up there had been squawking about. He felt every bit of bone-crunching brutality that took place, appalling and awful. Harry also "saw" everything—even Brian tripping over some stupid rock on the balcony, sending him smashing through the balustrades to the hard-as-fuck sidewalk below.

The freak on the balcony was supervising all this, making certain it sunk in …

Harry experienced each lope of fire in his guts, each muscle shredding from overuse. Then, the impact. Consciousness fading, precious blood leaking away. Barely turned when some stupid fucking car plowed into him, launching him through the air, the second impact scraping flesh off bone. Strangers poured in from all sides. The *Lambose jagoff* wanted to help!

Harry could feel it in the man's heart. Body shutting down, organs clicking off. The thought of happy things, moments he wanted to take with him. Harry-Brian… face up now… the stars wanted him.

Brian squatted closer. So close Harry could've slipped a finger through one of the moving holes.

No more blaming. No more false illusions. The artist was not at fault. I am responsible for the God-forsaken mess. Understand?

Brian hadn't considered his own child back home or his family. Lives were ruined. This was wrong. Destroying lives was evil. He'd upset poise in the universe.

You… got a break.

Harry was confused, but now comprehended that he had wrongly condemned the Lambose-dude. And his folks. Sorrow and sadness came to his core. They'd loved one another, very much. Harry asked for forgiveness. He feared for his soul, and burst into tears.

The verdict was still out with the silhouette on the balcony.

It was a woman, right? A normal woman? Hair flowing, clothes rippling …

Weird, shimmering lights materialized out of the ebony expanse above her, way in the distance, over the rooftop. Harry bet they were a part of all this, and the monstrous clouds. He became like lost laundry, abandoned and alone. Harry also understood that his cousin was indeed gone. Where to, he didn't know. The shadows under the staircase were there, but "cuz" wasn't. Brian was gone.

It *was* a woman upstairs. She started walking down toward him, glaring with that intense face full of freckles, hair blowing like in a beauty commercial. When she got to where Brian had been, through pain and tears, he dared asked: "What h-happened to them? Upstairs. The three …"

"That's not for you to know, Harry."

No holes were moving across her face. Wasn't she the same lady from before? "Y-you… know me?"

"Not in sum, but enough. Who do you have in life, Harry?"

"M-my—"

Constance cut him off. "—Family? Do you want to be with them?"

"Y-yes, of course …"

"Okay then. Someone will be visiting you. You're not going to remember me saying this—but when that happens—you'd *better* have your act together. You are *not* the center of the universe. Get up."

There was no waiting for his biochemistry to reboot.

"Get up," she said.

Harry grimaced, groaned, worked his way to his feet. When he was upright, the sounds of the city faded up into his ears. The world seemed to be returning to normal, and he was grateful for it. Wiping the tears away, aching to see his beloved family, he *knew* he had been given a break.

The lady continued to lord over him with the presence of a Viking fleet. "Go learn. And pray for your cousin. There's hope for him yet."

Harry looked up and down the alien street, keys to the Econoline van jingling in his pants pocket. He'd forgotten they were there. The major portion of the storm had dispelled, weird shit going away. As he tried steps, Constance shook her head, no smile. When he could, he bolted, tripping and falling once, then getting up again and running diagonally across Munnison toward Salmon, where he loped behind the sleeping houses, disappearing from sight.

Then alone, Constance removed the hair from her face, tying it into a natural braid behind her head. It had been a long night. Her hands and fingers were sore, and she rubbed them. She waxed sentimental, growing nostalgic. She ambled down Munnison in the opposite direction, thinking of the nights she'd strolled here with Trevin.

She would miss him. She would miss him greatly.

✳ ✳ ✳

The neighbors had been rendered to profound sleep. No interference was to be had. This was the maiden voyage of the mission, after all. They'd stir in the morning, agog with fantastical dreams of a great love watching over them. The majority would dismiss the ridiculous flights of fancy out of hand, preferring to stew over the shocking morning headlines with their horrid developments, wondering just how much more the world could take.

A few would journal their dreams with glee. Fewer still would share their experiences with spouses, lovers, significant others. A few would notice something significant in the swirling, circular motions set into ordinary things, relaying something weighty. A morning cup of coffee, for example—after the liquid is stirred with a spoon, settling to a gentle spin.

Wait until those people noticed the skies.

CHAPTER 41

—◄ ►—

Constance thought of Chicago. She knew it was the largest city in the state of Illinois, located along the southwestern shore of the freshwater Lake Michigan. With over 2.8 million people, it was the third most populous city in the country. The metropolitan area, referred to as "Chicagoland," consisted of Illinois, Wisconsin and Indiana, and had an extended population of over 9.5 million.

A lot of ground to cover …

That's why she was grateful when her new assignment came in so quickly. It had her quite excited. Two good ones in a row. The first time around had been challenging, but she'd learned to be more efficient, professional.

Terra Firma was over. Ancient prophecies, mythologies, suspicions, conspiracy theories, Doomsday scenarios. They'd all been correct. In a way. Perhaps not as dark. Her kind had managed to stay out of the limelight since antiquity. But now was their time. The Lambrose's comment about the angels had landed close. The startup effects had really heated things up, keeping humidity in the air. An unexpected byproduct of activation.

She'd heard hot autumn weather referred to as "Indian summer." She was in it now.

She crossed the busy intersection clad in another smashing outfit, admiring the beautiful Midwestern skyline gleaming in the bright sunshine. Perhaps, she thought, she was her own architect. All that engineering and planning. It felt good to finally spread her wings, so to speak.

A few commuters stared at the stunning brunette with the engaging freckles and arresting eyes. She never gave those people a chance. They'd get someone else. Most people were oblivious, however, imploding into their own private worlds of iPods, Blackberries and cell phones.

She cut a path across the depot's terminal, dodging exhaust-belching, primitive behemoths of metal, picking a shaded spot under a fiberglass overhang to wait. When the brakes hissed to a stop and her bus doors flapped open, passengers clambered on ahead of her, and she saw the hard-faced driver mutter superfluous greetings; a well-rehearsed conformity of society.

One fellow broke the monotony and attached his bicycle to the front grill.

She hadn't seen that before. Interesting.

She stepped aboard last, swiping her card, sensing the driver balking being so near to her. Deep in his mind and out of the blue, she'd inadvertently triggered a recall of something wonderful about an extraordinary day at the zoo with his big sister and aunt from childhood. He had no idea why, but he was suddenly very content. He'd been in a bad mood all day prior.

Constance worked her way to the vacant rear bench and sat, a comfortable perch from which to enjoy the jaunt to the northwest side. Fumes coughed and rose as the vehicle lurched forward, thumping its wheels over the rough patches in the road. Her window was open even as the air conditioning worked overtime.

Ironically, she could hear church bells somewhere. She craned her neck to see which steeple they were coming from. Couldn't find it.

Back in Rochester—and to a certain extent, Chicago—questions would be raised regarding the disappearances of the people named Lambrose. Investigations would be launched. Neighbors, acquaintances and old mean bosses would be drawn in, talking with authorities gathering information. But this wouldn't last either. Sooner or later, there'd be no one left.

Constance became captivated by the sight of twin babies in a double stroller five rows up. They'd just boarded, and their mother had positioned their device in the aisle facing backward. Direct eye contact with the adorable toddlers was impossible to ignore. They had the most innocent faces, simply precious. Mom pulled out a book. It took seconds for the cherubic children—boy in blue, girl in pink—to single out the nice man sitting behind them, dressed in a dapper suit and tie.

His face was at a three-quarter angle, but Constance saw he was handsome.

And he had freckles. A multitude of them. Like the stars above.

She wondered what body of water he'd splashed down into. The ocean in the west—same as her? The Atlantic? One of the Great Lakes? A deep river in Colorado?

Merely curious.

She could see his pronounced cheekbones rise, rounding into a glorious smile as he looked back at the children. He lifted one hand into the aisles where they could see it, and made swirling gestures, turning the wrist ever so slowly for them. Beaming grins bloomed on their pink, toothless mouths. In their brand new minds—somehow, vaguely—they would recall an intangible glee; their first cheerful memory.

"Aren't you two happy?" That was their mother.

She'd noticed them, and glanced back at the gentleman who'd been amusing them; the man with the most striking smile. Mom politely grinned, carried on with her reading.

At the next stop, he got off, noticing Constance, picking her out from all the passengers. He nodded before stepping to the street: a subtle recognition between colleagues.

Constance nodded back.

The twins had twisted as he moved by, straining to see him off, mom also giving one last glance. Such magnetism. As the bus motored onward, Constance watched the handsome man through the window as he met a random human and apologized after bumping into her. An adult female. Or was she random? They seemed to strike up an instant, friendly conversation.

EPILOGUE

Low on the horizon, cumulo nimbus clouds radiated with crimson light, gold ambers vivifying contours, ignited by a potent, setting sun. Exquisite to behold. These pre-twilight skies were also her favorite, and this one was at its peak.

A senior remarked: "Reminds me of Wyoming skies."

Constance turned, looked at the resident. She grinned at the elderly man who was outside near her, and moved for the entrance. She'd been here at the Lakebreeze Healthcare Campus for an hour now. But she'd been gearing to go in, gathering that last-minute nerve to do a better job, a quicker job. It had been great to digest the ambiance at the facility. The ginger globe at the sky's horizon was now only half a dome, sucking down into an extended landscape of buildings and trees. Flocks of zigzagging swallows swooped through the negative spaces between the branches and the sunset. The sound of the cicadas and crickets had long left the season.

Within the next five minutes, Constance had signed into the visitors log and greeted those around the reception desk. Each resident and employee found their spirits inexplicably soaring. Allison Pertina wasn't working this evening.

On the way to the atrium, the crossroads to the complex, a semi-familiar staffer recognized Constance and delicately stopped her. "Excuse me. Is Trevin Lambrose with you tonight?"

"No, I'm afraid he's not."

"Do you know where he's been? We've missed him."

"He's fine," Constance answered with utmost politeness. "He's doing his thing."

That seemed to appease the woman. Constance then learned of a most touching yet ironic development: Lakebreeze was to be the recipient of a generous donation from Mr. Eugene Joseph's estate. It had been in his will and his family was seeing to it. The facility was soon going to call Trevin and offer him a full-time position in the recreational arts program; a contract good for at least a year. When the conversation was over, the staffer nodded once, thanked Constance, turned and disappeared down a hallway.

Constance was the master of appeasement. She continued on as well.

The closer she got to Gladys Embery, the more escalated her excitement became. Constance paused outside the room, hearing the recognizable mumbles from the television set—the primitive device of plastic and glass. The sweet lady was here. Constance listened to the canned laughter cresting, waning. She paused, working so tenderly with a loving and caring approach.

Inside the room, Gladys halted as before, taking a break from the usual chores, sensing someone outside her door again. Earlier that day, the local florist had swung by, handed out cartons of fresh daisies. She'd been preening hers. Had they returned to deliver more?

No, Gladys knew. Someone was regarding her with powerful, extreme kindness. She turned down the TV. "Whoever you are, you can come in again. I can use the company."

Constance giggled.

Clever woman. She should've guessed.

Constance made the move and slipped into the room. Ms. Embery's eyes grew large, ecstatic. Then… relief.

The two women stared at one another with mutual admiration, crafting another precious and timeless moment between them. Constance ended the quiet first.

"Hello, Gladys." She was smiling from ear to ear.

Gladys smiled back. "Hello. I knew you'd come back."

"I have, Gladys. It's me… Constance."

"I remember your name, dear. Oh, I'm so glad." The elderly lady's eyes glistened with tears, putting hands to her wrinkled face, unable to contain the joy. "That smile. I was hoping I'd see it again."

Constance took another step closer. "I knew there was something about you when we first met."

"You did?"

"Yes."

"I've been so lonely," said Gladys.

"No longer," Constance said, and embraced the woman with ultimate compassion.

Gladys slumped into her arms, and like a little child, began to cry. "I'm so tired," she sobbed. "And I'm so ready."

Constance raised her face to meet her smile. "Good."

They continued to hold each other, then… laughed. Gladys felt the most heartfelt hug she'd ever experienced. Dabbing away the tears—or at least trying to—Constance next moved Gladys slightly back, then changed the energy, clapping her hands together in a sway of courage. For both of them. "A confession. After I met you, Gladys, I knew you were my next."

Gladys was overwhelmed. "Oh I'm so happy to hear that."

"There's no holding back," Constance gushed, holding back the tears of joy herself. "I have so much affinity for you; you're a sweet soul, Gladys. What gave me away?"

"When you're as old as I am," Gladys answered, sniffling full-out, "you know things. I've lived a long life."

"You have, my friend."

Yes, they were both content just being with one another, reunited. But there was work to be done. They smiled and cried until it hurt, no witnesses to this. Surrounding rooms had been recently vacated, ready for new tenants. Gladys asked if she could finish watering her plants.

"Of course," Constance replied, admiring their health. "Pretty leaves."

"It's the mayonnaise I put on them."

"I see."

The ewer within arm's length, Gladys took it and gave her prize just the right amount of water nourishment. "These will be taken care of?" she asked.

Constance was as tender as the setting sun now shining in from the courtyard across the hall. "They will," she answered.

"Goody."

Constance observed the room, fastidiously seen to: bed without a single crease, cream-colored comforter folded neatly at its edge. "All's in order."

"Preparation," said Gladys, putting the ewer down. "After you and Trevin left, I was sad. Did you hear me?"

"Recently, yes."

"And how is he? My Trevin?"

"More than excellent."

"He was such a good boy. I loved him."

"And he loved you, Gladys. Still does."

Gladys went to the sill, staring at her favorite bird feeder by the tree one last time. "Light's almost gone," she said. "You're my favorite scene now."

This got Constance weeping. She laughed through it, amazed at how much she felt for this beautiful human. "You're fantastic, Gladys," she said, wiping her face.

As they were both crying, Gladys snatched several tissues from a box and gave them to the radiant young woman in her room. "There, there, child. It's all right."

"I can't help it," said Constance, taking them. "How quickly I attached to you, Gladys. You are so very, very special. You are loved so very much. And you'll never be alone again."

Gladys announced that she was grateful for her life and all the people who'd been in it.

"Good," Constance assured. "It's good to be grateful."

When they'd gathered themselves, laughing more, Gladys joked. "We're like two emotional giddy-goos."

"Yes we are."

"And how …?"

"Simple," said Constance, finishing Gladys's thought. "I'm sending you home. You do want to go home?"

This is what the saintly senior had longed to hear. Her eyes twinkled. "More than anything. I want to go home to my mother and father."

Constance gestured affirmatively, then dug into her pocket and took out the crystal necklace Gladys had admired from their first encounter. The amulet spun, presenting all facets in pinpoints of golden-orange light from the sunset. Gladys recognized it, energized to the core.

"How many sparkles do you see, Gladys?"

"Countless …"

"That's how many good memories you'll take with you. You'll be happier than your mind can imagine."

"Could you… put it around my neck?" asked Gladys.

And that's exactly what Constance did. Gladys received it like a coronation, Constance tapping it once for good measure when in place. "It's you."

Gladys beamed as if she were the prom queen, turning to see herself—and the necklace—in the bureau mirror. Constance stood tall behind her, stating how stunning she looked. Then Constance caught a sketch on the vestibule, picked it up. "Yours?"

"Yes."

The drawing—rendered in colored pencils—was something to behold. It depicted a scene looking out an unknown window in an old-fashioned bedroom from days gone by. A private yard of full flowers and trees could be seen through it. At the bottom of the sketch, was a label written in two words: 'My Room.' Gladys' signature was to the right of it, perfect penmanship.

"Your childhood room?" Constance asked, tears almost gone.

"Yes," Gladys answered enthusiastically, back facing her. "There was no better day than when I would sit there, on my bed, looking out to our backyard—mother and father downstairs in the kitchen, preparing dinner together."

"No better day …" Constance parroted, admiringly, feeling her skin prickling: that warm, fuzzy feeling all over again. "That's exactly what I wanted to hear, Gladys. Tell me more memories about this room. What little girl had such a lovely view to the world?"

Gladys let go of the amulet, eager to recall such bliss. Once and for all, it might take care of her being a "giddy-goo." She asked for the drawing back, and set it on the bed, propping it against the pillows to access it for inspiration.

Constance shut the door, loosening shoulder muscles and rolling her wrists. This was going to be superb.

"Is that where you're going to stand?" asked Gladys.

"Yes," answered Constance, "if that's okay."

"It's okay."

With a youthful bounce in her step, Gladys positioned herself to the center of the room. Space was going to be helpful. "I was blessed …" she began, starting to sway to a song existing only in her mind. A melody light and breezy—perhaps a child's ditty—a lovely thing to dial into. "Blessed with a fantastically happy childhood. Lots of music was played in my room …"

The last cut from the sunset outside created a sudden, full spectral prism effect that blazed the walls up to the ceiling, irradiating the room with a magical atmosphere. Gladys began to dance, soft as air, back and forth across the room, more agile than Constance imagined possible. Her voice rose like a fountain on the ritziest terrace. And just as she had weeks ago, Gladys recited one of her best.

"Oh, I loved our house. Mother wanted the living room painted blue, but I preferred green. I've always loved the color green—olive green probably being the least fun. We'd quibble, we were broken records. But she loved me. I'd get my way in the end."

Gladys was in full-out waltz mode now, sweeping the room like a young girl dancing at her first ball, held in the euphoria of a best memory, moving this way and that, tears of sorrow evaporating.

"We ended up with pine green, not too emerald. I told her our neighborhood was like that, just look around. There were many trees. You see, father and I went to the store and bought the paint. We walked, held hands the whole way. He had such strong hands, I felt so safe when I was with him. There were big drop clothes all over the place—we had to wear our tatter clothes."

And Constance was enchanted. She was the perfect audience.

The End